The Painter's
Confessions

The Painter's Confessions

Philip Callow

Allison & Busby
Published by W.H. Allen & Co. Plc

An Allison & Busby Book
Published in 1989 by
W.H. Allen & Co. Plc
Sekforde House
175/9 St John Street
London EC1V 4LL

Printed and bound in Great Britain by
Bookcraft Ltd, Midsommer Norton, Avon.

ISBN 0 85031 905 6

For Anne with love

PART ONE:

Maggie

1

Even before my sister's violent death I had felt this urge to use words, to tell a story that would be my own, yet irradiated in some way by hers. For no obvious reason I couldn't take up a pen and start while she was alive. I had never sought approval from Vivien, or from anyone: all the same, something or other made me hang back. I was bashful, distrustful even. Looking for excuses, I told myself I was no good with words. Painting and drawing were more natural to me. Besides, I have always associated words with cleverness, facility. You can be an imbecile and still paint.

Once I did happen to mention the idea. She slapped me down, not playfully as I expected, but with the sort of inappropriate passion which leads one to suspect fear or shame. Surely she didn't imagine I could reveal something indecent about us both?

'Egotism,' she said. 'Vanity, conceit. Self-justification. It's your sly exhibitionism, which no one ever sees but me. All these years you've spent wallowing in paint like a . . . like a . . .'

'Pig. Go on, say it.'

'Francis, you're coarse.'

'I feel coarse. And soiled. I feel old.'

'You're not old. How can fifty be old?'

'I feel it.'

'And now it's going to be words, is that it?'

'You know as well as I do,' I found myself spluttering, and then shouting, 'the paint won't run for me any more.'

This was true, though I hoped to God not for long. I did no more about turning to words than speculating about it. 'So it's only talk,' I thought. After a while I forgot I had even mentioned the possibility. But what I had discovered in myself was the same need to confess as everyone else.

More than once I allowed myself to think that what Vivien and I had between us as brother and sister, the feeling we both called our bond, was a spiritual incest that could not be spoken, any more than could that other, taboo kind. Now she is drowned and dead I am drawn to her by a love I once took for granted and now long to understand. What do I mean? Was my deep distrust of her friend Celia my jealousy, or a foreboding I chose to ignore? Were the dangers plain for anyone to see who was not as guiltily implicated as myself? Am I now so lost without her that I have to turn to words in an effort to resuscitate her? And why not paint?

All I can seem to paint now are self-portraits, the blurred features of which stare back at me morbidly, full of accusation, scorn, duplicity. Even to write these lines makes her corpse live, stir a little, a trick of language that is perhaps as cruel as the trick of the light that evening, as illusory as the effect of the tide tugging at her clothes, her hair, her dead fingers.

Where to begin? With our longed-for reunion? I was still married then to Della, living deep in rural Cornwall. Vivien lived and worked in London. Our paths never seemed to cross, yet without knowing it we were making our way to each other as if from either end of a long corridor.

The once-derelict mill I had made into a home was at a spot called Chycoose. My American wife Della had said when we took it that it sounded Indian to her. The ordnance map marked it as a place, although the mill was the only habitation now standing. There must have once been a settlement of that name.

Della and I had each encouraged the other to feel remote there, but in Cornwall now no one really is. Nevertheless the site was impressive: stone buildings in a damp navel, tucked down snugly in a world of earth. Yet only a mile or two away was Devoran, or the tiny hamlet of Feock. When I climbed out of my damp sucking hole and stood on a ridge, a whole watery universe became visible to me, from Restronguet Creek, lying cold and sullen like slops, right out to Mylor and the broad waters of Carrick Roads flowing past at Falmouth to the sea. In the other direction, inland, lay Truro. That region too lived in a glittery mesh of rivers and creeks.

At first I loved it, and was lost in it, a stranger in a strange land. To live in Cornwall for a month or for twenty years is to be still a foreigner. Soon I hated it, and felt myself watched by close natives, mean and beady-eyed. Used as I was to hiding, I began to feel stalked by glances and asides. Was it my appearance or my speech which made me so conspicuous, or was it all imaginary? I imagined what I must look like – a thin, staring man, with a head of dense grey hair looking distinguished at a distance. Close up, I suspected there was something about the expression in my eyes which would create confusion, no doubt the look of someone perpetually unsure of who he was or where he fitted in. And I am a starer, I always have been. I've got hungry eyes.

Whichever way I walked or ran to get out of that place, Chycoose, it meant a hill. Usually I ran. I broke out. I have never been sure about my desires. Did I want to literally, physically get out from time to time, or was it just to make something happen that I ran? To shake something off.

Whatever it was, it refused to let go. While I was in motion it didn't seem to be there, and even sometimes when I paused on a ridge and stared around I felt free. Then, getting back and going indoors again I found I had trailed the thing in with me after all. My mind darkened again. Naturally it had associations with the black stuff I squeezed out ever more sparingly now on to the newsprint I used for a palette.

Desperate all of a sudden to escape the torments of my work I would drop everything and leave in a hurry, trot up the rough track from the slate-hung mill and feel myself shambling as if hunted, like one of the farmer's wild-eyed bullocks.

Reaching the cattle grid I would look back. The emptiness of the land was always a surprise, with nothing to see except my hiding place. There it was, stooped low in a way that fitted the ground it stood on. Once I had whooped with excitement just to think of it, living there and owning such a place. The novelty had worn off – like a lot of things. I would turn my back, fumble my feet over the steel poles of the grid and walk into the lanes to the left. Soon an even narrower gully branched off, rising between ferny banks to the right. It was steep as a staircase. With no reserve strength in my knees I ran charging full tilt. It soon stopped me. I would toil painfully upwards, gasping.

I knew of course what I was doing. It was the hill inside myself that I was attacking and could never surmount. It reared like a wall. It was the enemy. My legs gave up the struggle, I stood still and sucked in air. My chest rose and fell, I was lungs and slobber; I had turned myself into a pump. Nothing mattered but this rock in my chest I was struggling to swallow, while I trudged on upwards and my aching chest laboured. I was devouring air in lumps, and on the way down it rasped.

11

The heat generated under my shirt made the skin of my back prickle, but I would be too embedded in darkness to scratch. The hopeless animal I had become would carry me up the hill. When I reached the top by the clump of firs, and the huge flapping open light struck at me I would lift my head, amazed to find I had arrived. The space packed with wind changed me into a thistle. I would stand swaying, feeling greenly translucent, my back all prickles and my head as if about to sow seeds, blowing and wild.

Already, though I was high, the land would have twisted on itself and buried any sign of the mill. If I had any purpose then this was it, to give myself the illusion of a free being attached to nowhere. I would set off mechanically down the road towards Feock, which had a post office – not that I was in need of stamps or a telephone. The road carried me past Gweek Farm, where my friend Guy Franklin lived with his wife and child in an extension they rented to the rear of the main premises. Though it wasn't a time to call unannounced – and Guy would probably be out – I was usually driven to walk past, an exercise so pointless that I was obliged to deny what I was doing in the very act of doing it.

2

I remember one such walk. Gaining the respite of the Heights I tramped on, lulled by the aerial views and buoyed up in the blowy, soundlessly drumming light. Hearing the roar of tractor approaching I edged over to the verge. The machinery clattered past with its stink of silage, dripping black slime. A man driving, his thighs spread, his red cheeks shaking, calling out my name.

'Morning,' I shouted, lifting my hand in recognition but in fact not recognising the driver from his squashed-up profile. Feeling diminished and foolish away from my work I strode on as if purposefully, glad to be whipped by the wind and wanting to be scourged, even accused. In the lingering blast of diesel and silage smell I was left with something I was once again trying to shake off, a despair in my legs and shoulders so tangible, so physical, I half believed I could have got at it with a knife.

Near the milk churns standing on the gappy plank platform I dragged my feet, lingered, went on again. The churns marked the left turn down to Gweek Farm. Thoughts of evenings spent in near oblivion with my friend overcame me in a wash of sentiment. On the other side of the road a milkman I knew vaguely was dragging his battery-driven trolley. He turned his large head, fixed me with a fierce expression and bawled a greeting. I waved my hand. The dwarfish man kept moving, a canary yellow figure in his creaking and rubbing oilskins, his short legs synchronised to the chugging float. His full bottles and his empties danced little jigs over the freshly tarred and gravelled road.

I wheeled round in my tracks. Back again by the turning to Gweek Farm I wavered again. Thinking with anguish that all I wanted was to be poulticed by the soft brown eyes and warm tongue of my young friend, I walked down the lane towards Guy's door. Unless he had slept in, he would be away in Cambourne doing whatever it was that art students did. Yvonne, his wife, would be there alone. I didn't like her. Still I headed for their gate, and still hoped to see Guy's ready smile caught in the steamed glass of the kitchen window.

A sudden squall of hailstones, like hard sugar, and then an icy rain thick as gruel burst against my neck and shabby green corduroy shoulders as I heard her coming. But nothing happened. I banged harder. When the door opened, the elements were lashing at me at last as I had wanted, so viciously that I was galvanised into gasping, 'Yvonne!'

Yvonne's long bony face had a comic, impasted look. Her sallow skin was loaded with disbelief. 'It's you, Frank. Better come in.'

Her teeth gleamed a false welcome at me. They could be dentures, I thought, young as she is. But her greyish-greeny eyes – for some reason I never registered their colour precisely – were real, gnashing coldly with questions. Though I didn't care for her, I admired her steel.

Her mind was darting and spinning – I could see it – to sort out the problem of my arrival. She said, 'Guy's not here, I suppose you know.' Following her in, I stepped round the crawling baby.

'I didn't think he would be. I was just passing.'

I guessed that she would avoid picking Jasmine up. I was right. In a mood to confess things, I saw it was useless. As usual she shrank me into a perverse and unmanageable cold cat, bristling like her with premonitions.

'How are you?' she said stiffly.

'I'm fine,' I lied.

'Good.'

Hovering at the living room door I mopped with a handkerchief at my half drowned head, letting my hair drip into my collar and over my cheeks. Yvonne thrust a towel at me. 'Here, use this.'

Jasmine, a mute crawler, was dragging herself upright with the aid of a chair and a series of grunts. The chair toppled, and I nearly jerked out my arm to help. Just in time I remembered Yvonne's steely rules. She saw baby care as a refusal to intervene until absolutely necessary. The infant lay on the coarse ginger matting and struggled, getting redder, grunting once or twice, breaking wind once, not crying.

'Pardon?' Yvonne said.

'I didn't say anything.'

Could she hear my thoughts? The baby's grubby blue jersey rode higher and I saw the peach-soft skin, the twirled belly-knot. From the ballooning plastic pants that crackled with every move, biting in at the leg-holes, there rose a sickly-sweet odour.

I rubbed my hair partly dry and sat down. The sofa was old, and so low, with broken springs, that I sank into a hole. Wedged there like a frog, I was unable to stop looking at the child's skull, the pure line it traced on the wall behind, and its inadequate neck. Mostly though it was the tender nape – with its fluffy-chicken look – which had triggered my sensation. I thought the years had carried me beyond the reach of such pleasures.

As my wonder broke, my fingers itched for a pencil. I made an attempt to hand Yvonne the towel but was trapped by the hole I sat in.

'You'll have to stay there,' she scoffed. Taking it away abruptly, the efficient teacher, she called from the kitchen, 'We've stopped drinking tea and coffee.'

'Why have you?'

'Bad for the nerves.'

'Mine are past caring.'

'Do you like drinking chocolate?'

'Yes, yes I do.'

14

Stranded there ridiculously, I heard my voice rise too high, almost female. Something in me shuddered. I spun a fantasy of myself in a ward among geriatrics, and Yvonne the charge nurse. My voice fluting out would be in a dither to please and at the same time be difficult – an escapee's. Imagining it I was both shocked and pleased.

In the kitchen I heard the radio snap on. It played 'Satisfaction', and I was startled to hear Yvonne sing along with it in brief abandonment, a young woman who dressed and behaved so soberly. I was never sure of her, what was real and what impersonation, but I believed those sharp pointed eyes. I was even glad not to be liked by them.

Sucking hot chocolate over the rim of the crude stone mug, I got ready for her question – she always asked it – as she perched on a hard chair opposite. 'Della all right?'

She sat tipping her own drink from a tall glass in a cream holder with a handle – what my father would have called a bakelite. Telling her that yes, I thought so, I became aware of her body, her long figure inside the denims and hand-knitted navy sweater, and wondered what she did that was so dismissive of it. Her long brown hair was scraped back and coiled. Putting down her glass she raised her arms, clasping hands behind her head and twisting from the waist. I suspected that this was for effect. Her lips seemed to be regarding themselves, clever and inward. She had a bad habit of slightly smiling at everything. It could be Guy entering the room, or it could be the baby, spewing back whole spoonfuls from the fat pouches of its cheeks.

She smiled now. 'You say you think so?'

'Well, I haven't seen her lately.'

Eager to hear more, she was too proud to ask. She drew up her knees. At these moments I would feel myself heartily disliked, as our eyes met and we were connected. It was as if we each respected the boundaries of the other.

'Would you like a biscuit?'

'I don't think so.'

'Digestive?'

Like a wavering child who doesn't want anything but is troubled, who simply hopes to be comforted, I shook my head.

'Oh, go on. Do you like gingers?'

She was about thirty, and Guy at twenty-five was a kind of big child, as malleable as Jasmine. I murmured

15

again, 'No thanks,' just like a child with the devil in him.

'Another drink?'

'No.'

'So where is Della at the moment?'

'London. I haven't seen her for the past three or four weeks. You know how she likes London, Yvonne. It pulls her like a magnet. She gets bored with all this green. I suppose if you've got New York in your system then you need excitement.'

'Strange. I never do.'

For once I felt like sticking up for my wife. 'She misses the bad air,' I joked and defended.

'I hate big cities, but that's just me. Guy has a thing about the States, he says he'll explode if he doesn't go soon. Would he like it, though, I wonder? What do you think?'

'It's hard to say. New York's not America, they tell me.'

After our marriage Della went on using her professional name. I always thought of her as Della Burls. It isn't even a marriage in name only, I would laugh, frivolous as only the modern mind can be. Right from the start, at my first big show in London where we first met, I had got her wrong. From something she said I assumed she was a writer – and I was drawn to the idea of writers. It seems painters often are. No, she wasn't one, but explained that she was 'into visuals, like you.' In her case this meant photography. She called herself a photo-journalist.

Then she went on to explain that what she did wasn't so creative. There was the tricky business of deciding where the technology ended and she came in. 'I don't kid myself, believe me.' But soon after we commenced living together it rankled, and before long it was making her furious, what she saw as my primitive cave art with its damned pretensions. One afternoon we had a terrible row and it came spilling out, though her words were incomprehensible to me at the time. A cry of rage was torn from her that made my blood fall back appalled. From then on the entanglements of our egos and the confusions bred during our love-making affected everything, from meals and walks to the very glances we gave each other.

In the States, where I had gone hoping to spend six months, we lived partly in her apartment and the rest of the time visiting two Jewish acquaintances of mine who were admirers of my work. These hosts were generous and welcoming, but because of their connection with me Della could barely disguise her antipathy. 'Who the hell are you,' she howled once, 'to come over here and be applauded, when I've been sweating blood for years to get a look in?'

I cut short my stay and returned to London. Later, Della rejoined me in Camden, where I had a capacious, tottering old house. Getting married was my idea. I explained to her one day that my disorderly single life was unnatural, while she listened warily and subdued her own inner chaos – memories of two ex-husbands and innumerable lovers. She had been in group therapy and then analysis since 1966, dealing, she informed me, with the damage inflicted on her by her parents. I was too English to take this seriously. In those days I was a mixture of ignorance and arrogance. If I believed anything it was in my own instincts. And these were telling me to get married. As I see it now, my desire for marriage at any cost arose from my mother and father, both of them dead, speaking with one voice from wherever they were. I had mourned them long enough. Now I wanted to be reconciled to them by some act, by a ritual. Or perhaps I simply wanted to imitate them.

Yvonne and I had run out of things to say. I was trying edgily to leave and to find words for a goodbye. As a rule, even with Guy present, I would leave lamely, and then feel a perfect fool. At my age I still hadn't mastered this art. I steered around the wobbly astonished baby that was sitting up straight as it concentrated on the great moving universe I represented. 'Tell Guy to come down – and you too, any time,' I mumbled.

'Jasmine, what a lot of room you take up,' Yvonne cried, sounding triumphant for some reason.

'Pretty name.'

Yvonne smiled. She held the door open. 'Do you think so?'

'Why, don't you?' I must have looked surprised.

'No, as a matter of fact I think it's silly.'

'Then it was Guy's idea?'

Instead of answering, she smiled. As it happened, I knew already.

'Bye, Francis,' Yvonne said. She closed the door.

Women usually address me by my full name, and I am called Frank by men. I've never understood why this should be so.

17

My name is Francis Breakwell. On paintings I sign Breakwell at the bottom right-hand corner.

As a child, seeing boys exchange glances and titter behind their hands, I realised that my first name could be mistaken for a girl's. I quickly changed it to Frankie – for them. One day my mother heard a playmate use this altered name. She was indignant, not knowing I was the instigator of it, urging it on others and then disowning my action. It was perhaps my first conscious act of deceit.

I was already a compulsive starer. She would order me to stop. 'How many times have I got to tell you? What is it, what are you looking at?'

'Nothing.'

It went on all the time, an annoying habit no one could break. Later, as an adult, I thought I must have been like a fish, never closing my eyes. Yet often I wanted to be invisible, as I went swimming through time and space, my new fluid. I felt too naked. There was probably a gleam of fear in my eyes. Discovering art meant the discovery of a floating world, where I could swim in something more congenial – in my experiences, my memories, in my dreams and my thoughts.

The images of men and women in my childhood seemed immensely tall, huge with terror or joy. One Saturday night I was coming home with my friends Tommy Soames and Ken Abel, and we saw a drunk. As we watched, he collapsed slowly against a wall, choked deep in his throat and threw up a rope of pale glittery stuff on the pavement. Suddenly he rose up, black as a wave, lurching forward across the street in our direction. We scattered wildly. At a safe distance we formed up again. 'Whoa!' he yelled, jerking immensely long arms and wobbling. Twisting our heads in fear we ran for it, streaking off to the next corner where we always split up. On my own, I pelted along with the smell of vomit in my nostrils. Thoughts rushed about in my mind, my limbs, even reaching my toes. My whole body was in turmoil. I told myself that next time we did drawing at school, and Mr Edwards told us to make something up out of our heads, I would do a drunk man at night, bleeding the strange drunkenness all over the coarse sugar paper like sick, in red and yellow and black, colours as lurid and violent as my feelings. The black would be the huge gummy man rising in a soundless roar, and the night coming out of him.

3

On the way home I found myself recalling aspects of Yvonne for a portrait. Artists are opportunists. I knew that portraits of someone seen with a cold eye could have that extra bite. Back again at the mill, I skirted the primitive farm area – which amounted to a third of the premises – where the farmer stored fertilizer and implements. I heard a voice from the barn. It was the farmer, Luckcraft, grousing away to one of his labourers. Not wanting to pass the time of day I stood still like a thief, then slipped round the corner to my stone porch. Once inside I felt better at once.

It was a long low kitchen. The table filling it, covered in scars and gaps, shone dully under the light I had left burning by mistake. When I was in the mood, if I had the place entirely to myself, I spread paper on this table sometimes and worked.

I switched off the light, then worked the stiff bolt up and down cautiously on the door till it slid home. Now no one could get at me.

I opened the Aga and shoved in more wood. Left to myself, I hardly ever cooked. I had never bothered to learn how. All the stove did was keep the damp at bay and heat up the water. Once, however, starving and happy at the end of a good day's work, I did concoct a stew out of bully beef and some dried-out onions and carrots, wolfing the mess down without pausing long enough to ask what it tasted like.

I said 'Yvonne' aloud, since I was still thinking Yvonne thoughts. Since coming in I hadn't stopped moving, circling the table with my head down, peering into the yard from the narrow 'cat' window near the sink, left open permanently for the cats to worm in and out. 'You peer,' Della said once. It was true. Was it something you started to do at a certain age? I remember it of my father, and of his father: both of them peered.

Upstairs, entering the workroom where I also slept, I was too unsettled to begin a portrait. Even thinking of Yvonne so concentratedly was like manifesting a series – a series with variations.

As well as peering, I have become a potterer. I pottered about, picking up this and that, a sheep skull for instance, its teeth still intact, the cranium bleached and earth-stained, with blotches crying out to be interpreted. 'Not by me,' I said aloud, simply to hear the thought, and for the comfort of something human.

I moved again, made restless by my thoughts. Really my thoughts have always been feelings. 'Yvonne will think I called in because Della's away and I don't know what to do with myself. I don't care, let her think what she likes.' But the thought scratched away and I shifted again. 'When Guy comes home, running in excitedly all bright-eyed with a love he's been nursing all the way from Cambourne, will she tell him that I'm missing Della? That I'm lonely?' The truth is that I would grow lonelier with Della around. As soon as she became permanently installed my need to call on people intensified. I put it down to her implacable nature. She was now openly uncompromising in a way that she had probably always been inside herself. We had reached the point where we were talking past each other, that is when we attempted communication at all.

Friends such as Henry Duffin in London would tell me I was getting odd. Realising that I still had a friend or two left gave me a shock. I was more and more reluctant to visit. Any friends who cared enough were forced to come all the way down to Cornwall to ferret me out. It was only a matter of time before they stopped bothering.

Yet I wasn't quite a recluse. Dressed up I could still look smart. I would accept the occasional invitation to a party. There I would try to loll around with the best of them, but in fact doing what I always did, observing. A non-smoker, I would soon be in trouble with stinging eyes. Whatever was poured out for me I drank, till the heaviness behind my forehead felt like experience. Until that happened I felt peculiar, ridiculously innocent and lost.

I remember one evening in Cambourne. I had just reached the convivial stage when a lecturer in art history approached me. 'Hallo,' he said. 'Francis Breakwell, isn't it? What are you up to these days? Are you preparing earth-shattering surprises for us? I hope it's something thrilling, something *new* at any rate. My God, how we long to be rejuvenated!' He was terribly thin, and seemed to fall back inside his dusty green cord suit with the effort of saying this.

I gulped down more of the red wine. 'I live in hopes, like you,' I said. Then my nervous larynx developed spasms and I had a fit of violent coughing.

'My dear fellow, I'm sure you do.' His dry face buckled affably and he laughed.

Even red in the face, spluttering and feeling foolish, I was fascinated by the man's backward-sloping sheep's teeth.

It was March, the early spring of the south west. Soon I would be faced with the terrifying newness of real growth, exploding the seeds and splitting the winter crust with invisible shoots. Already the elms were lit by a reddish glow. I became aware of the stirring of roots. Almost horrible, because so relentless, it affected me like a torment. As always at this time of year I felt threatened by a force I knew I must emulate. I would ask myself in self-mockery: 'What do your puny efforts amount to? Are they necessary? Doesn't the huge outer struggle and your tiny one issue from the same darkness?' Surely this was true. What I thought of as the black orgy included me. I was attached howling to the same miry root.

I would light the big green oil stove and plant myself over it, rubbing my palms until the dry chafing sound reminded me of lonely old men. Once I saw a photo of Augustus John standing over an identical heater, his eyes bulging defiantly. The thing looked so nautical, so ship-shape that I went out and bought one.

There were also associations with poverty, and these I ignored. I preferred to think of myself as living the stripped-down-to-essentials simple life. Although no longer poor, I approved of thrift. There was always the possibility of a windfall, but in art nothing could be relied on. Changes of fortune were forever taking me by surprise. Random sorties as a visiting artist to colleges kept me out of debt.

By now, my stuff had stopped selling: the bonanza of the sixties was fizzling out. None of this bothered me. I had a place to live, plenty of space, and no visible bosses. Della had money, though I couldn't depend on her staying with me. When I thought of her as temporary I felt more relief than alarm. After all, my whole life was temporary. Only in the small hours did the prospect this conjured up twist my stomach into a sick knot. In the morning, out of the emptiness where nothing moves or hopes, I would be rescued by a collection of daubs, a mixture of paint and turps dribbling down in little helpless emissions, a jagged line or two going nowhere: nothing ambitious like a picture. But I would have left an audacious mark or two on the yawning void.

21

Della wasn't impressed. On one of the rare occasions when she looked in on me, she said, pointing at the canvas, 'Is that new?'

'Yes.'

'You're doing pastiches of your previous work. I noticed that before, the last time I was here.'

'Who better than me?'

'I'm serious.'

'I'm laughing.'

'Another thing, you're getting fussy. I used to admire your boldness. Now it's gone.'

'Della, be honest. When did you ever admire anything to do with me?'

'I did once, believe it or not. The first time we met, remember?'

'You thought I was an important person. That hypnotised you. Now you know I'm not.'

'And how!' she laughed, to express her pity for me, and then walked out.

I turned back to my pastiches.

I did have a daily routine, but the jumpy nature of my temperament made it seem botched and makeshift. My room reflected this. The sleeping area had been infiltrated by various objects picked up on my walks; bits of wood, stones, the chain-wheel of a bike, its teeth so congealed with rust as to look malignant, evilly decomposing. I was turning into a scavenger. But there was a Peruvian rug on the boards which had cost plenty, as Della would say. Every so often I noticed it, straightening it with the toe of my shoe to make it lie neatly beside the bed.

Della and I weren't sleeping together. That hadn't lasted long. After I developed the habit of working deep into the night – the electricity blinding me to the existence of shadows – I would lie down on the striped ticking of a button mattress on the floor. Beds worried me, and so did baths; they were too enveloping, like coffins and graves. Della would leave me in peace upstairs, but when her children were on vacation they invariably snooped up and then reported back on what they saw. She had two gangling sons from a previous misalliance.

If I was morose, I saw my marriage to Della as a sad joke. We were like conspirators, we deserved each other. The smell of my shirt under the arms in summer left me in no doubt that I was a bachelor. Della's method of handling the situation was by regarding us as business partners. I admired her tough realism, but not the lines digging down from her cheeks at the sides of her mouth. These gave me sensations of remorse.

It wasn't as though we were at each other's throats. On the contrary, we stepped around each other with the respect one might have for an unexploded bomb in the street. What kind of creatures were we to behave in this way? Was there such a thing in this day and age as a normal couple?

Before the subject of relationships I wavered like a ghost, partly because of my suspicion that what she said about me was true. I had a flaw, a split, she told me. When I wanted to indulge and excuse myself I saw it as a wound. From it came my work. I had become aware of this deep source, whatever it was, long before Della. It probably dawned on me during the time with Maggie that my disability was being put to good use by some inner agent, working day and night and with no more scruples than a gangster.

4

What I relished in Maggie was the directness I was incapable of myself. The very first time we were intimate she rendered me nearly impotent, in spite of my lust, by asking loudly, 'Are you what they call an arse man – or is it legs with you? What d'you like?'

I wanted her whole, I said, not in a selection of butcher's cuts. By 'what do you like' she meant, 'What would you like me to do for you?' No one had ever wanted to please me before. How could I have explained that what I liked was everything, what I wanted was to lose my raw unsatisfied self in her, bury the hard edges I had acquired in the effort to become a man and be delivered between her legs, born from a woman all over again? It was too preposterous, too shaming. She would see it as a kink or an insult, or think I was laughing at her.

'You're a funny cove, you are,' she would say in her strong Cockney, interpreting my silence as oddity, tousling my hair.

23

My hair was plentiful then, and black, sprouting thickly in uncombed tufts. She seemed to find it unusually soft and fine. It pleased her for some reason. She kept playing with it, until I grew irritated, feeling weak as a kitten.

She liked to call me Wes, from Wesley, my middle name. Long after we parted I would recognise her childish handwriting on the envelope of the Christmas card – in awful taste – which arrived without fail each year. 'How's the art, Wes?' she asked once, under her name – an after-thought. The irony didn't escape me. The card was a snow scene, pines and the roofs of thatched cottages sprinkled with glued-on glittery bits. Half of it was loose in the envelope like scurf. I laughed to see it, feeling a surge of idiotic affection. I doubted whether she had seen a thatched cottage in her life. It was impossible to imagine her out of London.

When we met, I had survived nearly two years in London. It was coming up to the sixties. Going round in a dream, concocting dream pictures. I found reality hard to grasp. Time seemed to elude me more than most. Also, I was still young enough to think I would live for ever. 'Life is frightful, but art saves us,' I thought – believing I knew from what, not venturing to ask what for. But two years! Sometimes it seemed two months, or it was like centuries. Changes in the light interested me more than the passage of time.

Plenty had happened. Most important, I had made a start on my true life. I thought of myself now as Breakwell, the name I scrawled on the bottom corner of anything I spared. I had become united at last with what I did, in spite of what I saw as the shame or stigma of art.

As for London, it was undoubtedly foreign and possibly depraved. I experienced the authentic illicit thrills of the born provincial. It frightened me to death, yet I liked it. I was alive with the fear of a threatened species. Not knowing the psychic language of the place meant that I was forced to use my eyes incessantly. Going for walks filled me up chock-full with visual discoveries, to be stored for future use or else forgotten.

Often in those early days I thought of the streets I walked down as belonging to an adopted land, hardly England at all. London seemed altogether too vast and too cold to connect with anything as small and safe as the other England I came from. Surges of exultation came and went. Nothing was expected of me here; I was free, I floated. Nobody gave a damn, I had no name, no history. I felt at times I needed lead in my boots to counteract the weightlessness.

It was weird, scary. At nightfall the shop doorways menaced, when the loneliness crept up and gnawed, the traffic swarmed, the millions of lights went on to create a glittering pie, where families clustered and homes were warmly illuminated in all directions. Then I cowered in my hole down by the river. Once or twice I howled into the pillow. One time after midnight I wanted to stick my head out of the window and scream, proclaiming to London and to the night that I belonged nowhere and was lost for ever.

'How's life?' a man said to me one night, as I hung over the rail on Westminster Bridge and considered suicide. The stranger went on before I could speak, but I couldn't have answered. The black water told me there was no answer. Loneliness, billowing up in the brown dusk over those thousand streets lit with sick yellow light, had I knew hollowed my eyes into black sockets. Once I caught sight of my face, reflected in the distorting mirror of a tube train window. It had changed into a skull. Within me, variations of the same fantasy raced through my mind, as Eros changed into Thanatos and naked women danced with skeletons.

In daylight it was better. Without realising, I had become a denizen of the great city, no longer the good little provincial boy having to behave himself because someone was always watching. In this sense of being free, which was a kind of voluptuousness, I began to exult. I had got out of the cage, I was on some road, on the dark side of a road going somewhere. One day the destination would be revealed to me.

I had begun to work seriously at last, and to admit the seriousness of what I did. Whether it would be of any eventual worth was still the agonising, unproven thing. Therefore I continued to suppress the use of the word 'artist'. When asked what I did for a living, on the rare occasions I was cornered – at the barber's or in a pub – I would say, 'Odd jobs.'

This was at least partly true. I saw the circumstances of my daily life as makeshift, which made the irksome jobs fairly bearable for longish periods. The servitude I had once endured, bowing my head to a life sentence in some office, now belonged in the past. Since coming to London I had taken and chucked up about a dozen jobs. Serving behind the Left Luggage counter at Waterloo had been the last, and the most mindless. My biro doodles were no doubt still there on the greyish worn wood for the next worker and the next to glance at and ignore.

Whatever the wage, I would accept it. Money matters were considered a problem when the cash dwindled, but not otherwise. On pay days I felt good, springing down the street with money in my pocket. I was prepared to go on working at something totally irrelevant as a means to an end, just to pay for the bare necessities of my two rooms and mouse-infested kitchen in the condemned house in Southwark where I now lived. My objective was simple: to hang on where I was, while certain inner changes were taking place. It was as though I was informed by an instinct or the stirrings of some power that I was heading in the right direction. Yet no one else could have seen my progress, any more than they could have seen the air moving in from the river or the onward movement of history, as inexorable and overlooked as the water rising and falling on each tide.

As if to reinforce these hunches, something extraordinary happened. In a cheap cafeteria run by Italians in Great Peter Street, Westminster, I found a big hectic woman, one of the waitresses, with the slow smile of a dairymaid, who was willing to take me on.

'Are you Maggie?' I asked her one day, sitting at my usual table eating breakfast. The grease from the fried egg and beans was still thick on my tongue. She stood over me unselfconsciously, strong-legged, with firm breasts.

'Who told you that, eh?'

I laughed. Pointing at the man behind the cash till, I said, 'He did.'

'Well, he's right. Have you got a problem?'

Amazed by my own boldness, I said, 'Yes, but I can't tell anybody. I'll have a cup of tea instead.'

The young woman smiled. I had aroused her curiosity. From then on she studied me as if looking for clues.

Afterwards, I seemed to remember that living together had been her idea rather than mine. But I was certainly agreeable.

Because of my vagueness and inexperience I regarded her as a girl, up to the point where she mentioned a baby, left behind with her mother in Battersea. Or so she said. If true, it was a peculiar arrangement, one that I was happy not to question. I understood from this admission that she had a past which she was unwilling to divulge. Well, what business was it of mine? Ashamed of my mistrust, I told myself that she would confide all at some future date, when sufficient trust had been established between us.

I now saw her as one of nature's mothers, though at times she acted like a girl. Was this purely for my sake? Gradually she let on that the other men she had known had all expected it. She liked to give rather than take, and she liked to please. When it came to giving men what they thought they wanted she was as protean as the next woman.

She had moved in without ceremony, and then gone sniffing about in corners like a cat. In her slovenly fashion she took over the whole set-up at once, including my impenetrable silences, when I withdrew as if to another room inside my head for a contest with my self-disgust.

At first she made a joke of it. 'Now where have you gone?'

'I'm still here.'

'Oh, are you? In that case, why haven't I heard from you?'

She was often lonely. I felt guilty, because I too had suffered from loneliness for years.

'Don't think I'm not noticing you. I am.'

'How would I know?'

Ashamed, but not really contrite, I made a decision to act differently in future. Before long I was drifting off again for long periods inside myself. I would announce my return with a remark about the meal she was putting in front of me.

'Oh, hello,' she would say. 'Come back, then?'

'Sorry.'

'That was a long trip, that was.'

I might grin, or give her a dirty look, depending on how the painting was going.

She would have unpredictable crying jags on lonely nights, when she was overtired, out on her feet. Soon my inflamed nerves were writhing in sympathy, or a mixture of sympathy and frustration. If she went on long enough, I put my arms around her. Then my own tears were liable to flow and mingle weakly with hers. She was shocked at first, and then moved by my exhibition of weakness. It was the same after a flare-up; we wept in each other's arms after the mutual abuse, rocking together on the floor like babes in the wood, getting soaked.

Often I felt exasperated to screaming point by the demands of her cheerful nature. Basically she was an optimist, she accepted.

27

When I needed her body, she gave it to me. In exchange for a bit of attention she flooded me with her love. I assumed it was either saintliness in disguise or a form of craziness, as a result of which I was bathed in an unstoppable simplicity. She kept bouncing the irresistible force of her satisfaction at me, whether I protested or not.

She was all light, I decided, flooding and squandering. Whatever she was, a shameless pervert in me wanted to fracture the goodness, to make some dark howling passion run out. The café-stickiness of her love would oppress me. My feelings, such as they were, seemed to be running away down the sink along with hers. It could have been her jubilant refusal to discriminate that I resented, since I was essentially a fault-finder. Yes, that, and her blind faith in life itself, rather than in me.

I suffered with the knowledge of how I was – my ungrateful grabbing when it suited me, my stiff neck and shoulders, my reluctance to pour everything down this channel we had in common, that she called love, when there were unborn paintings waiting to be dragged into the light.

But not only that. I was trying to bandage up my conscience for other, more material reasons, now that Maggie was in fact keeping us both with her earnings at the Cypriot restaurant in Victoria – she had been made redundant at the Westminster place. I told her, more as a sop to myself than from any conviction that it would really happen, that there was a chance of a dealer for my pictures when I was ready. This was true, but hedged about with imponderables. Telling Maggie the complicated truth in its entirety was a waste of energy, I reasoned, when an edited version was perfectly satisfactory.

'Will you be ready soon?'

'The way things are going, yes, with luck.'

'That's great, isn't it?'

'Not so loud. I'm superstitious.'

'Oh, so I am. Tell me what you're afraid of, go on.'

'Impotence.'

'Now what are you talking about? There's nothing wrong with you down there.'

'I mean the painting. I might wake up one day and find it's gone.'

Maggie stared at me. 'Which painting? Gone where?'

I shook my head. 'Never mind, forget it.'

'I'm superstitious about you. One day you'll disappear. Sling your hook.'

'That's not superstition, that's insecurity.'

'I'm that as well.'

I felt an urge to boast, and tell her about Charles Woodruff, my admirer in Staffordshire, who had interested himself in me when I was on the point of giving up art altogether. Thanks to him, I now had a connection or two in London which I could follow up at the proper time, when I was sure enough. I had gone snooping by the galleries in question. My postponements were not exactly failures of nerve, or not only that. What held me back for the moment was my own dissatisfaction, rather than fear of humiliation at the hands of cold strangers. Was I good enough or not? In my worst falls from grace these doubts became disbelief, and I came shuffling to a dead halt inside myself. Then I sickened, looked gradually grey in the face, and thought I could hear my own soul flapping feebly, in the airless room smelling of damp that was now a home.

5

At least with Maggie I had been left on weekdays to wallow in bed in the mornings without guilt. Della, being American, rose each morning like an eagle and levelled her beaky profile at the daylight, as if this was her first task, to splinter it. Then she would move about crashing doors and wrenching open cupboards. It was partly to escape this terrific dynamism of hers that I had tried to marry myself to my work again, with a domain of my own upstairs. But she was away, for how long I didn't know. I was not accustomed to receiving any communication from her, and none had come. There was no need to use the concealment of work or silence. Instead of being glad, I felt at a loss.

An afternoon sun was shining. The firs and beeches jostled the weak sun as it entered my grimy windows fitfully, wavering over the floor and the end wall. It lit up the patinas of dust coating everything, the dirty newspaper palettes lying where I had flung them months ago. I stooped down and screwed up a few of them, aiming the stiff encrusted handfuls at the cardboard box under the trestle table I used for watercolours and drawings.

I sniffed the sleeve of my jacket, wrinkling my nose at the stench. Halfway back from Gweek Farm and Yvonne I'd encountered a small olive-green truck parked on the corner. Its nearside door was ajar. Freddie sat inside, a youth who divided his labour between Luckcraft and a pig farmer near Devoran.

'Want a lift?' he asked me. The youth was pallid and thick-faced, with great pouting lips twisted up at one side. The profile was fearsome, until you saw the gentle cast of the eyes and were disconcerted.

'I won't say no.'

I tried to drag the door wider but the hinges were seized up with rust, so I squirmed through to the powdery seat as best I could. Freddie waited. He wasn't one for speech. The door clanged with a tin-can crash as I heaved at it. We set off. I sat slumped in a manner which I hoped conveyed gratitude, enveloped in the stink of pig.

A phone ringing below my feet put an end to this reverie. I let it go on making futile demands on the silence. Finally it gave up. Della handled what calls there were, since I was reluctant to break off whatever I was doing. Talking into what to me was a black threat she let herself flow with such ease that I could almost see the waves leaving her body to go lapping out through space.

Shaken by the disturbance, I waited for the silence to reform and settle upon me. To help matters I went over to the mattress and lay down fully dressed on top of it. With my hands behind my head, I let my gaze wander and my thoughts curl and loop the loop. I felt stupid and senseless, empty of meaning, as I always did when I hadn't worked for some time. I lacked inner nourishment, the spiritual food which came from what I did.

Waking in the mornings in this isolated spot with the place to myself, I was like a virgin or a nervy spinster, threatened by strange sounds. The rattling window down in the kitchen would intimidate me maliciously until I identified it. I had stomach cramps. Although reason told me that I only had to stand up for the pains to cease, I could spend an hour suspecting ulcers and worse. If Della was home, I lay flinching at the morning onslaught, following her progress from bedroom to bathroom, hearing the angry charge downstairs and the pans and dishes clashing as the breakfast warfare broke out. During college vacations, either Lee or Ben – they rarely came together – would get hollered at until they replied or went down.

A letter had come from my sister. I was saving it for the evening, as a treat, and to keep me company. Vivien wrote rarely, but when she did it was an event, as if she had stepped physically into the room and then kissed and hugged me. The words she wrote gave me intense pleasure, even though I usually forgot to reply to them. I was always promising myself a visit. What a pity she had been working elsewhere when I lived in Southwark, and after that in Camden. One day, I promised, I would drop everything and set out to see her. We would talk nonstop into the early hours and review both our pasts. It had been so long since we had last seen each other.

Vivien was now a supply teacher in London. Our mother had died when she was barely a fortnight old, so there was a gap of fifteen years between us. Now and then I wondered about her, well into her thirties and still unmarried, but with curiosity rather than surprise. I felt sure that nothing she did would ever surprise me. Her spirit was restless, her feelings volatile. She was a born wanderer. She had done VSO work in Africa, had lived in a kibbutz in Israel for six months. India beckoned, and so did China, so did Thailand. In her letters she always seemed to be revealing herself with delightful frankness, but what did I really know about her?

As a young girl she had been rather forbidding. Seeing her at our father's funeral I was quick to recognise a replica of myself at that age. But whereas she flared and was openly fanatical in opposition, my dissent would have been (and still is) masked by passivity. Meeting her again, I recoiled from her extremism as from a flame. Vivien, I thought, what's in store for you? In a world like this, built on lying and compromise, how will you cope? And how do I? Dismayed though I must have been, I was faced with beauty of a kind.

After the initial shock of the telegram I had tried to feel grief for my father's death. I ended up worried because I couldn't. Our inarticulate relationship had remained static and undeclared. When he married again it was as if I had been abandoned, cast out. I went to his funeral like someone with a strict task to perform, spruced up, but with no emblems: no black tie, no armband.

31

Vivien opened the door as I scrambled out of the taxi. For an instant, shocked by her pallor, I saw the face of an ingénue, tinged with hellishness. I gaped at her, this icily composed girl with a severe fringe, as if at a revelation. She was small and straight, flat-chested. I started believing in her absolutely from that moment; she was so evidently part of me.

'Are the others here?' I managed to say, meaning the uncles and aunts and cousins I hardly knew.

'I hate them all,' she said.

I looked at her aghast, then felt relief as she kissed me shyly on the cheek.

'How are you?' I said.

'Fine, thanks.'

I didn't believe it. Entering the tiny hall and following her into the packed room, I asked, 'Do you find this hard to take?'

'It's so strange. Who are these people?'

'Relatives. Don't you know anybody?'

'Aunt Lizzie and Uncle George, that's all. Who's that man over there? What's he laughing for in that horrible way? Tell him to stop it, it's disgusting.'

'I can't do that.'

'Then I will.'

Just in time I caught hold of her arm. 'No, Vivien! Try to understand. Things aren't what they seem at funerals.' I spoke as one would speak to someone who had taken flight back into childhood. 'People laugh because they don't know what else to do.'

A thin-lipped, orange-haired woman came up to us. It was Margot, our stepmother. She had never liked me. She had a small girl and an older boy from a previous marriage. She said disagreeably, 'It's you, Francis. Vivien, there's someone over here who hasn't met you before.'

Vivien jerked back her head as if stung. The blood rushed to her face. 'Tell them no, I won't. I won't meet anybody, I don't want to!' She ran for the stairs and disappeared.

'Now you see what I have to put up with,' Margot said bitterly. 'That girl's impossible, she always has been. Of course she hates me, that's the top and bottom of it. She'll do anything to spite me. God knows, I've done my best to fit in. I expect your father told you how hard it's been here for me.'

'No, as a matter of fact he didn't.'

'Is it my fault, then?'

'I don't suppose it's anybody's.'

'Oh, that's easy for you to say. You cleared out, you're well away from things aren't you, down there in London?'

'Yes, Margot.'

'You don't like me really, any more than she does.'

'Margot, I don't know you.'

She turned away. Over her shoulder, she said, 'You've always got out of responsibilities if you ask me. Your father said you'd got a lazy streak. He was right.'

She had told me this before, one Monday morning when I had overslept and stayed home instead of going in to the office. She and my father were newly married. As soon as I could I found a bedsitter in another district and moved out.

I went upstairs in search of Vivien. The door to her room was ajar. She stood inside with her back to me.

'You've got too much pride,' I said. 'So have I. It's no fun, is it, being an outsider.'

Misunderstanding, she shrugged her thin shoulders angrily and wouldn't speak. I could see half her face. She had pale doubting features. I kept staring, watching. After such a long absence I couldn't get over her sharp crystallization. She had changed into a stranger, a young person in her own right, pale as the cress sprouting in the cupboard that time – hundred of years ago in my childhood – from seeds sown on a bit of flannel in a cracked saucer. It was the only image I could find to convey her delicate blanched whiteness, and the impression she gave of a creature waiting blindly in the dark to escape. What I saw as her lonely vigil touched me, though it lay between us. My whole life up to that moment had been a struggle to overcome just such an isolation. I dreaded the fate she represented with such awful clarity.

'I'm afraid,' she said, in a voice hoarse with fear.

'What of?'

'Those people down there.'

'Why are you? They're only being themselves, like us.'

'I don't understand them.'

'But you will. Anyway, nothing lasts for ever. Our mother used to quote a framed motto she saw once at the dentist's. It said, "Don't worry, it may never happen."'

'Did it?'

I laughed. 'Probably.'

'Was she ever frightened?'

'God, yes. She was even frightened of being frightened.'

The faint smile raised by this nonsense of mine was my reward. Eventually I coaxed her back downstairs. She went and stood in the middle of the room like a post. Her very thinness seemed a reproof, addressed to me as well as to everyone else as she stood there in a frozen attitude, her stilted movements in marked contrast to all the relatives, pressing round the table with crude healthy appetites for the cold meat sandwiches.

Back again in Camden, in the draughty seclusion of my rattling, peeling old house in Valenciennes Street, I marvelled afresh at the uncluttered near-empty rooms as if I had achieved them myself by an act of sheer inspiration. Now that I was free, motherless and fatherless, I could reconstitute myself in accordance with my heart's desires. Successive blows of fate had brought me to the brink of the liberation I had secretly dreamed about. For a few moments at least, as I stood in the shabby kitchen, I wanted to thank what powers there were for bringing me to this point.

But grief for my father did exist after all. Suddenly it welled up from deep underground. I had sat down to a meal. Instead of sitting squarely I sat sideways on, as if about to spring up again – an old habit of mine. Like a powerful hand, the grief twisted me round, forcing my head down to the deal table. As I bent lower I began to croak, hearing it as though from someone else. I was weeping. I felt as old as my dead father. I had nothing after all. I was naked as the day I was born, yet old. Like a bereft old man I sat sobbing, swallowed up in my own abandonment. In the end it became a luxury I clung on to, unwilling to let go, as I dangled in the great vaulting space left by my father's death.

Emotionally worn out, I sat crouched at the table with the strange feeling that my body no longer belonged to me. I began to notice the fine wrinkles on the backs of my hands. It could have been the cold house. I chafed at the dry skin of one with the dry palm of the other, then got up and stood near the oil heater, another habit born of solitude. I would plant my feet apart like a nightwatchman, cupping my hands to receive the hot rising air. As my body enjoyed a sensuality of its own, my feathery mind drifted about. The column of green metal warmed my thighs, the heat rose before my chest in soft eddying currents. I would edge too close, and then the acrid smell of scorch in my nostrils warned me to move back, sometimes too late to avoid being branded. The scars of thigh burns across my jeans became slits eventually – evidence of my daydreaming.

Standing there now, I began guiltily, in the grateful warmth of my empty new life, to imagine colour and form for the tumult of grief I had just experienced. I was so humbled, so glad. To suffer is to live. I stood by the window, dreaming and postponing, waking slowly to an awareness of woodlice moving clumsily under the sink, feeling as I watched an emotion curiously like love. It was a side window where I stood; the house jutted out peculiarly at this point. There were no curtains yet. If I had been looking outward I would have seen the street. To anyone passing by it must have seemed as though I was gazing avidly at them.

6

Outside the mill, nothing stirred. I tore open the envelope.

Dear Francis,

I am writing this from my new address. Yes, I've moved again as you can see. Please make a note of it. This is what you do all the time in London. Why don't you come up sometime? I keep inviting you, what a stick-in-the-mud you are!

Or are you a hermit now? If so, how will I know? I only ask because I share a flat now (these two rooms) with a girl, Celia, who takes after her lawyer father and cross-examines me closely about you. What should I tell her? She's an *agent-provocateur* too – she keeps urging me to come and see you. Should I?

If I'm honest I must say that what stops me is Della, I mean the thought of her. Alas, she doesn't like me. That's a shame, because I was prepared to worship her. I'd never met anyone who impressed me more. Such confidence! I suppose what she hates about me is what everyone dislikes. She probably sees me as a prissy arrogant little bitch looking at her snottily in the worst English manner. Oh, dear, how unfair.

This letter was intended to introduce you to my friend Celia. Next time she will have top billing. What else can I tell you? This supply teaching is killing me. At the end of the day you go off crawling, fit for nothing and no one.

Celia is going to evening classes at the Literary Institute. A homosexual writer who also teaches there has her in thrall. She says I must enroll and see for myself. She's very persuasive. Over her bed she has pinned up a big photo of her idol, Sylvia Plath.

I'll sign off now, I'm falling off the bottom of this page as well as falling asleep.

Your sadly absent sister,
Vivien

Reading the letter again, I became conscious of a growing agitation. Upset, I started to trail up and down, hands stuffed into my trouser pockets. I knew what was wrong. My longing to see Vivien's face and hear her voice was turning into an obsession. Under it lay a desire to be reunited with her for good. Fantastic as this was, I began to ask myself in all seriousness how it could be achieved.

Glancing round at the clutter of my workroom, my eye was caught by a version of Guy Franklin's head among the propped slabs of masonite, his likeness barely identifiable because of the distortion and the blurring with rags. I went over and half-heartedly aimed a kick at it. Even my disgust lacked force. The afternoon had gone dark and opaque, and a lethargy took hold of me, glueing me to the spot. I must either move or petrify. I told myself I would go back up the hill as soon as it was evening and see Guy. The unfinished portrait would have to do as an excuse. Yvonne could think what she liked. Instead of keeping Vivien's letter for later, I had used it up. Reading it had made me more restless than ever.

I knocked on Yvonne's door, thought I heard my name called and went barging in. In my head I was engrossed, as I had been all the way up, with the multiple problems generated by Guy's portrait. It had reached that stage. A face provided so many distractions – the slope of a cheek, lighted pupils, the foxy cross-hatching at the edges of eyes. So many deceits, false trails: the opposite of naked, I felt. For the elimination of lies it would be better to paint a man's back. The truthfulness of a

36

back was sometimes too awful to contemplate – the equivalent in a man to a woman's bared breasts.

Yvonne said, 'Guy won't be a minute. He's just putting Jasmine to bed.'

I could hear her squawks from above. 'She sounds fractious.'

'A bit, yes.'

Things went quiet. The young father bounded down the stairs and came in. Guy looked flushed and happy. Of medium height, brown-haired, athletic, he was every girl's dream of a dark good-looking male. He looked gentle as well as strong. Unable to resist the commotion he caused, he was forever in woman trouble of one kind or another. This had more to do with his silver tongue than his handsome profile. Adoration of the female came naturally to him, and was indiscriminate. Yet he talked endlessly about his first love when he was sixteen, a country sweetheart enshrined in his memory and sought every-where in one form or another. Emotional excess could be found as easily with a mature woman in Birmingham inflamed by his romanticism as in the first sighting of a badger at midnight. I was another unlikely focus for his idolisation. I laughed in his face, but indulgently. It touched and warmed me even as I suspected it, I suppose because I liked him. impossible though he was. I liked his humour, his nimble mind, his thick brown eyebrows that met over the bridge of his nose, his big knowing eyes jumping with life at this moment from his wife to me as he flattered us both in different ways with his sly caresses. Because I was so much older he called me 'Young Frank' when he was at his most cloyingly affectionate. 'Hello there, young Frank,' he said now. 'I ws only saying to Yvonne when she told me you've been and gone – bloody hell, and I wanted to see him. I've missed you.'

'Really?'

'I have, Frank.'

Embarrassed by what I took to be sham love, yet with a sneaking wish for it to be true, I said, 'I'm not interrupting your dinner I hope?' It was the sort of thing you asked of a couple and then regretted, since it advertised the barren nature of your own life and it invited pity.

'We've eaten, thank you,' Yvonne said.

'Ah, we have,' Guy said. He rubbed his belly for emphasis. Then, warm where Yvonne was cold, he immediately asked if I was hungry.

'No, no.'

'I bet you could eat something. Like a bacon butty.'

'No, honestly.'

I wasn't hungry for food, but would have enjoyed sharing a meal with them, sitting at the table like a member of the family. I wondered if they ever suspected this?

We sat in the sitting room a little awkwardly. Yvonne's watchfulness made for a certain restraint. Alone with Guy it was somehow different. I would be the passive listener, amused by his pouring monologues, his fantasies and romances and his comic adventures, real and imagined. I never knew for sure if it was fact or fiction I was listening to. He invented a drama and then acted all the parts with gusto. The dirge he chanted one day would blossom into a rhapsody the next time we met. Everyday reality was always in danger of losing out to a golden age spun from the myth of his childhood. Like Dylan Thomas, the one poet he valued, he had taken a decision never to grow up.

There was also the inside knowledge I possessed, the blow-by-blow accounts of Guy's passionate affairs, confided in moments of crisis. How much did Yvonne know? If he was so confessional when we were together, then in all probability he poured out his sins to her too, when she intercepted a love letter or got wind of an assignation. Why did she put up with it? Did she hope to reform him, alter his compulsive behaviour, his falling in and out of love, as some women attempt to rehabilitate alcoholics?

I called once to see him when Yvonne happened to be out. To my horror, there was Guy kneeling on the floor in the living room over a half-filled tea chest, weeping brokenly into it. His head hung so low, I couldn't see his face. The room was in disarray, clothes and books scattered over the carpet. My first thought was that Jasmine had died or something equally terrible.

'What is is, Guy? What's wrong?' I went across and stooped down, and put my arm round his shoulder.

'She's found out about Pauline. She's leaving me.' He lifted his head, but only to sob, 'I can't bear it, I'll kill myself!'

Pauline was the married woman in Birmingham. She was just a name to me. Guy had been wooing her with letters and with poems set to music for months. A fortnight ago he had gone north for a job interview. The next time we met he was glowing to report on his reunion with Pauline. 'I rang her up and she told me to come round, she was dying for love. Christ, Frank, by the end of the afternoon I was dying after it. What a woman. She slithered all over me like a snake. Her voice though, it makes me tremble, she uses it like an instrument. When she kisses me, breathes into me, I'm all flute. Did I tell you she's a musician? A cellist, yes. She wraps her thighs round me like her bloody cello.'

Now here he was, the sorriest sight, sunk to his knees and all the cocksureness knocked out of him.

'Who told her?' was all I could think to ask.

'Nobody. She found one of Pauline's letters.'

'Where?'

'In a record sleeve where I'd slipped it. I thought she hated *Milk Wood*.'

'So now she's gone? Guy, I'm sorry.'

He jumped to his feet and began wandering up and down wringing his hands. 'No, not yet she hasn't. She's gone into Falmouth to buy the tickets.'

'Tickets? Where to?'

'She wouldn't say. I feel sick. I think I'm going to throw up.'

I felt groggy with shock myself. I had never seen him looking so awful, so distraught. 'Guy, listen, if she's coming back then you've still got a chance. You don't want her to leave, do you?'

He stopped in his tracks, clutching his head. 'I'll go mad if she does. She's my whole purpose, my meaning, her and little Jas, the core of my being. My eyes, my heartbeat. If I lose her, Frank, I'm finished. Washed up. Losing her would be like cutting out my liver. Bloody Pauline, she seduced my soul, tangled up my heartstrings and then twanged on them, just for the hell of it. I wish to God I'd never set eyes on that squelchy bitch. I do, I do!'

'What's all this?' I pointed at the tea chest. 'What are you doing with it?'

'Yvonne told me to pack all her personal belongings in it. Then she left. She wasn't crying or anything. I've been trying to do it but I can't, it's killing me by inches. What shall I do? God, what a mess I'm in.'

I opened my mouth to speak and then shut it again. For some reason, things already seemed less desperate. Was this a repeat performance, I began to wonder? Had I stumbled on a marital ritual which made sense to no one except the protagonists?'

Now, looking at them both this evening, exchanging pleasantries and smiles, I found it hard to believe I hadn't dreamt the whole episode. Naturally she hadn't left, or she wouldn't be here now. Guy's latest love object was a student of eighteen at Camborne called Marigold, who wore a bomber jacket and a leather mini skirt as brief as an apron.

For something to say, I asked how his art history thesis was going. He was in his final year at art school.

'Hell, it's agony. What a waste of effort, useless. A load of crap. It's not for us, the students, it's for the lecturers. Most of them are failed artists anyway. It keeps them in a job.'

'I've forgotten your topic again.'

Guy pulled a face. 'Modernism. And all the other isms.'

'Not only painting?'

'Oh, that, and how it relates to the other movements in the arts, starting at the turn of the century – music, literature, anything else you can lay your hands on. I haven't the faintest idea what the drivel I'm writing means, I just cobble it together out of reference books. I *am* modernism, isn't that right? You are, Frank. I should be writing about you. The trouble is you're not dead yet.'

'Guy!' Yvonne put on a shocked face, wide-eyed.

'If I feel a death coming on I'll let you know.'

Guy laughed his boyish laugh. The look he gave me at that moment was so ardent that I lowered my head instinctively, as if to duck the blast of love. I could feel myself smiling thinly. Hearing Guy's infectious laugh I often wished I could join in. We weren't introvert and extrovert exactly, but I would find myself feeding lines to him, as a stooge feeds a comic. If I had to describe him in a single phrase I'd call him a happy introvert. Again and again I would see through his shallow protestations of devotion, and then be won over, just like his girls, by that tender croak from deep in the throat, by those long-lashed, fluttering eyes.

'There it is – that look!' he crowed suddenly. He turned to Yvonne. 'Did you see it?'

'Pay no attention,' Yvonne said. 'He has these attacks from time to time.'

'Frank, you're a fox. You've been one in another life, haven't you?'

'You're fox mad.'

'I saw him the other night again. I did, Frank. I got close to him as you are to me now. He looked straight at me, straight in, and then whoosh! Gone. Beautiful, he was.'

Guy had a genuine passion for this animal he had seen on solitary walks near the farm at night. In some ink-and-wash sketches he had caught the authentic fox-spirit, the brilliant muzzle and the smoulder of coat and brush. The pang of envy I felt was also genuine, telling me how good the drawings were.

'When you come up here in the dark you might see him yourself one of these nights.'

'I didn't notice anything,' I said. 'I could have fallen over him and not seen him. I was working away at your portrait in my head.'

Guy's face opened like a flower. In those soft brown eyes I thought I saw a blend of cunning and innocence. He shuffled his feet bashfully, then croaked, 'I've started one of you, Frank. How about that? A memory one.'

'A portrait?'

'Well, you know me. I'd rather not say. Maybe it's a bit of landscape, with your nose sticking up from a rabbit hole. I can't stand labels.'

'But of me,' I persisted, surprised by my own curiosity. Was I hoping to find out what I really looked like, a reflection I failed to see in the mirror? This could be the greedy vanity of approaching old age, I told myself.

'Oh, it's you all right. All I've got so far is a pair of eyes and a mouth floating in thin air with nowhere to go.' He looked coyly at me. 'How do you feel about a sitting? Would it bore you rigid?'

'Not at all.'

'We can make it a duet, how about that? While I prod away at mine, you can have another go at solving your problems, sort of thing.'

Yvonne was showing signs of boredom. To change the subject I asked after Guy's father, recently a widower. I went on to say that my own mother had died after giving birth to Vivien, just as I was about to start my first job at fifteen. 'A long time ago.'

'How terrible,' Yvonne said. 'Were there complications?'

'There must have been.'

'What a gap that is, between you and your sister. I suppose you don't see much of each other?' Yvonne was probing delicately for details, so I obliged with a few. I didn't mind at all. Talking about Vivien was pleasurable. She entered the room and sat among us. I didn't attempt to explain the bond which existed between us, but said we hadn't seen each other now for several years. 'Yes, she writes to me. I got a letter only this morning.' I was on the point of adding that her letters were packed full of her, and nourished me like eggs. Shyness prevented me.

I must have drifted off, trying to recall her. Guy brought me back with a jolt. 'Sorry – did you say something?'

'Fancy making a start, boss?'

'I'm ready when you are.'

'Frank, this is smashing. I'm really glad to see you again.'

'Same here,' I mumbled.

We were off to an attic which served as a makeshift studio. Seeing the unfinished oil sketch gave me a shock, and not only because it was further advanced than I expected. The resemblances were undeniable. They had to do with the slumping of my thin figure on the canvas chair – as if bad news had knocked me into that position – and a suggestion of lobster claw about the long bony wrist and pink hand. The lips that Guy had already mentioned were there too, writhing shapelessly, in a torment of ambiguity that I feared was accurate.

Evidently Guy had planned and anticipated this moment. I was forced to revise my view of him as someone totally spontaneous. As well as the emerging picture clamped to the easel, there was a beach chair in green and white stripes which had been placed in readiness. This model's throne seemed to be squatting and beckoning with a peculiarly brazen air of its own. I sat down.

Guy said, 'I don't suppose you remember an afternoon last summer. Hot as hell it was. I knocked the dirt off that chair you're on now and plonked it down outside the back door. Then I wanted to see what you looked like in the middle of those blighted old apple trees in the orchard-that-was, so we shifted it. It must have been early August.'

'You were composing me. Yes, I remember.'

I was asked to place my right hand on my right thigh, in imitation of the art on the canvas, and to allow my left hand to clutch my wrist. This made me feel I was restrain-

42

ing my right hand from doing something indecent.

'Are you comfortable in that tatty chair?'

'I'm fine.'

'I've been giving it an airing in front of the fire, hoping your majesty would drop in.'

'It feels dry.'

'Thank you, your honour.'

Unaccustomed to posing, I soon felt my eyelids drooping a little. Also I was reverting in a stream of memory to the young man who had lived with Maggie. Once she was my constant, virtually my only model. I smiled, remembering.

'What's the joke?'

'It's private.'

'Beg your pardon, sir?'

'Well, no, it's nothing I wouldn't want to tell you about. But it would be too much of a rigmarole. That's the trouble with having lived as long as I have.'

'What is?'

'Knowing where to start. You pull at a thread, then before you know it you're trying to unravel something you thought was dead as a doornail.'

'Clear as mud.'

'You did ask.'

We fell silent. Guy forgot all about me as a person with a past and memories going back before he was even born. I could feel him wrestling with what he saw, with me, now. Gradually I became aware of a change in him. He muttered to himself, working himself up to a frenzy of dissatisfaction which was soon impossible to ignore. He blamed the light and his technique in equal doses. He cursed his luck, he castigated himself for all kinds of faults. 'I ought to stop, why don't I? Because I'm a bloody imbecile. Oh, look at this, I've buggered it up. No, hang on, Guy, don't do that, oh you silly sod . . .'

Finally he turned his back on me. I could see by his hunched stance that impotence had set in.

'Can I have a look?'

No answer. Standing up and flexing my stiff legs, I went over and peered.

Through gritted teeth, Guy said, 'Tell me the truth. It's a cock-up, right?'

43

'On the contrary. You've got a flair I wish I had. I've seen it in your things before. You can snatch at the essence of what a person is, or thinks he is. I'm not talking about anything facile like a likeness. I get a creepy feeling I'm in here somewhere, and it worries me. I want to peer round the back of it.'

Guy was momentarily speechless. He looked ready to cry angry disappointed tears. Finally he said pathetically, 'I don't know anything, honest.'

Somehow he had lost his fire, and was running discouragement into the surroundings, into the wall and objects, the chair emptily waiting, the dirty sill of the window, everything. I stared at him aghast, willing him not to collapse.

I made my escape by saying I had to write a letter to my sister. Turning to leave the poky room, I glanced once more at the focus of Guy's anguish, as if I wanted to catch my apparition unawares. It startled me for a second time as I saw the thin torso, even thinner than I thought I was, spiritualised by a sky-blue summer shirt I didn't possess. Those jutting knees – and the long fingers pointing at them – told my story so graphically that they dispensed with the need for a face. There I was, farouche. Like a spiritual lover, Guy had turned me into the wind-blown *artist maudit* he wanted to hero-worship. Only the clasp of rickety chair arms kept his vision from blowing away.

7

The theme of artist and model led me inevitably to thoughts of Maggie, reviving memories I'd assumed were lost. During my time with her I painted her again and again. Just because we lived together, she became the woman who stood in for womankind. At one time I had ambitions to be as domestic a painter as Bonnard. I have no idea what his wife was like at posing, but Maggie was a lousy model. She either couldn't or wouldn't apply herself. Who could blame her? To be a good model entails obliterating your personality to some extent. Until you did that, you squirmed like a maggot on a hook. Maggie acquiesced, protested, squirmed, all in the space of an hour. Basically she was a squirmer.

She used my middle name, shortening it to Wes, first of all mockingly playful, because of the bits of starch in me, and later as a pet name, affectionately. I didn't regret the loss of Francis. The prissy sound of it in some mouths, my stepmother's rendering in particular, had often irked me. I would have settled for Breakwell, but Maggie rejected this outright. She was too warm and generous – I would have said sentimental on my stiff-necked days – to consent to the use of surnames.

'You're my Wes,' she told me, laughing, but fierce with love behind the laughter. The next minute she was on me, all over me, flopping her soft warm arms round my neck as she thumped down on my lap like a sudden delivery of washing, only it was her big, loose-wrapped milky flesh making me spill my tea and curse, spluttering. I couldn't bear to be swamped. One of these days I would spell it out, brutal or not, and risk the injury to her feelings. The joke was, I was the one forever dreaming of abandonment.

'Me ole Wes,' she would giggle, nuzzling into my neck.

'Sounds like a piece of old underwear you're fond of – get off!'

Rolling round on my thigh bones, she chortled, 'Oh no, you're too special for that.'

Although she liked me thin and dependent and in need of sustenance, the mother in her wanted me fatter. But after a while she gave up, after steaks and large helpings of spuds, and porridge in the mornings, failed to do the trick. For one thing I was such a finicky eater, and for another, whether I ate loads of food or not seemed to make no difference. Yet I hardly ever fell ill, whereas Maggie was endlessly coughing, choked with colds, eyes and nose streaming.

She tormented me with her sneezes. I told her, 'Everything you do goes to excess.' One evening I counted fourteen in a row.

'How do you mean?'

'It's too much.'

'I've always sneezed a lot.'

'You do everything a lot.'

'Better than too little, like you.'

'What's too little?'

'Except that. Men are all the same, always worried about one little bit.' She looked at me ironically, but her voice was tinged with reproach. 'You don't talk to me enough.'

I hastily changed the subject. 'I'm built for speed, that's why I'm thin. Like a greyhound.' This was something I'd once heard my father say about the Breakwell side of the family.

'Is that it? You little rasher.'

She spoke irritably. I felt the need to defend myself. I said, 'Doctors always start off by asking if I've ever had T.B.'

'I'm not surprised. You could play a tune on those ribs.'

'I've never been any different.'

'They must have called you Oxfam at school.'

Needled, I said primly, 'There was no such thing then.' She should have known, she was older than I by two years. I would keep ferreting for her age but for months she put up a stubborn resistance.

'You don't ask a lady that question.'

'Who's asking one?'

'Go and boil your head.'

She was approaching thirty, which to her meant a crisis.

'I don't care how old you are.'

'I'm not old.'

'How young, then?'

'Why not just drop the subject?'

'There's no need to be secretive about it, surely?'

'Look who's talking! You're as tight as a duck's arse when you want to be.'

I realised I was now mildly obsessed. 'Just tell me roughly.'

'I shan't see twenty-one again. That's rough.'

'You're being childish.'

'And you're stupid. You don't know the first thing about women, do you?'

Apparently I knew how to rub them up the wrong way, I said, laughing.

She glared at me. 'Sometimes you're not funny at all,' she said.

She was even more reluctant about undressing, when I asked her to pose.

Maggie bristled. 'What? Not likely. You go to hell. I'm not sitting round here in my birthday suit for you to gawp at.'

'Why not? I've seen everything. I don't turn my back when you strip and wash.'

'That's different.'

'No, it's not.'

'What would my mam say?'

'I'm not asking her.'

'I mean about it.' She was perfectly serious.

'She's in Battersea,' I joked. 'She can't see you from there.'

I persuaded her slyly, by degrees, showing her drawings of the masters: Rubens, Courbet, Renoir, and Moore's stony giantesses. Her scorn for most of them prepared the way better than I could. But she was still suspicious. She had spasms of doubt. Then she questioned me closely.

'Why are they all fat?'

'Not fat, big.'

'Why?'

'Plenty to go at.'

'Is that why you like me?'

If not exactly happy, she was almost willing to be convinced.

'I might,' I said, 'If I could have a proper look.'

The next problem, getting her to sit still, was harder to solve. I thought half seriously of fastening her down with ropes. She was motionless for brief spells, then her tongue came fidgetting out between her teeth for a lick round her chapped lips. She developed excruciating itches in her armpits — and more inaccessible crevices. I didn't care about the odd squirm or two, but her selfconsciousness kept ruining things. Wasn't it tetchy old Cézanne who yelled at his model to 'be an apple?' It wouldn't have worked with Maggie. She had struggled too long with her recalcitrant body, coming to terms with what she considered to be its faults. The protective skin she had manufactured was even more in evidence when she was naked.

Her massed anxieties defeated me. Now and then I did succeed, simply by summoning up the full strength of my will and assaulting her with it. I would fix her in a succession of hard freezing glances, until she was forced into reluctant sculpture. For a few minutes, while I hacked away with brutal remote strokes, she became the inert natural form I was pursuing. Then she got sick of her victim role, the stone crumbled into words and fingers, scratching and complaining: 'I've got goosepimples on my pimples!'

Once, in a perverse, impish mood, she insisted that I should be naked as well, so that she too could have something to look at. I found the justice of this hard to deny. It was early summer, so I couldn't say I was too thin to be exposed to the cold air, even though the room only saw a slat of sunlight at around four in the afternoon. It never properly warmed up. Still, I stripped off my clothes.

'Okay now?'

Maggie stared with deliberate fixity at my groin, until lust affected me. The dark bush of my pubic hair hoisted a shameless member.

'Down in the forest something stirred,' Maggie hooted, beside herself with childish glee.

'Stop moving – you're like jelly on a plate.'

'Why don't you have a go with that instead of your crayon?' Her round breasts shook with laughter. 'Is it too blunt? Can't you sharpen it?' Her eyes gleamed with a strange light, as if she was about to jump up and begin dancing an obscene dance. I even imagined I could hear the clash of cymbals.

Suddenly my patience snapped. 'I'll blunt you if you don't shut up!' I flung the litho chalk at her, then myself. When we disentangled, the grain of the threadbare dusty carpet was imprinted on her white shoulders and the dimpled cheeks of her behind. It was my turn to laugh. She rushed off to the bedroom in search of a mirror, and to share the joke. There was always a certain pleasure for her in examining visible marks. It was the same with the teeth marks and small bruises of our lovemaking; on her flesh she scrutinised the undeniable evidence of my attentions. I speculated that she would have liked each one to be permanent, like a love tattoo.

On more edgy occasions, dangerously near her period, she would demand to know my opinion of her shape.

'Am I fat?' she asked once. She sounded plaintive, her gravity teetering towards outright misery.

'Ample.'

Leaping out of her pose, her face eloquent with a sudden suspicion of me and my words, not to mention my art, she rummaged through a dictionary for what I considered she was.

'It *is* fat,' she said, with the voice of a betrayed child.

'Abundant isn't the same as fat.'

'You said ample.'

Desperate to get on, I shouted, 'I like all of you, all of it,' with such conviction that her anger subsided.

But when I got her back into position it was no good any more. The spell was broken, the game was up for the time being. I set my bony jaw against her, for deserting me. She stared back, sad and bewildered.

I began to feel self-consciously defeated and pointless. The room felt disjointed, wrong. What was it? Troubled by an aching sensation, like a loss of being, I shivered, dragging on a sweater over my shirt. Then I felt hot. Perhaps I had a fever. I found I was rubbing my head in a faint delirium. There was Maggie, looking puzzled, gaping warmly at me. 'You seen a ghost, Wes?' She came forward, a wave of caring, then was halted by an invisible wire. 'Now what's up with you?'

'Nothing.'

My abrupt changes and withdrawals baffled her. It was no use pleading that I was as mystified myself. This time she retaliated. 'Who are you, God?'

'Don't get angry.'

'Up on your plinth again?'

But she came round – she always did – and I was grateful. I was acquiring wisdom painfully, sometimes by imbibing hers.

This was the first time I had been able to know the unexpurgated reality of a living woman. Wallowing before her, often at sea, absurdly youthful and foolish, I suppressed the impulse to fill canvases with her milky light rather than with representations of her actual body, which kept foaming at me in rushes of power and ecstasy. Unless I took care, her scepticism could bring the whole flimsy structure of my art crashing about my ears. Visions had to be tethered. Was it possible, I wondered, to grow forms organically, without apprenticeship, as a woman did? I was too unstable. I lacked roots. Patience, like the silence to be found deep underground or at the bottom of oceans, seemed totally beyond me. Yet a mother nursing a child could embody it, as the greatest pictures testified.

I had seen her as milky light, not substance. Once, as moonlight poured in and filled our poor room, she became shimmering blue water. Or as something glimpsed through mad hair, in the white smoke of a summer mist. Familiar or not, she exuded a mysterious bodily quiet. She was curiously pure and untouched, with the simplicity and fascination of a holy person. And she trusted me not to hurt her.

This meant, unaware of it though I was at the time, that I had fallen in love with her after all. She was a feast of blossom

49

which kept coming. In her absence I visualised her tenderly as a soft tree of growing light.

She belonged to me now. It was like being in sudden possession of the sun and moon and the seasons. Delivering her moon, dragging it free in tatters and flakes of white fire from her ragged rose petals, her loose breasts and belly, was where I came in. Studying her like a new creed, I went on a quest for her missing moon demon. Getting excited one day I tried to tell her. Indifferent to my obscure symbols, she didn't object to my rambling on. She liked the sound and ignored the sense.

'It sort of makes me feel special.'

'You are.'

'Shall I tell you what I like about you?'

'Yes, go on.'

'I like your man's smell. When you have a drink, I like to taste the beer when you kiss me. I like the stubble round your mouth if you forget to shave. Can I say something?'

'What?'

'I've known some crude, horrible men, but nobody as cruel as you can be sometimes. I know you don't mean it.'

'When am I cruel, Maggie?'

'You go away from me. You ignore me.'

'I don't mean to. It's nothing personal, you know that. I've told you, I have to struggle with things.'

'What things? You're so airy-fairy, all up in the air with your suns and seasons. Half the time you're on another planet.'

'I thought you said you felt special?'

'You're off out, just like other men. It's no different. You just dress it up different.'

'Don't say that, Maggie. Now you're crying.'

She wailed. 'I want to take care of you, and you won't let me!'

'I will, I do!'

We made love every night for a week. I lost my relish for the drawing and painting. This was my true work, ploughing away in her with love and humility. She lay beneath me like a field and I went rooting, planting and reaping in the same animal act. Harnessed joyfully to this new purpose I sowed emblematic seeds, delivered and baptised invisible babies.

I tried to make her feel as I did, twisting her hair against her scalp in my frenzy, groaning my wild desire. 'What's

50

got into you?' she protested once, drawing back her head to examine me with scared eyes, this crazy stranger who kept mounting her.

'Don't you love me?' I muttered into her throat, her flesh, hiding from her.

'Not if you tear my hair out.' But she ebbed and flooded under my hands, now sacrificial, now the priestess of a cult without a name, shrieking like a banshee.

Sometimes she was ocean, moaning and heaving. Often it was warm loam I was embedded in, or the earth-body of the planet itself, reeling through space while I clung on by hair-ropes. Afterwards, laughing helplessly in one of her sudden fits as if something ridiculous had tripped her up, she lay apart in her sex and femaleness, totally occupied and complete, with no need for my lust.

Even the sound of her mirth was now seismic to me. I heard the beat of tides, the faint roar of the cosmos in it. Now that the burden of creating order in space, with my inadequate colours and clumsy forms, had been lifted from me, I felt light, carefree, and even happy to share the love-language Maggie wrapped our lives in.

As for her, she was at peace with her contours at last, having herself appreciated *in toto* by me, each fold and bulge, even the hated jelly-wobbling areas, even the so-called dirty hair-sprouting secret bits. For that she adored me. My ramping lust became praise of her, worship of her. What else could it be but a form of rejoicing? Gladly I would shatter myself on her shores at night, then let her nurse me tenderly back into one piece on her thigh-ledges, squeezing soft handfuls of my behind, the only spare flesh she could find. 'You're such a bony bugger.' Shipwrecked but safe, I would doze off. My contentment was yet more praise.

Entering her like a fish, I would hear her gasp with surprise. She whispered once, under cover of darkness, that I still shocked her with my slithering bone thing, before it assumed flesh similar to her own, drooping when it was tired like hers on her skeleton after a long shift serving at the tables. Nothing I did was unwelcome, nothing mattered. Sometimes I seemed barbed, hooking viciously at her, or driving and punishing like a rod. She would gibber her mad love and slobber her delight, demanding everything there was, all of it – until the red poppy outbursts were flaming gaudily and softly with deep

51

black hearts in the dense heat at the centre of her body. Or so I imagined. How could it be the same for her as it was for me? Didn't she live in her body as in a black garden, with pools of succulence and damp tendrils I would never feel, teeming with spirits I would never know?

Afterwards, she would insist on looking after me. She made coffee, she asked if I would like a sandwich. A waitress again, she would see me as someone in need of help. She was never more contented than at these moments, putting me back in order and tidying me like a table.

8

Walking downhill in the dark I kept thinking of Guy, swamped by despair because he had failed. Would Yvonne nurse him back to his old perky optimism, or would she spurn him? Going past a holly tree rich with red berries I pictured his face, wearing the haunted look of someone who had gambled everything and lost. On the way up to see my friend I had been obsessed by fears of my own sterility. Now, by some curious twist of fate, I felt rejuvenated. Had Guy's energy flowed from him into me?

I scuffed my feet, stamping now and then to keep warm and to express my new robustness. The dark pinching night air felt good. I could feel my ears being nipped.

Something – a sudden luminosity – made me crane my neck upwards. A gibbous moon was humping out at me, surrounded by a brownish frost halo. The endlessly fluctuating Cornish weather would drive me mad, but this time it consoled me. It was temporary like everything else.

The mill stood silent and mysterious, veiled in white like the fields. Strange, it seemed to be waiting for me. I entered the grisly moonlit kitchen – the Aga was out – and walked straight through without stopping, trudging up loudly to my workroom. I switched on all three lights, the spots at the far end and the reading lamp by my bed. Instead of bothering with heat I shed my clothes, dragged on pyjamas and dived in, shivering violently and jerking my limbs about for the satisfaction. I soon generated warmth. Without getting out I hung sideways, rummaging among papers until I had what I wanted – Vivien's letter.

Talking about my sister had kindled a longing to read her words again. I saw now by the handwriting that her letter had been dashed down at speed. It gave me a vision of her hectically running down a city street. I dropped off to sleep with the sheet of paper in my hand.

I woke with a jolt, as if an alarm had gone off. It was daylight. My heart was still hammering violently. Was it a dream, a nightmare I had had? No, it was real. Underneath my head I could hear the familiar crashing to and fro of Della, back in occupation again. As I reached for my watch to find out if it was morning or afternoon, the coffee grinder exploded. My watch showed twenty past ten.

As if delivering a message the grinder howled and paused, howled and paused, in short frantic bursts. Knowing how I loathed the thing, there was a time when she would show consideration of a kind, yelling, 'Shut your ears!' up through the floorboards before she began. Now she just threw the switch and it screamed up at me without warning, maliciously, diabolically.

The aroma of ground coffee and then the hot coffee smell itself arrived next, like seductions. I wondered how she had travelled so quickly from London, then remembered that she would break her journey in Exeter if the mood took her.

I got up and dressed, dragging on the same wool shirt and baggy cord trousers I had been wearing for the past fortnight. Left alone I soon reverted to a tramp state. In the bathroom I passed water dismally, regretting the loss of pressure, squinting sideways at the mirror to inspect my parched gush of faded hair. The comb had gone missing, so I raked the mop flat with hooked fingers.

Following the delicious smell of toast, I entered the kitchen. Della sat hunched over the *Times* in an attitude I always thought masculine. She affected the long frizzy hair of a much younger woman, and kept the coppery colour burning which I had once mistaken for natural. When I complimented her on it, she said with her famous brutal frankness that it came out of a bottle.

Raising her head, she contemplated my appearance. The handsome face, I had long ago decided, was the result of character as well as heredity, when analysing her features closely for a drawing. In the part of me which registered shapes and colours I was still affected. She had long flat cheeks and high, foreign-looking cheekbones. Her mouth, wide as a Red Indian's, continued to exert its fascination, while her brittle movements, the tense positioning of her unhappy body, unnerved me as always. She had the American habit of devouring with her eyes, not from curiosity but lack of inhibition.

'You're a weirdo,' she said, in her matter-of-fact drawl which was without emphasis. She went on crunching at the blackish crusts of toast with her small, savage-looking teeth. I admired their action while her remark sank in. It came close enough to Maggie's 'funny cove' for me to assume it must be true. There was nothing to be done. Della referred to Maggie one day as 'the fat girl, the one who looks like a whore.'

'Maggie?' I was more flabbergasted than incensed. 'Like a what?'

'Those drawings of her you did make her look whorish.'

'Would you say the same of Modigliani?'

'Probably. If I bothered to rate his stuff, which I don't.'

I made an instant coffee, and stood at the counter stirring it. Della's 'weirdo' had catapulted me back to Southwark, and those studies of Maggie, images that bred from each other, showing her as lost and then recovered, sometimes half submerged in a baptismal river, changing colour repeatedly, always nude but once or twice curiously skeletal, with huge aboriginal eyes and toes splayed as if for mud. They issued forth in so many variations that I was gutted, denatured, yet I kept on until the last 'River Woman' sank away, extinguished like her creator, bleached to the colour of feathers by a surfeit of light.

Della was saying, in the hard, cheery, determined manner of New Yorkers, 'By the way, I've decided to go home for a while.'

'Home?'

'The States.'

'How long is a while?'

At my question, a flicker of gratification passed over her face. 'Why, what's it to you? How long is a piece of string?'

'A month, a year?'

'Say for an indefinite period.' She smiled across at me.

All at once, goaded by that smile and at the mercy of a passion which came bulging up through my body, as if through the soles of my feet, distorting me like a figure in one of my paintings, I said, 'Well, I hope you'll be happy. I hope you find what it is you're looking for, I hope you don't get sucked in again by somebody like me. I wish you luck, anyway!'

Della, clearly disgusted by this speech, shook her head. 'Francis, you're a creep.' Her greyish eyes briefly held mine. 'That's what you are. A little creep who can paint.'

I began to sink where I stood. To resist this, I said, 'We can't help what we are. If you're going to take yourself off, then do it. Just leave me myself.'

I moved to the door.

'Hang on, there's a letter here for you.'

I snatched it from her. 'It's from Vivien. But I had one yesterday!'

'You don't say. Lucky you!'

I crossed the quarry tiles without answering, clutching my precious envelope. As I gained the stairs I heard Della's hooting laugh.

Back in my room, I sat down in an arthritic wheelback chair to recover and to digest Della's news. A rustling sound to my left told me that I wasn't alone. On top of a pile of framed watercolours I had laid a thick brown paper bag over some newspapers as a bed for our lean, intractable black cat. Why she chose such uncomfortable spots was a mystery, unless she had a sin to expiate. Now I saw that they were both curled up together, the black stand-offish one and her house companion, a good-natured marmalade and white creature who had slunk up and ingratiated herself. They lay there snugly, deceptively lover-like. Seeing them I exclaimed in surprise, too loud. My voice jumped out, and in the same instant I jerked back my chair. Its legs grated. The two cats leapt down and streaked past me as if fleeing an ugly demon, bolting through the door like a single animal. I felt dismayed, absurdly so and beyond reason, by this latest evidence of desertion.

Della's announcement had left me asking whether her 'indefinite period' meant that she was leaving me for good. I was too proud to ask for confirmation. Reluctant by nature to admit the end of anything, to say of a situation that it was finally defunct, I wondered if there were in fact endings, if such a point could ever truly be reached. Even a death raised more questions than it settled. Beginnings were equally problematic, but at least we could say where and when we met someone for the first time.

I met Della at the private view for my second exhibition at the Montague Galleries. To explain how this came about I had better retrace my steps. After selling two large paintings unexpectedly, the gallery owners who had taken me on became suddenly attentive, offering to scrap the optional arrangement outright and put me under permanent contract.

Changes were in the air. I experienced the fluttery sensations of a balloonist, invisible forces propelling me upwards. My chest felt expanded, I felt giddy with the sudden rush of oxygen. Art, like everything else, was enjoying a boom. Expressionism, both pre-war German and post-war American was gaining steadily in popularity among collectors. The hunt was on too for exciting home-grown talent, preferably from the savage north. Of course in the visual arts one's origins were not immediately discernible. To compensate for this, attention would sometimes be drawn to it in the biographical notes printed in catalogues. Dealers were busy feeling their way in this tricky new business of the non-pedigree.

Harry Singer, the senior partner at Montague Galleries, was an assimilated Jew who liked to think himself something of a Maecenas, to self-taught painters in particular. This was no doubt because he had risen without formal training himself, unimpeded by culture. The driving force behind the acquisition of the gallery came from his wife, who had literary and musical pretensions. With her large floury face and subdued manner she looked rather meek. But she had a tireless will. This showed itself through odd acts of stubbornness over trivial decisions. Something about her black snake eyes and the wry shaping of her brown lips made you aware of how clever she was.

Singer was different – a coarse, vigorously thrusting man, unrehearsed in comparison with his wife. Tiny veins on the surface of his cheeks gave him a flushed, surprised look. His insistent animal body refused to be left out of anything; he liked nothing better than to push himself up close to you physically.

Matters of taste left him frankly uninterested. He left these frivolities to his junior partner, Simon Trench, while he took care of the financial side. Artistic fashion baffled him.

Everything had its price, but the price of a painting seemed to be anyone's guess. However, there were other considerations. Culture should be exhibited in his opinion, otherwise how did anyone else know you possessed it? Literal possession was surely not to be despised. One took a sensual pleasure in the ownership of cars, women, oriental carpets.

Harry Singer's grasp of the rag trade was more certain than his knowledge of aesthetics. He made frequent boasts to that effect. In his real trade, garments, he continued to make a killing. At dinner parties he liked to say that he favoured autodidacts because he was one, and painters because they could be seen at a glance, simply that. It was the next best thing, he joked once when he was drunk, to hanging their skins on the wall.

My sudden windfall went towards the purchase of the leasehold house in Camden. Amazing myself, I bought it without a second thought. I was intent on satisfying a burning desire for space, which became an identifiable craving one morning when I woke up after a bad dream. I had been lying cramped in a dank tomb, unable to breathe or even blink. With my 'Kneeling Figure on Bed' and my 'Bride and Groom' sold to the same buyer, an individual whose name – Roman – meant nothing to me, I was able to move into the house described by the estate agents as 'in need of renovation.' This, I understood, was the stock phrase for a property staggering on its foundations. The elderly surveyor, not too steady on his own pins, assured me that it was in fact structurally sound.

'A handyman, are you?' he said, giving me a fatherly smile.

'Not exactly.' The truth was that I had only half-heartedly decorated one small room in my life.

I went round entranced by it all; the newel post at the foot of the stairs, adorned with the fretwork of a more leisurely age, the leaded stained glass in the heavy front door – which had some of the raspberry bits missing and others fractured. The claw feet of the massive bathtub were reassuringly antiquated. I imagined myself wallowing here in private, forgetting about English winters and the problems of ancient plumbing.

The roof leaked. There was a council order for its repair. In strong winds all the upper sashes rattled their shrunken dry bones together. Signs of rot and damp were everywhere. The elaborate fluted cornices under the high ceilings hung there by a miracle, the plaster broken and mouldering.

Camping out on the ground floor during the first weeks I told myself what a fool I was to choose this ugly echoing barn, with its ominous crack zigzagging up the stairwell from basement to attics, in this neglected street of blistering facades. It was the street name, Valenciennes, which had attracted me in the first place; that, and the wicked, unfamiliar voluptuousness of abundant space.

I was now signing Breakwell almost truculently in the bottom right hand corner of every canvas, though in a diminishing squiggle that was hard to read beyond 'Break'. My first one-man show, in the Lower Gallery, was hung on the fawn hessian walls of a room seeming smaller than it was because of its L-shaped plan. Was I being gambled with, invested in? The Montague itself had just completed its third lucrative year. After this I would have a name, a reputation, or could it turn out to be a mirage?

Recently I had been working very hard and very fast, hurled along in a gathering momentum. Whatever I came across had the effect of stimulating me, as if left in my path deliberately. One rainy afternoon in Charing Cross Road I picked up a folio in Zwemmer's and leafed through. It was from Goya's 'Black Series' – painted straight on the walls of that house they called the House of the Deaf, after the ageing Spaniard's wife had died and he was 'deaf, shy, infirm'. With the sharp eyes of the assistant trained on me I drank in the pages, and then went out into the street with Goya titles erupting in my head: 'It is All Lies,' 'No One Knows Himself', The Sleep of Reason Begets Monsters', 'There is No Remedy,' 'Were You Born For This?'

My own paintings were getting bigger, in a progression, each one spawning a mass of drawings. Almost overnight I had become the deliberate artist, that is to say a quiet force, connecting the dream which comprised my life to the dream of art like a skilled electrician wiring a circuit.

Where was the struggle? Who was it who had said that failure is the beginning of success? I could do no wrong. While the trance lasted, every one of my strokes went home. I kept uncovering birds in my paintings, one newly-hatched bird face after another. Their blind gape could have been a judgement, or it represented my joy in this apparently senseless stream of images. Maelstrom-like cityscapes of my imagining alternated with thickets full of birds, feathered masks that were sometimes Maggie with hair down over her face, and one street in particular which I searched for in dreams but was never able to locate. It surfaced in paintings as a smear of lit windows beckoning.

If I had loaded up a van with this exuberant production, emptying the house, I could have filled both galleries with ease. But they were too recent, not to be trusted. What if they turned into revolting muddy slabs, post-mortem effects, created by demons in order to mock me? Oils could do this, but watercolours and drawings were not treacherous as a rule. I was falling more and more in love with watercolours. I depended almost helplessly on the translucence of the washes to float me through to the next period of fecundity.

At the private view – the junior partner insisted on calling it a *vernissage* – I was accosted at once by a youngish American writer, or so I thought. Della Burls wasted no time on viewing; she simply stood in front of me and grinned.

'I guess you're the painter, right?' She lifted a hand to her dense, burnt sienna hair. Bangles and assorted charms and chains jostled on her arm for attention.

'A painter. One of many.'

'I mean of these.' She waved impatiently at the room, to a more fervent clashing of cymbals.

'Yes.'

Della laughed. 'You English. I never know whether to believe in your modesty or not, you're such kidders.'

'It's diffidence,' I said. 'Speaking for myself, that is. I've yet to meet a modest artist of any race.'

'Whatever.'

The sherry, sampled hastily on an empty stomach before the doors were opened, fumed in my head. I said, to my own astonishment, 'Humility is the goal.' What did I mean, if anything?

'Somebody or other once called the English the Japanese of Europe.'

'I've heard so.'

'How does that hit you?'

'It hits me.'

'Anyway, these painting of yours are the goods for me. No bullshit, they really are terrific.'

'Thank you.'

'Why is the show entitled, let's see – 'Figures, Masks and Faces'? Doesn't that leave plenty out?'

'Yes, you're right. It wasn't my title, or my idea to have one.' I wanted to say that foetuses would have been more accurate than faces, but didn't. I should have insisted on my own title, I realised. 'Wishes, Lies and Dreams,' I said aloud.

'Is that a picture?'

'No, no. I was talking to myself.'

Pictures in an exhibition were to me like babies in incubators. The one painting in the whole show which I felt belonged to me was entitled 'Flowering Head'. A Jungian might have called it 'My Lady Soul'. It was both a soul adventure and a self-portrait. Solace and danger stared back at me from the nub of this tender image. I went over and stood before it.

Della followed me over. 'How long have you been at it?'

'What?'

'This show. Did it take long?' She shook her thick frizzed hair like a girl. 'It must represent one hell of a lot of sweat. Not to mention passion.'

'We shed our sicknesses in art, somebody said.'

As if I hadn't spoken, she went on, 'I know what it costs, believe me. Why do we have to suffer, huh? Why should it be so damned hard?'

Over near the entrance I caught sight of Simon, the junior partner, signalling to me excitedly. 'I think I'm wanted,' I said to Della. 'Excuse me, will you?' Then as a reckless afterthought I added, 'I'd like to come to New York one day.'

She smiled a broad, vermillion smile. 'Sure, why not? Listen, when you do, be sure to look me up. I can be your guide, how about that? I live on the edge of the Village, and that's where the action is. Plenty's happening right now.'

'Good.' I nodded my too-heavy head, moving away.

'Are you married?'

'No.'

'You live alone or what?'

'I do now. We've broken up.'

'Too bad. It's the same for me. I've got room for one in my apartment.' She fished into the mouth of her sack-bag and gave me a little printed card.

'Thanks.'

'My pleasure.' Then she laughed wildly, harshly. 'Be warned, though – I eat men like air!'

I was unfamiliar with the quotation, but got the message. 'With or without ketchup,' I mumbled, grinning.

Simon Trench had come over. He took my arm. I was steered over to meet Keith Fulcher, a Marxist critic who had a series running on television. His thick black eyebrows, straight as a rule, were in deadly earnest. Fulcher scowled up from under his tangled fringe and champed on a hand-rolled cigarette. Simon Trench backed away discreetly, after first murmuring that the critic was favourably inclined towards my work. I had heard this already. Though he struck me as an unlikely ally, I waited politely for his questions.

He said abruptly, 'May I ask if you care for Turner at all?'

A small man, he sounded friendly. As he spoke, he raised himself on his toes. I wondered if it was a nervous habit or a desire he had to be taller.

'Very much.' On the point of saying more, I spotted a trayful of glasses of white wine hovering nearby, and reached for one.

'We all accept him now, of course, as the forerunner of modern art as we know it.'

I nodded in what I hoped was an intelligent manner. The level of wine in my glass had sunk mysteriously. Conscious of a damp feeling, I supposed some must have splashed over my left knee.

Fulcher went on, 'Have you ever made a deliberate study of him?'

In my fuddled state I found it hard to make sense of this question. I began to ramble. 'A long time ago I waded through a nineteenth century biography of Turner.'

'Not Thornbury's? Enough to put you off for good. Slovenly as hell, didn't you find? Chock-full of inaccuracies. A complete disaster of a book. Probably accounts for the reason we've been so long cottoning on to Turner's significance.'

'I can remember the anecdote concerning him and Haydon. It stuck in my mind for some reason.'

Fulcher shook his head. 'I don't believe I'm familiar with it.' His mouth twisted unhappily.

'Well, it was when somebody told him that Haydon had killed himself. Turner kept on painting. All he'd say was something incomprehensible about Haydon stabbing his mother. "He stabbed his mother, he stabbed his mother," he said over and over to himself.'

Fulcher's blackest scowl had come back. 'Haydon did?' he said. 'Are you sure?' He stared at me in genuine pain and bewilderment, as if stabbed himself.

'No, he didn't.'

'He didn't?'

'No. Turner was referring to Haydon's attacks on the Academy.'

Fulcher's face cleared at once. 'Ah, I see. *That* mother.'

I seemed to have mislaid my glass. Another trayload came by and I helped myself to a replacement.

Fulcher took over the conversation. I was more than content, since my contribution had become a series of grunts and nods. I had a longing to lie down. Fulcher, oblivious to me, got on to the subject of forces. He talked in a steady stream and I listened. 'I only bring up Turner because of his obvious dynamic constructions, the delicacy and violence combined, and that gushing light, that whirl towards a central hole – all that tugging and twisting of contrary forces. What I call his vortex-vision.'

'Do you?'

'You have a similar drive, it seems to me – in totally different terms of course. The tensions you create, forms banging together, the clashes, resistances. Is this presumptuous on my part?'

'Not at all.' I smiled agreeably, not just at him but at the whole room.

'Naturally it would be stupid to interpret your images and rhythms in terms of sexual disturbance. I'm not doing that.'

'Good. That's good.' Suddenly I felt a surge of joy, or liberation from the bonds of myself. The wine had done its work, I was ready to kiss and embrace the whole world.

'Yes, well, congratulations,' the short man said, through the fence of his teeth. He disengaged himself abruptly, ducking his head with attractive bashfulness. 'You have a success here, in my opinion. Powerful stuff. Very.'

'Here's to your health,' I said, smiling and feral. Unashamedly incoherent. I lifted my glass tipsily, watching in astonishment as it went higher, higher. My left arm extending itself grotesquely seemed nothing to do with it, or with me.

★   ★   ★

Months passed. An airmail came from Della Burls. I had difficulty in recalling her name. The letter arrived with the onset of spring, as I was being afflicted by a bout of acute restlessness. As usual I blamed this condition on the season. Slitting open the blue envelope, I read:

Dear man,

I hear from artist friends here what a name you are making for yourself – getting established and so forth. It's great to know, even at second hand, that you're so continually productive. At the risk of amputating you from your primal sources, so to speak, let me renew that offer of hospitality I extended in person, in all sincerity, when I was being slugged between the eyes by your work, during the best vacation I have had in years. I don't find your policemen so hot but I adore your pubs! Believe me, your preview event was *the* climax – I had a dream of a time. Altogether memorable in every way.

With love and friendship.
Della B.

9

I didn't realise it, but Della, who dressed and acted like a young person, was in her forties. Comparisons are odious, but Maggie would never have gone to such lengths to fool people. Eighteen months after we had parted I was still appreciating her qualities, things I had taken for granted when we were together.

As my passion for her body intensified, naturally it was easier for her to pose naked in her 'birthday suit'. Yet the fact is that she couldn't see the point, or make head or tail of the result afterwards. An unregenerate philistine she might be, but because I was in deadly earnest and I had this obstinacy, she submitted.

Once, looking at one of my hasty oil sketches of Maggie as I paused for a breather, after daubing and thinning, then rubbing with palms and fingers and with rags, fouling the hafts of my brushes and finally disgusting myself with the infantile excretory mess I was in, I became aware of her behind me. In a stupor, absorbed in the problem, I hadn't notice her get up and come over.

'Where am I, then?'

I feigned puzzlement. 'Pardon?'

'My body. What you've been painting. Is that it?'

'You're the starting point,' I said wearily, wiping at my hands with lumps of encrusted rag. Whatever she was, I had bungled it. I was the one who had perished, not her.

'Looks like a lorry-load of orange and lemon slices. Where's my head?'

'I'm not interested in your silly head!'

'What's silly about it?'

'Nothing. But it gets in the way.'

'You can't leave it off, that's stupid.'

'I haven't left it off. Use your eyes.'

'Where is it? Where's my chin?'

'It's there somewhere.'

'Show me.'

'No!'

The next day she came over for another inspection, curious in spite of herself. It was barely recognisable as the same picture. I had darkened everything, spilt blood, allowed the night to take possession, on my way up a different, more tortuous track still. Apart from her scarlet gash in the midst of some orange-pink candy floss, anything resembling the human in her had been obliterated.

She stood scratching her knee and looking. 'Now what?'

'Tell me what you see.'

'It's a pile of rocks at the bottom of a mountain. Is that blood, there? Whoever's been and gone has sacrificed an animal in that ravine, before they hopped it. Am I getting warm?

I wanted to laugh, thinking how near to the truth she had come. Cleaning up, I just smiled to myself. Failures like this made me cataleptic.

She was without shyness now in front of me. She washed and sponged at herself without shame, hanging over the crude phlegm-coloured trough while I sat and watched, my hand sneaking towards a sketch block. 'Stop looking,' she would scold, but half pleased, not really meaning it. Now and then she seemed to be suggesting the opposite.

Looking at her, full and slack, rounding her flesh, I not only admired her big softnesses, I tangled with the problem of how to convey the gold shadow down her sides, the silvery glisten of her shoulders as she sluiced the water over. And those breasts, the loll of them, swaying like fat yellow roses in the breeze.

I have never mastered the play of light, and never will, partly because of ineptness. But it is also my impatience, hearing a voice in my ear demanding that other, inner light. There are many ways of seeing, and as many distractions. The bountiful surfaces of things, the alluring multiplicity of textures, these have always tended to defeat me. It's a kind of conspiracy.

The temptations abounded. Soon I was hungry for more nude studies, for another approach to her rosy abundance.

'How do you want me this time?' she asked once.

Life is one irony after another. She was now shyly proud of her role, while I was in sporadic rebellion against mine.

'Take off your clothes and walk up and down.'

'What, like a show girl?'

'Like a human being.'

'No, I'm not doing that.'

'Why, for God;s sake?'

'It's not natural.'

These days there was hardly need for her to strip. Now I had knowledge of her, the clothes revealed more than they hid. I didn't despise naturalism, I admired the patience and fidelity of those who employed it, but it was too laborious and superseded an operation for me, and it put obstacles in the way of the shapes I hoped to fish out of her gambolling belly. What I sought were lightning methods, impromptu strategies. I got hold of a sketch book and filled it in a matter of hours with excesses, deformities, Maggie-monsters, all of them feverish with mad energy. They were ejaculations rather than drawings. I went on banging them down, page after page, while the goat lust was jetting.

There were times when my very hand seemed infatuated. At others, it was as if its sole purpose was to feed the ever-hungry white ground of the paper. As my mind grew supple, greased on visions, as I turned into a blend of thought and intoxication, my body fell away and ceased to exist. Later, when I flapped through the desecrated sheets, the cut and thrust of my wild jabbering lines amounted to no more than I had known instinctively at the beginning. The modern lust to dismantle was in me. I was driven by an urge to hack to pieces, decapitate, dig deep into the body's mud that might have risen from the darkness of centuries or the slaughterhouses of our own time. Conscious of corruption on all sides, and most of all in myself, I wanted to cut through to the heart of the matter. Before anything worthwhile could emerge, it seemed to me that this surgery was called for. I would lose my bearings, my nerve, and sit flinching, confronted by the reality of what I had done. There was Maggie's rosy joy, dismembered.

Staring aghast at the butchery, a tattery crayon between my fingers, I still believed I was right. Either the battlement I felt was a technical thing or it was a measure of my own monstrousness. Was I a kind of demon? I would go to any lengths to tear away her sham surface – and that included her simple, rubbery-textured nipples pink with love. I was after the sinister radiance of another reality. The misunderstandings between us could all be blamed on this monomania of mine. I was as hurt by them as Maggie, but veiled my eyes, on a journey to an eventual painting which I thought might be called 'Anatomy of a Woman'.

Reading somewhere how the modern nude began with Goya, I went around for days pondering the statement. My face wore such a vacant expression that Maggie started to worry. She wondered if I had perhaps met some girl, say a student, a clever half-starved little bitch who could talk flatteringly in art lingo. This fear became her main source of insecurity. One day she faced me with it directly, swallowing her pride and looking furious.

'Where would I meet anybody,' I countered, 'when I never go anywhere?'

'Whose fault is that?'

'Am I complaining?'

'You could be anywhere, I wouldn't know.'

'Now you're talking rubbish.' The words she wanted to hear, I couldn't say.

'You go on walks, don't you, all over the place. So you say.'

'By myself, yes. In streets. Half the time I don't know where the hell I am. You can't stop people in the street and have affairs with them.'

'I didn't know you wanted to.'

66

'What?'

'Stop people.'

'Did I say I did?'

'Yes.'

'I said nothing of the kind. Maggie, it's about time you trusted me. Do you trust me?'

'No.'

She did and she didn't. What I did all day long was a mystery to her. A day seemed an immense amount of time to squander on yourself. Guilty about this, and of her working all hours, I would try to occupy myself. I read, I walked, all the time planning my next moves in my head. One evening Maggie watched me ferreting about under the plank bookshelf, and in the damp flaking cupboard among piles of rubbish.

'Now what have you gone and lost?'

'My Goya book.' I had picked up this book from a barrow in Shepherd's Bush market, mainly for the introduction. It was a cheap find, with lots of black and white plates, a few in rather insipid colour.

'What's it look like, this Goya?'

'It's got a man on the front in a white shirt, holding his arms out, just before they stick a bayonet in him.'

'Gawd strewth!' Her voice sounded horrified, but she was keener now to help me track it down.

Finding the grotty thing, she held it up by one corner. 'This it?'

'Yes.'

'Why paint a picture like that?'

'To illustrate the horrors of war. It's a protest.'

'Horrible.'

'That's the idea.'

'Who wants an ugly thing like that?'

'The truth's not ugly. Not to a Goya.'

'Oh no? He should see my gran when she's eating.'

'He's dead.'

I was flicking through the book to find the two Maja paintings, both for myself and to show Maggie something different. Leaving me to my picture book she went to make the hot chocolate. I could hear her sighing like a tired dog, back there in the alcove.

Bending my head, I pored over the little monochrome pictures which opened on facing pages – the nude Duchess with her wide-apart high moons and broad hips, then the same lady corsetted and dressed. As I did so, I returned again in my thoughts to the idea of the first modern nude. What did it mean?

The secret, surely, lay in the woman's eyes. I looked up her name, for that too was part of it: the modern nude must have a personality. Dōna Maria Teresa, Duchess of Alba. She gazed back at me boldly, as if to say, 'Well, what do you think?' At the same time she lay regarding herself in an invisible mirror, the identical question jumping out of her eyes. African carvings, such as those in the British Museum, could never have worn that look. Neither would the Renaissance goddesses with their emptily abstract faces.

Now I thought I knew what was 'wrong' with Gauguin. His women were in a paradise that didn't exist. Was that why I felt such a need to fragment the luscious wholeness of Maggie, before she turned to sweet syrup in my mouth?

Gauguin's savages had been Frenchified into self-regarding moderns, scissored out of cardboard and propped against jungle backgrounds. I admired – if that was the word – only one, a corrupt beauty from Martinique, dragged back to Paris and shown flaunting in a carved chair. She was a modern studio nude, modern as one would say 'rotten'. She was bad news. Her depraved primitivism had the sort of license Gauguin understood perfectly, since it was the mirror image of his own diseased freedom.

Lautrec was, I thought, better. Instead of trying to have his cake and eat it he told the truth, wrenching it from his freakish body, a sad and ugly truth to do with perverts, whores, brothels. His pictures touched me, and made room for my own weakness, as well as embracing the dissolution sliding round me now on all sides, for which my symbol was the great oily debased snake of the Thames, once an enormous open sewer. It flowed and oozed just beyond our front door and almost washed against the walls. In one form or another the river coiled and twisted through all my work.

I clung blindly to my belief in the importance of nudes. It was a sort of blind faith I had. How else could I reach out for those virgin elements I sought to rediscover and celebrate? Ever conscious of being in some sense exiled from the human family, I tried to feed my starved eyes on the lambent body. Too often I gagged on the cold remains.

When it was the season I filled a chipped mixing bowl with yellow roses and painted them as straightforwardly as I knew how, making honest copies in honour of Maggie, to please her, to see her smile, and her eyes light up, above all to do homage to her body's extravagance. Any attempt to repay her more directly seemed to go awry. In my paintings I used bits of her without owning up. Any part I focussed on, whether her rich belly or her newly hennaed hair or her big toe, would be absorbed in a grand design I often despaired of controlling.

Knotted up at times by the strains and contradictions involved I would become madly irritable, flying off the handle for no reason. In bed, twitching, I would have trouble keeping my legs still. The joints of my knees ached, and my taut calves, like growing pains. Was it rheumatism? The rooms we lived in reeked of damp. My feet rasped together under the sheets, an old habit from my monkish earlier days. One night Maggie suddenly struck out, fetching me a thump on my back with her round fist. I lay smarting, infuriated, not from the blow to my back but to my ego.

'What was that for?'

'What do you think? I can't get to sleep if you keep that going. You're like a bleeding grasshopper. Either that or you're half over this side like a carpenter's rule.'

'That's a slight exaggeration.'

Moonlight was filling the room. I could see the stains on Maggie's palms and fingers from the red dye she had used to set fire to her hair, which lay over the pillow in dark charred heaps.

'It's all right for you,' she moaned. 'I've got to get up early.'

She heaved around herself now in her frustration, sighing her heavy dog-sigh.

'I'm sorry. I've always had this. It's only tension.'

'Who cares what it is?'

'I said I'm sorry.'

Her temper soon fizzled out. A home-body, she couldn't bear the prolonged cold of an estrangement. Within a matter of minutes she was her old self again. She snuggled up in the dark, fitting herself to the lean nobbly back she had just struck fairly hard. 'I'm a silly cow,' she whispered. 'What am I?'

'Go to sleep.'

I spoke gently, humbled for the hundredth time by the sweetness of her disposition. My buttocks felt the warm cupping of her soft groin. In the summer I slept naked, and she wore her short shift. The night was hot, so I got her to peel it off.

Falling asleep, I dreamt I was in a jet plane hurtling over the Atlantic to America. Nothing seemed strange, but the pilot was a young woman who sat in an open cabin in full view of everyone. With her back to passengers she made cutting remarks in reply to questions, so that people fell silent. A famous man, a film star, wearing round glasses and with boundless assurance, told us of his intention to live at the film studios in order to save time. His face was nondescript, yet I felt envy for his exciting life. The woman captain put the plane on automatic pilot and then hosed down her back with water, drenching her skirt. As she did so she gave a running commentary on her sensations to someone on a lower deck. Smiling, she jumped up and disappeared. The plane sank lower, and before long was just skimming the waves. An ocean liner loomed up, directly ahead of us.

I woke up violently, gave a terrible jerk and cried, 'Look out!' Maggie groaned, stirred in my arms and went back to sleep. We had reversed in the night, and now I clung to her back, which was damp from the heat we had generated together.

The next morning I lay listening as she got ready for work. Always late and in a hurry, she would bang about clumsily in the light like a moth hitting a light bulb. In her haste she shut the door behind her with a crash. The silence that descended was almost solid enough to see.

I was fully awake, but fighting off the temptation to close my eyes. Getting up robot-fashion and pottering around on stilt legs like a soiled old man, I avoided paintings and drawings as though they were mirrors. In any case, I had taken precautions: the few surviving large canvases were turned to face the wall.

I made tea, and then didn't drink it. After sourly reviewing my lack of progress, though without actually looking, I got myself out. Rain or shine, it was nearly always better if you were moving. Maggie would have taken one look at my stone face and given me a cuddle, and of course it was no solution, and anyway, where was she? Sparks of hope flickered and went out. The work I had done was all botched. I knew them in minute detail, even the destroyed ones, as a criminal does his crimes. They dragged at me, dragged me down, heavy in my blood.

Outside, feeling ill and unspeakably haggard, I still enjoyed the lumpy feeling of the cobbles under my feet. Heading instinctively for the river, though with no desire to gawp at it, I fixed my gaze on the stone wall serving as a parapet. At some time it had been slopped over with cement and painted a cream gloss, so that now it looked slimily unpleasant in the strong scraping light. I stared with distaste at its stains and cracks. Even when despondent my eyes refused to stop storing up these useless impressions.

Leaning there against the parapet, I turned my back on the water. I stood opposite Cardinal Alley, near the crumbling tall house where Wren lived – I had read the plaque – during the building of St Paul's.

A cat with its greys and browns muddled together, scraggy about the head, had changed itself into a giant caterpillar and was stalking a live milk-bottle cap. The tinkling sounds as the breeze shifted the tinfoil were barely audible to me. The animal's mauled ears were so sharp with instinct, so electric, that I felt obliged to move, as though to prove that I too was capable of pouncing on something.

6

The whole thing was a puzzle. When did the thought first enter my head that I could be an artist? What on earth could have sown the seed of such an idea, and what made it grow?

To have even articulated such a notion in the world I came from would have been preposterous, not even a subject for ridicule. I grew up in a poor terraced house in Gallipoli Street, a warm nest till I was too big for it. Everything I needed for growth as a small boy I had – a loving mother, a father who was strict but not cruel, who provided for us through hard times and kept his thoughts to himself. Suddenly I had a sister, my

71

mother died, the war broke out and I went to work as a goods station clerk, all in the space of a month.

My small universe throbbed with the life of a tidy slum, extending over a grid of back streets to a scrubby park in one direction, an old cemetery in another. Where did art come in? The only pictures were calendars, cheap framed prints to cover damp patches, bundles of sepia snapshots. And all kinds of knick-knacks. Culture was as rare as leisure. So why me? To this day I have remained mystified. Basically, I am still that boy. Maybe, influenced by my mother's religious upbringing, I simply wanted to sing hymns with what I was given.

One Friday, coming back from school, I was urging my bicycle down a long hill in the direction of home and I noticed the sky. Being winter, it was in tatters, looking as if a giant brush had been swirling round in it. Then this brush had slashed the whole space with indigo-grey diagonal strokes like an enormous act of cancellation.

I pumped furiously at the pedals and attacked the next rise, in a hurry to get inside and spread newspaper on the kitchen table, and then use my watercolour box. I longed to run colours as freely as that sky all over the paper in the Woolworth sketchbook, steering them round with a fat brush just to see what would happen. My tongue crept out and licked my lips at the thought of that wetness.

Once I said, 'I'd like to draw you, Mam. Can I?' Suddenly it was urgent.

'Oh, I don't think so. Wouldn't I have to sit still?'

'Yes.'

'Where would I find the time?'

I was stumped. 'You can if you want.'

'I can't, Francis. Draw your grandpa, he'll be pleased.'

'Why not you?'

She said illogically, 'I look such a sight.'

'I want to.'

'Well, we'll see. Now clear the table, there's a good boy.'

That evening I started a head of my grandfather, burning with eagerness to please, and to win my mother's approval. With this end consciously in view I strove for a likeness, something I knew would produce admiration. Before long, this ceased to matter. I was enmeshed in the intricacies of the old man's moustache, its stains, its ragged fringe. Then there were the strands of larded hair and the flesh folds of ears, sprouting their coarse tufts.

Displeased with the skull, I covered it with an imaginary cap. My grandfather sat up straight, neck stiff, a funny crimped smile on his mouth. Once he bared his front teeth, which were set in a trap.

'How much longer?' he complained at last.

My mother came over to see, feeling obliged to show an interest. The artist at work always attracts attention. I had failed, I only wanted to disown the thing.

My mother said comically, 'I like his cap.'

Although I knew she was only trying to spare my feelings I hated her for her dishonesty. To make her gasp I tore the paper in half, the halves fluttered to the floor, and then I saw it, upside down, the glaring beast head which no one could possibly admire except me. There and then I began another portrait.

My father married again, two years to the day after my mother died. As his brother remarked disparagingly, he went up in the world. Margot saw to that. His railwayman's wage alone would never have paid for his new standard of living, but Margot managed a tobacconist's shop in town. Soon they moved to a better district, a semidetached with stone bays, the garden fenced with thick privet at the front. To the rear could be seen a rustic arch crawling with roses, a crazy paving path, plump flower beds. The place where they ate was actually called the dining room.

Usually on a Sunday, when I couldn't bear my broom cupboard of a bedsitter any longer, I would visit my father and stepmother. As much as anything this was to escape the permanent smell of insecticide I lived in. The landlord had daubed daffodil distemper over the walls, leaving smears and drips on the skirting here and there. Mr Kelly occupied two rooms underneath on the ground floor. On Saturday he called for the rent, and his greeting never varied. 'All right, are we?' he said. He had a beer-belly, which shook when he tittered.

In those days I enjoyed seeing Vivien because she was so outspoken. Since she was a child this was excusable, charming. It was only later that it became alarming. For the present her only crimes were physical, handling the gold brocade curtains with sticky fingers or swinging her muddy shoes up on the speckled green expanse of the settee.

The spontaneity of her welcome delighted me, even if it did only spring from excess energy. I didn't mind her rude questions either. I took it all as a sign that she was glad to see me.

One time I remember, she ran out of the front door after spotting me through the window, and asked, 'Why have you come?' I was startled anew by her mass of bright bubbly-yellow curls that jumped about when she ran.

'To see your ugly mug,' I said, knowing it was the kind of answer she liked.

'Mummy will tell you off for saying that.' She hadn't yet been told that Margot wasn't her real mother.

'I expect so.'

Fidgetting about, scratching rudely between her legs, she moaned, 'I want a puppy. Why can't I have one?'

'Don't ask me.'

Abruptly she changed tack. 'Take me to see where you live.'

'No.'

'Why not.'

'Why should I?'

This baffled her for a few seconds. 'Mummy says it's because you're ashamed.'

'What of?'

'I don't know.'

'Well, I am.'

'Ashamed?'

'Yes. I don't live in a house, that's why.'

'Everybody does!'

'Not me.'

She sucked her thumb avidly, giving me her whole attention. 'Why?'

'Why do you always ask why?' I laughed.

'Where do you live? Why can't I see it? I want to see it, I want to!'

'How can you? I haven't got a house.'

'You have.'

'Not like this.'

'What is it like?'

'I live in a concrete pipe, on a building site.'

'That's a fib,' she said, looking at me uncertainly.

'It's nice and dry, only the walls are curved. When you lie in bed your back's bent.'

'I don't understand. What's curved?'

'Curved is the opposite of straight.' I picked up an apple from the fruit bowl and held it out to her. 'Curved, look.'

She stared at me in silence for quite a while. 'You're so thin, you could slip down a hole, down a crack,' she said suddenly in her clear high voice, eyes shining.

'I know.'

'Why are you thin?'

'You tell me.'

She turned into a woman, confident and knowing. 'Because you don't eat properly.' I heard a version of our stepmother.

'Except raspberry jam,' I told her. 'I eat tons of that.'

'Is that why your lips are so red?'

'Probably. And all the blood I drink.'

'I think you wear lipstick.' She gave a little squeal of triumph.

'I'm going in the garden,' I said, and got up.

Vivien leapt up and shot through the door ahead of me, to be first. 'So am I! I've got my own garden, Daddy made it for me. I'll show it to you if you're good.'

Margot was busy in the kitchen. We had to pass through there to reach the back door. Vivien had already disappeared down the garden path, and the door was left swinging open. Margot shot a glance in my direction and muttered, 'That girl.'

I followed hastily. Because of our differences and her disapproval, there was nothing I could say to my stepmother without selfconsciousness. We had achieved a truce of sorts based on mutual avoidance.

A cold wind sliced across the garden. I had come out without my top coat. Beyond the rose briers on the lopsided wooden arch I nearly turned back, daunted by the wintry expanse of roughly dug ground. I had no idea where my father was. Vivien crouched over a patch of raked soil which looked barren, at the far end near the compost heap. Her corner was marked by a little border of half buried house bricks planted in the earth to create a saw-tooth profile. She had her thighs apart, straddling. She was poking and scraping with a piece of broken garden cane and looked thoroughly preoccupied. Obviously she had forgotten me. Who could have forseen her transformation from this child without problems to a young girl steeped in despair, intent on cutting herself free from every tie, even if this meant pulling down the whole house, the street, the town?

My father appeared behind me and opened his shed without a word. Although this was a safe district he couldn't break with his old habit of keeping it padlocked.

I followed him inside, as much to establish contact as to escape the cold. It struck me then that sheds were more than cobwebby interiors full of old junk that might come in handy one day, they were refuges for men. I hadn't grasped this before. The boards creaked around us in sly complicity. Standing together against the workbench out of the wind we grinned at each other, fleetingly in touch. My father was searching for something, digging with his fingers among nails and screws, tin tacks and cup hooks, odds and ends of all kinds, in the nests of boxes within boxes which I remembered from boyhood, intricate with points, spirals, edges, steel worms.

He said, without glancing up, 'How's the clerking going?'

I didn't know how to answer without disappointing him. The misery of my weeks in that office kept adding to a sum total which had reached, unbelievably, three years, and still I lacked the courage to leave. I was now a gas board clerk. Hating the boss in one department I transferred to another. Lately I had become so sharply aware of the absurdity of my position that I felt at times in danger of splitting in two. The double life I was leading inside my head was so plain to me, I couldn't believe it was unsuspected by everyone else.

'Stick at it, son. You've got better prospects than I ever had.'

'So you tell me.'

'I know what you think. That you've got all the answers. I did. The young always do.'

I shook my head. 'I haven't got any answers.'

The fact is that I was exactly as he described, only worse. Arrogant was the word for it. I swung between stammering timidity and an overweening conviction that I was right and the rest of the world mistaken. My favourite reading during this period was Bernard Shaw. The jaunty mockery of his letters was a joy, confirming everything I suspected about the morass of stupidity and ignorance in which I found myself.

Now and then, on a Saturday, I caught an excursion train to London. As well as this I ransacked the public library for biographies of artists. These I read indiscriminately, no matter

76

what the period, leaving off as my interest waned, which was when all struggle ceased and the rigor mortis of success set in. Sometimes I wondered if it was only the ordeals and significant sufferings of painters that appealed to me. But martyrdom, suffering for the sins of others, would have earned my contempt. What uplifted me were examples of winning through against all the odds – heroism, in other words. Heroes of art were my exemplars.

My knowledge of modern art, such as it was, came from the lush books of reproductions I leafed through ravenously in the reference section, and from visits to the Tate which were like guerrilla raids. I would race out of one room into another, quickly becoming sated and then nauseated by the genuine article. Tramping along Millbank after an hour of viewing, dazed by the rush of traffic and light, mistrusting the canvases I had seen, their slickness, their too-easy solutions, I gulped down the fresh air which was not so fresh, dreaming of the contribution I would make which would have little in common with theirs. As I raced back northward in the train, sneaking glances at my reflection in the carriage window, I wondered at the nonentity I saw there, who had the effrontery to believe he could create a domain for himself.

In my bedsitter I studied a book on loan from the library called *Expressionism*, which included Munch's swirls and screams, his dripping candle-heads, his oval mouths. I thought of his work sardonically as depicting 'misery on the melt'. Yet the energy and raw emotion ran into me direct. My eyes gulped it down hungrily. Later I would be fearful of where it might be leading, as if the chaos underlying it had opened a chasm in front of my feet. Was it black magic, devil's work? A fear of losing my balance, of a dizziness, of falling and plunging would grip me.

Then a Rouault folio I saw in Zwemmer's in the Charing Cross Road took me into other waters, stunning me with its veracity and calm. I began experimenting in watercolours with black outlines. The book was far too expensive an item to buy, and in any case I was afraid of its potency. The pictures burned in my head and refused to die down, those ash-and-cinder suburbs, bloated judges, emblematic flowers, Semitic kings, syphilitic whores. I loved this man for his nerve and his vision, for saying so much with so little, by such humble means. Even the scum and rags of my own life seemed to have a purpose, to take on a glow, become sacrosanct.

Visits to London were now essential, even if they entailed the skirting of pitfalls. I suppose I fell under the sway of artists without realising the extent of their influence, even as I tried vainly to find a style which owed nothing to them. Their example was another matter. They flouted conventions, rejected laws and restraints. What was to stop me from doing the same? I was a blank page, a virgin. I was unloved. In those days, the West End streets at nightfall were alive with prostitutes. I would be leaving it to fate, I told myself, if I just stood on a street corner behind Piccadilly and loitered. All the time a voice inside me was saying, 'Now or never, now or never,' until I broke out in a sweat.

It was a rainy summer evening, perversely cold in the best English tradition. I thought it must be obvious that I was there for a purpose, but giving up now was unthinkable, even worse than going on. 'Now or never', the voice said. Feeling like a pariah, outcast from the world of decent people and disfigured by an interior ugliness that might erupt through my skin at any moment, I stood back against the smart shop front with its blinded windows. Sick with guilt, I was only thankful that my mother was dead.

A thick moisture crawled down through the air. Suddenly my heart leapt. I had seen one. She could have been an evangelist out to save me. I yearned and shrank, the bellows of my lungs strained in and out. She turned the corner and crossed over with insufferable slowness, making a bee-line for me. Struggling to hold my ground I watched from the corners of my eyes. Never had high heels sounded so insolent.

She sauntered nearer, twirling her umbrella like a parasol. Terrified, I also worshipped her cold insouciance. She went past, just a fraction, her timing impeccably professional. I heard her say, 'Lonely are you, darling?'

That was it, that's what they said. But my knowledge was deplorably academic. Blinded by confusion I mumbled something, aware only of a fall of black hair.

'What a beastly evening. Shall we go somewhere warm and dry? You'd like that, darling, wouldn't you?'

It was like the night itself speaking. This was its queen.

We were in motion together. Miraculously my legs were functioning. As we walked or floated along, natural as lovers, she asked me tenderly how long I'd been waiting in that draughty spot.

I didn't speak immediately. My throat gulped and nothing came out. I said at last, 'About half an hour.' It was more like an hour.

'Never mind. Let me make it worthwhile for you.'

She began to put on speed. The alteration was so rapid that I couldn't have said when it started, how it was that she stopped being a mother and became a panther, prowling along with a slither of haunches. I darted shy glances at the gaily smiling face, smelling the cosmetics. 'Now it's too late,' I thought, and struggled to breathe normally. I was trembling from head to foot.

To halt suddenly in front of a door painted blatant crimson seemed the inevitable thing. As the tallish woman shook the rain off her umbrella and collapsed it, then fished a Yale key from her shiny black bag and let herself in, motioning me to follow, my abject terror abated. The fear seething through my veins, by some mysterious variation, became a quiver of excitement.

The woman tripped up the narrow stairs ahead of me. Following, I wanted to touch the swell of her hip, the bare flesh of her calves, It was mine, all for me.

Every brisk, efficient movement she made seemed a further proof of her sexual expertise. I wandered dumbly behind her, into a small room. At moments or stress or anxiety my hands would shake. They were under control, but the cold vigil had turned my nails bluish. I was deeply ashamed of my unfledged, red knuckles, my proppy, coltish legs. While the woman bustled about, igniting a gas fire, getting rid of her wet mac, I hung there in a kind of limbo in all my dripping ineptitude.

Professionally cheerful, she cried out, 'Come along, you poor boy.' She sat on the plumped-up bed and extended her hand. A luscious bedside lamp of milky alabaster with a fringed red shade was glowing seductively. The room wore an expectant, arranged look, and yet seemed weirdly unreal, a stage set – as if the walls and doors were of compressed cardboard. She was in her thirties, I guessed wildly.

'Take off your raincoat,' she ordered. Her white teeth were shining a smile at me, her voice taking on an edge.

'Look, you're wetting the carpet. Goodness, the maid will kill me.'

Conscious of the ugly swallowing of my Adam's apple, I did as I was told. 'Where shall I –?'

'On that chair. That's better. My, what a starved boy you are! Are you starved of love, too, darling?'

I could only nod speechlessly like a found-out child. Nothing mattered, there were no witnesses.

'You are, yes. Now, shall we play a little? What are you staring at? Is this your first time with a woman? Does the cat have your tongue perhaps? Oh, warm your hands first, there's a nice man. Want to look some more, yes?'

She had removed her skirt. Now her heavy white thighs sank into the bed, in the lacy cami-knickers that were black as my fate, black as death, black as disease. A swaying hot wave went over me.

She said impatiently, 'What is it? Don't you like what you see? You don't know what to do, eh? Well, all right. Unfasten your trousers, silly boy. Stop gaping – I have another appointment, so be quick. Quickly!'

'I . . . can't –' She had become my hateful nurse.

'Then that's too bad, you'd better go. This room is shared, you understand? Do you?' She lost patience completely and pushed me aside, shot to her feet and began dressing rapidly.

There was cash ready in my pocket. 'Will you –'

'What for? Pay for nothing?' She waved me off angrily. 'For wasting time? All right – give the maid something as you go out.'

She left the room, waving her arms in exasperation. I thought I heard a low volley of French to someone outside, perhaps the maid, before she hurried downstairs and the street door banged.

With money in my hand I looked out on the landing. There was no one; not a sound. I coughed loudly, then went back and dropped a pound on the bed, followed by the other notes I'd expected to hand over. At the door I stopped, returned to the bed and retrieved the extra money. Abasement was one thing, crazy extravagance another. For a person of my upbringing, the waste was as bad as the disgrace. Going down the stairs I thought I heard a voice, high up.

At the end of the street I faltered, the burn of shame so intolerable that I nearly ran back to beg cravenly for another chance. I did in fact retrace my steps for a few yards, until I realised I had lost direction and was walking blind. Streets surged their walls and openings at me. The red door could be anywhere.

I thought the redness would go on burning in my mind for life, like a buried secret or a recurring nightmare. There was no way I could ever do penance for not being a man. Mercifully, the door, room and bed sank from my consciousness after about a week. So did the woman's red mouth, which had become hard and stinging when I failed to co-operate – like the mouth of my stepmother.

11

I moved into yet another bedsitter, and for once it was a move with far-reaching consequences. In a fit of desperation, horrified by the sterility of my attempts to break out, still a beginner in every respect, I tore up my roots and left town. One day I simply went to the station with my cardboard suitcase and boarded the first available train. I got off at Nottingham, sixty miles to the north. I didn't know a soul. I marvelled at my own daring, feeling in my shoulders the authentic shiver which told me I was embarked on an adventure. I was lonely, frightened, and there was nothing magical about my situation, but at least I had elected to choose my servitude, instead of having it imposed on me from without as a life sentence.

For the first time I had acquired a view. My room was on the third floor of a tall gaunt building, on the corner of it, so I had plenty of light flooding in through the two windows. From one window I gazed directly down a long broad road which had hefty, old-established limes set in the pavement on either side. This road, running downhill to the city centre, was called a boulevard. The word was new to me, as were the trolley buses that hissed and rolled along it, forward and back.

I soon got myself a clerical job at an ordnance depot that was also an army camp. During slack spells I slipped out of the records office and found my way to the wire fence dividing us from the soldiers. Squads of men drilled, roared at by a sergeant. In the evenings, stupefied with boredom, I was released along with hundreds whose work was a mystery to me. I felt again the sensations of triumph and daring, making for my boulevard, familiarising myself gradually with the strange street names, their peculiar layout, seeing buses trundling past marked with destinations unknown to me.

It was autumn, an Indian Summer. Although near the end of October, a warm and mellow sun kept shining. In a civic building near the Arboretum I enrolled in a life class already in progress, meeting on Thursday evenings at seven.

Susan Hines, the teacher in charge, did nothing which could be described as teaching. If someone raised his or her hand, she went over. Otherwise, after arranging the pose and collecting the fees, she settled herself behind her own easel and got to work. Since I only wanted to draw the model and be left alone, this suited me fine.

On the evening of the third week at the class, bored by the model, I watched the teacher surreptitiously. Did Mrs Hines, as they called her, have a husband in tow? Somehow she had the air of an unattached person. Her figure was slight, her dark hair cut in a style which suggested a schoolgirl, but under the makeup her face showed the maturity of a knowing woman. Her chin was small and pointed, her putty nose childishly short, with oddly wide, rather unattractive nostrils. So where did the attraction lie?

It could have been her eyes, bright with amusement and appraisal whenever our glances met. It occurred to me that she wasn't so much flirting as issuing a challenge, as if to say, 'Make your move, go on, I dare you!' Of course such initiative was totally beyond me. Surely that was obvious to an experienced woman? I began to suspect a game she was playing. Even the occasional eye contact made me blush and look away as if stung. How could I have controlled my wavering mouth long enough to even speak to her coherently, and what would I have said? I could only study her when she was seemingly preoccupied with her work. Yet in the fantasy I created I was definitely infatuated, and she the pleased recipient. Her skin isn't good, I told myself. It made no difference.

Watching her in conversation with others I was struck by her unsmiling demeanour. Humour she did have, however. She expressed this by a certain forthrightness, a peculiar set of the jaw at odd moments, a toss of the head as her eyes ignited.

Sooner or later I would have to find the nerve to write, and so declare my interest. Should I ask her to meet me somewhere? The fear of ridicule struck dread into me, and the thought of an actual confrontation was worse, but I knew I would do it: I had gone too far now inside myself. I sat down one night, my fingers clumsy with tension, to compose a message. Handing it in to a porter the next day tormented even more than the ordeal of writing it. Immediately I wanted to ask for it back.

Her reply came in a matter of days, swift and decisive. She used green ink and a calligraphic script. 'Who are you?' She wrote. 'I know your name from my class list but I'm so hopeless at putting names to faces, or I should say the other way round. Meet me in the Starlight Restaurant this Thursday at nine, can you? I go there usually on my way home. By the way, you aren't black, are you?

I was there too early, thinking it an advantage to be sitting there calmly. As the minutes ticked by, my nervousness mounted to near hysteria and I had to fight to remain where I was, my heart booming and huge, bursting with sick thuds beneath my shirt. An old woman moved from table to table with bunches of Michaelmas daisies for sale. Nobody bought any. As she came up to me I shook my head. Part of me said yes, but I would have looked a perfect fool with a bouquet to present at a first meeting. For the umpteenth time I composed my hands around my coffee cup, looked at my watch, fought a losing battle to stay calm.

She strode in bare-headed from the cold street, wearing a dark wine-coloured coat. I signalled with my hand, and she advanced springily. She did have a smile after all.

She said, 'So you're Francis Breakwell.' This perfectly simple remark took my breath away with its naturalness, sweeping away all difficulties and putting an end to my torment. The waitress came up, and she ordered a coffee for herself. 'Would you like another? Yes, go on, have one. Have one with me!' She unbuttoned her coat rapidly. Everything she did was quick, certain.

'Thank you.'

'Now tell me about yourself. Yes, I remember you now, of course I do. You keep looking at me! And I look back. Do I or don't I?'

'I believe so.'

'You're honoured, let me tell you. All I'm concerned with usually is getting on with my own work. Selfish bitch, aren't I? You noticed that, did you?'

'Well, no.'

'What, then? Obviously you miss nothing, you notice things. Tell me.'

I stammered, 'I can't think of anything.'

'But you were watching me.'

'Yes.'

'Naughty boy. You're supposed to be looking at the model. Even if she is dull as ditchwater.'

'I know.'

'Well, I don't mind you looking at me instead. I'm very flattered and pleased. Thank you.'

I saw that she wasn't laughing at me. On the contrary, she gave me the whole of her attention, and by doing so made me feel that I had been craving secretly for years for this very moment to arrive. Her eyes, blue with flecks of violet, had points; she had gull's eyes. She gazed at me without subterfuge, so avidly that I was forced to look down.

'You're a shy young man. Should I call you Francis?'

'Yes.'

'You don't sound like a native of these parts. You're not, are you?'

'I've been here six weeks.'

We stared at each other. Her lips wore an inquisitive smile. More than once I've been reprimanded for covering my mouth with my hand in the act of speaking. I did so now, feeling scrutinised like the model.

Susan Hines sat back and sipped her coffee. She said tartly, 'You mustn't leave me so completely in the dark. Tell me a little about yourself. Don't be shy. I don't want to feel like a detective.'

'I'm of no interest.'

'Oh, aren't you?'

'Nothing's happened to me. I've had a completely dull life.'

'Is that so? You poor old man – you sound as if you're at the end of your days! How old are you?'

'Twenty-three.'

Her eyes flared with mischief. 'Are you really?'

I felt the blood rush to the roots of my hair. 'That's right, laugh.'

'Who's laughing? I'm envious. Don't be so touchy. Listen, I want to know why you're living a dull life. If you are, what about me? Men are free, they don't have to be bored.'

'I'm a clerk. Nothing happens to clerks.'

Her face intense, unsmiling, she learned forward across the table to ask, 'And what would you like to happen? You can whisper if you want.'

'You're laughing again.'

'I don't laugh at such things. Let me tell you something. Laughter kills desire, did you know that?'

'No.'

'Well, it does. If you won't say anything else, what about your work? Are you passionate about it?'

To dignify what I did with the word 'work' was both thrilling and absurd. 'I'm probably wasting my time.'

'I know, you're your own worst critic. That's the trouble when you're so isolated, the doubts swarm in. A response, an honest but sensitive one, that's what you need. When can I see some?'

'Oh, not yet.'

'Can't I come to your room?'

'No, it's too horrible.'

'I've been around, you know. I'm a working-class girl, and anyway, who cares? What's it matter? I wouldn't be coming to inspect your curtains.'

'There aren't any,' I lied.

Her eyes widened. 'Are you serious. How do you get undressed?'

'In the dark.'

Suddenly she laughed, a high ringing peal. 'I'd definitely like to see something of yours. In fact I insist.'

'I'll look something out and bring it in to the class.'

'What a spoil-sport. Another thing, what about your favourites? You must have painters you adore. I do.'

Talking rapidly, she explained that at home she painted surrealistically, not as she did in the life room. She mentioned Redon and Ernst. I responded by blurting out the names of my own idols, Blake, Van Gogh, Rouault, Beckman, and a new discovery, Emil Nolde.

'Ah, you're a visionary!' She glowed at me approvingly.

Ambivalent as ever, I slid my eyes away. I didn't know whether to rejoice or slink from her in disgrace, not because I was nothing, but I had achieved nothing, and here I was being regarded with perfect seriousness. Anything I might do was far ahead of me, unused, waiting – like the life I would live one day.

I met her again at the restaurant, and once or twice at a pub round the corner. As the time crept up to ten, she would begin glancing at her watch. She was afraid of missing her last bus.

'You could do with a car,' I told her.

'We've got one. Victor uses it. When it's not broken down.'

Victor was her husband. They had met at the art school in her home town. He was an illustrator and printmaker, but he refused to teach. They lived on the income derived from a newsagent's he ran, and from her part-time earnings. The shop was in a mining village, five miles out of the city. They had two small children, 'flukes' she called them, Kara and Tom. I gathered that the husband, Victor, was embittered by his uncreative life, chained to the shop at all hours.

'Never get married,' Susan said, and pulled a wry face.

'I want to.'

'Why, for God's sake? Stay as you are, enjoy your freedom while you can.'

'That's the trouble, I'm not enjoying it.'

'Why aren't you?'

'It feels pointless.'

'Is your work pointless?'

Her use of the word 'work' still embarrassed and challenged me. 'It might be, I'm not sure. Even if it's not, it should flower out of things shared, out of life with a woman, out of a family.'

'Francis, you're so sweet.'

'You think that's stupid.'

She sighed. 'My dear, it's naive. And sad. What you think you're missing blots out the rest. Everything gets gobbled up, there's no time.'

'So art's a compensation, is that it?'

'I don't ask such questions. But don't say I didn't warn you. Try it your way and see. I have tried it, and I'm telling you it doesn't work.'

Taking leave of her at the bus stop, I asked, 'What's it like, where you live?'

'The village? Ugly. Ugly as hell. If you think that's what you want, you're mad.'

'I didn't say that.'

'Living life in a dog kennel isn't for me. Streets of dog kennels, with backyards clamped together in a long line like poultry runs. Got the picture?'

'Why stay there?'

'I told you, the shop. Victor's crucifixion. Money, my love.'

'So what do you want?'

'Me? To be left alone, so I can think, so I can paint. If I didn't have that, my God, I'd hit the bottle. Now what are you staring at?'

'You.'

'Is my mascara smudged?'

'No.'

She squeezed my fingers as her bus swung into view and lumbered towards us. Tilting her face for a kiss, she whispered hoarsely, 'Let's have an affair.'

'I don't believe in them.' I had only the faintest idea what an affair was.

'Suit yourself. Goodnight, idiot.'

I stood smiling stiffly, and the bus took her away, back to the over-full life she seemed to decry, though I was never convinced by this attitude of hers. It always struck me as a pose she had to strike. To be a wife and mother was déclassé. If she was such a free spirit, I argued, why not strike out on her own? I stopped short of thinking it should be with me, but the more she disparaged what she had, the more I wanted it for myself.

It was December. The classes came to an end. Susan wrote a hasty note to say that Kara was ill with chicken pox and so she, Susan, couldn't see me for at least a fortnight. There were also other family demands, relatives to meet, a Christmas party to arrange. The note expressed no regret, no affection. I held it in my hand, in a room which didn't belong to me, part of a city in which I had no place. I felt totally superfluous. I might have been on the moon. There and then I began to suffer the tyranny of coveting what wasn't mine.

In the New Year we saw each other as before. Once I took her to my room, unwillingly, only because she insisted. I had been putting her off with various excuses, but the truth was that I feared the lingering of her presence after she had gone. I lived like a monk. Would a vibrant female make my dreary surroundings uninhabitable?

The reality was different. We were so late heading for my district, and her actual stay was so brief, it was as if she had never been.

The door was without a key. A previous tenant had screwed on a padlock. I opened it and we went in. I smelled dust, saw the dinginess of the ceiling, the stained wallpaper.

'What's wrong with it?' She ran over to the window and exclaimed with pleasure at the view.

'It's just a room.'

'Think of what you could do with it! My God, you're a lucky devil. A room of your own. I'd love it. Nobody would dig me out. I could work happily here. If this was mine I'd cherish it, and put a damned great notice on the door saying "Mine".'

I pulled a folio of drawings from under the bed and she inspected each sheet, turning every one with care like a privileged person, kneeling on the carpet to do so. Reaching the end, she started again from the beginning. Everything became silent, charged. I held my breath. No one had looked twice at anything of mine before.

'Thank you,' she said. 'I'm not disappointed. I knew of course I wouldn't be.' She glanced at her watch and leapt to her feet. 'Help, I'm late! If I miss that bus it'll be a taxi, and that'll be a row because we're broke again.'

We ran down the street together. Scrambling on to the moving bus platform she called to me, 'Don't waste your talent. I'll help you. See you next week, barring domestic disasters.'

The bus conductor, a young black-haired fellow, was grinning intimately at her. Susan waved and winked.

On our evenings together, since the time was so short, we walked the streets if it was fine. Rain or intense cold would force us indoors. I wanted to catch a bus and walk by the river but the distance was too great.

In the Gay Dog one evening we had our first real quarrel. As is often the case, the subject was no more than a pretext for the real protest I was making, a complaint about her treatment of me which I could never have justified out in the open. A hypocritical puritan in me clamoured to voice objections, level accusations, attack her character, insult her for God knows what faults or defects, but what we were discussing was Gauguin, an artist she adored and who interested me not at all. Her attachment to his art was as good a reason as any for despising him, since I was now jealous of every one of her attachments. I had even asked about the bus conductor.

'Is he a friend of yours?'

Her eyes twinkled. 'Oh, I wouldn't be surprised. Anyway, an admirer.'

'What's his name?'

'I haven't the faintest idea. I'm not even sure who you mean. Is he dark, young?'

'Yes. Good-looking.'

'Isn't imagination wonderful. To tell you the truth I think he sees me as a tart.'

'Why should he?'

'I've no idea.'

'You don't mind that?'

'No, I rather like it.' She laughed.

'Am I the customer you're leaving? Is that what he thinks?'

'Probably. Obviously you're not amused.'

'Obviously you are.'

'Oh, don't be stuffy!'

We returned to Gauguin. I racked my brains for some derogatory remarks. Finally she was stung to say coldly, 'I think you're missing the point entirely.'

'And what you're talking is aesthetics and nothing else. Is that all art is to you?'

'You know it isn't.'

'How would I know?'

'Look at my work, that's how.'

'I'd like to,' I said.

An inner voice told me this wasn't true, and that it would only confirm me in my dislike of her. Susan's candour, which I had so admired in the first place, now seemed one aspect of an actress intent on displaying herself, and in so doing, dramatising everything. I saw drama as the most obvious of the arts. My view of Susan was confused, and so were my feelings. Shamed by my boorish behaviour I wanted to be worse, like the masochist who falls ill in a desperate attempt to gain love.

'What's the matter?'

The alarm on her face gave me a measure of satisfaction. 'Nothing,' I said.

'I must go in a few minutes.'

'Yes, I know.'

'Will you ring me at the usual time?' This was an arrangement we had.

'On Saturday, yes.'

'Promise?'

She reached for my hand and pressed it. Her eyes sought mine, but when I looked at her it was sadly and ironically. I read falsity in her every gesture, which could only mean that things were nearing an end. Irritated by her hurt expression, I said, 'Let's go.'

The following Thursday she asked me without preamble to come and look at her work. It was high time, she said.

'Where?' I said, amazed.

'At the house, where else?'

'Can I?'

'Victor's away at the moment,' she said shortly. 'How about this Saturday afternoon?'

I was expected around three. When I located her road – I had come by train – and approached the semi-detached house in a developed part of the village, I was bewildered to find no sign of a shop. As Susan let me in, she explained that Victor rented a lock-up premises in the high street.

'Where is he at the moment?'

'Victor? He went to his father's in Leicester. Or so he said. I believe he's having an affair. Well, that's all right. I wanted one myself, remember?'

'How can you be sure?'

She laughed her unexpectedly high laugh. 'How do women know things? It's so funny. We've got a mutual friend, Jenny. Victor asked her to be his go-between, so he could receive letters from this woman of his, whoever she is. What he didn't allow for was Jenny's loyalty to me. She passes on his mail, or rather he collects it, and then she tells me what's going on. Isn't that absolutely priceless?'

'I'd use another word.'

'What word?'

'Treacherous.'

'Oh well, we all enjoy the intrigue, I'm sure.'

'So you're not upset?'

'On the contrary. No doubt Victor's got himself saddled with this creature and can't shake her off. I know he doesn't want an affair really.'

'Then why do it, what's the point?'

'I'll explain, shall I? Couples are mysterious to outsiders, who never know the inside story. The fact is that Victor and I love each other. What he's on with now is only something to punish me with. Yes, I'm sure of it. If it's still going on, that is. He hates deceit and so ends up punishing himself rather than me. Poor Victor, he's actually an honourable man, better than I deserve. Nicer than you, probably.'

'Aren't I nice?'

'Yes and no. You tend to be unstable, Francis.'

'Thank you.'

'But so sweet when you want to be.'

'I've got another question.'

'Quick, then. Before I proceed to stagger you with my brilliant work.'

'How can you be sure Jenny's telling the truth?'

'Very clever, yes, and I've thought of that. It could be Jenny he's having an affair with, is that what you're saying? Well, it's possible of course. Except that it's happened once already, and I can't see them reviving it, they've moved on from there, they have a brother and sister relationship now. Either way it makes no difference, none whatsoever.'

'Because you love each other.'

'Precisely.'

'Might he be punishing you, or trying to, because he's got wind of me?'

'Oh yes, he might.'

'Or because of someone else?'

'Now, now.'

'Have you had many lovers?'

'My dear boy, do you want the story of my chequered career?'

'I feel like a simpleton.'

'Believe me, you're not that. You're just young.'

I asked after her children, and Susan said they were with Jenny. The obstacles were all cleared away, yet I knew this was the end of our intimacy. Entering the largish house, I had been astonished to find it in complete disorder; uncarpeted stairs, naked light bulbs, dust and cobwebs in corners, large prints and canvases hanging unframed and askew on walls of bare plaster. Building alterations seemed to be in progress. Children's toys were slung down in doorways and on landings, so that I had to pick my way through.

Susan led me upstairs to the chaotic room she called her studio. Her eyes on me, she propped boards and stretchers against the walls and on her easel. There was a trestle table under the window piled with drawings and prints. I stood nodding, murmuring appreciatively, unmoved. These surfaces were highly decorative, tastefully coloured, cleverly designed, pleasing. I took note of the skill and admired coldly, diguising my true feelings as best I could. The spark which had flown from her to me was not here, among these toadstools, plants, spider webs, imaginary birds in imaginary foliage. Ribbons of vines fluttered leaves like farewell letters. I could see nothing in them, nothing that could only have been done by her, nothing that *had* to be there.

Edgily alive, she took me down again to the kitchen. Unwashed pans and pots choked the sink. Over coffee, she mentioned a friend she would like me to meet, an autioneer with a firm of fine art dealers.

'His name's Charles Woodruff. If I can get him to come to the pub one evening when we're there, I'll introduce you.'

'Why?'

'Because he's a protégé-hunter?'

'What's that?'

'He loves to be in on the discovery of talent. Who knows, you could be his next find.'

'My stuff might not appeal to him.'

'Oh, it will. Anyway, I've told him about you. Together with a reference so glowing it could get you into heaven.'

'When was this?'

'Oh, weeks ago. He's definitely interested.'

'You're full of surprises.'

'Aren't I!'

'I never dreamt I'd be sitting here in your house drinking coffee, and now this.'

'Do you like me again?'

'I didn't say I'd stopped.'

'No, you never say anything. Come here and give me a kiss.'

12

Charles Woodruff looked staid enough to be forty but was probably much younger, with a full head of stiff yellow hair, parted as if by a hatchet. He was dressed conservatively and his lounging stance was so assured, so worldly, that I thought there must be some mistake. But no, here was Susan taking me up to the bar. She said brightly, 'Charles, this is Francis Breakwell, the young artist I was telling you about.'

We chatted lifelessly for a few minutes. The conversation soon foundered, but before it did I was invited to visit him at his home. Woodruff said, 'Here's my card. Ring Pru, my wife, and fix up an evening with her. I'll look forward to it. Any friend of Susan's is sure of a warm welcome at our house.'

'That's kind of you.'

Later, Susan asked me, 'What did you make of Charles?'

'To be honest, not much. He's going through the motions because of you.'

'Does that matter? First impressions are often misleading. Anyway, go.'

'I might.'

'Francis!'

'All right, I will.'

'Behind every man there's a woman. Wait until you meet Pru Woodruff.'

'Now what are you getting me into?'

'Silly boy, it's not me. I didn't make the world.'

I rang the Woodruff number as arranged. A precise female voice gave me a date and expressed pleasure at the thought of meeting me. I was too flustered to ask whether I was speaking to Mrs Woodruff.

When the day came, I vacillated, on the verge of not going. My mood swung between a debilitating timidity and bursts of wild inner truculence. I was shaving, trying to make myself look presentable. I put on an ill-fitting brown suit which was beyond redemption, the only suit I possessed.

Unable to settle the question of what to select, in the end I left the folder of samples behind, turned my back on the drab room and its contents and rushed out angrily, empty-handed, in search of Mapperley, the suburb where the Woodruffs lived.

I got off the bus as instructed at Victoria Crescent, then turned left into Private Road. Passing one impregnable large house after another I felt my skin start to shiver in anticipation. Soon, in spite of the March wind, I was sweating and wilting inside my clothes. The very grit of the drives around here looked sharper, harder. Entrances were raked and weeded, with no mark of a human foot, no children, no dogs. I found the place – a tall, mock-Tudor facade, with broad thrusting bays and lifeless curtains, and rang the bell. The heavy oak door, studded all over, was swung open by a small girl with a bright ginger fringe. She gazed at me in silence through her mask of freckles.

Though the words I'd rehearsed down the road sounded foolish and inappropriate now, I still said, 'I believe Mrs Woodruff is expecting me.'

'I'll fetch Mummy,' the expressionless child said. But she didn't move. Her eyes, plunging everywhere, ate me up. Suddenly she went clattering away into the silent depths.

I waited on the long steps, hearing nothing. Then a loud female voice was saying, 'But that's rude isn't it, darling – you must ask our guest to come in. Whatever will he think of us?'

Smiling and apologetic, the woman appeared at the door. 'I'm so sorry. You must be Francis Breakwell. My husband's a little late. I'm used to it. He did ring though for me to pass on his apologies.'

I followed her in. Never good at first meetings, I was more than willing to encounter one person at a time.

Pru Woodruff was a billowy, black-haired woman. She moved like an empress, and wore a magenta sweater that seemed calculated to knock my eye out. Averting my gaze, I noticed the contradiction of a small-boned face, so tightly composed that I was thrown into nervousness.

We went into a fine drawing room. Reddish furniture gleamed richly. A glass cabinet sparkled with crystal and silver. The walls were so thickly covered with pictures that at first I couldn't take anything in. One was a gay primitive, facing me as I passed through the doorway. It was of a frozen Rousseauish cat, the stripes decorating rather than enveloping the greenish animal, which was flattened against a zigzag assortment of multi-coloured cushions spurting red and yellow tassels and flaunting blue stitches. The pale eyes of the cushiony cat were devoid of expression, like the girl's at the door. This was Jessica, who turned out to be the artist.

Pru Woodruff said, 'So you're the young painter I've been hearing about?'

The word 'painter' was easier to live with, because more workmanlike, than the ridiculous 'artist'. Nevertheless, in those days I would automatically refute the charge. 'I'm a clerk,' I answered. To my dismay I felt the hot flood in my cheeks and neck which I could never control. Facing the woman, I saw that I wasn't so much being looked at as pored over by Pru's liquid eyes. The fixity of her gaze was extraordinary. Beneath it, there was her social smile, as if pinned on. My ridiculous bashfulness intensified. I was afraid my lips might be helplessly twitching. My hand flew to my mouth.

She said calmly, 'Please sit down.' While I did so, and she moved about the room touching objects on the tops of low bookshelves, she added, 'I mustn't embarrass you by staring, it's an awful habit of mine. Really I must be worse than Jessica. Charles is always telling me off.'

'I do it as well,' I murmured.

'I can't say I've noticed.'

'Oh.'

I sat drowning foolishly in the deep comfort of a Knole armchair with high velvety wings. At least now I had some protection.

'Would you care for a drink? We have everything here, more or less. Sherry, perhaps?'

'Thank you.'

She poured pale sherry into a long-stemmed glass, and one for herself. As she arranged herself decorously on the carved settee opposite, I stared at the bric-a-brac everywhere with a display of interest. The glass paperweights, semi-precious stones, jade bowls and an ostrich feather swam into focus as my gaze flitted wildly about.

Something about the way she was presenting herself gave me confidence. I was her captive audience. Nothing I said or did would go amiss or be unacceptable. It was her show, and the show was herself. Her brows had been carefully plucked and redrawn. I took in her long legs, swelling unexpectedly into broad, darkly swathed hips and that assertive jut of magenta. The thick metallic collar round her neck seemed responsible for the way her face suddenly diminished, too small and crushed for the black hair, dressed high in a glossy dome. Something about her features reminded me of beetles.

It was difficult for me to forget my gaucheness. I was ridiculed by my knees, my limbs strewn as if helpless in the unresisting gold upholstery. 'It's a lovely room,' I said, for some respite from my own self-rejection.

'Yes, isn't it.'

I was aware of her faint smiling derision, either at my social failure or the tactics of my eyes. The slight tang of an accent betrayed her local origins.

'Beautiful things you have.'

'Oh well,' she laughed, 'you mustn't think we're wallowing in *Vogue* richery, because we're not. You can pick up gorgeous items in junk shops even now, if you persevere. I suppose I've been lucky. And I couldn't care less personally about the odd crack or two.'

'No.'

She went on, pointing, 'That jade bowl over there for instance, was in two bits when I found it, absolutely buried in rubbish and covered in muck. A pound. I glued it back together again. It's quite worthless but it pleases me. What does it matter?'

'If it gives pleasure.'

'Exactly what I say.'

We were interrupted by a silent apparition in the doorway. It was Jessica, demure and soft like an angel in pyjamas of some furry blue material. I could make out the sprigs of tiny flowers.

'Who's the beautifullest!' her mother cried, holding out her arms.

'I am.' The child walked forward solemnly for her goodnight kiss. It was a ritual. She disappeared as softly as she had arrived.

'She's very sweet, really,' Pru said, towards the door, like a parting caress.

For a few minutes we discussed painting, but in such a desultory fashion that I began to suspect she had more interesting topics in mind. The subject apparently left her cold. Was I to be the recipient of some confidence, or perhaps a revelation of her true nature? I hoped not.

Whatever it was, she had left it too late, tightening her mouth in annoyance at the sound of tyres crunching over the gravel outside. 'Here's Charles now,' was all she said. By the look she gave me, she might have been signalling details of an assignation. I got up, telling myself I had nothing to be guilty about, but as though I had.

'My dear chap, I've kept you waiting, I'm afraid,' Woodruff said, striding in.

He had changed. From being the rather colourless individual I had met in the pub he was now a person who exuded the power of ownership. He went to his wife and pecked at her as she offered her cheek.

'I said, 'There's no hurry. Mrs Woodruff has been taking care of me.'

'Good.' Woodruff acted as though he hadn't heard. Pru gave me a thin smile, and a look of strange complicity which struck me like a snake.

Charles Woodruff was a sensible, definite man. I got an impression of certitude and impatience. Art, I imagined him saying, was a business like any other. If nuances and atmosphere were to be of interest, frames were necessary. He took me lightly and courteously by the elbow and paraded me up and down before the layered pictures. He was a man who believed in concentrating totally on the matter in hand.

Swamped by so much variety, I mumbled my apologies for not bringing along something of my own to show. To my surprise, Woodruff seemed genuinely disappointed. 'That's a pity, I'm sorry,' he said, twice. 'Never mind, you must come again soon. For supper. I understand you're mainly a water-colourist, is that correct?'

I blurted out that I hadn't settled for any one medium, that I was still experimenting. The word covered a multitude of sins.

'Yes, of course,' the man said rapidly, 'but I take it you do have preferences?'

'I don't have the space for oils.'

'One day you will have, if what I hear is correct.'

What had Susan been saying about me? Taken aback, I was glad to be on the move again, to view the collection in an adjoining room. I glanced over my shoulder to locate Pru. She had disappeared. Now she was no longer accompanying us I stopped thinking of intelligent things to say which might have impressed her.

I saw first a large, expensive reproduction of an Etruscan tomb painting, a male dancer, stepping out like a peacock.

It glowed splendidly in a gold frame. Then I found myself confronted by a study of a woebegone adolescent girl, sickly pale, with forlorn squashed nipples. I recognised a famous Münch.

Woodruff saw me admiring, and laughed. 'My wife's choice. Myself I don't care for Expressionism, unless it's the abstract sort. Mind you, I can appreciate the force of it. No, it's altogether too disturbing, too loony for my taste.' He laughed again, as if mocking himself. 'Which tells you more about me than anything else no doubt.'

I liked him better for this admission. It was on the tip of my tongue to ask him about some unframed canvases I'd seen in the hall on the way in. Were they the work of prótegés too? If they were, I thought, in a sudden access of pride and arrogance, I had nothing to worry about.

Determined not to overstay my welcome, I invented someone I had to visit. I was unnerved, standing so close, by the taut skin of Woodruff's face, and by his pained eyes swerving away from any contact. He was more genuine than his wife. 'In hospital,' I added, compounding the lie because my excuse seemed impolite, feeble, transparent.

Going down the road I mused over Pru Woodruff's disappearance. No explanation had been given by her husband.

A fortnight went by. One morning there was a letter for me on the doormat. I picked up the small square envelope to guess at the author. Only Susan very occasionally wrote to me. It wasn't her. Tearing open the envelope I walked down the street to work, reading first the large scrawl at the bottom of the notepaper. Pru Woodruff. The letter said:

> Dear Francis,
> I must ask you to forgive me for my apparent rudeness the other evening when you called. I had a sudden blinding headache and went to lie down – always the best thing. I had no idea you would be leaving so soon. Charles should have called me – too bad of him. He did say you would be coming again, with something to show us this time. He is terribly vague about important things, though very efficient in practical matters. He can be pushy – which could be to your advantage. Vulgar though that sounds.

If you are ever free in the afternoons and feel like dropping in, I promise not to do another vanishing trick! You have our phone number I believe.

At work, I sat on my clerk's chair with this letter in the back pocket of my trousers. In blank spells, when I was supposed to kill time by rearranging the filing system, I reached for the sheet of paper and examined it again. It had an embossed address. By the end of the day I had made up my mind to ring next Tuesday. I got a form and applied for a day's leave. If Pru Woodruff said no, there was always the gallery at the Castle to visit.

The day was long in coming. I couldn't wait to set out. This time I would make a better impression. In my mind's eye I sprang about like a tiger before the alarming Pru Woodruff, outlining my plans for the future. My reservations about her quite blotted out, in their place I imagined a warmly welcoming woman, pressing me to accept her help, encouragement, praise, glasses of sherry. In the same way, my diffidence was no longer a feeble quality but a tender vulnerable nakedness which she admired. Hungry and eager, I would be the raw material this woman of refinement was waiting for.

In the afternoon I dialled the number from a phone booth. The directory, dangling on a string, looked as if a dog had mauled it. Two rings, and I heard Pru Woodruff's voice: 'Hello?'

'Mrs Woodruff?'

'Speaking.'

Overcome by anxiety, I gulped out who I was. 'I wondered if I should call round.'

'When, now?'

'Well, yes, if it's not inconvenient –'

'It isn't. Come right away!'

I put down the phone. The ideal picture I had been painting in my head with such verve had gone up in smoke. Why this was so I couldn't understand. I saw myself now as pathetic and naive. But stepping out into the street I headed straight down the hill towards the market square, heading for the Mapperley bus stop, as determined to go as ever. Shy people who shrink from others are sometimes crazily reckless. I walked along frowning, driven by a relentless and angry mood, not giving a damn for anyone.

The door opened before I could even press the bell push. Pru was dressed differently, but made the same regal impression as on the previous occasion. In her eyes I saw a worldly gleam which threw me completely. Any confidence I may have mustered left my body. To add to my confusion I was being tossed violently to and fro inside myself, feeling important one moment and a fraud the next.

'That was quick. Come in!'

'It's a good bus service,' I muttered, and she said, 'Yes, we're very fortunate on this route.'

I was given wine, white and sharp. It had a fizz to it. Pru allowed me a few sips, then bore down with questions of an appalling directness. Her twinkling looks when at the door had been merely to disarm me.

She leaned forward eagerly. 'May I ask you a personal question?'

'Yes.'

'Artists have a curious way of looking at you. They examine you as they would a still life.'

'I hope I don't, Mrs Woodruff.'

'My name is Pru.'

'Yes, I know.'

'Do you like me?'

'Yes.' It came out as a croak. I had become aware, too late, of her unassailable single-mindedness.

'You can be perfectly honest.'

'I am.' I felt I was being braided, by eyes instead of fingers.

'Don't look so alarmed.'

'I'm sorry.'

'Can I ask you something else?'

'Yes, if you like.'

'You needn't answer if you don't want to.'

'Answer what?'

'Do you have a sweetheart? Are you infatuated with somebody?'

'Not any more. It's ended.'

'You sound very definite.'

'I suppose so.'

'I know it's dreadful of me to ask.'

'No, it's not.'

'Let me refill your glass.' Her shimmery coral-red blouse seemed to be sewn with metallic flecks. 'What must you think

100

of me with these questions. I have to know things, you see. I can't bear mysteries.'

'If you want to know something, ask,' I said toughly. And then wanted to bite off my tongue.

'All right, I will.' She spoke calmly, slowly. 'Something is puzzling me about you. It must be the insight you have as an artist.'

'How do you mean?'

Pru Woodruff crossed her legs. 'You're a virgin, aren't you? Yet you seem to know about women, about what they want, what they dream of. About me. I find that intriguing. I'm sorry, am I embarrassing you?'

I got out of there as fast as I could, with what was left of my self-esteem, its rags and tatters, in a turmoil that was part revulsion and part lust. The vulgarity of Pru's will made me sick and exposed me as a hypocrite, both at once. I walked away furious with her and with myself. Life being what it is, I read once in Gauguin's journals, one dreams of revenge.

13

Right from the start, beginning with my mother, women have drawn me to them like iron filings to magnets. A life going nowhere would be transformed, quivering in new expectant clusters around the power they gave off. The trouble was, there was no happiness. I wonder why. Did I dislike them secretly? Could it be that I'm an emotional cripple? A moment came when they would cry out, as if gripped by an ancient fatalism, 'You hate women!' I half expected to hear next, 'That's how it's been, it's what we're here for, nothing changes.'

I thought with Maggie it was going to be different. She aroused desire and yet we stayed friends, and out of our friendship grew a kind of dumb love. Vivien apart, none have wanted to stay with me. It must be more than just bad luck. Maybe I don't have what it takes to share a life with someone and at the same time be kindled enough to want sex with them. Who can fathom love? It's more honourable in such circumstances to stay single, but it feels abnormal, as well as selfish and cold. Vivien saved me from the barren existence a man knows when he is deprived of a feminine presence. Wasn't a woman brought into Christianity by popular demand?

Maggie and I were drifting apart, and all the time I did nothing. Totally absorbed and obsessed by my work, I did nothing. I hardly noticed. Then it dawned on me, too late. The rot had set in.

I fell to pieces even before she walked out. In losing her I lost touch with the best, happiest, most wholesome part of myself. She was the kind of woman who comes along once in a lifetime. If my mother had been alive, how she would have grieved! She would have wanted me married to Maggie, if only so that she could have stopped worrying about me. She seemed to have premonitions, forebodings where I was concerned. I think she saw my future as a dark one, fraught with the difficulties of a withdrawn personality: in other words, a fate like her own. I was a mother's boy.

When Pru Woodruff wrote to me at Southwark, Maggie was still installed. The letter contained the bombshell of a proposed visit. I didn't want her to come there, or to see her at all. But the letter dangled an enticing carrot at a time when I was earning nothing, living on dreams and on Maggie's slave labour. It said in part: 'You might even be amenable to my bringing back something for Charles to see. Apart from the dealers he mentioned, he has business associates who are potential buyers – and I have friends here eager to collect. Yes, really!'

Apart from anything else I was reluctant to stop work, even for a few hours, on a large ambitious painting I had just begun. My meanderings through the streets had borne a strange fruit.

During that early period in London I liked to get lost in streets. I couldn't have explained to Maggie what it was I did on some days, but it had to do with the sensations of half fear, half excitement I felt when I was without bearings, wading even deeper into unknown territory. The further I strayed from my base, feeling the thrill along my nerves that perhaps an animal feels, the more acute was my eyesight, the more alert my responses: or so it seemed. Partly it was being in London, a vast city that would remain for me essentially foreign, where no demands were made and where I was unrecognised. It was the immense city labyrinth, lubricated by money, which made the river of dissolution flow. The sour damp of this artery, and the seething decay that went with it, was never far away, like the smell of a cistern.

Crossing over the sludgy ebbed river one morning and on into the City district, my painting suddenly flashed into me, complete and achieved in every detail. The pictures you dream or see in your head are always the ones that get away, the most beautiful, the truly satisfying and eternal creations.

I not only dreamt the picture, I walked on encapsulated in a dream or transparent womb where I breathed freely and was perfectly content. The traffic ground past, ripping and beating to no avail. Nothing could disturb the sleepy musing which had drugged me into believing I was unique and fulfilled, and not absurd in an absurd world like everyone else.

I went on past a huge magisterial building fitted with imitation bronze doors. As if nudged, I craned my neck suddenly to look upwards. High on the walls, the leaning gold words spelled SUN LIFE ASSURANCE. These words became at once mingled with the hallucination I believed I could transfer to canvas without lifting a brush. In my mind's eye the canvas skin grew luminous. Miraculously appropriate forms were breeding in a procession, like a triptych. Wet and brilliant jewels, as if fished from a uterus, they came to rest inside me. I stood at the kerb, reeling in my marvellous catch, wanting now to run back to my room and yet fearful of disturbing what I had been given. Would they go pop and vanish like beautiful irridescent bubbles if I took a single false jolting step?

Moving like a somnambulist, I passed a street cleaner. A middle-aged ginger man, he poked away in the gutter with a stiff-bristled broom at coatings of dust and nothing else. He shuffled along without raising his head.

Later, preparing a canvas hastily, I conceived the titles 'Sun Life and City Death', 'Bride and Groom', and finally 'Weddings of Light' in a desperate attempt to pin down and hang on to my vision. One pair of bloody, new-born lovers would represent the mystical union, with a smudge of sun raining seeds into an area ringed about with buildings that were sharp and pointed like iron, gouged from the living darkness. Born out of decomposition, they would glitter with an awful knowledge. The same forces were endlessly at work, whether mangling or renewing. From this senseless activity would arise my lovers, heavily erect like strange purplish tulips, bearing

103

on their limbs, their cheeks, their hands the marks of experience which disfigure us all; a bride and groom in the midst of festering shadows.

Going over to the window in a daze I mentally retraced my steps. I saw everything in pointed form, pointed seeds, pointed roofs, the prows of boats, boards, railings, even the pointed Adam's apple of the street sweeper. What did it mean?

Then in the small hours, with Maggie breathing loudly beside me in her drugged state, whimpering now and then like a dog dreaming, the sickening feeling took root in me that my powers were a delusion. I lay sweating in the cruel light of this fear, whimpering once myself in self-pity and imploring Maggie with my eyes. I fell asleep at last, daybreak came and I woke up to the same nausea, curled around it in a mess of tortured sheets. How things got better again was a mystery I never fathomed, and don't now. I touched bottom. I was always amazed to find myself no longer suicidal but normal, ordinary, and free again, free to glance about keenly, to make plans. I walked again with the characteristic nervy step others have commented on, leaning forward nervously, jumpy with the possibility of visions, imagining them in my blood or wherever they secrete themselves, prodigious and teeming inside my skin like the huge city itself.

Maggie wasn't all light. I handed her Pru Woodruff's letter to read, and her face clouded. To see her bowed over it, absorbing the contents laboriously, exasperated and hurt me. As she read she was kneading at the lobe of her right ear with thumb and finger.

She gave the sheet of paper back with the consideration she reserved for something official. 'When is she coming?' she asked, in a scared voice.

'I'm not sure that she is.'

'She says she wants to.'

'I know she does.'

'Well, then. What's wrong with letting her?'

'She wants a lot of things. She's a kleptomaniac.'

'What's that?'

'A person who grabs things.'

'Does she do that?'

'In a way, yes.'

'Is she poor?'

'Hardly. Compared to us she's rich.'

'Then what d'you mean, she thieves things?'

'No, she pays. She just has to have them, that's all.'

'Why?'

'God knows. Because they're there.'

Changing her tone, Maggie said, 'I don't get you. She sounds nice and friendly, real helpful.'

'Oh, she is.'

'Now you're being sarky.'

I shook my head. We fell silent. I said, 'Perhaps I'll meet her at the station and head her off. Take her for a walk round.'

She was silent, absorbing this. She gave the impression of someone tussling with a knot which wouldn't come undone.

'Why haven't you told her about me?'

Caught out, I said defensively, 'Who says I haven't?'

'Your face.'

'Why shouldn't I tell her?'

'You're ashamed of me.'

'That's stupid.'

'Bring her round here then.'

'Not likely.'

'I don't mean when I'm here.'

'You don't understand. She wants to poke about in my stuff and cart something off.'

'Only to help you.'

'So she says. Well, I don't want her to.'

'Well then.'

'Stop saying that!'

Ever practical, she asked, 'Doesn't she have a car?'

'I don't think she drives.'

'What's she look like?'

'Maggie, I haven't seen her for ages.'

'Can't you remember?'

'Sort of. Vaguely.'

'I bet she's beautiful,' she said wistfully.

'She works at it. Elegance they call it.'

Pursuing a different train of thought entirely, she said, 'You must have liked her once, for her to be so friendly.'

I had made myself fairly presentable in a clean shirt and trousers and a new pair of cheap sandals. The one snag was my partly grown beard, which had reached the scruffy stage. What did it matter? If the woman wanted to fraternise with budding penniless artists she would have to put up with it.

She materialised out of nowhere, while I was gazing at pigeons in the elaborate ironwork of the station roof trusses. Wings flapped. A filtered yellow sunlight shone down.

She wore a black duster coat of some thin material. Where it gaped open I saw flashes of her taffeta peacock colours. I still hadn't admitted to myself that I was taking her back to Southwark, even though I could see no alternative. I thought naively that if we went first to the National, then the Tate, sheer fatigue would sabotage any plans of hers.

She soon asked, 'You are taking me back to your studio, I take it?' The plaintive, little girl's voice she used made me wince.

We were sitting down at last, supposedly contemplating the dark varnish expanses of a vast painting with a classical theme. Even in sandals my feet were killing me. But she gave no sign of the slightest discomfort.

When I didn't answer at once, she said, 'I'd like to see your work there. May I, please?' She placed a gloved hand on my arm.

'It's a hovel, my place. It smells of cat. We've got a cat now, a stray one.'

As delicate as any cat she retrieved my word. 'We?'

'Yes. I'm living with someone.'

Her eyes shone, as if I had said something amusing. I found myself staring at the details of her mascara, thickly applied but in perfect taste. There was one crumb working loose on the underside of an upper eyelash. Pru was as I remembered her, opulent, assured, her colours unnerringly right. I began asking myself unwilling, not for the first time, how I would tackle the portrait of such a woman.

'Now what are you looking at?'

'Nothing.'

'You're a dark horse, Francis. Why on earth didn't you tell me?'

'I didn't think.'

'What's your girl friend's name?'

'Margaret Fisher,' I said stiffly, giving the name in full to avoid divulging anything personal. But now Maggie sounded anonymous, robbed of the intimacy of our life together. 'She's not a girl. Have you seen enough here?' I went on rudely. 'Shall we go?'

'Yes, I'd love to meet her.'

'Some other time. She's at work.' I was discovering strange loyalties inside myself. Maggie's voice was in my ear and I heard its kindness. It was ordinary and yet unique, it belonged only to Maggie.

We entered the park and sat on a bench in St James's, looking out over the tranquil water of a pond. I said, 'I've got nothing worth showing you at the moment, as I said in my letter.'

Pru smiled her maddening smile. 'I shall still enjoy myself. How do we get there?'

A bus would have been easy, but she insisted on hailing a taxi and also paying for it. When we got out, the heat trapped between buildings was stifling. Leading her into the dirty cobbled alley I thought I caught a whiff of the invisible river, sunk away at low tide with its faint rotting smell.

Though I had resolved not to apologise for a thing, I took her in muttering excuses for the uncleared table, the wicker basket of unironed washing, noticing with dismay that the walls, with their rips and damp stains and rotten plaster, had somehow maliciously closed in. I gave up. 'Now you know where I live,' I said. 'In a rabbit hutch.'

Back again in Southwark that evening after escorting my visitor to the station, then wandering aimlessly into several bars, not wanting to drink, not knowing what I wanted, I knew that Maggie would be home and waiting. Turning into our now absurd medieval alley I went in and upstairs to our deplorable flat. On the stairs I smelled the stench of cat, and groaned.

Maggie was collapsed in the burst armchair with her feet on a stool. She looked too exhausted to be more than mildly curious. But I was wrong. She asked immediately, 'Where is she?'

'Gone home.'

'She came here. You brought her back.'

'Yes.'

'I can smell her cigarettes. What are they, French?'

'American. Philip Morris.'

'It was the first thing I smelled when I came in.'

'Anything else?'

'Yes,' she said. 'Her posh scent.'

Just then the offending cat sauntered through, a young black female with supple flanks and curiously splayed hind legs. The top floor tenants had left it behind when they moved out. I pointed at it. 'Has she been perfuming the stairs again?'

'How would I know? You and your ladyship have been here half the day, I haven't.'

'Two hours. She insisted.'

'I bet she did. Curious, I expect. So would I be curious.'

'To see how the other half lives?'

'Something like that.' Then, as I guessed it would, her sense of decency got the better of her, and she added, 'That's not fair. I expect she's very nice.'

'I expect so.'

'Is that what you think?'

'No.'

'You're terrible, Wes. You always criticise everybody.'

'Who's criticising?'

'What did you tell her about me?'

'Your name. That's all.'

'Thank God for that.'

'You're worth a hundred Pru Woodruffs.'

'Did she take anything with her?'

'Yes, an oil sketch. I was going to dump it anyway.'

'Was she pleased?'

'Over the moon.'

'It might bring you luck. You work so hard, you deserve it.'

'Maggie, you bring me luck. I don't need any more.'

A sweetness that was never far away ran into her face. 'Liar!'

14

Della had gone, there was now no doubt. Her final departure had caught me by surprise, just as Maggie's had done. Would I ever learn to anticipate what was about to happen to me?

I was alone at the mill now with a vengeance. Glancing at my reflection in the glass of a framed watercolour I saw the wary eyes of a recluse. When did Della leave exactly? I had lost track already. It was December before I noticed that the season had well and truly changed.

Guy and Yvonne were talking of moving, either to Exeter or London. He was applying for teaching jobs in both places. If they left the area, my isolation would be complete. I was in contact with no one else. This was due partly to misanthropy, but I avoided people now for another reason. I was working flat out again, with a fixed programme. An outburst of totally unanticipated creativity was threatening to swamp me. Often I wanted to call a halt, my mind overheated, my nervous system begging for a respite, whether I was at work or in bed or in the act of hunting impatiently for a tin of food to open. Each boiling wave would be succeeded by another. Subjects for paintings kept surfacing in this tide with the insistence of dreams. At one point I was forced to abandon colour and simply draw from memory, like drawing an endless thread out of my body. I seemed to be trying to obtain rest and deliverance by capturing objects in outlines.

It didn't once occur to me that it might not be art at all, but therapy. It had been such a long barren time. I had survived, risen from the dead. Who knows, perhaps an artist's labour was merely a form of benediction, an offering of thanks to whatever it was that made everything grow.

At times I felt an urge for seclusion so fierce that I began to dread the slightest disturbance, barricading myself in with my fears and manias like an old maid. When the milkman knocked on the door, usually a Friday, I would be lying low, an envelope containing his money propped against the empties. Once, though, I forgot. He banged and banged until I answered. I must have looked wild, needing a haircut, unshaved, a half frightened smile on my face. His startled expression brought me back to my senses. I went off, back to work, ready to laugh at the mad ruler who had taken possession of me.

Paintings which arose directly from dreams were often abandoned in half finished states, I assumed because dream material is inert when brought up to the light. I called one such picture 'Water-walker'. Like the others, it was a failure. I had meant to work late into the night, fell asleep in a chair and was walking over Restronguet Ferry towards Falmouth instead of sailing in a boat. For some reason I could touch bottom. The wateriness was curiously firm, a pale brown treacly fluid. It was night. I walked hand in hand with a small chain of women and girls, tugging them forward insistently. The turbulence and dark swirling of the surface ahead caused the hands in mine to drag back in fear. These females who were in my care didn't trust my judgement.

One day, crossing over by this ferry to do some shopping, I made mental sketches for yet another painting. The chugging white boat carried its few passengers like a mother, plucky and reliable. I sat in the bows, my favourite spot. By my side sat a thick-necked fisherman whose hands and feet were massive enough to belong to one of Guy's idealistic friezes depicting noble workers. Behind me was a pale anxious woman whose unfortunate child kept wobbling its hydrocephalic head. I was torn between studying this poor creature and rejoicing in the clumsy animal-like butting of the prow as we were dragged sideways in the powerful current. The salt water swirling in eddies was being sliced like material by the bows, blunt as they were. The fisherman's hands, clasped together and bulging with sausage fingers in his lap, were one detail I noted down in my head. Another was the retarded child. His red-rimmed piggy eyes brimmed with depthless love, as if a speechless rage at his condition had become, through some remarkable transition, reversed. He held his gaze fixed to his mother's face the whole time in a look of utter devotion. When we disembarked he was still doing it.

It was gone one. The little twisty streets were congested, though it must have been late October. Falmouth holidaymakers paraded up and down, groups of families, old men and women, entwined lovers. The pavements were too narrow and I had to keep stepping into the road to make progress. Cars crawled, braked, hooted. Reaching Swanpool Street I slipped round the corner. At the base of a steep hill I went through the swing doors of Antonucci's celebrated fish and chip parlour.

Antonucci's was small and clean, with a reputation for quality and fast service. The shiny zinc counter nearly always had a queue before it. Further in, and upstairs, booths with tables and chairs waited invitingly. The red-and-white check tablecloths were changed regularly.

Jean, the waitress, was gathering up her pad and pencil as I entered. My spirits lifted. For all kinds of reasons and unreasons she reminded me of Maggie. I also liked her for herself. She smiled at everyone in the same unaffected way, familiarly, not cheeky. Her flesh was plump, warm-looking. Obviously she was a country girl, as much a native of her region as Maggie was of hers. Probably she had been on her feet for hours. It didn't show. Not at all like Maggie facially, she had, I felt sure, the same basically modest and cheerful disposition. These are the salt of the earth, I thought, the ones who give the world what virtues it has. Jean flushed red and laughed a lot, opening her mouth generously. I came in for the food, but she was equally nourishing. If she didn't appear to serve me I would experience a pang of disappointment.

'She served a woman sitting alone and came to me next. 'What is it for you, sir? The usual?'

'That's right.'

She laughed. Her cheeks turned red. 'With a cup of tea?'

'Yes, afterwards.'

'Peas or no?'

'No thanks.'

'Bread and butter would you like?'

'Oh yes.'

'Two slices?'

I tried to make up my mind. Jean stood over me, smiling. Under the pale blue pinafore her flesh was pressing forward as if spontaneously offering itself, not just to me but to the room, the town. At the same time her unwavering look seemed to say that it was nothing to do with her personally.

'Four, please,' I said, surprising myself. Was I bewitched? I smiled after her childishly.

Watching her cross the room with my full plate I felt no uneasiness, though I didn't deserve to be waited on by her or by anyone. She widened the space between my knife and fork a fraction before lowering my meal.

'How are you, then? I haven't seen you for a while.'

'No,' I said.

'Keeping busy?'

I opened my mouth to say something noncommittal, but my voice said of its own volition, 'Yes, I am, as a matter of fact.'

'That's good,' she said happily.

As far as I knew she had no idea what I did for a so-called living. 'One thing leads to another,' I told her.

'I'm sure,' And she nodded, as if to say, 'That's true, and I understand perfectly.'

I sat concentrating on my fish. It flopped there in its batter like a fallen sun, knocked out of shape but molten, bubbling its thick yellow skin. Suddenly I realised how ravenous I was.

Jean brought the bread and butter and I mumbled my thanks. Already at work, I filled my mouth gingerly with hot delicious morsels, taking pieces in with little wincing lip movements. The white succulent flesh steamed up under my nose.

I gave myself up to sensuality, but it made no difference – the mental work, powered by its own intentions, went on unabated. Nothing turned it off. In that hiding place where ideas geminated, racing out of nowhere, I could almost visualise the study generated by the boat trip – the water, light, movement, passengers huddled like a tiny congregation. At home these studies would be executed at speed in coloured pastel and Indian ink. My neglected paints were in such a filthy condition, I had been unable to unscrew half the caps. I would use tattered crayons, and finally a quill pen to defeat the onset of good taste, injecting the necessary savagery by the use of villainous squiggles and inky clouds of cuttlefish black.

If art taught me anything, it was that the forms of life came out of chaos and fell back again into the same chaos, to emerge once more, metamorphosed by natural agencies. And so on, in an eternal recurrence. I was involved daily in these weird complexities, yet the growing complexity of my involvement with Maggie had found me unprepared, inept. Like a fly, I only began struggling when I was already trapped. Her simple view of things misled me; I had been lulled into thinking that the relationship we had was a simple one. Suddenly I was in the midst of disorder, rising chaos, and finally that old teacher, jealousy, aware too late of the fragility of the status quo. Maggie had moved away, gone beyond me, out of reach of my puny powers. I imagined a black tide flowing in under the door to claim her in the night, old demons, stealthy and inexorable as lovers. Was this nonsense, when I could reach out and touch her?

We lay together one night in the dark, listening to river traffic. It was New Year's Eve. At midnight all the small craft in the vicinity would signal the end of the year by giving prolonged blasts on their sirens. There we were, waiting for this moment, when Maggie decided she had better broach it about Gregory. Did the time have some special significance for her? There were mysteries embedded in her past which I hadn't bothered to probe, dismissing them in my mind complacently

112

as unimportant. I listened now in the vague expectation of another.

'Who's Gregory?'

She snorted her impatience. 'Gregory – you know. At work.'

I recalled the name, nothing else. 'One of the waiters?'

'Sometimes. He's the middle son.'

'A Cypriot?'

'What do you think, an Eskimo? When did you last listen to anything I say? Your head's too bunged up with pictures and books to take in what I tell you.'

'Tell me again.'

I could feel us hanging in the silence. She shifted uneasily. 'Well, I've been thinking,' she began, and stopped. She seemed to be simultaneously firm and irresolute. 'Are you sure you're awake?'

'Yes, yes.' But I was dozing off as I spoke.

'I might bring him round to meet you.'

'Who?'

'Oh God. Gregory!'

'Maggie, why are you telling me all this?'

'Don't you want to know?'

'But why?'

'To find out if you mind.'

'I stifled a yawn. 'No, I don't mind. Is that all?'

'Yes. Forget I mentioned it.'

Ten minutes later, the sirens sounded in unison. Maggie didn't even wake. She was snoring and muttering in her sleep. Her hair carried a whiff of fish from the restaurant. I rolled over with my back to her.

I thought dozily of us as a couple, of our oddity, of the fact that she had a child but made no mention of it – not that I ever asked. All at once I was wide awake. A thought had stung me. I twisted round and shook Maggie.

'What's up, what's the matter?' she moaned pathetically. 'I just got off.'

'This Gregory.'

'Who?'

'Gregory.'

'What about him?'

'You knew him before, did you?'

'Wes, I'm half asleep. Can't it wait till tomorrow?'

'It is tomorrow.'

113

'Jesus, so it is.'

'You knew him before the Italian place, then? Where you were working when I met you.'

'Yes, all right. What if I did?'

I was getting to the truth in stages, like a partly realised painting. 'So he's the father of your child, I take it.'

There was such a prolonged silence that I thought she had either dropped off again or was refusing to answer. I wanted to see her face, but was afraid to switch on the light.

'Not just that,' she said finally, her voice curiously hoarse and low.

'No?'

'What I mean is, it's not so simple.'

'Why isn't it?'

'Oh God, I'm tired. I'll tell you in the morning.'

'Tell me now.'

After another long pause, she said flatly, 'He wants us to get spliced.'

'He wants what?'

She sighed. 'Now you know.'

Because I didn't answer she slipped off to sleep again. Not realising I was alone, I said loudly, in what was meant to be a voice of outrage, 'What kind of stupid yarn is that, for Christ's sake?'

I lay there with a sensation of hollowness, trying to convince myself that the whole business was no concern of mine, that it left me untouched in some peculiar fashion. This Gregory might want to marry her, but she hadn't said she had any intention of obliging him. If his proposal appealed to her, why hadn't she married him years ago when she had his child? Was he tied then, but not now? Solving one mystery had uncovered several others. Not least was Maggie's crazy suggestion that I should now meet the father of her child. To what purpose? What was her motive, and how would this confrontation affect us all?

I woke early. I was cold, desolate, as if blasted by a terrible light into fragments. Maggie's body, sunk in sleep beside me, seemed heartbreakingly separate and baffling. Shifting up closer in an attempt to draw warmth from her, a warmth to which I felt no longer entitled, I understood for the first time that I was in hell and suffering from jealousy. I groaned a little, letting out animal whimpers in the vain hope that she would wake and turn to me. She slept on.

Gregory Tabalis, when he did come, sat looking distinctly uncomfortable and talking in monosyllables. Maggie fussed over us both at the table. We ate generous helpings of shepherd's pie, followed by tinned pears and thick custard. Watching the stranger, deriving some satisfaction from his discomfiture, I was impressed in spite of myself by the young man's head of tight black curls. He had a bullish neck, broad shoulders. I studied his swollen mouth surreptitiously, and became professionally engrossed in his skin's olive colour.

'I don't even know your daughter's name,' I said.

He answered hesitantly, shooting a glance first at Maggie, 'It's Rina.'

'You see her a lot?'

He looked puzzled. 'Me?'

'Yes.'

Maggie went over to the alcove to make coffee.

'I have her,' he said. 'I look after her.'

'Oh, I didn't realise. By yourself?'

'With my mother.'

We sat over coffees. Gregory stirred sugar into his, two heaped spoons, and said nothing. He seemed more at ease, like a friend or a relative who had called in by chance, a man we had known for years. I felt a desire to get to know him better. What was he thinking about me? I kept studying him with the fascination of someone who has stumbled on the missing piece in a puzzle. We came from different worlds, different cultures, and yet shared the same woman. It was like the bond between a husband and his wife's adulterous lover. Which was my role? I wondered if he was likely to be more talkative in other, more propitious circumstances, for instance if we were two men sitting together. It would give me intense pleasure, I thought, to hear his impressions of Maggie, and to be able to swop my impressions with him.

It was now Maggie who was acting as though embarrassed. Her speech was abrupt, blurting. She nearly spilled her coffee, and looked more and more flustered.

'What's the matter?' I asked her.

'Nothing, why?'

'By the way, I thought it was your mother who was taking care of your daughter. Didn't you say that?'

'You got it wrong, as usual.'

Gaining confidence, I said lightly, 'Did I get it wrong about Gregory as well?'

Maggie became tense. She glared angrily at me. 'I don't know what you mean.'

As if to reach an understanding with Gregory without addressing him directly, I went on, 'Has he slipped my mind too? Until you mentioned him the other week I could have sworn I had no idea who he was.'

'Are you trying to be funny?'

I noticed Gregory smiling at me in a friendly fashion. I smiled back.

'We might as well laugh,' I said.

The little triumph of my cruel irony was short-lived. Soon after Gregory's visit, Maggie stopped undressing in front of me. At first I didn't grasp the significance of this. When it dawned on me what she was doing, and that a process of withdrawal had commenced, I was too overwhelmed by a huge rage to speak. She was lying demurely in bed reading one of her women's magazines. Kneeling down, I grabbed her shoulders and began to shake her. I shook and shook, as if to shake the last crumb of truth out of her. My throat was congested. I was faintly, comically growling, my face felt convulsed, as if madly disintegrating. Her head bobbed on her neck and she didn't speak or resist. It was like shaking a doll.

When I stopped at last, she said in a low voice. 'That's it, then.'

The touch of pity I heard in her voice caused me to tremble all over like a dog. Standing irresolutely, with dangling hands, in the rocking space of my own madness, I saw what I had done. Instead of forcing the truth into the open for us both to see, I had shown her the wretched lie of myself. Hatred, not love, was consuming me, and it was her love that my black vindictive will was intent on destroying.

To avoid the humiliation of her departure I wanted to clear off until the coast was clear. Even this proved impossible. I found myself caught in the snare of her silent reproach. Besides, we had delivered up more of ourselves to each other than either of us had bargained for. In the bitter effort to retrieve these pieces, which seemed suddenly so essential for our future survival, over the next few weeks we fought endless fights. There were many painful scenes. Maggie drowned us in tears.

'He wants me, anyway,' she wailed once. 'He won't make me soft, either. You don't want me, you never did!'

Standing before her, with my head down, as though to guard against being struck in the face, I muttered. 'Why didn't you say you wanted to get married?'

'Oh you fool, it's not that.'

'All right. For the kid's sake.'

'No, no,' she sobbed. 'You don't understand a thing, you never did. You haven't got the brains of a rocking horse, you. Why can't you understand?'

'Make me.'

She stopped crying suddenly, presenting her stained, gargoyle face to me, bunched like a fist with misery. 'You can't be in charge,' she gobbled. 'Because you don't want to, do you?' Her eyes were stricken.

'In charge? In charge of what?'

'Of us. Of me. Oh what's the use!'

She was issuing a challenge I was incapable of taking up. It wasn't in me to be in charge of anyone, least of all myself. Even now, clinging to shreds of hope and wanting her to stay on any terms, my legs wouldn't move towards her, my arms wouldn't embrace her, my tongue refused to utter vows.

She said, 'Have you had anything to eat?'

'I can't remember.'

'You're hopeless. How are you going to look after yourself?'

'The same way I did before.'

'And end up a starved whippet.'

'I can't be what you want, that's the trouble.'

'No it's not. You don't know what you want. You never did. You haven't got a clue.'

'Gregory has, I take it?'

'He wants me for a wife.'

'Why's he taken so long?'

'Ask him. He's been married, his wife went mad, he went through a terrible experience, she's a schizophrenic. Anyway, it's taken him this long to get a divorce.'

'I get the feeling you'd choose me even now, if only I could find the right words.'

'Words! Is that all it is to you, is that all I amount to, a pile of bloody words? You go to hell.'

117

'I can't help how I am. Things have always happened to me, I can't make things happen. If you like it's weak, it's pathetic. I can't help it. I have to leave the initiative to others.'

'I might have chosen you once, not any more.'

'What would happen if I begged you to stay?'

'You won't.'

'I can't.'

'Anyway it's too late.'

'When are you leaving? I can't dangle like this, not knowing. Fix a date, or I will. I'm not living, I'm just waiting to live.'

'Whose fault is that?'

'Tell me when.'

'Soon.'

She had hennaed her hair an even deeper rich red that before. I would be intimidated by this blazing victorious crown, and then think I saw signs of wavering and pathos in her eyes, in the lower part of her face. Was she hoping even now for a change of heart in me?

I said to her one day in a dull voice, 'Where do you get it from?'

'What?'

'The henna.'

'Morocco.'

'I mean which shop.'

'You wouldn't know if I told you.'

'Oh.'

'Anything else?'

'It's a powder, is it?'

'Yes, yes it is, yes!'

I blocked her path as she tried to move past. Her face tense, she said, 'Don't.'

She looked me in the face. Her eyes expressed such derision that I could hardly speak. I said with difficulty, 'I want you.'

'You don't want me, you never did.'

'I needed you. I need you now.'

'That's not the same as wanting.'

'What is it, then?'

'Sex. You barely kiss me, you never mention love. The other thing you could do with anybody. Sleeping with a woman isn't personal.'

'To me it is.'

'How many have you said that to?'

118

'You're the first.'

'So you always say.'

'It's true.'

She went on in this scathing vein. I got angry, thought of a cutting retort, was about to let fly with it and then was dismayed to see the tears running down her cheeks.

'Please, don't cry.'

She sobbed. 'It's not you I'm crying over.'

'I didn't think it was.'

'This is the only home I've ever had.'

'Maggie, please. You don't have to leave.'

'Yes I do.'

I would be assailed by doubts. Sometimes a wave of anguish would mount in my chest. I've lost her, I can't live, I thought. I exhibited the classic symptoms of the neurotic, a chronic inability to lift a finger to save myself. Instead, I took to following Maggie about, driving her mad with my stupidity. It was all I could do not to trail after her to work in the mornings. What would I have done then, stand outside in the street like a stray dog? If she asked me outright what I wanted of her, I couldn't say. It's possible that I simply wanted to be forgiven. I seemed to have become that most pitiful of specimens, a person emotionally as well as creatively bankrupt. Days followed one another in a grey numbness.

I came in from an aimless walk to find her packing. 'You seem all right, anyway,' I said, half relieved and half appalled that the moment had come at last. Where did she get her strength? I watched her lug clothes from the wardrobe with the determination of someone mortally afraid of stopping.

'Have you got to stand there looking?'

'I can't believe you're so sure.'

'Somebody's got to be,' she said, in the frighteningly cold tone she used nowadays.

'Have they?' I tried to sneer, but failed. My shoulders drooped.

Maggie said, 'Ah, Wes.' She stopped what she was doing and came over to me wearily, as to a child who must be scolded into commonsense or else pitied.

'Why, Maggie, why?'

She put her arms round me, all-knowing, infinitely maternal. 'Why can't you stop kidding yourself, eh? You know as well as me it's no use.'

Gregory was calling to pick her up. We still had a few hours to suffer. Maggie kept returning to examples of my complacency and neglect, which I countered with accusations of heartlessness as best I could. Finally she lost patience. 'You'd better put a sock in it,' she warned, 'or you won't see me for dust.'

'I won't what?'

'You heard. We won't have nothing to do with each other ever, not even as friends.'

Weakly hoping, I said, 'Is that possible?'

She looked at me calmly. 'It depends.'

'On what?'

'You.'

Now she was set so unassailably against me, she became stronger by the minute. Any resolve I once had seemed to have left my body and flowed into hers. Where was the soft and floppy Maggie I once knew?

'I don't get that. How do you mean? Doesn't Gregory enter into it?'

'He wants his wife to be his. With him the boss. It's the Greek thing.'

'So?'

'I can be that, can't I, and still have a friend?'

'I doubt it. Not if the friend's me. He won't wear that, surely.'

She stuck out her jaw belligerently. 'Who says so?'

Left alone at last, I crept about for nearly a month in a state of near extinction. One morning, shaving with nerveless fingers, I gazed disgustedly at withered skin, at eyes bloodshot and without light. But deeper down, I was alive. Little by little my self-respect began trickling back from where it had secreted itself. I peered through a cracked pane at the drizzle and went out for my normal makeshift groceries. On the stairs I groaned aloud like an old man.

Outside, I blinked around in bewilderment. The whole enormous city seemed to have shrunk in the night to a few miserable streets. I saw how stale and drab and unredeemed everything was. Really I must have been blind and deaf for years. Without my work, what was I? Nothing but torn newspaper, a tin can in a dirty gutter. Passers-by were glancing at me uneasily. I felt like a ghost. Did I resemble a vagrant, someone out of a hospital? Was my gaze empty like an addict's?

Maggie dropped in to search for a pair of missing earrings, and to see how I was. I sat before her gratefully, warming myself at her warmth like a baby. We avoided touching one another. She restated her belief in the new arrangement she had proposed. Later, I went round to her a time or two, to where her baby was crawling and dribbling on the gaudy carpet, in one of the poky flats above the restaurant in Victoria where she still worked. There were exotic cooking smells I couldn't identify. She fed me heaped platefuls of spicy food, with the same generosity and concern she had shown at the beginning. I took this as an expression of her modified love. Or it could have been guilt.

Gregory's old mother would shuffle in and out, not speaking unless addressed. When she did, I found it hard to tell what she was saying. She dressed sombrely in black, and her brown face was incredibly wrinkled. Though she looked ancient she was probably only in her sixties. Her rasping voice seemed to say one thing, her twinkling eyes another. I got the impression I was being deferred to as a male rather than a person.

Once, Gregory came in. His mother was out. Maggie took Rina downstairs and we were left alone in the flat. I wondered if she had done it deliberately. We were both bashful, seemingly hapless men. He didn't know where to look and neither did I. It got easier when he poured us a glass of wine. Our exchanges were funny, now I think of it. It was hard not to like him, and anyway I wanted to like him. We sat there. Something in me laughed.

'Have some more,' he said, and filled up my glass.

'This is strange.'

'Like a lot of things.'

'I'm not dreaming, am I?'

'If you are, so am I.'

'I'd like to know what you think.'

'What about?' he asked. He seemed genuinely startled by the question.

'The way it's all turned out.'

He grinned sheepishly. 'I just get on with life, I suppose.'

'Did you want a family?'

A sly expression flitted over his face. 'Don't tell my mother. No.'

'Now you've got one.'

'That's all right.'

'You don't mind?'

He shook his head slowly. 'Why should I? It's happened.'

'What does Maggie feel?'

'I wouldn't know. She does what she wants.'

'How does she speak of me?'

'Friendly. Know what I mean?'

I gave up. He was gently mocking, whether of me or himself I couldn't be sure. I tried one more time. All I got was a shrug. We heard Maggie on the stairs and exchanged little smiles.

I look back now on this period and can still feel amazement. My recovery took place literally in the void. There I was, the painter-spectator, a failure on all counts, lost, finding my way suddenly in the blood-red and purple masses and rushing blue lines of a new work. I could only make sense of it by regarding my painting as something aimed directly at the reconstitution of me, the disgraced artist. I was soon embarked on a whole series to do with the strange ritual of burying and recovering figures in webs of my own making, leading from darkness to light. These rites of passage were to be my salvation. Forces that would brook no argument yanked me upright, planted me on my two feet, and these same powers drove my brush strokes. My fortunes changed, I sold the two big canvases, acquired a dealer and an exhibition, and brought the house in Valenciennes Street.

This was all some way ahead. One day in Southwark, the light failing. I squinted through a pane at the one piece of sky allowed me and saw the carmine sunset stain spreading. My shaky, reborn spirit wobbled out towards that. I stood rooted, hands grasping the window pane.

PART TWO:

Vivien

15

In Cornwall I often hoped for the certitude I had known in London, which burned brightly in my memory as a place of deliverance. But the self-doubt and self-hatred preceding it I conveniently forgot. Is it the Chinese who have the same word-picture for opportunity as for disaster? Life in the south lacked calamities. I moved from the doldrums to mad activity and back again, brooding over my idleness but not desperate enough to break out of lethargy.

Then one morning, jittery for no reason – unless it was the endlessly perverse weather – I felt uniting in me the desire to move, to run loose, and the longing to see Vivien. I got myself tidied up, forgot breakfast, and made my way with a duffle bag to The Dell, the tiny halt in Falmouth. Trains shunted from there to Truro for the expresses to London.

It was summer, the kind that is forever promising to deliver and never does so. Gales sprang up in the middle of July. Heatwaves began one day and collapsed the next in thunderstorms and squalls.

The branch line train slowed down and stopped. We sat in the middle of fields within sight of the estuary. I spent over an hour stranded in Truro before my next connection arrived. In the station buffet I sat trying to interest myself in the comings and goings of passengers, drinking the stewed tea. A doleful woman serving behind the counter stared into space. On the platform, I marched one way towards Penzance, and turned on my heel and made for Plymouth. Now I had resolved to make the trip I wanted to get going. A childish impulse to surprise Vivien had prevented me from ringing her in advance. I could do so now, but it was a Thursday; probably she would be teaching. My plan was to reach her place by late afternoon. What if she were away herself on some visit? I decided not to worry about that possibility until it became reality.

At the thought of seeing Vivien again after all this time I felt a tingling sensation along my nerves that was part excitement, part anxiety. It seemed incredible, but we hadn't set eyes on each other since the day I climbed aboard the Jumbo at

Heathrow and flew to America. We met in Piccadilly on the day of my flight, and that afternoon she insisted on seeing me off. Later, she and Della became acquainted, an occasion engineered by Della so that she could get to know my sister. My kin, as she put it, was now hers too. She bought two tickets for a West End farce and persuaded Vivien to join her and then have supper later. The evening was not a success. Vivien hated the play, and was convinced that Della was jealous of her for being so attached to me. It was the only time they were together.

I reached London just after two. Estimating that I had time to spare, I left the station and entered the wet maze of rainy streets. The rain had eased off. A wind gusted warmly in bursts. Sometimes it was pushing on my back like an impatient hand, urging me to hurry when I wanted to loiter, or it hit my ear and the side of my head as I passed openings, negotiating the wash and litter of gutters with my head lowered.

London seemed dirtier than ever. Nevertheless, I somehow contrived to get lost. My instinct was always to abandon myself to its enormities. Not so very long ago I had made my mark here, achieved some recognition and a measure of success, yet I reverted after a few steps to the boy from the provinces I had once been, and probably still am. I sniffed suspiciously at the foreignness, glanced tensely from side to side, noticed the haste and the preoccupied airs of Londoners and felt contemptuous, forgetting that I had lived here too and been proud to live here. My upbringing told me as always that it was a cruel hell, the rebel and exile in me found it fascinating. It was dirty, sophisticated, a powerhouse, a shambles, a world falling to pieces, inhabited by robots. Rustling seductively behind its walls lay the dressing and parading women, the lure of money, the organising deals and conferences.

Straight ahead, a well-dressed group of people just delivered to a hotel by taxi were being accosted by a vagrant. He harangued them incoherently and then stood sucking on a bottle. They took no more notice of him that of a fly. As I went past on the other side the man opened his black hole of a mouth. He threw back his head and howled violent abuse at the sky, swaying on the spot.

Once or twice I asked for directions. I was heading vaguely for the river, seeing in my mind's eye the wide expanse I had known at Southwark, gleaming dully beneath skies that were often soiled, defeated. The river, bulging as if full of dead bodies, floated a scum of refuse under bridges, moving surprisingly fast. I was about to see it again.

Somewhere near the Strand I asked for help. Spruce young men hurrying along in wool business suits clutching bulky buff envelopes were too busy to be of use. I knew this from past experience, I merely asked to find out if anything had changed. 'No, I'm sorry, I don't know this district.' Others fended me off with violent head-shaking and a volley of broken English.

Once in the heart of the West End I intended to get a tube out to Kew. Needing to slow down my progress, I blundered into an elegant print shop. I saw my reflection in the plate glass as I went in, flattening my hair with the palm of my hand. The glassy silence inside made it too uncomfortable for a long stay.

Out again, I was caught by a lashing rainstorm. Refusing to take cover I ploughed on, butting through the downpour with bowed head. By the time I backed gasping into a shop doorway my grey thinning hair was plastered darkly to my skull like a baby's. In another reflected image I stared with distaste at a soaked derelict whose face was covered in a scrabble of pencil lines. I wiped the rain and saliva from my lips.

I waited for the next lull and then ran, a long distance, between buildings that were growing immense as they angled me from one to the other and then flung me off at an intersection, against the endlessly grinding traffic. 'Where is this, please?' I asked a startled long-haired girl trotting lightly down the steps of a towering arched entrance.

I thought at first she wasn't going to answer. Clearly this dishevelled, scrawny man who was staring too hard alarmed her. She wrinkled her smooth forehead. 'Bush House,' she told me, without stopping.

'I want the Strand,' I called out hoarsely.

The girl smiled a shadowy smile, like a reward to me for not being as dubious as I looked. She pointed in the direction she was walking. Then I saw where I was. Descending on the great roaring thoroughfare from an unfamiliar street had totally confused me.

It was just coming up to four when I emerged at Kew. If Vivien was in fact still a supply teacher at secondary level – I had only the vaguest notion of what that meant – then I was too early.

A growing tightness in my chest caused me to take deep breaths. I tried to bring up wind, thinking it was indigestion.

Nervous indigestion bothered me at moments of stress. Also my stomach didn't feel right. I decided to delay another half an hour before making for the address. For the umpteenth time I took out Vivien's letter and read the road and house number. Absurd to get knotted up at the thought of meeting your own sister. The element of surprise that I had felt was in my favour now displeased me. It seemed a foolish tactic, stupid, like wanting to jump out and shock someone.

I located the road I wanted and then walked deliberately away from it. A small park to my left seemed a good place in which to kill time. It was deserted. Beyond the high wrought iron gates a winding path let to a rustic shelter with a bench inside. My legs and feet ached, so I sat down. To my left and right behind my head was a mass of graffiti, most of it incomprehensible, in signs and codes.

There was an elderly man on his way up the path. Ahead of him ran his dog, a white Jack Russell terrier. The animal trotted up energetically on short legs and sniffed around my shoes. I got up, perhaps too abruptly. The little dog backed away, barking insanely. When the old man ordered him to stop, the barking ceased as if he had thrown a switch.

I returned to Vivien's road and wandered down it, feeling odd and conspicuous among the rows of sedate houses. Everywhere spoke of emptiness, with no sign of a car, let alone a person. Then an old van swung into view and went trundling past, the kind electricians or builders use. No one knew of my existence here, yet I felt observed from behind curtains, the little bits of pointed gravel trained on my skin. Even the leaves of privet looked hostile, all with their cutting edges. Telling myself not to be an idiot I walked along with calm strides, gazing critically at the yellow brick houses like a prospective buyer.

I became aware that I was delaying so as not to be disappointed by Vivien's absence, if indeed she was still out. I would explore the adjacent street and then come back. But which way? Something prompted me to double back on my tracks. I sniffed at the sleeve of my top coat and discovered its damp musty smell. With a need to leave it behind I broke into a stumbling trot. I went careering round a blind corner of dark overhanging shrubbery, past the plaited strips of some new chestnut fencing, and almost collided with a young woman. My arms jerked up of their own accord, I nearly fell against her and she lifted her free hand to ward me off.

Without looking at her face I said, 'Sorry.' I stepped aside.

'Francis! I don't believe it!' the woman cried.

Stunned to hear a voice I recognised, I said in a dazed voice, 'Yes, it's me.'

'I don't believe it,' Vivien said again. She was staring goggle-eyed into my face.

'I thought I'd pay you a visit.'

'I can see that! Why now? Why on earth didn't you tell me, I could have been looking forward to it? You're quite mad, you rotter.'

I didn't know whether to feel ashamed or delighted. My body, however, was certain, knowing the sure pleasure of its sudden relaxation. Although I hadn't expected a young girl, the image I had of Vivien in my memory had stayed intact and unchanged. Though I had seen her since, somehow she was stuck at the age she had been at our father's funeral. Smiling happily at her, I could still see this girl. Of course her face bore the marks of experience. As then, she wore no make-up, but her eyes looked drawn, her hair different. She was sharp-faced, taller than I had expected. In one hand she held a shopping bag.

'Is it all right – I mean convenient?'

'Now what are you babbling about? It's wonderful!'

'Let me carry your bag.'

'Don't be silly, no, there's nothing in it. I was on my way to the corner shop for a few things. Come with me?'

'Of course I will.'

'I can't believe it,' she kept saying. 'I'm amazed.'

She shot unbelieving glances at me, amused and delighted, but mostly she walked with her head down, a habit I remembered. She frowned slightly, with the look of someone tussling with something, catching at her upper lip with her teeth, which I saw were stained. She was a smoker, then.

I could almost see her stream of thoughts by her innocent absorption in them. Another person would have worn a mask, behind which they lived. It pained me that she hadn't grown one, after so many years of independent life. Would it ever be accomplished? Yet I saw that she was also resolute, unjaded, hopeful, essentially unharmed. The world hadn't deformed her or beaten her down. In some recess of herself she was tough, indestructible even. Or was this wish-fulfilment on my part? I tended to endow women with qualities which set them apart, in another realm from the one I inhabited. It was a world which combined exaltation and resourcefulness, and I suppose I turned to them in the hope of entering it.

Vivien laughed, coming to a halt on the pavement. 'I keep wanting to pinch myself.'

'Me too.'

'Is it really you?'

'It's me all right.'

'Turn left here. Not far now.' We were moving again. 'Are you sure you don't mind trailing along here? I won't be a minute, I only need a few odds and ends. Where are you staying in London?'

'Nowhere. Here.'

'What? You've actually come all the way from Cornwall to see me?'

'Of course.'

'Good God.'

'Listen, if you can't put me up, don't worry.'

She said simply, 'It's so nice to see you, Francis. You've no idea how lovely it is.'

I met her gaze, then hastily looked away, embarrassed by the ardour in her eyes. 'Same here,' I said gruffly.

There was nothing I wanted to say, so I fell silent. The fact is that I was perfectly content, trailing along docilely beside my sister, being led. It was like coming home. My head drooped a little, like hers. If it had been possible I would have held her hand.

We came to a shop and entered it together. The worries which are never far from my mind vanished. Like a simple-minded person who regresses whenever he can to his childhood, I waited contentedly. It was easy to imagine I was back in the past. I looked around curiously. Without noticing as we walked along, I saw that we had come down in the world – one of those bewilderingly swift changes which occur only in London. An old-fashioned bell was still quivering above the door behind us.

I glanced slyly at my sister. It was hard to believe she was in her mid-thirties. Again disturbed by the girl I saw in glimpses and then lost, I listened to her light quick voice as she made her purchases. She caught me observing her, and smiled radiantly. Her pale critical eyes moved swiftly over my face. I could almost feel her gaze soaking me up in a delicate sponging process.

The shop reminded me of ones I knew as a boy, and yet was unlike any particular one. As though trying to account for this I stared at the shelves and into over-stuffed corners. The fussy grocer had finished serving and was counting out Vivien's change. Protruding teeth fixed his mouth in a peggy grin. He spoke pedantically and made a disagreeable impression, with his soft, old woman's hands and shifty eyes.

Out in the street, Vivien said excitedly, 'Right, that's done. Come on, you must be dying for a cup of tea. Are you hungry?'

'I'm past bothering.'

'Well, we'll see. Is that bag of yours heavy?'

She smiled fondly, like a mother. I noticed again the girlish narrowness of her face. I shook my head. 'Only a shirt, pyjamas, toilet things.'

We walked steadily, not in haste. Vivien stepped out briskly. She was wearing jeans. Her manner of walking had something wide-legged and unimpeded about it. 'I'm perfectly happy,' she said, 'just looking at you. Don't mind me, will you.'

'What do you see? Am I still the same person?'

She took my arm. 'I suppose you are. But I've got to discover you all over again.'

'I feel the same.'

'Good.'

'I haven't changed, then, not dramatically?'

'If you have, I'll soon find out.'

'Not visibly?'

She laughed. 'No, it doesn't show.'

'You look fine,' I told her. 'Why don't you get older, like me?'

'Oh, I'm a wreck. You'll see soon enough, when you get me under a strong light.'

We were appreciating each other with the concentration of old lovers, but without the teasing banter of sex. At the next corner, I went one way and she another. We collided, our bodies muddled for an instant. Vivien laughed, 'That's one thing I remember about you. No sense of direction.'

'I'm a stranger here,' I said indignantly. 'How do you think I found my way here from Cornwall?'

'I can't imagine. Tell me.'

'By a series of accidents. One leading to another. The way I paint a picture.'

'I'm sure you can do absolutely anything you decide to.'

'Are you serious?'

'Of course.'

'You don't see me as incompetent? A day-dreamer, not really here, no idea what time it is, a man made of smoke?'

She slowed down. As if reading my thoughts, she said, 'Is that what Della thinks? No, I don't agree.'

'Maybe I should talk to you more often.' Her high clear forehead was slightly bulbous, I noticed, the line of my imaginary pencil tracing it.

'You should.'

'It's not only Della who thinks so.'

'Well, it's an impression you like to give sometimes, perhaps.'

'What, of a helpless artist?'

'I don't know,' She shrugged her thin shoulders. 'Good lord, we only meet once in a blue moon.'

I stopped talking. Vivien's shrug of dismissal was enough to remind me of her as a teenager, and I recalled how prone she was to impatience. This talk of mine was only a kind of ruse, so that I could, as it were, become her, absorbing her into myself. In fact, I felt sure the opposite was taking place. My absorption by her was happening with the rapidity of a chemical process.

Totally preoccupied, I failed to notice what kind of house we were entering, only that it was large, faintly musty, the high ceilings encrusted at the corners with ornate plasterwork. I shook off my musing, soft, benificent sensations to do with Vivien and registered things. We walked over the scarred parquet flooring and began to ascend a wide staircase.

It was the tall newel post, darkly varnished, which gave the clue to my strange feeling of having been here before. I could have stepped back into the turn-of-the-century house I once owned in Camden. Unlike mine, however, this place was cared for.

'I shan't stay away so long again. Neither should you,' I said, astonished to hear such a positive statement issuing from my mouth.

Vivien flashed me a bright, elated look. Exhibiting teacher-like efficiency she led me upstairs to her flat. I was both pleased and nervous. I had forgotten her eyes, their stabbing intelligence. I was aware now of her pallor, her fine bones, the veins in her temples. Something tightly wound up and spring-taut about her, a smiling tension, a malaise, cast a fear over me. The next instant it seemed too silly for words.

132

She led me into a large square room, generously lit by two heavy sash windows.

'You've got plenty of space,' I said, nodding approvingly.

There was a massive old sofa stretching along one wall, and on the floor enormous garish cushions, red, green, blue. The faint exotic aroma I identified as joss-sticks.

'Yes, we're very lucky. Except that it's a devil to heat and stay warm in. Sorry, did I say we? I mean I am. Did I tell you anything about Celia in my letters?'

'Your friend, yes. Just a bit.'

'Well, last week she moved out of here, back with her husband.'

'Oh, she's got a husband.'

'Didn't I say that? As a matter of fact, yes, she's very much married. That's the trouble. She came here in the first place because she can't stand her marriage, and because I wanted her to, of course.'

'Didn't she want to?'

'Francis, don't be sly. You're asking me what there is between us? I can only speak for myself. I'm sure she's fond of me, and I've become terribly protective towards her. If you meet her, you'll perhaps see why. She's terribly sweet, a sweet child who's got herself into a situation that's essentially false, I think.'

'How old is she?'

'Oh, about my age, a little younger maybe. I've never bothered to ask. I keep saying a child, so did you think a teenager? I see her as stuck there in adolescence I suppose. But it's Jake Samuels, he's her husband, who I believe stops her from being an adult. Yet he can't stand the child in her either, which he himself brings out and perpetuates, with his idealistic game.'

'His *game?*'

Vivien laughed sharply. 'Sit down. I'll be brief. You shouldn't ask me these questions, I ought to be looking after you. In a minute I'll go and put the kettle on.' I rubbed one hand over another, a nervous habit, and she said immediately, sensitive to me, 'It's a little chilly in here. Let's have a bar on. What a glorious summer we're having.'

She switched on a small electric fire with a concave reflector, the chrome showing patches of rust.

'What does this Jake do for a living?'

She said, smiling, 'That's a man's question. All right, facts. He lectures in English somewhere, a polytechnic or a university. If I'm so vague it's because he's changed his job at least twice. Apparently he's brilliant. I've met him, I can believe it. He also writes poetry, it's his first love, but apart from a Gregory Fellowship he hasn't got anywhere with it. Celia's the real poet, though how original I wouldn't know. Sylvia Plath's one of her idols. Oh yes, another thing – Celia's an ex-student of his. What Jake's trying to do is turn her into a genius, as a way of getting vicariously what he hasn't been able to achieve for himself. She's his literary goddess. He shouldn't have tried to write poetry, he knows too much. He nurtures her, feeds her with knowledge, never stops telling her she's destined for great things.'

'Is this theory?'

'No, observation.'

'You mentioned a game.'

'You may doubt this, but I like Jake. He's sweet, like her. The trouble is, he's a dreadful masochist. That's my reading of the set-up. The game he's playing does two things for him. It sets aside his own dreams of glory and it gives him a self-sacrificing role, that of the devoted patron. He gets punished for this by Celia, every time she acts capriciously and turns into a fickle child rather than his creation.'

'I see, I think. So where do you come in?'

'A good question. Look at it like this. By coming to me she was taking a deliberate step towards claiming her true self. To him this was just one more example of her childishness, this running away, it was the reverse of her gift. It's so easy for a man to make a woman feel infantile. I see *him* as the real child, the boy who won't grow up. He can't bear it when she usurps this favourite aspect of his own character. Then there's another factor – the snare of the material benefits he bestows on her with his salary, so she can never escape a feeling of ingratitude whenever she goes against him.'

'And now it's back to square one. Will she stick it, do you think?'

'Celia?' Vivian grimaced to express her concern. 'God, I hope not. She was so down when we first met, I went round for a week expecting to hear she'd killed herself. She's deep into the Plath legend. Going back like this is a final throw of the dice, she says. No, she's not at all sure she'll stay. On the other hand, if he goes down on his knees and begs again, I don't know. Abasement, that's his trump card. The trouble with clinging things is that they often win.'

'You sound pessimistic.'

'Yes, well, who understands couples? They're a mystery unto themselves. Francis, I vow I'll never consent to being half of a couple. One complication I haven't mentioned. You see, we shared the rent of this place. It's too expensive for one. Celia's asked me to wait a month before looking for another flatmate.'

Listening, I was full of admiration for Vivien's account, its adroit summing up, its clever analysis, but her annihilation of Jake, whoever he was, had aroused an obscure sympathy or fellow feeling which I couldn't have explained or defended. She's being too clever about it all, I thought, not judging her. Her cool detachment would have chilled me if I hadn't seen at the same time the flow of feelings on her face, hearing in her voice at the mention of her friend a tender affection.

I followed her into the kitchen. She said, 'I was seeing her tonight as a matter of fact. 'I shan't now.'

'Why not?'

'Because you're here, that's why. It doesn't matter anyway. She's got herself involved with a group of kids who live in a squat. If you ask me it's another slap at Jake's authoritarianism.'

'Where is it, this squat?'

'They've taken over a big house on the edge of Holland Park that's been standing empty for years apparently, just crumbling to bits. I was supposed to meet her there, but only if I felt like it.'

For the second time I astonished myself. I blurted out, 'Why don't we both go?'

The rather antiquated kitchen, large and bare, smelled faintly of gas. Whereas the sitting room had been cherished and adorned, the kitchen still wore its rented, impoverished look.

Vivien smiled. 'I couldn't possibly drag you over there, not tonight.'

'You won't be dragging me. I'd like to come.' The word 'squat' and her description of her friend's predicament had combined to awaken my curiosity. What were they like, these squats I had only heard about? I toyed with obscure images of devilment, people peering from holes, a toad-like existence. I wandered back into the sitting room with its welcome splashes of bright colour, and the flood of summer light. Following me in, Vivien said, 'Well, if you're certain. See how you feel after I've made us a meal. Can you eat an omelette?'

'I'm sure I could.'

'That's easy, then. And Francis, take your coat off! You look like a visitor.'

'I am.'

'You're my special guest.'

'Yes,' I said, to her departing back. Taking off my coat I sat hunched over the dully glowing fire, smelling the hot dust as I chafed my palms. Suddenly abashed, I waited for her to ask me about Della. Instead, she called to me in a worried voice. 'Are you sure you're looking after yourself? I don't suppose you're much good at it. Do you eat properly in Cornwall?'

'When I remember,' I called back. She came at once to the door. Seeing that I had succeeded only too well in alarming her, I added hastily, 'I'm fit enough.'

'I suppose so. You're never really ill, that's true.'

'You talk as though I live alone.'

'Well, don't you?'

'Now, yes.'

'You always did, if you ask me,' she said, and turned on her heel. She poked her head round the door to ask comically, 'Who'd live with a maniac like you, anyway?'

'Good question.'

Our eyes met. We smiled happily at each other.

After the omelette, rolls and coffee, I sat wiping my mouth with the paper napkin she had provided. I asked about her job. 'Is the school where you teach far from here?'

'Not at the moment, no. Twickenham. Before this, I was right out at Wandsworth, and then Westbourne Grove. Horrible. There I was in the headmaster's office one morning, breaking down. I wet the poor man's suit. He told me he was surprised I'd lasted so long. Francis, I felt such a failure.'

'Poor Vivien. Were you scared?'

She nodded, as if still afraid. 'All those resentful kids unable to cope, immigrants and back street whites, the words they can't understand, can't pronounce, don't know how to write. You see with your own eyes how *angry* it's making them. If any violence erupts, a single incident in the playground, it sets up a force field, they flood to it as though magnetised. You don't teach, you scream.'

'Shall we have another coffee? Let me do it.'

She jumped up. 'Stay where you are.'

When she came back, I said, 'How well do you know the immigrants? Could you get close to them at all?'

She sat back in her chair, her eyes veiled. 'Sort of. I've got a West Indian boyfriend.'

She had spoken matter-of-factly, with no more than a hint of shyness. I must have looked dumbfounded, though I said at once, 'Go on, I'm interested.' I was aware of the pleasure she took in this revelation. As well as this, it must have been the first intimate fact about her I had learned, and from her own lips. She had tossed it out like something quite inconsequential, and now she was laughing silently at me.

'What's so funny?'

'Your face.'

She sat enjoying my bemused and pained expression. I rubbed at the stubble around my jawbone. 'Doesn't he have a name, your friend?'

'Michael.'

I nodded. I thought I knew what was biting me. I had become my father, with his blind objection to sudden change. Now I was Vivien's father too. I seemed to sit in the confusion of my body, out of sympathy with it, but encumbered with its hateful slow processes, a body that was somehow wormy, katabolistic, writhing now with dubious questions.

'Is he nice?' I asked, and then immediately wished I hadn't.

Vivien said, 'He's a good lover.' Then she added for good measure, 'They have quite a reputation, you know.'

'No, I didn't know.'

She got up, abruptly enough for me to see that I had upset her. 'I'm, having another coffee – how about you?'

'I've still got this.'

Coming back, she said calmly, with a touch of defiance, 'Have I shocked you?'

Though we sat only a few feet apart, I couldn't believe we had just been so close, warm and open with each other. 'No,' I said. 'I'm too old in the tooth.' I wanted to say that I didn't understand what I felt, and that in any case it was no business of mine what she did. Instead, I continued to sound falsely tough. 'Nothing anyone does surprises me any more.'

'Worried you, then.'

'No more than I worry myself.'

'Drink up your coffee, it's getting cold. Shall I make you a fresh one?'

'No, no.'

'You see me as someone who needs looking after.'

'Do I?'

'I'm a big girl now.'

'Yes and no.'

I saw with relief that she had lost her momentary distrust of me. Was I trapped between vague fears, protective and possessive at one and the same time? Vivien watched my face and seemed reassured, even flattered by what she read there. I said, 'This Michael.'

'Yes.'

'He's not a pupil?'

No sooner had this left my tongue than I was deriding it. She shook her head, smiling, not in the least offended. 'In a way I'm his,' she said enigmatically.

I gulped down a sudden thought with a mouthful of lukewarm coffee. 'I'd like to meet him.' Whatever she did was her, I went on to think. Then an anxious yearning rose into my consciousness, a voice in my ear whispering, 'Is there a place for me in her life?'

I stirred pointlessly at my cup, feigning disinterest. Vivien, who had apparently come to a decision, told me suddenly, 'It's not what you might think. There's nothing cut and dried about it. We're both restless creatures. Michael comes and goes when he likes, he just suits himself. The last time he dropped in I said he needn't bother. The laughable thing was, I was the insulted one. He's laid back, as they say. I suppose it's the secret of his charm, at any rate for me.' She laughed, and added wryly, 'Frying his bloody bananas.'

'Is that what he does?'

'Plantains, they are. The two nice ladies who live below here, the owners actually, they object to the smell. Otherwise they're amazingly tolerant.'

'Like me.'

Vivien broke into laughter. 'Oh yes, but you've had a shock. Anyway, you're my big brother. I expect you to advise me.'

'I wouldn't know where to start.'

'You must have learnt something from your mistakes,' she said, gently teasing.

'Evidently not. I'm still making them.'

She considered me seriously. 'Tell me one thing you lack more than anything else.'

Without a moment's hesitation, I said, 'Confidence.'

She sighed, all sympathy. 'I know. It must be so hard these days, being a man.'

'Hard?'

'Wearing.'

'In what sense?'

Following her own train of thought, she said, 'Apart from Michael, who belongs to a different culture, all the men I've known are in trouble when it comes to acting freely. They're so ashamed of expressing emotion, so crippled by their egos.'

'Yes, I know.'

She went on solemnly, 'This leads them to try to impose restraints on women.'

'All the men you've known?' I said ironically. We both laughed. We were friends again.

'The several men,' she amended.

'Why are men in trouble rather than women?'

'Haven't I already said?'

'You've only pointed out how they differ from each other. Women are free now, but is it what they want?'

She sat eyeing me calmly, an unsurprised, free woman who retained a curiously timeless and unmodern appearance. 'The Middle Ages have come to an end,' she said.

'True.'

She got up. 'I think we ought to make a move. Are you positive you want to?'

'I'm looking forward to it.' As much as anything I was speaking in order to convince myself. My curiosity about Vivien's friend had waned, together with any nostalgia I may have fleetingly felt for a life of squalor. I got up stiffly and went for my coat.

Vivien left the room. She returned almost at once, wearing a dark blue blazer with white piping. On one lapel she had pinned a flat broach, depicting in blaring red plastic the silhouette of a parrot. She drew my attention to it with her finger. 'You see this? Another symbol for you to conjure with.'

'Am I a symbolist?'

'Well, aren't you?'

139

'I hope it's not that obvious. What's it a symbol of?'

'I'm becoming steadily more raucous.'

'I can't see any signs. Maybe you're signalling something which hasn't surfaced yet.'

'I expect you're right, as usual. Awful though it may seem, I fully approve of this parrot.'

Over the brooch and blazer she pulled on a dashing raincoat of creamy oatmeal colour with a big floppy collar, tying the belt in one swift flourish. 'Right,' she said.

16

In the street she strode vigorously, no longer strained or weary around the eyes. She had stepped into the twilight as if into an element which magically renewed her.

The tube train was half empty. We sat side by side on the bench seat. I waited for her to speak. She smiled at me and glanced away. In public I saw another person, blandly competent, a little distant.

I wasn't myself either. The underground always made me apprehensive. In its gusty tunnels I often felt hollow and papery, and was forced to contemplate the waste places of my own spirit. The glazed tiles, deserted platforms, scraps of blown litter, huge strident posters – everything looked slightly mad, a madness disguised as order. In the evening these effects and portents were somehow accentuated. For once I longed for the seethe and bustle of daytime crowds. I said, 'Does Michael have a job?'

'Oh, he goes for months without one, then he'll announce casually that I won't see him in the evenings, he's driving taxis, or else working at a nightclub.'

'What's he doing now?'

'At the moment he's a postman. Well, a sorter – at the enormous sorting office at Rathbone Place. He tells me about men who virtually live there. Sixty-to-seventy hour weeks are normal.'

'He complains about it?'

'Never. No matter what. Of course I find that infuriating where it concerns me. For instance, he's so casual – you'll be expecting him and he'll just forget. Ask him what happened and he'll say, "I forgot, man." End of conversation. I sit around fuming, I sulk, it's all useless. Anyway he's told me the truth.'

'Are you sure?'

'Oh yes. If he'd gone drinking instead with his pals, or gambling, or slept with another woman, he'd tell me.'

'And you can cope with that?'

'I have to. It's deceit I can't stand.'

'It's because he's straight and consistent that you admire him, is that it?'

'In theory, yes. Often though it's hell.'

'You put up with it though.'

Vivien was silent for a moment. 'For the time being,' she said. We pulled into a station and she gave a start. 'Here's our stop.'

Up on the street now it was nearly dark, with a strong wind blowing as we left the station entrance. The wind suddenly died away. Banging against my sister on a pedestrian crossing, I said, 'Sorry.'

'Nearly there now.'

I wanted to ask her what Michael thought of Celia, whether they had met, but when I came to speak I put it the other way. 'How does Celia get on with Michael?'

'She's antagonistic. It's funny. I'd like to think she was jealous, but it's not that. I don't think she even knows what jealousy is. She evaluates people in terms of weak and strong. I'm strong, and she sees Michael as a weak person. A degenerate, she calls him. Not to his face – not quite. She's quite bitchy towards him. I think she sees in him a side of her she condemns, so really she's being severe with herself. They have one thing in common.'

'What's that?'

'They both go their own way regardless.'

'How does she regard her husband?'

'Jake? Basically as a sentimentalist, for all his brilliance. She wanted a stern hero to worship and she finds him sickly, a sick lover who leaves her frigid.'

'Yet she's gone back to him.'

'I imagine it's terribly hard to leave someone who can't stand up.'

'It must be hard too, knowing you're so despised.'

Either she didn't hear what I said or she had no comment to make. She kept forging ahead, leading me. I had to quicken my pace every now and then to catch up. I trailed after her alongside the railings of a run-down square. Peeling houses faced an area in the middle which had once been a private garden. Some of the white buildings were in reasonable order, others were like bad teeth, rotten with decay. I caught my toe in an uneven paving slab, tripped, clutched at Vivien's arm. 'Whoops, steady!' she laughed.

Further on we had to step into the road to avoid barriers. Pavement had been torn up. 'This is the place, here,' she said.

A flight of cracked steps, sprouting weeds, led up to a once-grand porch with fluted columns. Lumps of plaster had worked loose. All the tall handsomely proportioned windows were blinded by unpainted plywood shuttering, crudely nailed up. A man as old as myself hung about at the bottom of the steps, hands in his pockets. He looked the other way as we climbed up to the door and Vivien banged on it. Nothing happened. She looked at me, shrugged, banged again, this time with more force.

The door opened. 'I'm a friend of Celia,' she said to a woman, who stood aside drably without answering. I followed like a shadow. We were standing in the wrecked hallway, on a layer of dust and plaster. As we walked down corridors towards the rear of the house it got cleaner, so far as I could make out in the dingy light. At least the grittiness beneath my feet seemed to be lessening. Vivien poked her head into an open doorway, then we went on again.

We passed into a lofty, frowsty-smelling kitchen with a broken ceiling. A long scrubbed table, minus its drawers, was littered with miscellaneous crockery and scraps of abandoned food. There was a smeary mess at the far end where something had spilled: it could have been beans. A hard chair painted bright blue was hung with a child's woollen cardigan and some tiny dungarees. Light came from a naked low-wattage bulb on a long flex. Candles stuck in their own wax stood unlit, several on the table in saucers and two on top of a cooker. The vinyl floor, a sea-green tiled design, was startlingly clean and shiny, as if someone had just finished mopping it.

Vivien turned to me and shrugged again, impatiently. 'They said she'd be down in a minute.'

I asked stupidly, 'Who said?'

'A man I just spoke to.'

'How many live here altogether?'

'I've no idea. I imagine it varies.' All at once her face brightened. 'Listen – I can hear somebody.'

It was a young man in jeans split across the knees, tee-shirted, with a dark moustache, who lolled his head in what may or may not have been a greeting. Ignoring us, he mooched over to the cooker and stood with his back bent. He sniffed at a saucepan, his nose almost in it. I heard scraping sounds; we were both staring. After a while, feeling that I was dreaming, or about to petrify, I coughed loudly and shuffled my feet. Even that seemed part of the scene, which was without substance and made no sense. Just as in a dream, I struggled to make myself act. I had a sudden desire to run out and find a phone box and ring Maggie. She would provide the antidote to all this, I thought, wildly and without hope.

Then a young woman came in, making hardly any sound. I was released. Celia glided, almost on tiptoe. It was such a stagey entrance that I wanted to laugh, thinking it the sort of thing girls do in their bedrooms or in front of the mirror. She was taller than my sister. So this is the love object, I thought.

'Celia!' Vivien cried. She ran over in one graceful joyous movement. The two friends stood whispering together, heads and tongues wagging, their figures avid. At one point Celia burst out laughing, a high, forced peal, and I thought, she doesn't have a laugh, she's like me.

Vivien hooked me over with energetic arm gestures. I crossed the space diagonally, skirted the table and found myself in the path of the other man, who was heading for the door without looking at anyone. I muttered an apology and stepped aside. The man kept on. His oily black hair lay in long strips on the nape of his neck.

'This is Celia,' Vivien said needlessly.

The formality of an introduction struck me as funny in these surroundings, and I smiled. I was met by a wide-eyed stare.

'You're Vivien's brother,' the woman said, wilful and keen. I took her to be thirty or so.

'Yes, I'm Francis.'

'And a painter.'

'Endeavouring to be.'

Vivien said, 'Don't let him kid you. He's very good.'

'I'm still a beginner. At least I hope so.'

Celia stared at me inquisitively. 'When you paint, is it like dancing?' she asked.

Was she joking, being clever? I couldn't decide. Not knowing what to say, I confessed, 'I don't dance.'

Suddenly she stopped focusing intently on me. Her gaze swerved about, she looked apprehensive. Vivien asked her quickly how she was, and she seemed to recover her composure. As these two engaged in gently bantering conversation, obviously a continuation of some long-established ritual, I backed away little by little, coming to rest against the edge of the table.

Celia wore Turkish trousers of some cotton material, seagreen, and a purplish shirt top. Around her shoulders was draped a white fringed shawl. Despite the determined femininity of her attire, something about her, what it was I couldn't have said, reminded me of a boy. The more I studied her surreptitiously, then openly, coldly even, as one does with a model, the more I felt she was a boy disguised and acting awkwardly as a woman. A boy, not a man. Following this search to find out, I went plunging back into an adolescence which came and went on her face as I watched, perplexed.

What about her body? The top half was long and flat, surmounted by the contradiction of a delicate moon face, plum-cheeked, not quite pretty, with big greenish eyes and a doubting mouth. Her short fair hair was a mass of tight curls, called I think a bubble-cut. Below the waist she swelled out, ungainly almost, with heavy thighs of which she disapproved, so I was told later. Hence the baggy trousers. Downstairs, as it were, she was firmly rooted and secure. Up above, all was threatened, precarious, narcissistic.

I must have been irritated by her at the outset, to have gone in for such analysis at such short notice. I reacted as some people do who are averse to cats, when one ingratiates itself slyly by degrees, with the suppleness of a snake. I even decided at that moment that her demure greeting revealed the timorous nature, which seeks to please in order to disarm and make safe. Behind these moves, in her witty eyes, was the ruthless person who believes in nothing, least of all in herself. She seemed to look out of the corners of her eyes at a world of menace, as if being urged towards it against her will.

Much of this of course is hindsight. Meeting her for this first time I though she was posing. Now, I understand the quality she

144

had of seeming to stand aloof and arrogant. She was horrified by the world.

I knew next to nothing about her death obsession. From what Vivien had said to me I pictured her as someone who had fallen for the myth of the artist as sacrificial victim, perhaps to justify a need for the dramatic. In short, I was out of sympathy with her from the start. It could be that my antipathy was sparked off by traits I detected in myself and found abhorrent. Dislike can lead to recognition.

Between them, Celia and Vivien had decided to make coffee and carry it upstairs. 'Come and experience the nether regions,' I heard Celia say. She went over with Vivien to the cooker, opening a cupboard. 'Francis, how do you like yours?' she asked, and before I could answer, my sister said, 'I know.'

We left the kitchen, each clutching a mug of coffee, and began to climb up through the house. After two floors, passing rooms showing light under their doors, hearing a sudden flood of rock music from another quarter, the stairs narrowed and tilted up yet more steeply. There was inadequate light, then nothing. Celia produced a torch. 'Can you manage?' Celia asked from the front, supposedly for my benefit.

'Yes.' I was clumping away at bare invisible wood. 'Are we nearly there?'

'Yes, nearly. These are the attics.'

Behind me, Vivien called, 'It's damp, Celia.'

'You don't smell it after a while.'

We entered a room. Someone was inside, a youth, who clambered to his feet with difficulty. His right leg was encased in plaster and he had a steel crutch. 'Steve's broken his leg in the dark,' Celia said, by way of introduction.

'Hi,' the rather pretty youth said, docilely. He lowered himself again.

The dusty coloured light in the L-shaped room came from a large sphere of brown pleated paper, dangling from a flex to within a foot of the floor. All I could see in the near gloom was a pallid rug and a mattress covered with a travelling blanket. What am I doing in this miserable dump? I asked myself. I was too old now for roughing it. When you're young, everything is novel. With imagination you can persuade yourself that you're having an adventure. I can't, I've lost my illusions. My eyes were growing used to the murk and I could see that the ceiling

145

sloped like a garret. For something to say, I asked, 'How did the juice get switched on?'

I thought the youngster might answer, but it was Celia who said, 'It's all a mystery to me.'

We sat in a row like Indians on the bed and sipped our drinks. I had been wondering what a squat was exactly. Now I knew: you squatted. As I got down on the mattress, knees jammed up under my nose, one of my joints gave a loud crack. I sighed under my breath for a decent chair. In a matter of minutes cramp would set in, I thought gloomily. My flesh shuddered. Winter seeped from the walls; I had lost touch with the summer outside. If I wanted a toilet, what then? Did they have such things? As far as I could see in the pinkish brown glow, the room was clean.

A peculiar silence extended itself. Vivien leaned her spine against the wall. I had begun to doubt everything in this house, in this light, except the existence of my own body and its complaints, looking at my thin wrists lying on the blanket.

'Where do you live, Celia?' I asked. Her profile, what I could see of it, was enigmatic, impenetrable.

She said, without moving a muscle,. 'I've been sharing with Vivien. I thought you knew.'

Stung by this reply, I said, 'Yes, I do know. Where's your home?'

'Chalk Farm.'

The name meant nothing to me, except as a tube station. 'No, I meant originally, where you grew up.'

There was a moment of strained silence. 'Why did you want to know that?' she asked sweetly.

I stared blindly at her round blurry head. In my mind I had the picture of her face in the communal kitchen below to refer to. Down there she had had milky freckled skin. Her eyes seemed devoid of lashes. I remembered that as she talked, and I watched, she kept clothing her bald Gothic forehead with thoughts, and these thoughts were creased like a book down the middle, above the bridge of her nose – two fiercely questioning perpendicular grooves. What about the rest of her? I thought of her already as a Cranach nude, the pure and the perverse inextricably mingled.

Her question had stumped me, and it was a rebuff. Still I had to go on. 'I suppose I'm curious. Don't you have family there, wherever it is?'

146

Vivien, sitting beside me, had apparently withdrawn. Here I was, sandwiched between neutrality on one side and near hostility on the other. But I was past caring.

'I'm going to be rude,' Celia said, in a louder, firmer voice, 'and say that's my affair.'

'Excuse me.'

'What for?' Now she was being light and amusing. 'The only time I feel homesick is when I see a flooded field. I come from Norfolk, on the coast.'

'Do you, Celia?' Vivien cried. 'I didn't know that.'

Celia went on, 'A place doesn't exactly exist for me when I'm not there. I'm sure it should. I must have been born with that bit missing.'

'And people?' I found myself asking. 'Don't they exist for you either unless you want them to?'

Bright and prompt, like a star pupil eager to shine, she said, 'As long as I'm away from there, no, they don't. It's not a matter of wanting. My life's all holes, perhaps that's it. They drop through the holes. Unless someone reminds me.'

'Excuse me if I've reminded you.'

'It wasn't you I was thinking of.'

I thought, now I've been firmly reprimanded for my egotism. I imagined her waiting, maybe with relish, for my next rejoinder. Suddenly she put her hands to her head.

'What is it, what's wrong?' Vivien said, leaning across me towards her friend.

'Nothing,' Celia said. Her voice had changed. There was fear in it. She got up. 'I shall have to go, I can't stay here. Will you come back with me?'

'Yes, yes,' Vivien said.

'Please, will you?' Celia actually swayed on her feet.

I scrambled up to help, though unsure of my role. The change in Celia, when I glimpsed her face, was unbelievable. She looked withered, she stared at me venomously, in terror, her hands were bunched up like a baby's and pressing into her cheeks. What had happened to the cool stand-offish person who had just been speaking in such measured tones?

'Francis, run out and get a taxi, will you?' Vivien was saying, her voice calm yet intense. She had her arm around her friend's shoulders. Celia shrank against her.

'Yes, right.' I was grateful for the task. The boy with the plaster cast sat there as if turned to stone. I blundered out on the landing, immediately lost my bearings in the dark, turned back and collided with Vivien in the doorway. 'I can't see a thing, I need a torch, who's got it?'

'Wait a minute, I'll look. It's in here somewhere. No, it doesn't seem to be. Celia, have you got the torch, darling?'

No answer. Vivien tried again. 'Francis wants the torch, have you got it?'

The stricken woman shook her head like a dumb animal. She whimpered in her throat. I said, 'Never mind, I'll manage. See if you can find it for yourselves.'

Somehow I crept down the two narrow flights, feeling my way blindly along walls with my fingertips. The rest was easier. I rushed out of the house, fumbling for coins in my bewilderment. Did I have any? What street was this? Where could I find a phone box? Everything which had looked so unremarkable on the way in was now somehow nightmarish.

I began to have some luck. Looking up, I read the name of a square. I had plenty of loose change. A man pulled up in a car almost beside me and I asked him to direct me to a phone – I needed one urgently for an emergency, I explained.

'What kind of an emergency?'

I said the first thing that entered my head. 'I think a woman's having a fit.' Running down the street from the house I had begun to suspect epilepsy.

'Better come in here, old man,' the stranger said. He took me into his brightly-lit hall. Everything was order, sanity, cleanliness. The phone stood waiting on a little table. Beside it was a seat, joined on to the table. There was even a list of taxi firms before me. I chose one at random and dialled. A woman's voice answered at once and I babbled my message. The man whose house I had entered was nowhere to be seen. Wanting to thank him, I hesitated at a closed door, then changed my mind and ran out, back to the squat.

I had seen everything as lost, ill-starred, the dingy streets part of a maze which led to nowhere. Sirens wailed in the distance, rushing to the scenes of other disasters. Doorways that I passed were sunk in shadow, and seemed to be inviting break-ins, crimes of all kinds. Then the man, whose face I couldn't even recall, drove up out of nowhere and gave assistance without being asked, in this district where I thought no one was to be trusted.

Vivien and Celia stood waiting in the portico, the sick woman like someone prematurely senile. The way she hunched up her shoulders, she looked smaller, shrunken. Vivien still had her arm round her. To one side I noticed the middle-aged man we had seen on the way in earlier. He was there still. As I reached them, Vivien spoke to him. 'Hello, Al. Aren't you going in?'

He grunted something inaudibly, not moving, standing there in an attitude of dejection with his hands sunk in his pockets, his collar turned up.

The taxi came. We drove in silence to the address where Celia lived. From time to time I peered into the night, completely at sea. The taxi stopped. Vivien helped Celia inside the building.

'Is this Chalk Farm?' I asked the driver.

He was listening to music on the radio. He turned down the volume. 'Come again, mate?' he said, without bothering to look over his shoulder. He fished about in the glove compartment and found his cigarettes.

Vivien came out. She asked the driver to take us to the nearest tube station. When we finally reached Kew and came to her street door, she said, 'I'll tell you later, Francis, what that was all about.'

'Does it happen often?'

'Thank God, no.'

'Is she seeing anybody?'

'She's tried that. Freudians, Jungians, acupuncturists, you name it. I'll say this for Jake, he's not stingy.' We went upstairs. She was dragging her feet, and I was just as tired. 'Let's have a coffee. Oh hell, I've got to go to work in the morning.'

'Can't you be ill?'

'Me as well?' She laughed harshly. 'I can't tell lies. That's to say, I'm a lousy liar.'

In the kitchen, she did things and talked simultaneously. Women do this all the time, men hardly ever. 'Before that seizure, before we went upstairs even, she gave me some news.'

'Celia did?'

In a transfigured voice, still with her back to me, she said, 'She's had enough, she tells me. She's coming back to Kew.'

'Back here with you?'

'Yes.'

* * *

149

The next morning I travelled back into town. When Vivien set off for work I walked down the road with her. It was early, but the sun bounteously shone, and the urge to move, to move anywhere, was upon me. I might ring Maggie, I might not. Happy though the thought of seeing her made me, I would have preferred, as always, to leave the initiative to her. One day she would look me up of her own free will; she had promised as much. The last time we had spoken on the phone, she said I was on her mind a great deal. I hadn't forgotten her either, far from it. Maybe the future held a few surprises for us both.

At a corner, Vivien walked off one way and I another. 'See you this evening,' I called. She waved goodbye to me.

In town again, I mooched aimlessly as I always did in this vast beehive of a city. Where was everyone going in such a hurry, with such determination, such importance, so grim-faced? People in London seemed caught up in some rite which excluded me, into which I had never been initiated. Thoughts of the evening before came over me, its distress, its disturbance. I felt nauseous, shaken, as if haunted by a bad dream.

It was all baffling. In the big-city turmoil of Charing Cross Road I crossed to the railings and descended the wet shining steps of the public toilet to urinate. Down below, the attendant slopped away at the white-tiled floor with a mop. I stepped gingerly over his work and stood examining the shiny brass fittings in front of my nose. The pipes were old, stained with verdigris. How had they survived all the development? On street level, buildings were being torn down and plywood fencing erected around the perimeters of new premises-to-be.

In the open street and part of the stream again, I stared at faces of men and women, asking myself the usual questions: why were they so preoccupied, what was happening, was it as grim as their expressions suggested? Did they have any choice? Does anybody? I often wondered if we were all part of some cosmic joke which we helped to perpetuate unwittingly. In the midst of this musing I suddenly understood that I had made a decision. I wouldn't call Maggie, that was too fraught, but Simon Trench, my dealer. Perhaps, like everyone else, I was being driven to seek a niche, a purpose for myself. The very tempo of the city seemed to demand it.

I turned into an arcade and made for a phone box. Then a doubt attacked me. Did I really want to risk the disillusionment a gallery visit would almost certainly produce? But this was so feeble an evasion that I dismissed it and then actually speeded up, reaching the booth and yanking the door open before a woman heading the same way could beat me to it. She stood nearby glaring in as I put through my call. If Simon Trench was out, a voice inside me said, that would be that.

The fact is that I shrank from meeting him and yet was driven to meet him for conflicting reasons. My shyness, never totally vanquished, would reappear if I gave it the chance. I had come too far now to regress. Sweating palms and a sick stomach belonged with those other miseries and inhibitions of the past. But there was now an additional complication, a cultural one. Charles Woodruff, and now the gallery, had imposed on my work a cultural value which was nothing to do with me personally. Culture seemed to have no connection with what I did, which was something compulsive, savage even, something that propelled me. One day I would be found out and exposed. What a joke, to have taken seriously an activity which could dry up overnight or be condemned one day as a sickness.

Yes, he was in, the receptionist informed me, but a conference was in progress. Would I mind phoning back, or did I have a number they could call? I said I would ring again.

What were they conferring about – my paintings and why they were now piling up instead of selling? Were they fed up with my recent work, the compositions of crushed figures, babies, heaps of stinging nettles, all rendered from the same restricted palette of sombre grey-greens, paintings that looked faded and mauled like old washing?

To kill time, I went into a smart bookshop and pretended to browse. The slick glossy jackets had a sameness about them, seeming to say in one voice that there was nothing fresh to be discovered, it had all been said, there was just froth and no substance, repeated endlessly. A suave young man approached. 'Can I help you, sir?'

'I said, 'Just looking,' and then felt obliged to continue doing so.

After a decent interval I left. I was now vaguely anxious, unable to concentrate on anything until the accursed phone call was made.

Trailing up and down obsessively, I spotted another call box. When I picked up the receiver it was to find it had no dial tone. There was a stench of urine, mingled with tobacco and stale sweat smells.

I sprinted round a corner. Hunting for another box, I saw a group of three in the distance and ran some more. Panting to a halt, I lugged violently at a spring-loaded door.

This time I spoke to a secretary, the female voice oiled and bland. When I tried to explain my intentions my voice was jerkily short of breath.

'Anybody who is available will do,' I spluttered. 'No, I don't have an appointment. Somebody might find it useful to see me, I thought . . . as I was here . . .'

'Francis, how nice,' a voice I recognised said. It was Simon Trench. 'Where are you, by the way?'

The fug in the tiny cell clung hatefully. I visualised how I must look, my ear sprouting wires, growing a black shell. 'London.'

'Yes, but where, roughly.'

'The lower reaches of Charing Cross Road.'

'Good. Come round now, will you? I may have to keep you waiting for just a few minutes.'

'Right, I will.'

'Splendid. I look forward to our chat.'

I walked through Bloomsbury, past the British Museum. A thoroughfare enlarged and swallowed me. Soon afterwards I lost track of where I was. I kept asking for the Angel, the one landmark in Islington I was familiar with.

At the Montague Galleries I sat in a little screened-off area which served as a waiting room, fiddling with my fingers as I watched the woman intercepting calls in between leafing through a newspaper. I expected Simon Trench to come out of a door that was nearly opposite. Instead he drifted round the corner of the partition, a typed letter between his fingers.

We shook hands. The slender, softly spoken man was bright-eyed and attentive. He excused himself, spoke to the receptionist like an intimate friend, using her first name, then came back for me. Shown into a pleasant small office, I noted again the dealer's keen young face, the fair fluffy moustache. His blue-green shirt seemed to glow as youthfully as its wearer. In Simon I admired the opposite of what I was.

He murmured, 'I must say you're looking extremely fit,' and waved me to a chair.

'Thank you.'

'What brings you to the city? Is this a holiday, Francis?'

'Yes, I suppose it is. Just a few days.'

I sat thinking of the side streets outside, the spilling refuse, broken paving stones, fences scrawled with graffiti. Simon Trench, polite, cultivated, exquisitely shaven, was a startling contrast. The world outside might never have existed. His presence exuded a confidence which I absorbed gratefully. I began to enjoy a sense of privilege, though nothing could have convinced me that I was entitled to it. Simon Trench smiled easily. I smiled back, as relaxed as I would ever be.

'I've only French cigarettes, I'm afraid. But you don't smoke any more, am I right?'

'I never started.'

'How very wise.'

'I suppose so.' Smokers were forever saying this, and still I hadn't worked out what to say in reply.

'You don't mind if I do?'

'No, go ahead.'

I looked into his intelligently working eyes and thought that it was easy to like Simon, at least when you were faced with him. His quiet charm was on show the whole time, like a tangible asset. He touched his moustache with his fingertips, smiled again, and said, 'As it happens, your timing is excellent.'

'Oh?'

'Yes, I'm expecting one of our clients any moment now. In fact he's late. An American, Dr Marshall Walder. Over here on one of his trips, making a few acquisitions – I hope from us. He's got a fine modern collection, so I believe, quite valuable. Though I haven't seen it myself.'

'Where do I come in?'

'I was coming to that. As a matter of fact he owns at least one, possibly two Breakwells. I seem to remember him launching into a quite passionate appreciation of one of your New York pictures – that period.'

'If you can call it that.'

'It was brief, I agree. More's the pity. Anyway, I'm sure it would be beneficial if you met this man. What do you say?'

'I don't mind in the least.'

153

'Excellent.' Simon finished his cigarette and plaited his fingers together in mid-air, his elbows on the desk. 'I thought we might go round to the Pear Tree for a drink.'

'Is that nearby?'

'Only round the corner. Very pleasant.'

We soon ran out of things to say. Simon was too diffident to be an easy talker. Topics would be raised, only to run into the ground after a couple of stilted exchanges. He was no monologuist either. I began to feel sorry for him. I even saw myself in him. He exclaimed, 'Ah,' with obvious relief when his secretary poked in her lacquered head of motionless waves to announce a caller. 'A Dr Walder to see you.'

'Show him in, Margaret.'

Dr Walder astonished me with his youthfulness. He filled the doorway of the office, which suddenly became even smaller. I had expected some kind of leathery veteran, maybe with a Stetson balanced on his head like a solidified cloud. This individual was no older than my sister, I estimated. Tall and rangy, he was wearing a safari suit of light brown linen. He beamed effusively.

We settled down for a few minutes before transferring to the pub. From time to time Dr Walder broke into wild laughter which had no apparent cause and was prolonged alarmingly. Simon explained, with a tentative smile in my direction, 'I asked Mr Breakwell here to hang on, knowing you'd be delighted to make his acquaintance.'

'You bet,' the leggy young American said. He exploded a few more laughs. 'You're telling me you haven't set this up, you weren't holding out on me, this is a coincidence?'

'Indeed, yes, I am. Absolutely fortuitous. Of course you're an old admirer of his work.'

'I'll say,' Dr Walder said, grinning broadly. 'Fantastic.'

'Do you know his later things? Apart, that is, from examples we have here in the gallery?'

'I've done some browsing you might say. Beautiful, great!' He was addressing me as if we were alone in the room. 'Who knows, one day I might be able to meet with you in your studio. Would you object to that, sir?'

His eyes were jovial and yet earnest. I liked him. Putting aside my misgivings, I stammered, 'Not at all.'

'I'd be privileged if you'd allow the intrusion.'

'When I get back I'll look in the book,' I said, inventing an engagement diary out of panic on the spur of the moment.

'Surely,' Dr Walder said equably. Then he added, 'May I inquire – are you based here in London?'

'No, I live in Cornwall.'

'Cornwall. Can't say I know the region. Is that south from here?'

'It's the south west,' Simon Trench put in. 'Francis isn't far from Land's End.'

Dr Walder was nodding. 'Let's see now. I understand you have a thriving art colony down on the south coast some place. Am I getting confused here?'

'No,' Simon said, 'you're absolutely right!'

'And you're part of this colony, Mr Breakwell?'

I shook my head. 'I don't know any artists.' I remembered Guy. 'Well, one. The only creatures I can see from my window are four-legged, such as cows and sheep. I can go for a week without setting eyes on the forked variety.'

The tanned client grinned, staring with frank admiration. 'You're a recluse?'

'When it suits me, yes. It gets the work done.'

'Francis has an American wife,' Simon said suddenly, and I thought, 'My God, is she up for sale too?'

'That a fact?' Dr Walder said, with notable lack of interest. But no doubt he felt obliged to ask, 'Which state?'

I was surprised by my own response. Because Della had always hated her origins, disowning them whenever possible, even glad to be mistaken for English a time or two, I said loyally, 'She's a New Yorker.' In fact she came from Ohio.

'Is that so?' Dr Walder's mind seemed to be elsewhere. His gaze was roaming idly over the walls.

We went around the corner for our drinks. The pub was called a tavern, Virginia creeper clothed the porch, the interior had been 'designed' to look rustic. After a few drinks, if you shut your eyes to the clientele you could imagine you were in the country somewhere. Whisky flowed, tongues were loosened and thickened, nothing of any consequence was said. Thank God, I could go back whenever I liked to my rainy hole in the west. I began to feel strangely bodiless, as I sometimes

155

did in London, a naked soul floating between one body and another.

Getting out and making my escape, I considered I had lived through one of the longest hours of my life. The bituminous decaying streets now had my full approval. A bleary sky, wheeling between gaps in buildings, half blinding me at intervals, freed and exonerated me somehow from the drivel I had been uttering. I loved the grimy brick. The very banality of the voices I heard gave me a grace I had thought woefully lost.

Whenever I drank too much I inevitably speeded up. The neat spirits on an empty stomach seemed to be fuelling my reckless unstable walk. I crossed over blithely and then was unable to remember looking for approaching traffic. A couple turning the corner ahead of me caught my attention. The woman was dressed like Celia, in identical baggy trousers, and she held on decorously to the hand of a West Indian whose headgear was outlandish, the crown of his cap so large it seemed to be inflated. I told myself I must be mistaken, how could it be? Before I could even rub my eyes she had disappeared.

The brief talk of Cornwall had stirred longings for an arcadia which remained buried and unacknowledged while I was there. I presumed it was submerged in the paint too, surfacing in the form of innumerable images of seduction. The very thought of spring, a season I associated so naturally now with Cornwall, evoked the narrow granite land in all its glory. As if pricking in my blood, the willow, hazel and hawthorn rose before my eyes, leafing tenderly with sharp lyrical outbursts. Remembering that aching fresh green, which I always wanted to lick at, to stroke, the sloe blossom exploding in white puffs over the hillsides like gunsmoke, I strode on with large happy strides. Then a moment of acute anxiety stopped me in my tracks. I searched drunkenly in my pocketbook for the return half of my ticket, as if for a passport guaranteeing my safe passage across the Tamar. Failing to find it, I broke out in a sweat. It wasn't there, but it was in my back pocket.

Intoxicated with the new power to accomplish things I would have found impossible when sober, I explored Soho and then Mayfair. I was still moving at speed. Finally a reaction set in. I felt ill, weak. I thought that maybe if I ate something it would

156

settle my outraged stomach. Soon I found myself approaching a large restaurant, Cranks. I went in and sat down. Though I wasn't a vegetarian, over the years meat appealed to me less and less. Slowly it dawned on my fuddled brain that no one was taking orders. I got up and joined the small queue at the self-service counter.

17

As I walked from Kew Station towards my sister's road, I was in control of my stomach again and my speed of walking had returned to normal. All I suffered from was a sick headache and a sad feeling of disorientation and lost vitality, after the briefly soaring euphoria.

My pace quickened as I reached Vivien's road. It was good to think of her there in her rooms, awaiting me. I looked forward to telling her about my day. What of hers? Her daily life was a puzzle, and not only because I had no real sense of it. I couldn't imagine her being fulfilled for long by an occupation, but neither could I recall her ever speaking of a cause or purpose or career which might have satisfied the demands of her nature. Was she searching for something unattainable? Did she have a secret store of love which she held in readiness and would deliver up one great day? I saw her as passionate, not amorous. Anything she did, even promiscuity, would be taken intensely seriously and dedicated to an end, on the road to this goal I believed she hugged to herself and told no one about, possibly because there were no words fitting enough. Was she hoping to discover a love which would consume her utterly, and meanwhile keeping clear of matrimony, so as not to put out a fire that went on burning away inside her, if nowhere else? Did she want children?

I rang the bell of her house, then stood waiting. My fingers touched a strange object in my jacket pocket. It was the key ring, with two keys, which she had given me that morning and I'd completely forgotten.

Vivien opened the door. I held up her duplicate keys. 'I forgot.'

'Come in,' she said. 'You'd forget your head if it was loose.'

'It is, I think.'

'What's that?'

'Loose. My head. I'm no good with whisky.'

'Then why drink it?'

'I'm no better at saying no.'

As we climbed the stairs, she said 'I was wondering what time you'd get here.'

'Are you waiting to eat?'

'No, not yet. How about you – I hope you've had a meal somewhere?'

'Oh yes.'

'That's good. I'm making scrambled eggs with toast. Will that do for you?'

'Beautifully.'

'I've been thinking of you quite a lot today,' she said fondly, her voice pleased and light.

'You've been on my mind too.'

But something was amusing her. She hugged a secret. Revealing it with a smile, she said, 'Michael's here at the moment. I think he's going, though. I told you, didn't I, what a dropper-in he is.'

We had crossed the wide landing. Vivien was about to open her door when it was yanked open from within and Michael emerged. On his head was a large floppy corduroy cap in bottle-green, the one I could have sworn I'd seen in Islington only a few hours ago. I stared at him. He gazed back impassively, a thin, loose-limbed black of medium height. I was as fascinated by his outsize headgear and the sewn segments composing it as I was by the face underneath. A portrait jumped up in my head, with that cap filling the entire top half of the picture. Really I would have liked to have studied the stitching.

'Where d'you think you're going?' Vivien asked him roughly, in a dry humorous tone that was new to me.

'Out, man.'

She said sarcastically, 'You just got here.'

Michael murmured, 'I know, I know.' He edged past us slowly on the balls of his feet. He opened his hands to Vivien ironically in a gesture of mock helplessness.

'What a funny person,' she said.

'See ya, honey.'

'This is Francis, my brother.'

'Hi, brother Francis,' he called gaily, waving, already halfway down the stairs. He disappeared. The front door banged.

We went in. I gazed round the room, enchanted by it, grateful for its familiarity. Like someone coming in from work who belonged here I dropped down where I had sat before. Vivien stopped to look at me a moment, smiled, then passed through into the kitchen. I heard her say, 'That was Michael, that was.'

'So I gather. What was that visit about?'

'Nothing. It never is.'

Suddenly I felt regretful, and realised that I hadn't wanted Michael to go. The clue to another, very different Vivien had just gone slipping down the stairs. Now this other self would be withheld from me. I said, 'How long was he here?'

'About fifteen minutes.' She stood in the kitchen doorway.

'And that's a regular occurrence?'

'Fairly.'

'Did he come with a message or anything?'

She laughed. 'I suppose you could put it like that.'

'How would you put it?'

She went back into the kitchen. From there she called, 'He'd brought himself, that was the message.'

'Decipher it for me.'

She came out with two coffees. 'We'd had a row, you see.'

'Again?'

She laughed, and at the same time seemed puzzled by her own reaction. 'I haven't a clue to what's going on, not really. Sickening, isn't it, to be so at the mercy of your emotions. I'm getting to despise myself. My soul's not my own.'

I thought for a moment, then said carefully, 'Why not stop it?'

'Apparently I don't want to. Or else I can't.'

We sat together gloomily for a while. To be gloomy on purpose, as it were, in order to be at one with someone else, was something I had not experienced before. 'So what was the message?' I asked gently.

'He's simply saying, here I am, no hard feelings, let's get on with life.'

'Wise man.'

'Selfish bastard!' she laughed, too fiercely. She sprang up violently and clutched her hair. 'Oh Christ, what a stupid idiot I am!'

'What happened next was in the air above me, away from me, as I sat stiffly embracing my knees, like a father whose paternal advice has been flouted. Vivien was crying silently behind her hands. I got up clumsily, frightened to see this bright capable adult turn so swiftly into a lost helpless child. Putting unsure hands on her upper arms I stroked up and down them compulsively, not knowing what else to do or what I was trying to express.

'It's all right. I'm sorry,' Recovering almost at once, she dabbed angrily at her eyes with a tissue. 'Just ignore me, will you?'

'I can't do that.'

'I wish you would. I'm over-tired, that's all. Look, if we sit here mulling over my problems it's going to be a disgraceful waste of an evening.'

'What would you like to do?'

'Well, I've tentatively said we'll go round to Jake and Celia tonight. I rang Celia from work and she said fine.'

'What time was that?'

'Time? Why do you ask?'

'Tell me first.'

'Oh, four-thirty it must have been.'

'Because I thought I might have seen her today but I can't be sure. It was around two I think.'

'Where was that?'

'Islington.'

'It's possible. Why didn't you speak?'

'I wasn't near enough. Celia had her back to me – if it was her. And she was holding someone's hand.'

'Oh?'

'You'll say this is crazy. It looked like Michael.'

To my astonishment, Vivien smiled knowingly. She said, 'Really? Oh, I hope so!'

'You do?'

'Yes, yes, I do.' Her bright face expressed an inner transformation. I thought she was about to clap her hands.

'Now I'm really confused.'

'Poor Francis, you must be. Shall I tell you a little story?'

'I'm all ears.'

160

'Well, putting it crudely. Celia and Michael were lovers, then they fell out. I met him through her, you see.' She grimaced, laughed. 'It's all her fault. No, of course it isn't. But if you've seen them together and on friendly terms again, that's wonderful, I can't tell you how happy that makes me feel. All the time with Michael I've felt I was betraying Celia in some peculiar way. Now I'm free of that. It was horrid, I hated it.'

'I'm still in the dark. What's the nature of their relationship?'

'You mean now? Oh, it's platonic, bound to be. It was when Celia told him she was going to abstain from sex that he washed his hands of her and they broke up.'

'Did she think he wouldn't mind?'

'I've really no idea.'

'Now he's had second thoughts apparently.'

'So it seems.'

I sat digesting what she had told me, while tantalising smells of toasting bread wafted in from the kitchen. She called out, 'Turn on the TV if you like, I expect you want to see the news.'

'Why should I?'

'You're a man.'

It was a novelty to me, so I switched on. The neat packaging and presentation of other people's misfortunes at first fascinated and then repelled me. I switched off again. In the kitchen it was roomy enough to eat, and there was a table, but instead we sat side by side on the sofa and ate from our laps. 'Are you sure you don't want the TV?' I asked.

'No, it's you I want to hear, while I've got the chance.'

She asked if I was happy about going to Jake's place. 'Naturally I'm curious to meet him,' I said.

'I thought you might be.'

'That's at Chalk Farm.'

'Yes.'

We had a second coffee. When I attempted to wash up, she shooed me out of the kitchen. 'Later, not now. Come and talk to me.'

'What about?'

'Mind if I smoke?'

'Go ahead.'

She picked up a vintage tobacco tin. It looked pleasantly old and worn, the lettering rubbed off in places, the corners burnished. I admired it.

161

She nodded. 'Michael gave it to me.'

She began to roll a cigarette deftly, using only her right hand. By the grace of her movements, the lizard lick of her tongue along the glued edge and the way she struck the match, I guessed that the ritual was as soothing to the nerves as the smoking itself. It might be all illusion, I thought, but I envy it. The wobbly nervous machinery inside me was not yet under control, yet Vivien's collapse into tears already seemed like a dream.

'Do you smoke much?'

'Only in company as a rule. I like to have something for my hands to do.'

Somehow our mother came into the conversation. She said thoughtfully, 'I was eight when they told me. I suppose you knew that?'

'What?' I asked stupidly.

'When they broke the news about Margot not being my natural mother.'

'I had no idea you were as young as that.'

She urged me to describe our mother and I did my best to raise her from the dead. I ransacked my memory for anecdotes, crises, character-traits. Getting across the living reality of a person was even harder in words than it was in paint. I talked about her fear of authority, her anxiety about money, her thin figure, her scarlet blushes, her sallow complexion. As I talked she came closer, then retreated, as elusive in death as she had been in life. Vivien listened to the most trivial details with hunger in her eyes. I was pierced by a realisation that she could never know what I had known. With all her being she reached out for a parent she hadn't seen or heard, like someone eager for evidence of a maternal love she has only read about or heard spoken of, or witnessed in the lives of others.

Then by a lightning switch we moved from my mother and were back to Michael. This time I was the one asking for enlightenment. Vivien spoke without inhibition. Her free thinking was a revelation, and a reminder of the age gap between us. Without lifting an eyebrow she told me, 'There's a certain type of West Indian who enjoys having a white girl on his arm. He sees her as exotic. It's not necessarily sexual. They have a more relaxed life style than ours. Look at our pornography, we're drowning in filth. We've got sex in the head, we're obsessed with sex. For all that, you get the feeling there's not a lot of it about.

Jamaicans have a sexual experience when they dance, play their music, sing, eat their food, talk, it's all a lazy communal sex life, they're enjoying without strain or effort. Nothing personal in it at all, or it's truly personal, who knows?'

'Are you saying Michael is this type?'

'I wouldn't put him in any category. I'm only talking in general terms.'

We set off for Chalk Farm. On the way, Vivien explained about the Samuels' home, and the curious set-up, as she called it, which they had jointly decided upon. They had split their house in two. It was on three floors, and Jake occupied the first two floors. On the top floor Celia lived separately in a large room which she called her loft. In it – apart from a bathroom and toilet – was everything she needed for an independent existence. The bathroom was next door, and there was another below. She could enter and leave her accommodation by a steel fire escape which had been erected recently at her request. She and Jake met now and then downstairs for an evening meal. Otherwise they communicated by internal phone. It was agreed that he should only enter her domain if invited by her.

'So what does she do up there all day?'

'Lives. Writes, reads. Entertains her friends. Most mornings she gets out her bike from a garage in the garden and goes off to Swiss Cottage where she helps run an adventure playground. I believe that's where she met one of her squatter friends.'

Listening to my sister, I was reminded painfully of my withdrawal from Della, and of her acquiescence. But the two set-ups were fundamentally different, I reflected. Mine had evolved without thought, provisional and not divulged to anyone or admitted by ourselves, while theirs was it seems a civilised arrangement, decided in advance and carried out by deliberate acts of will. Underneath both, however, lay the same age-old problem of a man and woman failing to understand one another.

I asked, 'But now she's moving back to you?'

'Yes, so she said. She finds living in such close proximity to Jake intolerable now. All I hope is she doesn't change her mind again. An inability to reach a decision, isn't that a symptom of mental illness? What am I saying?'

'If it is, I'm ill permanently. I'd say it depends on how extreme the condition is.'

163

'Oh but it's sad. I feel for them both. They're my friends.'

'Isn't it going to be a strain tonight?'

'No, don't worry, we'll see them one at a time. Jake first, then upstairs to Celia. Crazy, isn't it?'

'The psychopathology of everyday life.'

'Is that a quote?'

'It's the title of a famous book.'

'Yes, who by?'

'Freud.'

'Yes, of course. Have you read it?'

Vivien looked sideways at me. I said with a smile, 'I've been too busy living it.'

At the house, Vivien raised her hand to press the bell-push and Jake opened the door to us. 'It's out of order,' he said, 'like everything else. Come in, come in. Welcome to the madhouse.'

Vivien was nursing a bottle of white wine in purple tissue paper. She handed it over. 'Let's think of something to drink to, Jake.'

'We're alive, that's something. So I keep trying to persuade myself.'

'This is Francis.'

'Hello. Your brother?'

'Yes.'

'He's as thin as you. It must run in the family. Does he eat enough?'

'Ask him.'

I said, 'When I remember.'

'Is he an absent-minded professor?'

'An artist.'

'I'm only joking. Celia told me she'd met you. Her voice came down from on high. These days the phone rings so rarely, I think it's God.'

He spoke wryly, with a bitter edge. I should have assumed from his name that Jake Samuels was a Jew, but in fact it only dawned on me gradually. Then I was prepared to like him at once. It was an instinct with me to idealise Jews, in the same way that I idealised Celts, Italians, Greeks, and the black originators of jazz. None of this had any foundation in reality, but was something generated by my repressed nature and the trail of indignities which have stemmed from it. In my youth, an almost pathological shyness threw me back on myself, making

164

me first of all a passionate reader, then a man mad about art. My hero worship of art heroes extended later to include anyone fortunate enough to possess the gift of intimacy I so desperately lacked. Jews, so I believed, were a mixture of the devout and the iconoclastic, the hot-blooded and the astute, but at all times they were intimate, like members of a close family. In my ignorance I embraced the whole race indiscriminately.

The fact is that Jake Samuels looked anything but Jewish. A man in his forties, his sparse hair was bright red, his skin freckled, his eyes blue. But his first words addressed directly to me were no disappointment. He said worriedly, like an intimate, 'I'm not very happy at the moment. How are you?'

I felt an urge to laugh. I was also delighted by his blend of seriousness and farce. Jake was tall, broad-shouldered, his face plump. In the midst of large lumpy features you came with surprise on a small curly mouth. His cumbersome physique contrasted oddly with the nimbleness of his mind. He wore gold-rimmed glasses, and spoke with an exactness of speech which one associates with the prissy person. If I had met him in other circumstances I might have thought him gay. He was at once flatteringly attentive and annoyingly self-absorbed. He gave off an aura of loneliness, and of someone who had formed the habit of constantly observing himself.

He disappeared, and came back with two kinds of cheese, one smoked, one flavoured with herbs, together with wine glasses and Vivien's bottle, now uncorked. 'I've forgotten the crackers,' he said snappily, and made another trip.

We sat around a circular coffee table made from a huge slab of pinkish grey marble. Our surroundings were tasteful. Lamps with big shades shone in all the corners, controlled from a dimmer switch. Jake got up and twiddled with it. 'That's better.' It was still light outside. Then I realised that the heavy curtains were half drawn. Prints on the walls were by Hockney and Kitaj, framed in white metal.

Vivien asked Jake why he wasn't eating cheese.

'I've got a weight problem,' he said fretfully, then shook his head and laughed.

'You're not fat,' Vivien protested

'I need to lose twenty pounds. I was a fat, unhappy child. It's true. I don't want to be a fat unhappy man.'

'How's the new job working out?'

'Fine. The head of department's a man who makes time for you. Not an intellect, but who cares? Most of my colleagues are pleasant, friendly. Yes, and kind. There's one though, I can't stand, a principal lecturer who seems to be afflicted with a persecution complex. That's all. Students the usual mixed bag. One, a mature student – a woman – has it in for me. Thinks I have it in for her. Says I treat her with condescension, won't let her speak freely. She's one of those people who hog the limelight out of a kind of compulsion and intimidate the nervous and timid, in other words the majority. One day I jumped on her, metaphorically speaking. She's now put in an official complaint.'

'Is that serious?'

His eyes sparked mischievously, as if for a moment he had forgotten his troubles. 'No, it's normal. Why should I put up with her nonsense? I never have before and I'm damned if I'm going to start now. Last week I ordered one of my students to leave the room if she wasn't prepared to participate with the others.'

'Another woman?'

'A girl this time. Why do you ask? Don't think I haven't wondered whether my bad temper isn't the result of frayed nerves. I'm sure that's so, but I let fly at males as well as females. I'm not a woman hater, Vivien. These days I'm on a short fuse, I admit it.'

'I do wish I could help in some way.'

'Nobody can. It's got to work itself out, or through, like an attack of shingles. I thought this arrangement would ease things, and what's happened? Things are even worse. I got all these alterations made, showed them to her, and she said, "It's intolerable to be under the same roof with you." Am I repulsive now or what? I can't stand much more.'

'Is she writing poetry?'

'I wouldn't know. It's forbidden to mention it. The last communication we had on the subject ended in disaster. She read out a beautiful poem about her father, the dark man in her life, and her love for him. I wasn't allowed to touch it, only listen. A tragic voice came out of her. This poem was quite something, an all-embracing lament, a dream of love that drew in everything, and I said why didn't she tackle something small-scale next, just for a change. As a challenge, I think I said. She flew into a rage. I was patronising her, I was saying she suffered from inflation, I was jealous, and so on and so forth.'

'But are you speaking to each other?'

He groaned aloud, drained his glass, stood up and sat down again. 'I tell you I'm going mad down here. The phone rang one night, it was her. She's an insomniac now, did you know? In the nicest voice she said she was a real pain in the ass, she understood what I was going through, I was right and she was wrong. She even made an attempt to explain what happened as a consequence of our lovemaking, her extinction as a person, her loss of self. I sat listening to this long involved monologue, feeling useful as an ear if nothing else. When she showed no sign of stopping, in fact she was now talking faster than when she started, I interrupted to ask if I could come up for an hour, half an hour, ten minutes, and she shrieked down the phone, "You spoil everything, you're impossible!" The line went dead.'

At that very moment, the phone rang. Jake whispered, 'It's her. She's clairvoyant, I'm convinced of it.'

He picked up the receiver and listened. 'Yes.' He hung up. 'She wants you to go up when you're ready. Are you ready?' His mouth twisted up in a painful smile.

'Oh, Jake.'

'Finish your wine first.'

As we got up to go, Jake said to me, 'My apologies. Let's have a real talk one day. I've become the world's biggest bore, the person of one obsession.'

He was looking into my face, though like many obsessed thinkers he had rarely done more than glance fleetingly at us. I answered promptly, without having to lie, 'I wasn't bored.'

'You're a kind man.'

'No, I'm interested. That's too callous a word, I'm sorry. You see I'm a monomaniac myself. I tried to find the word monomania in a dictionary once. Apparently it doesn't exist.'

'It exists,' Jake said grimly. 'Throw your dictionary away and buy another.'

I followed Vivien through the house and up thickly carpeted stairs towards the top of the building. Halfway there, she paused to issue a warning. 'Francis, try not to stray on to the subject of Celia's family if you can possibly help it.'

'Am I likely to?'

'Last night you did. That's why she was short with you.'

167

'I don't understand.'

'It's her father.'

'What is?'

'He's dead. He died tragically, less than two years ago. They found him in the garage, sitting in his car. He'd switched the engine on, and run a tube or something from his exhaust. Celia was there when they discovered him.'

'She actually saw him?'

'I'm not sure.'

We were on the top floor. Vivien put a warning finger to her lips. My stomach tightened. She banged on a blue door, and I heard a voice inside call out. She went in and I trooped after her.

The room we were in looked enormous. It was square. Celia wore a dark green dress, pinched in at the waist with a broad glossy belt. She stood by the window, which was open, smoking a thin cheroot. 'Do come in. Have a seat. I'll join you when I've finished this.'

At the far side of the room was a sofa bed, already pulled out and made up for sleeping, the sheet and duvet disarranged. An alcove was filled from floor to ceiling with books, mainly paperbacks. Towards the window against the wall was a cooker, then a porcelain sink and draining boards. A refectory table stood in the middle of the floor, on it a bowl of fruit, some newspapers, a typewriter. The hard chairs up at the table were painted Chinese red. There seemed no other seating.

We sat down like conspirators awaiting their leader. Conscious of Jake prowling about under our feet, tormented by God knows what, I wondered if we would just sit in silence mourning his plight. I was now identified with him to some extent. Celia came over and sat down with us and I eyed her warily. She said stiffly, to no one in particular, 'Would you like something to eat or drink? Sherry? Shall I make some tea?'

'We've been drinking wine,' Vivien said. She might have been speaking to a child.

'Oh, have you?'

'Celia you do look pale.'

'I've been asleep. I didn't sleep a wink last night.'

'Should we go?'

Celia gave a start. 'Whatever for? No, stay.' She managed a ghost of a smile. 'I'm rotten company.'

'Have you got any pills?'

'I took three. They didn't do anything. Then there was the noise outside.'

'What noise?'

'Cars, car doors, people screaming, laughter. I stuffed up my ears and I could still hear.'

'With your ear wax in?'

'Yes.'

I sat listening to a conversation in which I had no part. Passivity comes naturally to me. Even so, I felt unreal, overlooked in some abnormal way. Celia's poise was disturbing. Her tension was visible in the rigidity of her neck muscles. Her grey-green eyes were dilated and almost frenzied, like someone about to crack. Yet she sounded as she had sounded the night before, perfectly in control, coldly knowledgeable, rather amused.

I began to speculate. Was the terror I read in her eyes brought on by the discovery of a desert of nothingness inside herself? Was that what ailed her? I wondered this because I had known it myself in Southwark, living through the desert left by Maggie's departure. I fled from that into a fury of work, creating in the process one slimy uterus of paint after another. One is rescued by forgetfulness. I forgot I was deserted, suffering a suspension of life, I forgot how sterile I'd become. I was living actively again and with pleasure. I hadn't ground to a halt, failures were of no importance, death didn't exist.

Celia said, 'I hope you heard illuminating things downstairs.'

'Not particularly,' Vivien said.

'All about me, no doubt.'

'More about Jake, as I remember.'

'And now you feel frightfully sorry for him.'

'Celia, I did before.'

'I've castrated him spiritually. Even you think so.'

'Nonsense!'

'Men do like to be treated badly, isn't that strange?'

'Do they, though?'

Celia said, 'Ask Francis, he's a man.'

'Perhaps they do,' I said without thinking, perplexed by my own words. I had no firm theories about man in the plural.

Vivien took me up. 'Why?'

'Oh, it confirms their worst suspicions,' I said lightly.

'About women?'

'Naturally. Then at least they aren't in the dark. They fear that most of all.'

169

Celia began to speak about things which bore no relation to what had been said before. Suddenly she was saying, 'I woke up one morning when I was a young girl, and I had this obscure rage, impelling me to quarrel, smash things up, get into trouble. Until that moment I'd been a model child. My father adored me. I sat on his knee like a doll. I thought he was God, literally.'

'How old were you?' Vivien asked uneasily.

'Fifteen. I liked to play with make-up. I was good with it. If I took care, I could pass for twenty. Anyway, I thought, I know, I'll be a prostitute for a few hours, but how? That was the most disgusting thing I could think of. Eventually I did.'

'You did what? Stop acting the goat – '

'I didn't think you'd believe me.'

'Of course I don't believe you! You're in a funny mood tonight, aren't you? Why don't you lie down and try to sleep?'

'I *can't*.'

'All right, be perverse.'

'No, I'll shut up. You talk.'

Nervously, as if torn between a need to humour her and to call her bluff, Vivien said, 'I'm curious now. I want to hear this story.'

'Are you sure?'

'No. Yes!'

'Once I'd made my mind up, suddenly I wasn't panicky about life any more, I was excited. I've thought since that it was a girl called Lynda who made it possible, but it wasn't, it was my fear of boredom. Have you ever been so utterly bored that it frightens you, when the thought of an hour to be got through is like an eternity, and a whole day stretches out like a lifetime? When you know there's nothing, absolutely nothing you want to do. I suppose solitary confinement must be like that. But in that case you're forcibly prevented from doing anything. To find nothing in yourself to do is much, much worse. You stare into this empty cupboard which is you. You've simply condemned yourself to stop living.'

'Who was this Lynda?'

'I met her in a Wimpy bar. Unlike me she was brimming with absurd hope, yet she seemed about to fall to bits. Whenever I saw her it was the same – that's how she was. Half destroyed, yet always bouncing back. I got to know her. She made a terrific impression on me. She was rough, bright, game for anything, not stupid. She had hilarious tales to tell of her experiences at the hotel where she'd once worked as a chambermaid. She made you double up with her stories. She knew things. What men were after, what they were prepared to pay for. Corruption to her was just a fact of life she accepted. I thought I could be like her, learn from her how to survive, be as hopeful as her. What I wanted to do really was apprentice myself to her.'

'Celia, you little idiot, I love you! Is that all?'

'Would you like me to confess everything?'

'Only if you want to.'

'I don't know what I want. Lynda took me one day to this house in the red light district where she lived. A group of prostitutes operated from there, run by some man, though I never set eyes on him. One Saturday I turned up by arrangement in my gear and they let me go out to a customer. They sidled up to the house after nightfall and stopped their cars under the street lamp. I wore a white skirt under my mac, to stay pure. Isn't that touching?'

'I don't believe you again!'

'Would I lie to you?'

'I'm not sure. Don't be hurt, but I believe you're capable of deceiving others, never yourself.'

'Vivien, really. Well well.'

'I think you're trying to torment me. Am I being put to some sort of test?'

'What can you mean?'

'No, all right. Tell us some more. You're out to shock us, aren't you, with this nonsense. Or it's something you've written especially to degrade us.'

A little smile came and went on Celia's lips. 'There's no more to tell. I got in the next car that drove up. Then I knew I'd made a terrible mistake. How do you act, what do you say? The man was scared, he was more scared than me. It was a new car, smelling of leather and metal. I can smell it now. Men are such bluffers. He cleared his throat several times, I could see his Adam's apple working. Lynda, the liar, had told me how simple it would be. My body was a mass of contradictions, complexities. On top of that I was a fraud. He might kill me when he found out. It must be strange being a man, having to get rid of something, get something into you. Afterwards he talked, and lit cigarettes for us, like on the films. In a way it was exactly as Lynda had said. Men do what you want. You have to tell them, and they do it. "They expect it, see?" '

It came as a shock to hear Lynda's voice with its northern accent issuing from Celia's mouth.

Vivien wasn't amused. 'Is that the truth or isn't it?'

'Lynda was. I couldn't have invented her. Never have met anyone so disorganised. The emotional mess she churned around in – I used to ask myself, did she manufacture it or go looking? Did it just descend on her?'

'So you didn't get in the car?'

'I did. Then bolted. Chickened out, as Lynda would say. That's the rotten truth.'

'I believe you now.'

'Because I fail at everything, I know.'

'No!'

Celia said bitingly, 'It was despicable. I wanted to sink to the bottom, don't you see, then I might have been Lynda's equal. I didn't feel the slightest bit besmirched by the idea, that's the point. There was no need for the white skirt. I even remember feeling elated, stumbling on this ancient secret.'

'What secret?'

'I was in possession of something men wanted, and handing it over for a price was known as prostitution. How simple, I thought, how right! When I became Jake's student and he discerned qualities in me, I loved only clothes. I was a poor student, my grant went nowhere, so I fell in love with his readiness to buy me skirts and boots and blouses. Boutiques were forever sucking me in, I was addicted. I buzzed in through the open doorways and saw the pollen, racks of flowery open things everywhere. Pop music played, I was in paradise till I came out and the drab squalid world hit me. I don't see it as cynical at all, my attitude.

'Then I got sick of my addiction, I hated myself for it, for the abject weakness, the endless craven yearning for pretty things. Knowledge was the next price. Jake paid for me in knowledge. He bought me loads of books, he spent hours of his time tutoring me. I've sucked up all the knowledge I need, now it's solitude I demand from him. I told him I'd have to abstain from sex, it was a diversion of energy. He agreed, resentful at first but then admiring. This latest move of mine he interprets in terms of ethics. On the contrary, there's nothing moral about it, or about me or anything I do. I think I'm essentially an amoral person. He's fixed up this top floor for me to be solitary in, self-contained, so why can't I accept my ideal situation? It's all *him*, that's why, paid for by him. In his mind I'm still his. Well, I'm not. I've given up having sex with men, but as I see it I'm still his prostitute. That's intolerable. I intend to give up prostituting because there's nothing else I want. That's why I have to leave here.'

Throughout this monologue I had been sneaking glances at Vivien, who sat motionless, on her face an expression that for some reason reminded me of my mother, a woman so anxious to please everyone. Yet Vivien was in many ways fearless, calm. Celia looked at us both in turn. She began to laugh uncertainly, artificially. The cracked high note made me cringe back inside myself.

'Vivien said, 'What's funny? Us?'

'Would you like to hear how I was raped by my father at the age of seven?'

'No, I've heard enough. Shut up, Celia.'

'It *might* have happened.'

'Yes, and it might not.'

'Or I could be out of my mind.'

Vivien said urgently, 'Celia, are we friends or aren't we?'

'Oh, I don't know. Who'd want me for a friend, I'm nothing, everything I touches goes bad.'

Leaning forward, Vivien took hold of Celia's hand. 'You've got no choice and neither have I. We *are* friends. Do you understand what I'm saying? We're friends and that's that. It's happened.'

Without letting her eyes leave the other's face for an instant, she raised Celia's fingers to her lips and kissed them fervently. Celia seemed unaware of what was happening. She sat staring at Vivien's head with a frozen expression. Then I saw that she was trembling uncontrollably. 'I'm ashamed, I'm so ashamed!' she called out suddenly in a stricken voice.

Vivien looked furious, then anguished. 'No, you aren't, you mustn't be. What are you saying?'

'I can't get into life. I've got stuck. It's horrible. Do you understand?'

Vivien patted her friend's hand distractedly. 'Don't say any more, stop thinking, you're only wearing yourself out with this despair, aren't you?'

We sat on in silence. Celia's lips were moving but no words came out. I'm at a seance, it's ridiculous, I'll get up and go in a minute, I thought. But the logic of my curiosity overcame my pride. As though to solve a riddle or unlock some secret that was vital to me, I sat where I was.

Then Celia smiled, radiantly self-possessed all of a sudden. I was flabbergasted by the transformation. She said, 'Yes, I am. Now I'm going to read you a new poem.'

'Wonderful,' Vivien said. She flashed me a look of triumph mingled with immense relief.

Sitting there, struggling to understand and believe the evidence of my eyes, I thought, This is a fairy tale, not a nightmare at all. I tried to see in Celia the friend Vivien had first described, an angel in need of help and protection. What I saw was a rude, hard, impossible female, out to dominate by means of weakness, dominant as only a born victim can be.

Celia pulled out a white sheet of paper from the typewriter. At that moment, the internal phone rang once. She shrugged her shoulders contemptuously and began to read. Her thin voice took on astonishing resonance. It rang out, rapt as a sibyl's. I listened amazed, like a person being tricked, enchanted by the sound and yet unable to grasp or make sense of anything.

Back again at Vivien's, I said I would probably return home next day. She seemed preoccupied and didn't answer. As she made no reference to the evening either, I took it that she was unwilling, or else too worried to confide in me. For my part, I felt I had walked miles through London in a huge circle and got nowhere. Even though I had been alone a good deal of the time, the sense of oppression that crowds bring me was always present. I needed to get right away from people. At the thought of my work waiting, unsullied because not yet grappled with and spoiled, I felt better, light-hearted, as if the far-off unstirring countryside had suddenly moved its irresistible purity nearer.

That night I fell asleep and dreamed of a woman who was bitter and depressed. She kept repeating in a whisper of despair, 'What am I going to do?' The woman was a stranger. Vivien sat in the room, but with no words to say. I realised I was observing myself, like someone in an audience watching an actor. To blot out the unanswerable question which was driving me frantic I got down on all fours barking and howling deep in my throat. The woman fell to her knees and joined me. She climbed on my back and rode me like a horse triumphantly, her face blazing with weird power. Watching, I saw that she was cured, but at the cost of my freedom. I woke up making choking sounds in my throat, twisting as though to throw off a burden which had become unbearable. My heart beat violently and I was perspiring.

The room where I lay on the sofa was pitch black. I saw the the bluish light of dawn begun to appear through a chink in the curtains. A car door banged, an engine started up, the car drove away. Then I must have dropped off again. Vivien was shaking me gently. She bent to say goodbye.

'Will you write?'

'Yes.'

'Are you just saying that?'

'No, I promise.' My voice sounded croaky. 'I want us to see more of each other.'

'So do I, we must. That's settled, then.'

She smiled down. I wanted to lift my arms to her, but felt drained, whether by the night's events or the evening before I had no idea. Anyway, we weren't accustomed to embraces. She hurried off, I heard her steps, doors, then her footsteps outside on the pavement going away. In the dead silence a sadness took hold of me, then a nameless grief. Lying there enfeebled, unequal to life, I thought of my mother with deep longing. With an angry movement I forced myself to sit and then stand up. As I went to the kitchen and filled the kettle, a child in me still mourned for something irrevocably lost.

On the way to the station for the journey back to Cornwall, I stopped, entered a phone box and called Maggie's number. When she answered, asking at once if it was me and where I was ringing from, I said guiltily, 'Falmouth.' Otherwise she may have asked me to visit. What a temptation that would have been! I though that by telling one lie I could avoid the necessity of several. Then I was startled to hear her say, with obvious relief, 'Oh, Wes, you sound just round the corner. I couldn't have done with you, not now, not the way I'm feeling at the moment.'

'Is anything wrong?'

'Not so you'd notice. Anyhow, I can't explain on the phone.'

'Then how else am I likely to know? Maggie, please. Is it money trouble?'

I heard her draw a deep breath on the other end of the line. 'I'm pregnant again.'

'Well, congratulations.'

'Are you being funny?'

'I'm sorry. You don't want another one. Why, don't you like children?'

'I can't say I'm mad about them.'

I shook my head. It was all I could do not to burst out laughing at myself. Whenever I fantasized about a new heaven on earth I always enthroned Maggie for its queen, the natural goddess and earth mother, her heart ruling her head, her instincts paramount. One fact over the phone and all the hocus-pocus was blown to bits. Kill the ideal, a Chinese sage had once said.

'Well, that's all right,' I mumbled.

'No, it's not.'

'Tell me why.'

'Not on the phone. It's personal. Somebody could be listening.'

'How the devil could they? I haven't come through an operator.'

A loud clicking began. Someone else's conversation crossed momentarily with ours.

'Wes, is that you?'

'Yes, I'm here.'

'Isn't it funny, after all this time I still miss you.'

'Same here, but never mind about that. Listen, Maggie, you could have an abortion.'

'It's too late. I couldn't anyway. If I killed it, Gregory would kill me.'

'How is Gregory?'

The line started to crackle and fade. I thought I heard, 'Ask his mistress,' but it didn't seem possible. Maggie's voice was now terribly far off.

'This line's awful – what was that? Speak up! Maggie, put your phone down and I'll ring again.'

The line cleared. 'No, you can't, somebody's come in. Goodbye.'

18

September came and went. October began, sharp with frosts in the early morning, then each day rounding like a fruit. One after another the days bloomed, soft and still, like the same beautiful day repeating itself. A full moon, yellow as butter, touched the field hugely one evening and then slowly diminished as it ascended. I stood outside the mill and watched. Going indoors again, I found I had reached a decision. No doubt it had been ripening in darkness for some time, no more mine than was the moon I had just left.

I sat quietly, and considered the practicalities of the situation. I told myself it was time to go, time for a change. I needed the stimulus of a city – though not London, never London – if my work was to take off and develop. Behind all this rationalising was Vivien, my thoughts dwelling on her, her spirit pressing against my consciousness and refusing to go away. Not that I wanted her to stop insisting. Any move I made would have to satisfy the aching wish to draw closer to her.

Providentially, I bumped into Lotte soon afterwards in Falmouth. Lotte was Polish, married to a Cornish boatbuilder. She owned an upstairs teashop in the High Street. Trudging up there for a cup of tea one vacant afternoon I had been accosted by this warmly gushing, rosy-cheeked woman. That was months ago. Now, on the narrow pavement being jostled by shoppers, she voiced my thoughts. Though I hadn't realised, the whole country was caught up in the convulsions of a property boom which accelerated daily. 'The gazumpers, they are having a field day,' Lotte cried.

As though reluctant to know more, I asked what that had to do with me. The uproar of the last removal day still lingered in the memory, and that was with Della in charge of it.

'Goodness, Francis, your gorgeous old mill would go like a shot. Within twenty-four hours I'd like to bet. And for at least double the price you paid for it.'

'Even in the state it's in?'

'Why, of course! Places like yours in this county are at an absolute premium. Are you telling me you didn't know?' Her business acumen was outraged, and at the same time she thought it hilarious. 'You'll have people falling over themselves, fighting each other on your doorstep probably.'

'The English don't do such things, Lotte.'

'You'd be surprised, my word!'

'Sounds like a scrum I could do without.'

She hooted with laughter. 'Silly man, you don't have to be here. Clear off and let an agent handle it. That's what I do. They see to everything. This is our fifth move. Or I could do the necessary for you, gladly. Now there's an offer!'

Alarmed, I fended her off with uncertainties of various kinds. The next time she spotted me she ran up and launched straight into the subject. 'Don't forget my offer.' I thanked her, saying I would definitely think about it. 'Why does property excite people?' I asked myself.

Feeling trapped, I confided in Guy Franklin, and wished I hadn't. He fairly jumped at the chance of becoming my unpaid assistant. Soon the prospect of my move absorbed his young energies to an extent I hadn't foreseen. He came back from art school one day with the news that a potter and his family, friends of a friend of his, had put their warehouse in Plymouth up for sale. Guy suggested a trip down in his old van to view the place. That weekend we were on our way. All I said was, 'I suppose if I could get it cheap enough, that would offset my living expenses for the next year or two.' Guy took my words for an unequivocal yes. He sprang outside to tinker with his van as if he would have liked to tear down the road that very moment.

Why was I so beset by doubts? In the city I longed for nature, in the countryside I missed people. Tranquility didn't seem to suit my nervy disposition. I wouldn't miss the country, only the country of my lost routines, I assured myself. In the early days, before we were so at logger-heads, Della would call me an old stick-in-the-mud. For her that was coming close to a term of affection. Once, in an access of sentimentality, she had thrown her arms around me impulsively. I was deeply ashamed, as if implicated in some grievous misunderstanding.

To be isolated in a remote spot and free from distractions, one could fall prey to strange lusts. One fantasy, to which I yielded now and then in bed, was of being pursued by bacchantes. In a mad painting or two I had continued the chase with a brush and pursued the resulting turmoil, depicting a white moon-faced hairless man, his arms elongated, sausage fingers and toes grabbing at air, tipped into a green bath and the vermilion and blue females piling after me, soft and fluid and delicious as warm scented water.

I sat beside Guy as we drove down for a quick inspection of the vacated warehouse. In my hand I held the agent's leaflet. It drew attention to the advantages for any purchaser of 'the historic Barbican, wherein this spacious and unusual property is situated, only a stone's throw from the Mayflower Steps and the Elizabethan House'.

'I said, 'Thanks for the lift. Does Yvonne mind?'

Guy grinned broadly. 'She's used to me taking off. I like to get out from under her feet when she does the housework.'

'She's a good wife, is she?'

'The best.'

I knew this was sentimental nonsense and meant little. But even as something in me mocked Guy's platitudes I felt the common man's desire to be the family man he was, enjoying the experiences most people had. An anger against my fate rose up and thickened my throat. Why had so much been demanded and so much denied me? What choice did I have? Were the consolations of art in any way comparable to these everyday joys? Yet here was a man with his feet seemingly in both worlds. I glanced meanly at him, not wishing to change places but as if seeing him for the first time. Guy loved driving. He bent eagerly to the task, and the journey rewarded him. He was given purpose, he steered, he was his own man. We sped on, each with our secret regrets and expectations.

As we got nearer, I tried to anticipate my feelings, should I actually move here. I thumbed through the pages of the road map to convince myself that I would be on the same coast, by the same sea. I was not convinced. Maps were imaginary charts, like paintings. What I did know was what I'd known already, before even starting out. There was a luminous Cornish sea living inside me. And I could look forward to a city, and I would have shortened the distance between me and Vivien. I was not really convinced. I missed something in the world, and though Vivien was not wholly it, she represented a direction towards which something in my heart sought to turn and align itself.

We arrived in the old quarter of the city. Streets narrowed and became cobbled, leading down to the harbour. Alleys ran off to the right, stone staircases rising steeply, with tall buildings overhanging, some scabby and others freshly painted in pastel

179

colours. Shops for tourists were next door to ship chandlers and little bakeries. A post office also selling knick-knacks had racks stuffed with picture postcard views of the real world just outside.

The initial view of the building for sale, as we stood staring up at it from the other side of Basket Street, filled me with dismay. I gaped at dingy rows of bricks and accusing dead window lights, the two right at the top reflecting a sky coiling ominously like grey intestines. The place loomed too high for us to see the state of the roof.

I tried to joke. 'What was it, a factory?'

Guy, uninvolved with the need to make a decision, took a cheerful view. He pointed out that the facades on either side had their brick skins gaily painted, to the left a shell pink and on the right pale blue. 'It wouldn't look so grim, Frank, if you gave it a slop of white. With black window frames.'

'Paint me while you're about it, I feel starved of colour.'

'You look a bit pale.' Guy shot a funny look of concern at my face. 'Have you seen a ghost up there?'

'It was probably you saying I ought to paint the place. Suddenly I was up there, balancing on an enormous ladder. I got a touch of vertigo.'

Guy laughed. The huskier of the two, he enfolded me briefly within a comradely arm. 'Fancy a drink and a sit down? The pubs are open.'

'No, I'm fine now. Let's take a look.'

'Great.'

I took the large rusty key, with the agent's tag attached, out of my pocket and opened the door. 'After you.'

Bursting with impatience, Guy shot in with a childish eagerness. I followed doubtfully. Inside, I was glad of his chatter, wondering if I had ever known, at any age, that kind of headlong optimism. I felt instead the caution of an old dog who wonders if the next thing will be a kick or a caress. I stood hesitant and wavering for a moment, feeling crushed by the weight of silence that descended. It was like entering a sepulchre, or some great upended monument. What did it commemorate? I was surely out of my mind to be even considering it.

Guy of course had no such foreboding. He shot to and fro like a squirrel, heartlessly exhilarated on the uncluttered floors, burrowing rapidly upwards from one storey to another. 'Hey, this is great, this is terrific,' I could hear him bubbling to himself. 'You could really do things with this, wouldn't you say so?'

Certainly it was not anything which could be said to resemble a house. Unlike the mill, it wouldn't have been feasible to convert it into even the semblance of one. But was a house what I wanted? Were the potter and his family happy here? And even if they were, was the world of the happy for me? Apparently they had lived in the gaunt draughty spaces above ground floor. Down on street level were shop windows and a glazed door and shelving, no doubt for the display of pots.

I clambered up crude baulks of timber stairs twisting about in lighthouse fashion. Ships' rope from the chandler on the quay served as handrails, looped through massive cast iron rings. Where the previous occupants had lived *en famille* the high lengthy area had been split in two by a partition. Up on the next floor was a bathtub, plumbed in to hot and cold but stranded on bare boards in open space.

The floor above this one had been a workshop, judging by the clay splashes everywhere, the pottery shards in corners. Bony sash windows overlooked the street gully at the front. To the rear were the slummy sunless backs of condemned workshops which stood empty, a vista of corrugated iron, rusted or in holes, smashed windows, rotten wood and festooned gutters.

We came across no fireplaces. This didn't surprise me. After all, these had once been commercial premises. The floor divided for living and sleeping sported a stainless steel sink jammed up against the back window sill. Above it, a wooden rack made of unpainted dowelling was screwed to the wall. It hung there like an art object. A gleaming futuristic electric cooker waited in the corner, so robot-like that it looked capable of propelling itself on its castors.

I followed Guy stiffly, objecting silently to his exuberance, resisting everything because it was strange. 'Don't you like it?' he kept asking. 'Look at all this space. Fantastic!'

Rebuked by his shining eyes, his health, I fell back on facts. 'The rates are heavier than I'm paying now. If the roof leaked, how would you get a builder up there? I'm not happy about tall buildings.'

Try as I might, I was unable to throw off an instant dislike of walls scarred and fingerprinted by hands other than my own. On the top floor – which Guy had already christened 'the penthouse' – I was woefully affected by the melancholy wash of autumn sunlight. Nevertheless, I padded submissively on the accumulated dust over to the rear window. Guy struggled, swore, got the window open at last, then hooted with delight at a vision he glimpsed of a grey sliver of sea. 'A sea view, look!' He was craning his neck, his head fully out.

'But I've got the sea where I am now – the open sea.'

'Can you see it though, Frank?'

'Do I want to? I know where to find it.'

'You said once that being near the sea inspired you.'

'Inspired? Did I throw that word about so lightly?'

'Now you're having me on.'

'No, I don't remember.'

'I do.'

'Then my memory's going. A first sign.'

Guy roared with laughter. 'Another reason for being here. Otherwise, just think, if you can't see the sea you might forget where you last saw it. Then what would you do?'

'Very funny.'

A shiver ran through my shoulders. Della would have known instantly what to do, how to get rid of these ghosts. Get a stiff broom! This echoing four-chambered cave was someone else's discarded womb. I would have preferred the skittering of mice to the children's feet I might imagine hearing if I came to live here. Drifting around stunned in the wake of Guy's enthusiasm, I thought grimly that I would have to commit a form of matricide before I was properly installed.

What would Della have said? She relished nothing more than a fresh start, clearing the decks for action. 'Simplify your life,' she used to exhort me, 'organize it, make it serve you.' This whizz-bang philosophy undoubtedly worked for her. I was never sufficiently clear as to my direction. If I wanted to annoy her I would say that such an approach didn't suit the effete English, so slothful and evasive behind their veils of progress and fair play.

'You mean lazy.'

'Yes, and degenerate. America is full of children masquerading as adults. You don't understand degeneracy. Corruption's a mere game from one of your fairgrounds.'

Her patriotism was easily inflamed. 'What's more corrupt,' she said once. 'than your public school system?'

'That's not what corrupts us.'

'What does?'

'Mother love.'

'You should know, honey.'

'I beg your pardon?'

'From what I can gather,' she said darkly.

Now, while Guy Franklin dived downstairs again, kicking up dust as he went, I wandered up and down disconsolately, asking under my breath, 'How, how can I live here?' I was on the point of adding, 'What would my mother have thought?' but suppressed it, remembering the age I had reached.

19

Two years later, I was still unused to the change. I still stepped through the glazed and frosted front door and then was shocked to find myself on pavement, in a cobbled street, wondering stupidly for the hundredth time if it was all a mistake. It took so long to grow into a new place – perhaps more time than I could spare. I still marvelled at my decision, and for the hundredth time dubiously congratulated myself, sometimes forgetting that I had reached the point where shortage of funds had made a move from Cornwall inevitable.

Now I was beginning to like it, but in secret, not admitting so in my consciousness, as if aware of resistances yet to be overcome in dark corners of myself. The chief test, whether I could feel sufficiently at ease – I didn't ask to be happy – to do continuous work, had been passed. The evidence littered the top floor, where I had established a studio and living room.

Deciding where to paint had been an old agony revisited. I usually solved it, over a period of weeks or months, by a process of trial and error, moving from one temporary site to another. When it came, the solution seemed to include all the other changes in one act of Providence. This time I was helped by something which Keats recognised as negative capability. A sense of emptiness which came and went, afflicting me at times like a spiritual toothache, ruled out any thought of duplicating that void by the suspension of an empty floor over my head. After fruitless hours of dithering, tramping up and down, standing in doorways with my head cocked to sniff at atmospheres, I moved up there, as permanent as I would ever be. It felt right. Perched under the eaves with the gulls, hearing their heavy landings on the slates and their frequent ugly screams, I reasoned that I would be immune from tourists and visitors alike.

Below my feet, little had changed. The chaos of moving day, later overcome by inertia, was now petrified. What remained was a wasteland, a deep bin littered with packing cases and old newspapers, a storage hold. Letting myself in through the glassy lower regions, I left behind the ghostly vestiges of shop and clambered up to my eyrie. In my imagination I was the one surviving tenant in a doomed and shattered building awaiting the *coup de grâce* of the demolition men. This was patently false; the structure was perfectly sound. I lived in a city section of historic importance, protected by a preservation order. All the same I encouraged the fiction, for the sake of the pictures and composition-studies it produced. Sometimes it is necessary to live one's inventions. Scores of recent drawings came under the heading of 'rooms'. Many of them were of caverns jagged with hard-edged objects flung together pell-mell, as if a bomb had exploded and the windows had caught the full force of the blast. An almost human electric cooker kept reappearing, and sometimes an effigy-cat stalking along a moonlit ledge, frozen at the sight of an upside-down wicker chair brandishing a black oval.

At the start I had gone through a period of desolation, unable to lift a brush or even stay long enough in the place to do so. For company I was driven to unearth an old Bush radio, its plastic back cover buckled from when the set had fallen on to the hot plate of the Aga. I clicked the sound on, off, then on again, hating the babble and not fit to face the silence. Music, with its emotional excesses, was just as bad, a tormenting reminder of what I had forfeited in order to live my own life.

I went out a lot. The salt water lapping in the old harbour and the smell of mackerel from the fish dock usually drew me by the nose in that direction. I roamed the alleys and cobbled streets, sat in the local cafes, the pubs, keeping well clear of the shopping centre a quarter of a mile to the west, with its windy new thoroughfares like landing strips, its chain stores crammed with goods I had no intention of buying. Each time I returned I half dreaded, half hoped to find some mysterious silent female installed who had arrived for the express purpose

184

of civilising things. Who in God's name did I have in mind?

Seeking a bigger area to wander in, I walked up towards Tinside and along the foreshore on spring evenings. I liked to walk close to the rails, staring out in the direction of the breakwater. Family groups, as I skirted them, taunted me without knowing it, creating pictures from bygone years that I thought I had repudiated. I passed by with my pangs of envy, which I pretended, for my pride's sake, were more intense than their ordinary pleasures. If to be an artist was to live twice, and art a means of preventing time from slipping away, was this better than a conventionally rounded life, even allowing for the cruel world as it was and all its limitations? Then one evening, as if to keep me ploughing the same lonely furrow, I caught sight of a small girl, wailing and sobbing in a frenzy of unhappiness. Her father, his red face congested with anger, aimed ugly flailing slaps at her bare legs. Tearing herself free, she ran howling in my direction. Her wild misery struck at my heart.

I went several times to position myself against the rails just beyond the Royal Western Yacht Club and its white flagstaff, gazing down on warm afternoons at the curved plinth and inviting yellowish rocks of the Lion's Den, a spot reserved for male bathers. Of course I had a painting in mind. I forgot to bear in mind that my intense scrutiny might be misinterpreted. One day a gang of youths and girls passed close behind me, nudging and grinning. Hearing giggles, I twisted my head round. A strong breeze blew away the words I only half caught. A prowling ice-cream van let loose a jangle of canned music. The youngsters were going towards the harbour, probably to the amusement arcade. They shoved one another, laughed, broke up and formed again. I gave them a few minutes and then followed, cutting off to the left by a seaman's bethel and coming out in Basket Street very near to where I lived.

On my way upstairs, soothed by a quiet that stirred around me, alive and welcoming – yet I had wanted to get away from it only an hour before – I thought of the room above my head as a snug nest. Like a gull, I drifted about on air currents, drifted back, picking over whatever I had found for my eyes to feed on, as birds feed their bellies. I stopped halfway and peered into the tarnished mirror in my make-do kitchen, as if to catch unawares what those youths might have seen. Who was this sorry-looking specimen? I found a smile creeping on to my mouth and wiped it

185

off, touching the greying stubble of the artist-tramp who glared back defensively at me. Deciding to clean myself up, I turned on the hot tap. The water was tepid. I boiled a kettle and had a shave, unearthed a clean shirt and a pair of unstained trousers and in a few minutes was diving out again for a haircut, before the resolve weakened.

Turning my back on the harbour I followed the twist of the street towards the town. As I walked I sniffed up the various smells from doorways. I went past an antiquarian bookshop, a print shop, the distillery where sloe gin was made, a fruit stall, a cafeteria that was also a store, selling everything from sheepskins to backscratchers, then turned right and climbed uphill. As often happened when I decided to do something purposeful, I was moving too fast. I slowed down at the Golden River, a Chinese restaurant I sometimes used for a late supper if I had forgotten to eat during the day. I preferred Indian at the Khyber to Chinese food, but it was too far to go. Also I liked the impersonality of the Chinese waiters.

At the top of this hilly street, on the very brink of the city centre whirlpool I habitually avoided, I opened the peeling brown door of what looked from the outside to be a squalid little hairdressing salon, of the kind familiar to me from my childhood. The interior was in fact remarkably clean and neat.

Sitting down to wait, I examined the mail gathered up from my doormat as I left. Apart from an airmail envelope, containing only a scrawled message on the back of a picture postcard, there was one proper letter. This was from my London accountant. He wanted to know how I was managing to survive on virtually no income.

The postcard was from Della. Six months must have elapsed since she last wrote. I looked again inside the envelope, wondering if there might be a cheque to help tide me over. Did I really hope for miracles? It was in any case a preposterous thing to expect. No, nothing. I deserved nothing, I thought, and that's what I've got. Before absorbing the message I took in the picture, foolishly searching in it for something of special significance. Why this particular painting? It showed Manet's *Dejeuner sur l'herbe*, the black, grey and brown rabbinical men gathered in the woodland clearing, the hamper of food, tablecloth, the decorative stream where a girl paddled and hoisted up her skirts. In the foreground the white nude, vivid

186

as a magnesium flare, had about as much sex as a mushroom, I decided. Could that be the message?

The words scribbled over the back in thick black jabs of the pen, said,

'Dear Francis, no doubt about it, I am ten times more energetic and hopeful here. Guess I'll always be an unregenerate barbarian. Autumn was superb – best time to be in New York. Winter went fifteen below. Waiting for a cab it nearly froze your pom-poms off. Is it spring where you are? In Cornwall I could never tell the difference between one season and another. I have no concrete news. Hurdles insurmountable in England are obstacles no longer, now I've regained my natural rhythm. Enjoying a slow unfolding as I establish contact with resources I thought lost for keeps. Peace and joy, Della.'

Two men and a mother with her child sat waiting on the row of hard chairs. There were two cutters, one a young woman from the ladies' salon next door who was helping out. As my turn approached I began to hope I would get the woman; she seemed without patter. But my luck was no better here than it had been for several days running up in my studio dust-heap. I thought, I must go back again to that bathing place, I haven't seen enough, the alchemy is held back. An over-ambitious 'Lion's Den' would have to be scraped off for the fourth time, or else ditched altogether. I had started in too much fear and been premature. It was like a sexual excitement which became anxiety, then a compulsion to act and get rid of the fear. Joy was lost, and with it the alchemy.

'Right you are, sir.'

The breathy, unctuous barber settled me in the chair, lagging the gap around my neck with those long wads of cotton wool I particularly loathed. Was it the cotton I hated or the man's horny fingers, prodding and insistent? Soon the same interrogation started up that I had experienced before.

'You don't work then on Saturdays.'

'No,' I said.

'Not a shop assistant then?'

'No.'

'Tradesman?'

'That's right.'

'Whereabouts is that?'

'Here and there. I work for myself.'

'Self-employed.'

'Yes.'

'Like me.'

'That's right. I can please myself.'

'Of course you can, yes. And give yourself an afternoon off now and then.'

'You've got it.'

'What's your line exactly? If you don't mind my asking.'

'Painter.' I saw in the mirror that I had swallowed my lips.

'Very nice. Bet that keeps you busy. No shortage of work there.'

'No.'

'I've got a nephew does painting and decorating, in his spare time mind.'

'Ah yes.'

'Not a professional like yourself.'

'No.'

'Anybody working for you, or on your own are you?'

'Single-handed.' Improvising a private joke, I added, 'All my own work.'

The man scissoring away at the back of my neck broadened his Devon accent. 'Lovely jaarb. Nice to be independent and that.'

'It is,' I said.

Socially acceptable on the outside at least, I sat, in my freshly barbered state, in one of the wooden shelters on the Hoe provided for holidaymakers and the retired. It was the following day. In fact the view from here was rather humdrum. The rough bulk of Drake's Island lay directly in front and below, though I was not looking at it, or past, or anything. It was a fine, imperceptibly blossoming May evening. Springtime trees and shrubs at a distance combined with flowers, gauzy clouds and a restless breathing sea to intoxicate the atmosphere, as if a vast conspiracy was under way. I was feeling strangely happy.

I was in a queer, almost truculent state of mind. The morning post had brought news of another sale to Marshall Walder, who was now converted to perversities of Cornish origin, a phase of mine the gallery owners were still regretting. That was one triumph. The other, more dubious, was a typically flamboyant letter from Pru Woodruff. All the same it was warming to hear that she had acquired my 'Nettles and Arums' and was 'transported' by it.

The letter gave me a gush of longing for the hedgerows I had left behind. I had gone through a short irradiated period when I was forever painting and drawing small icon-like pictures of lords-and-ladies, enigmatic presences suggested by those large glossy arrow-shaped leaves on long stalks, and their curious inflorescences. The thin dark purple club enclosed by its pale green floating hood, delicately pointed, became a carnal metaphor I reproduced at first naturalistically, and then grossly distorted, with growing savagery and pleasure.

I sat with veiled eyes, inwardly active. I became conscious of someone sitting beside me. As I began a drawing in my head, starting with the eyes and circumflex eyebrows, the pent-up, redly shining little man whose breathing I could now hear burst into speech.

'My name's Charlie,' the man said helplessly.

I started, my eyes shot open. The stranger's bald head and full cheeks were sweating. Though I was too close for comfort, I couldn't draw away without giving offence. I sat transfixed by the man's damp blazing skin. In the half trance I was in, I could have reached out for that cranium like a wet beach ball which had suddenly come within reach, it looked so invitingly round and solid. Then I registered the eyes. They too gave the impression of boiling, while pleading speechlessly with me. Instinctively I shrank back.

'You understand?'

Baffled, I found myself nodding. 'Charlie, yes.'

'I got nobody out here,' the man nearly wept.

'What's that? Where?'

'They discharged me too soon, they did. I told them that, didn't I?'

'Told who?'

'The hospital. Marytavy. They should have known better, wouldn't you say so?'

'Excuse me, where is this place?'

'I've been in there six months. They're the experts, they should have seen the signs. On Sunday they should.'

'Was that when you left?'

189

'I can't cope at home. How can I?'

'Isn't there anybody there to help you?'

The distraught man shook his head violently. Beads of sweat flew off and hit me in the face. I felt scooped out by the other's anguish, in danger of being scalded by my closeness to such heat. Charlie seemed to be both melting and bursting out of his flesh. He launched into a muddled account of his family troubles. There was the son whom he adored, the wife who refused to take any more, an interfering brother. It was this intermediary, Stanley, who was making things so much worse with his meddling – if that was possible.

The air was warm. It wasn't that, though, which made me feel I was steaming. With my fingers I jerked at the opening of my shirt. The sky, above the humped land to the west, was rent by fingers of lowering sun. In front of the blackish island, where the sun struck, the placid water of the Sound was now a shimmering pool.

'I love my little lad, he's smashing. He's not afraid of me, neither. Sits on my knee like a bird he does. That's it, you see.' Charlie was gabbling, getting faster. 'It doesn't bother me in the hospital, I've got a nice room, they like me in there, everybody knows Charlie, I do jobs, help sweep out the dining room and lay the tables, if only I didn't miss my lad but I do, I do something horrible, that's what the missus can't understand when she says I shouldn't come out, not even at weekends she says because I lose my temper and get excited . . .'

Wanting to halt this flood before it swept me away, I couldn't think of anything. Then I stammered, 'What's his name?'

'Who's this?'

'Your boy.'

The small, boiled-lobster man curled back his lip and laughed in a wild blurting, the joy and pain spilling out together. I shrank back.

'His name is Tom,' Charlie cried, uttering more splurges of weeping laughs. 'He sits so quiet on my knee, like an angel he is, a bird, I tell him stories and you should see him there with his eyes getting big and shiny. She's got plenty to put up with, my missus, I don't understand her though . . . .' He fell silent a moment, then was muttering to himself. 'What does Stanley say to her about me? He's not helping. Why doesn't he keep his nose out of my affairs, eh?' Crestfallen immediately, he rushed on, 'I shouldn't say that, I know he means well, only . . . .'

I waited a minute. 'Before you had to go into hospital, what did you do for a living?'

'Me? Oh hell, that's another thing, that is.' His scarlet forehead corrugated with thought, Charlie hammered with his fists at the bench on either side of his thighs and swayed to and fro. 'It's too frustrating to think about,' he groaned.

'That's all right, don't bother.'

'A chippie in the dockyard, I am. A good job, that. Twenty-five years I was there. A chippie, that's a joiner. A carpenter, see?'

'Yes.'

We sat in silence again. Charlie clasped and unclasped his wet swollen hands. Once he dragged out a huge white handkerchief and mopped over his head. I sniffed up the aroma of the salty air. Then suddenly Charlie turned to me, pleading with eyes like a fugitive begging to be caught. This was more that I could bear. Trying to appear casual, I got to my feet.

'I'm forty-one this August,' Charlie said. 'That's amazing, that is.'

I said, 'I shall have to be going,' pleading myself now to be released.

'How old are you?'

'I can give you ten years.'

I saw this was a ruse to keep me there. Charlie showed no interest. 'Getting on for twenty brain shots I've had,' he said, as if he was boasting. 'I can't remember things, not like I used to. I get these blinding headaches.'

'Will you go back in?'

'I shall have to, shan't I?' He sounded sorrowful, yet he was staring at my face belligerently. Then he seemed to forget me. He rocked his body to and fro.

I walked off, expecting any moment to hear myself hailed. Dropping down over the flights of stone steps I walked along the paths of terraces, descending the landscaped shoulder of cliff with its flower beds and rockeries and green-painted council benches. Only when I was crossing the tarmac road on my way to the foreshore rail did I crane my neck upwards. There was nothing to see. Charlie was hidden by a fold in the cliff. I imagined him lost in it like a hot churning baby.

Later that night I sat up in bed, exhausted, doodling in a sketchbook as a means of cooling my thoughts. I hoped to cast out a spirit rather than call one up, but this snaking pencil line

191

seemed to have a will of its own. The likeness to a bald man hurtling out of a wheel, with a diminutive figure clasped in his arms, gave way after a few pages to a wild arum which was patently obscene, a phallus sprouting hairs deep inside a woman's diaphanous belly.

Tired though I was, my hand wanted to go on. My mind raced, tumultuous as ever with thoughts and images. At last I lay down and covered myself with the sheet, my eyes wide open. The night was warm and I could have thrown off the sheet, but the pathos of my arms and shoulders, what I could see of them, brought back Charlie's plight and my own defection.

Falling asleep, I ran the gauntlet of subliminal fears. In one dream, a woman who seemed to be Celia had just had a baby. She sent her husband out with the baby in its pram to sit in a park. It was winter. I asked her why she didn't like the child and she said blandly, 'I did when I first had it. Now it keeps crying I hate it.' We went to the park. The husband sat on a bench overlooking the Sound. He was both Gregory and myself. He sat shivering in lightweight summer clothes. The woman spoke contemptuously to the husband and he got up and pushed the pram behind us. I told the woman that if she spoke to me in that fashion I wouldn't stand for it. She pouted, pretended anger, stalked ahead. The buttocks of her large behind made their own derisive comment.

I woke up with a gasp as my hand reached out for a starfish lying exposed and radiant on a beach. The brilliant sun was hitting the wall of my room like a gong, up near the ceiling. It was nearly noon.

I still felt exhausted, but got out of bed, put on trousers and went wading downstairs in bare feet to the sentry-box lavatory on the second landing. Someone was banging loudly and continuously on the shop door below.

'All right, I'm coming,' I shouted, in a cracked voice. As I descended I tried to buckle my belt with numb fingers. I shouted again, using an expression of my father's: 'Hold your horses!'

Guessing that I must look deplorable, with a pallid face and gummed eyes, I scraped down my hair with one hand while the other fumbled to unlock the door. The woman outside on the sunny pavement could have stepped out of a carnival. I recognised her only gradually. Before I had the door properly open I was already gaping through the glass panel at the large green velour hat, its band garnished with silver feathers.

The street was empty. My unfocussed eyes blurred over the face and took in a voluminous oyster shirt, grey cord jeans and cowboy boots. Was she collecting for something? Then I saw who it was. I stood cursing myself, for opening the door, for losing the morning sleep, for my churlishness and ingratitude.

'I'm so sorry,' Pru Woodruff said. 'Am I disturbing you?'

I held the door and felt I would have fallen over without it. 'No, that's all right,' I said in a choked voice. I tried to laugh. 'I must have overslept.'

'Now I feel terrible. I've got you out of bed.'

'No, not exactly,' I mumbled, lying without reason, or to salvage my pride. I dredged about in my fuddled wits for her first name. 'I was about to get a bit of breakfast.'

'You'd forgotten me, hadn't you?'

I denied it. Yes and no was the answer. Pru put her hand to the antique silver and turquoise necklace she was wearing. She wore a chunky silver ring in the form of a snake swallowing its tail. I remembered how I disliked it.

'You didn't even recognise me. It's been so long.'

'Pru, I've just got up.'

She smiled. 'May I call and see you tomorrow?'

'Come in now. I don't mind if you don't.' I made haste to amend the tactlessness of this. 'Would you like a coffee?'

'No, thank you. I'll call tomorrow.'

'Where are you staying?'

'I'm at the Holiday Inn.'

Her gaze went over my shoulder appraisingly. Then she thrust a paper bag at me. It gave off a savoury smell. I saw by the lettering on the paper that it was from a chicken take-away down on the quay. 'I thought you might enjoy this for your lunch. Or your breakfast.' She laughed. 'Eat it while it's fresh.'

'What is it?' I asked stupidly.

'A steak and kidney pie.'

'Thank you.'

She was moving away. 'Till tomorrow, Francis.'

On the spur of the moment I called out, 'Come around six. We can go out to dinner later. How does that appeal to you?' The paper bag oozing grease and warmth on my palm prompted me to smile gratefully after her in the bright sun.

'Very much,' she cried back, and waved gaily.

20

Why hadn't she got in touch by phone? Did she hope to catch me out? Well, she had succeeded. Then I remembered that I was ex-directory.

I had always detested phones. I boiled with silent – sometimes not so silent – rage whenever it rang at the mill. I would feel hounded, bullied, worst of all racked with disappointment or guilt afterwards at the thought of whoever it was that I had forsaken. There was a phone hanging on the wall near the street door, left by the potter and perhaps the owners before him. It sat on its hook, black and squat, a picture of invincible stupidity. No matter what abuse I hurled at it, the thing rang, smug with its rightness, a servant that pleased only itself.

I had left it disconnected for months. Letters came from my dealer and my accountant expressing surprise that I was not wired up to London. Thank God, I thought, I am spared the discouragement of bad news poured straight into my ear.

What really impelled me to call in the engineers was the thought of Vivien. Her letters now were unsatisfactory, simply because I now needed to hear her voice, to have the illusion of closeness which a phone conversation brings. If the phone rang and it was her, it transformed itself magically into a friendly instrument. I would say 'hallo' and 'yes' and then relax into the warm bath of her voice, allowing the rippling flow of her feminine chatter to run over me, hardly taking anything in but feeling delightfully 'in touch'. The dislocation as her receiver went down and I hung up was like a physical pain. Then I was plunged into a silence made restless by echoes of Vivien; her voice, her laugh, her breathy pauses.

But my aversion remained. I told her to reverse the charges whenever she wished, but refused to ring her. If I left it to her initiative, I was thus slyly persuading myself that I used the phone passively rather than from choice.

Giving way to an impulse that last day in London and ringing Maggie I now saw as unfortunate. Ever since I had been asking myself what, if anything, was wrong, but obeying a voice

194

telling me not to get involved. One evening, the phone rang. It was Vivien. With Maggie on my mind yet again, I steered the conversation round to her. I was tired of talking to myself about her without getting any answers.

'Where is she living now?' Vivien asked.

'I think over the restaurant still. Yes, I'm sure she is.'

'You're not saying you haven't heard from her? I thought you two were in touch?'

'Only in our hearts,' I half joked.

'I wish I could meet her. I feel I do know her, Francis. I ought to. She's become a part of you.'

I was jolted by her words. The idea of Vivien and Maggie sitting in a room together, perhaps becoming friends, hadn't once occurred to me, not even as a remote possibility. Suddenly it had become spoken, wished, and so to that extent feasible. The thought pleased and excited me, though in a part of myself I was objecting, 'What could they possibly have in common, apart from me?' When I put this to Vivien she said, with a little snap in her voice denoting disapproval, 'We're two women.'

'Is that enough?'

'It should be.'

'So what happened between you and Della?'

'You know very well what happened. She saw me as a threat. I was eager to be her friend, I admired her even.'

'Maggie couldn't be more different. What would you find to admire in her?'

'I resent that remark.'

'Forgive me. It's my generation. How can I put it? Well, she's a mother for one thing.'

'I'm fascinated by mothers. I admire mothers. I think mothers are incredible, mysterious, especially when they're pregnant, absorbed as they are in such a source of wonder and joy.'

'I didn't realise.'

'Perhaps it's because I didn't know my own mother.'

'But you don't want to be one.'

'How can you say such a crass, such an idiotic thing!'

'Sorry, I'm sorry.'

'Cancel my previous remarks about mothers, they're so patronising and insufferable, an insult to Maggie.'

'It's all right, she hasn't heard you.'

The upshot of this was that she did get in touch with Maggie, and then was invited to call. The next time Vivien rang, I was told this. Very pleased, I then explained my worries concerning Maggie. Now at last, I thought, I would get put in the picture.

'Is she in good health?'

'She looked fine to me Francis, I do like her.'

'Good. I'm very glad.'

'We got on like a house on fire.'

'Who did most of the talking?'

'I'm afraid I did. I suppose you know she has two children now?'

'Yes.'

'The toddler, Rose, is a real heart-stopper. She comes running over, her face wreathed in smiles. Her smile breaks me in two. I love babies, but I never thought I'd want one of my own. Now I do.'

'Would you say Maggie was happy? How are she and Gregory getting on?'

'I got the feeling things weren't as they should be. For one thing he's never around. She's very lonely, I think. Nothing much was said, but I picked up a few undercurrents. I'll let you know if she confides in me.'

'She will, don't worry. If you confide in her first.'

'I wouldn't know where to start if I wanted to tell her about Celia, for instance.'

'Start anywhere. She'll listen.'

'Oh yes, but Maggie lives in a different world.'

'How is Celia?'

'She'll need a phone call to herself,' Vivien said. She laughed unhappily. 'I'll tell you next time.'

'Anyway, she's alive.'

'Yes. With the aliveness of someone who talks about dying all the time. Staying where she is could be a madness in itself. The last time I called, she let me in and then dragged the table against the door. There's no key, she said. Her eyes rolled in a frightening way.'

'What's the matter with her, really?' It was on the tip of my tongue to add, 'Is it genuine?' My instinct was to resist anyone's conviction that the world around us is a kind of hell. It is easy to agree, but I prefer to see it as absurd.

Instead of answering directly, Vivien said, 'Sometimes I think she flirts with the idea of death as you would a lover.'

'Is that her, or is it the Plath business you mentioned once?'

196

'Francis, no! You can be so crude and trampling sometimes.'

'Now what have I said?'

'Never mind. Forget it. If you don't know, you don't.'

'But I want to know.'

'Celia's a person in her own right. Does that answer your question?'

'You still care for her?'

'Yes.'

'As much as ever?'

'More.'

I snuffled a laugh into the phone, then apologised hastily. Vivien was indignant. 'Would you mind telling me what's funny?'

'Nothing – it's not what you said. I was just laughing in amazement. Marvelling.'

'What at?'

'You, you're so positive, you people with the power to assert yourselves. How do you do it? I'm the docile type.'

'You want power too, in your quiet way.'

'If you say so. Vivien, we'd better stop. This call has no logical end. It could cost a fortune.'

'What d'you mean? I didn't reverse the charges this time.'

'You didn't? That's right, I'm sorry. Keep talking.'

The morning following Pru's surprise visit I was hard at work, labouring to create a makeshift sitting room. I had visualised it in bed in the small hours. There were various items of dusty junk at my disposal, and now a garishly painted screen, bought earlier from the antique shop up the street. I lugged it back triumphantly and unfolded it around the eyesore of my sink and cooker, then sneered at myself for attempting to hide these necessities.

Switching off the old vacuum, I thought I heard rattling knocks on the shop door. Surely it wasn't Pru already? Two boys stood scuffing their feet in the doorway. They each held dog-eared sheets of paper. Would I sponsor them for a charity walk over the moors? I began searching automatically in my trouser pockets for loose change. They both sniggered. 'We don't want any money yet, not till we've done it.'

'No?'

'You have to put down how much.'

'Oh, right.'

197

I scrawled a version of my painter's signature with their oily biro.

When Pru did come it was seven-thirty, late enough for me to realise that I was now in need of her visit; unless, that is, I was desperate suddenly for any company. Did I mean male, or female? If I had the choice, someone unlike me in every respect. I badly wanted a rest from myself.

This time she was hatless, showing her legs below a short skirt printed to look like leopard skin – unless it was a dress. She wore a cable-knit sweater, the sleeves shoved up unceremoniously to the elbows. Her small shoulder bag matched her gamboge shoes, with their high teetering heels and ankle straps no thicker than parcel string. Her stocking-masked toes were poking through. I remembered her flamboyance from the old days. Now she was older she seemed to have gone to extremes and become even jauntier, more exotic.

'I'm rather late.' You'll excuse me, won't you, her smile said.

'Come in for a moment.'

I led the way, not wanting to linger because she seemed inclined to stand goggling at everything, and it was just emptiness and dust on the ground floor, and probably mouse droppings on the bare boards. I hadn't noticed, but had heard sounds of life. I found it hard to believe that we hadn't met since that day in Southwark when she had inspected my squalor, followed by my paintings.

'It's been one of those days,' she was saying behind me. 'I've left clothes strewn everywhere. Nothing seemed right.'

'You look fine.'

'Francis, you're sweet. But you can be cruel as well. Ignoring me all these years!'

'I don't write letters.'

'There are phones. I see you have a phone.'

'Loathe the things.'

We were standing on an area, on a turkey carpet, which until a few hours ago was like a huge dustbin with a path running through it. Facing me squarely, Pru said, 'You're looking amazingly well, I must say.'

'You too.'

'I've powdered over the cracks. You haven't needed to.'

'Well, I'm fit enough. On the outside.'

'And what does that mean?'

'You can't go by surfaces.'

198

She laughed. 'Not even those signed Francis Breakwell?'

'Especially those.'

'Oh well, you wouldn't believe if you didn't doubt, surely.'

I blinked, obliged – not for the first time – to take this dressy, egotistical woman seriously. 'Haven't you got that the wrong way round?'

'Probably.' She had lost interest already. 'You're not angry with me, are you, for getting hold of your address?'

'Do I look angry?' I fenced.

'Simon, your protective dealer, didn't want to give it to me. But I got round him.'

'I can imagine.'

She made eyes at me. 'He gave me to understand that your insistence on privacy verges on the pathological.'

'But you're a client. Was that what you said?'

'No, I didn't. What a vile word, client. Can't I be something nicer, after all these years?'

Embarrassed by her play-acting, I said hastily, 'Come up and inspect a few recent things. Then we'll go for our meal.'

'Oh yes,' she said, and went up on her toes like a girl.

Again I led the way. When alone I charged up and down the stairs in a hurry, desperate or preoccupied or both. Now I loitered, conscious of Pru behind me picking her way carefully on those ridiculous heels. Near the top I glanced briefly over my shoulder. Her mouth set, the lines betraying her age, she clutched nervously at the rope rail. Something about her, a worldiness and resolution, reminded me of Della, even of Lotte in Falmouth.

I reached the landing. 'Are you all right?'

'Perfectly,' she answered.

I thought she looked a little drawn, and sounded out of breath. Not wishing to humiliate her by seeming concerned, I took her into my sanctum.

She gave a cry of pleasure. 'Oh, what's that?' She pointed to a slapdash oil sketch, one of a number of 'Artist and Model' imaginings I had done on odd bits of board and left propped against the walls. I did them like keyboard exercises, mere strummings, while waiting for the next thing to arrive. The trouble is that a sketch, thrown off in an hour, or minutes, can ignite a whole room and put everything else in the shade.

'How intriguing. How very interesting!'

'What about the others? You haven't seen the others.'

'On the same theme as this? Let me see. No, wait a minute, don't rush me.'

'Take your time,' I muttered, gratified in spite of myself. Damn the woman, she had good taste.

'*Le pauvre*,' she said, still hanging over the small picture I had condemned and then reprieved.

'What?'

'This poor man. Oh dear. He's a bit diminished, I must say.'

It was true. The whey-faced painter, whether squatting on a three-legged stool or upright at his easel, was eclipsed in every version by the variations of glowing nude. One showed the artist peering myopically through his spectacles. In another, the female being painted had a sleek black head like that of a somnolent black cat. I busied myself at a marble-topped washstand, cleaning some brushes.

'Picasso did a series of these.'

'I know.'

'Have you left me to it?'

'Yes, look where you like.'

'Are you sure you don't mind me intruding?'

'You're lucky to get in. Sometimes I don't answer the door for days.'

'You would for me. I'd have made a scene in the street.'

Normally on my guard with this woman, I forgot myself and smiled. 'Have you still got the Alma-Tadema?'

She snorted impatiently. 'That dreadful thing.'

I agreed. All the same I had a sudden longing to see it. Somehow it was bound up with my beginnings. On my second visit to Charles Woodruff's house I saw the painting and was seduced by it, by the skin of the creature reclining classically on a marble bench draped with animal hides, her shoulder and one indolent arm sunk in a large fleshy pillow. She lay nakedly swelling and pink-tipped, seemingly transfixed by a phallus-asp she was holding in her hand behind the line of her upraised hip. In the reference library later I tracked down the weirdly named artist who had helped to make eroticism respectable for Victorians by the application, so I read, of classical gloss. The tawny ostrich feather screening the groin had made me laugh. It did now.

'You got rid of it?'

Pru shook her head. 'I've no idea where it is. Charles took the beastly thing with him.'

200

I stared at her. 'Took it where?'

'I forgot, you wouldn't have heard. Charles cleared off, oh, three years ago now.'

I didn't know what to say. 'I'm surprised.'

She said hoarsely, 'Why, did we seem a loving couple?'

'I wouldn't know.'

Strangely glassy-eyed, she went on abruptly, 'By the way, whatever happened to that waitress you were cohabiting with once in Southwark?'

'Why not say copulating and have done with it?'

'Yes. Excuse me.' She drew back her head. 'I'm being coarse and insensitive in my middle years.'

'We parted.'

'Living together was naive, I thought. Not that we ever met. How could you expect someone like her to understand you?'

'I didn't. She loved me.'

'I see. How nice for you.'

'Not for her. She was the unlucky one.'

'Because you didn't love her?'

'I didn't know how.'

Pru threw back her head and laughed. 'You reprobate! Men are all the same. Why, are you discontented with yourself?'

'Aren't you?'

'It's different for me. God help me, all I have is this face and this body. I've got brains, but nobody's interested, certainly no man. Of course you're discontented – isn't that why you paint?'

We stared at each other, like enemies who had suddenly revealed their true colours and were nonplussed. I had misjudged her. She could be quite frank when she wished. Respecting her judgement, I asked her to look at the narrow little board clamped to my easel. She walked over.

'The colour's rather unpleasant. if you'll forgive me,' she said, almost crossly, and stood regarding it with her hip thrust out. Unpleasant, yes, that was correct. I paid attention to her.

On the acid-green ground the two figures were bathed in bluish light, flowing up vertically to a wavy brown stain

201

of horizon near the top edge, like keyholes placed side by side. In my mind the picture had a title, 'Luna', because I had begun it one night under the sway of a blazing full moon.

I went over and stood beside Pru, squinting to restore the lost illusion of a squatting odalisque, one breast rolling free, stick arms bent in a hoop round the moony head. The scarcely human male figure to the left was streaked with blood. This armless and bloody trunk ended in a bulbous growth on which the pink clottings of nascent features were emerging.

'Is it Adam and Eve?'

Unwilling to go along with this, I shrugged. 'Male and female, certainly.'

'The Adam thing looks – nasty,' she complained. She squirmed her shoulders in a gesture of revulsion. 'Why does he have such horrid bulges?'

I considered the question. It was a better one than those raised by critics. 'Perhaps he isn't born yet,' I suggested. 'Isn't he pretty enough for you?'

'On the contrary. Only too convincing.'

'So what's bothering you?'

'I don't wish to be rude, Francis.'

'Say what you think, or there's no point in talking at all.' I heard myself speaking decisively and was astonished. I imagined a power emanating from my work and flowing into me, calmly and steadily, even altering the sound of my voice.

Pru said, 'I'm sorry, it's just repulsive to my eyes.'

'There's no answer to that.'

'I mean the left-hand side only.'

'You can live with the right?'

'Well, yes – '

I nodded. A funny silence began and I wanted to laugh, tell a joke. 'My man hasn't any feet,' I said suddenly. 'I've only just noticed.'

'I wonder why?'

She had now entered a game which it seemed I wanted her to play. 'I don't know.' I pretended to ponder upon a mystery. 'I've got it. It's obvious why. He's not going anywhere.' This idea had simply wandered into my mind.

'How true,' she said bitingly. 'Just like a man.'

202

'Here's one who is.' I pointed at my own chest. 'He's hungry. Shall we go for our meal?'

Standing there, Pru's face seemed older. She turned to me, the heavy lines around her mouth deepening. 'Yes, let's!' she exclaimed. 'What a good idea!' The fleeting tiredness of her eyes was snatched away, to be replaced instantly by a new vivacity. I saw again the merry, indomitable woman who had confronted me yesterday at the street door, dressed to kill, able to surmount years, lack of love, anything.

21

Months of time would pass in a long dream, a monotony during which one worked because there was nothing, absolutely nothing else to do. Then suddenly everything happened at once. People turned up from the dead and forgotten past who were not dead but very much alive and kicking. The phone rang, the door knocker banged. What had been for so long internal became externalised. No sooner had Pru gone than another visitor from the past came knocking, only this time not in the flesh.

A letter arrived out of the blue from, of all people, Joseph Meckler. Always one to identify my correspondent from the handwriting, I was baffled by this hand. The postmark was too blurred to decipher. I tore open the envelope and the name Meckler took me back in a great rush at least twenty-five years. Here he was, actually in touch. How had he obtained my address? He must be old, an old man, I thought. The handwriting was firm, neat, every word legible. It was the first letter I had ever received from him.

Some time before I left for Nottingham, to find a bedsitter and then take a leap, at last, into the dangerous world, Joseph Meckler must have had a one-man show of his paintings in that city. If I had been there then, a few months earlier, would I have gone to see it? Probably not. In those days I was the kind of art snob who lost interest if a local artist was mentioned. The classes run by Susan Hines were under way, I joined, but wasn't yet involved with her. Then by chance I picked up the *Evening Post*, opening it to read a profile of a painter who lived and worked in a large village on the other side of Mansfield. Among the trite, journalistic phrases, Meckler's remark, 'I go round looking, and then remember,' convinced me that the person talking was the genuine article. A photograph, badly reproduced, showed the gaunt worn face of a man who could have been any age between forty and fifty. The feature was headed misleadingly, 'Artist in Brick'.

One day I opened the door of the Starlight Restaurant and there he was. He sat alone at one of the tables sketching. The photograph had shown a bearded man but I recognised Meckler at once. Fascinated, I went and sat down as near as I dared in order to observe him and find out what he was doing. He kept grubbing away with a pencil or crayon stub, his head lowered. His mouth jerked every so often spasmodically. I noticed the sickly pallor about the jowls of someone who had just shaved off a dense beard. In my thirsty eagerness for mystery and a certain strength I connected the man's head, and the thick shells of his eyelids, with portraits by Rouault which I had seen in books and admired tremendously.

After a while I forced myself to go over and make conversation. The *Evening Post* article would serve, I thought, as a means of introducing myself. I declared my own interest, stressing that I was a novice.

'Aren't we all,' the man said dourly.

'Mind if I sit down?'

'Help yourself. Mind if I go on with this?'

'No, of course not. Thanks.'

It was a head that the man was now smudging in. 'It's like an itch, drawing. You can't stop scratching.'

'I know what you mean.'

Meckler's accent was broad Sheffield. Wanting to idolise him, simply because he existed and looked like a workman, I thought of his tongue rasping at the blunt words like a trowel. Casting around desperately for something intelligent to say, I could only think to ask whether the place described in the newspaper was his permanent home.

'Scrapcroft? You could say that.'

'I haven't been here long, so I don't know the country in that direction.'

'You could call it country I suppose. Some wouldn't. It's like the tag end o' summat.'

He was taciturn, but seemed perfectly willing to discuss his work. I said eagerly, 'I'd very much like to see some. I missed

your exhibition. Meeting you is a real stroke of luck for me.'
When this brought no response, I blurted out, 'I hope you
won't think I do this sort of thing all the time. I just came in
and spotted you.' Hot in the face, I fell silent.

'You come out and we'll have a talk,' Meckler said. 'Mind
you, I haven't got much I'm on with at present.' The skin of
his face was rough. He rubbed at it with bony fingers. 'Come
on Sunday,' he added. 'Dagmar is there on Sundays.'

Dagmar was his German wife, or woman. She worked as
an auxilliary in a nursing home. Meckler dug in his pockets
and came out with an empty cigarette packet. Tearing it apart,
he scrawled away carefully in a large hand, writing down his
address. 'Not that you could get lost. Folks know me.'

I could hardly wait for Sunday to arrive. At last I was getting
somewhere – I had made contact with the world of art, not at
second hand through books and museums, not out of the past
but here and now, incontrovertibly, in the shape of a live artist.

Approaching the village I wanted, the bus started rattling
violently as if protesting about something. Everything rattled,
the windows, seats, not to mention my bones and my teeth. Still
delighted with my initiative, I was even pleased by the unholy
racket we were making. What was causing it? The approach
seemed all potholes and building litter, between scrubby hedges
and then down a long grimy channel of brick uniformity.
Terraces of artisans' houses gave way to a cleared space, half
of it dug up for pipelaying. In the middle of this ramshackle
square the bus shuddered to a halt. I got out.

Behind me the only other passengers, members of a
squabbling family, filed off the bus and then disappeared down
one of the mean openings. I looked round. An old woman, bent
and creased like a jumble-sale shoe, seemed to be waiting on
her doorstep for me to come over. I went across and asked for
directions.

'You want Joseph's place, eh?' she said, and gave a sudden
flapping laugh.

'That's right, Joseph Meckler.'

The woman sighed, folding up her face. 'I know the one you
mean. I never heard of his other name. Joe they call him round
here. He's been in the paper they say.'

Finding in myself a patience and respect for the very old
which I didn't know I possessed, I asked courteously, 'Is it far
from here?' I showed her the scrawled address.

'Oh, you'll walk it fast enough, you're a young un!' she screeched, and rocked to and fro.

'The Hermitage' was a blue-painted shack of wood and iron, with a brick chimney piece supporting one wall like a buttress. A border of dying marigolds led round to the extension, which I saw was a kitchen. Inside, though the glass was fogged, I could make out the figure of a woman moving. On the far side a long trench of live water went gurgling over stones. Lines of cabbages stood in soldierly rows.

The door opened as soon as I knocked. A tallish woman in a dusty blue housecoat faced me dumbly, her mouth grim. I heard Meckler shout uncouthly from within, 'Let him in, Dagmar, for fook's sake. I told you about him.'

The woman stood aside, unsmiling. She was middle-aged, with sunken rouged cheeks. As I went past her I got a whiff of her hospital smell. Joseph Meckler levered himself up from a bulbous armchair. I realised for the first time what a scarecrow of a man he was. His short greying hair stuck out from the sides of his head in tufts. His face looked blearier than I remembered. Now that he was minus a jacket I could see how scrawny he was. One of his bare forearms carried a small violet tattoo of a thick snake with a twig flowering in its jaws.

The little room, neat as a caravan, presented an interior I hadn't expected, with fussy check curtains tied back with ribbon, hearth rugs underfoot, ornaments on shelves and in corners. At my back, the foreign woman announced, 'You are welcome to take tea here with us.' Surprised by this speech, I turned to find her smiling, lifting her upper lip to expose broad protruding teeth. 'You like tea?' she asked.

Meckler bellowed out a harsh laugh. 'He's English, so I daresay he does. Tea and buns we'll have in a bit. After I've taken him down the garden.'

'Oh yes, he will like that.'

'It's what he's come for.'

'Of course,' the woman said, 'and it is what you want too.'

'It won't take us long.' Meckler made for the door.

'As you wish.'

I followed the painter out. We were heading for a large asbestos building at the far end of the plot, beyond a clump of gooseberry bushes and raspberry canes. The straight flow of water to our left sounded louder now. Its bright rapid surface fed under the light with the bluish glint of steel freshly machined.

Inside, I peered into the gloom. A powerful electric light snapped on. 'I keep telling meself I'll fix a couple of skylights in here,' Meckler said, in his flat thump of a voice. 'That's as far as it gets, like.'

He got down on his hands and knees by a work bench, dragging persistently at whatever was half stuck under there. Soon he had unearthed a disorderly pile of drawings for inspection, and had gone to a large cupboard in the corner to plunge in his arms. Paintings of assorted sizes came spilling out and were propped on any available surface. Finally the floor itself had to be utilised. Still they kept coming, deprived of any commentary from their creator. Jumpily active, he shifted pictures about needlessly to other levels. He seemed anxious to mount the show and at the same time conclude it.

He straightened himself, scowling round, then dragged out an upright chair with a broken stay, rainbow-coloured from the paint splashes and wipes, and sat gazing ahead with a blankness similar to that of Dagmar. His work stared back at him through the startled eyeholes of all its masks.

A curious tense silence descended. My hearing fastened on the ceaseless rustle of water in the trench outside and magnified it in my mind to a river. Once or twice I blinked my eyes, as if to get rid of water. The panorama of scenes and figures I confronted, itself a frozen river, recalled the macabre paintings by Ensor I had seen once in a book. But the procession before my eyes lived in a universe of brick. I was gaping at a composite portrait of a place I assumed must be Scrapcroft. The essential brick fabric of the town had been worked over and reassembled. As I gazed at this livid facade, it seemed to breathe, pullulate, to sweat and glisten with moisture. The lines of grubby mortar and ridged soot, the flakes of rust and baked clay changed into human features and dissolved again as I watched. I could have sworn there was an odour of decay, the vegetable smell of old sumps and buried rivers, given off by these masses, effigies, from their skins. I was looking at an abandoned Scrapcroft, at its rotting wood, crumbling brick, its permanent ooze of damp.

Meckler seemed in a trance, as if saddened by the sheer volume of his unwanted production. I glanced at him again. The fact is that he was in the act of picking his nose with total absorption. He glared back at his work balefully, then shook himself like a dog.

'When did you do all this? Does it cover a long period of time?'

He shook his head. 'See that one over there? It's still unfinished. I've been tickling away at that one for so long now, I can't remember when I started.' He pointed. 'See that? It's got all the backyards and sheds and allotments for miles around embedded in it, you might say. My "Allotment Gothic", that's what I call it.' He laughed coarsely. 'You must have noticed on your way here what a godforsaken hole this is. I like it though for that, I wouldn't have it different. It never could make up its mind whether to be a town or a village, industrial or rural.'

'What's the appeal of it?'

'Appeal? Its appeal is that it's got none. It's given up expecting anything. You take, say an old man on his allotment smoking a Woodbine, an old soldier most likely, with half an eye on cats snooping past on their bellies like snakes, like great hairy caterpillars. He might lob a stone at one, nothing nasty mind, just to keep them off his seeds. There he is, gawping at the patch of damp spreading on a piece of old sacking in the drizzle. A rich man, that.'

He pointed out a profile whitened to feverishness, heavy-lidded, the lips long and corrupt. 'Now you look at that one. Him. That Romeo. Street-corner shark. Go in any billiard hall and you'll find him basking in a corner. Or in a pub, at a dance, gobbling at the girls. He's got the looks and knows it. All there it is in that greedy gob. He'll make himself ill, sick, then go out and spew up on the pavement and come in again for more of the same poison. The whiter he gets, the better he attracts. That's his glamour, where he's been. Get his mouth right, I said, and you've snapped up that Romeo once and for all. Swagger, spew, the lot. He's our local dago, you might say.'

I was listening but also looking, unable to stop my gaze wandering over these crowded figures and faces. Suddenly I discovered Dagmar, looming larger than most – a flat matriarch on stick legs like a sheep, dressed in smouldering red feathers dowsed here and there with ash, cheeks inflamed by a brick-dust erysipelas. Her brown uncomprehending teeth were decently covered.

There was something I burned to ask, since these images were neither abstract not naturalistic, and I could detect no obvious influences. I was working round to my question covertly. Meckler beat me to it. In an expansive mood, as if a current had been reversed and his arrayed work was now swarming with friendly presences, he said genially, 'If I had to name a

favourite, I'd say Picasso. I love his energy. Oh I know what
you're thinking – where is he then? Nobody but a fool would
imitate an artist like that. For one thing he's a con man – okay,
a trickster who lets you in on his act. That's all right, it's the
age we're in, anything goes now. I used to have a photo of him
stuck up on my wall when I was a youngster, and I'd look at it
and think – what eyes! Never in my life have I ever seen such
magnetic eyes as that man has.'

Too shy to propose another visit, I never encountered him
again. But I remembered to send him an invitation to my first
private view. He didn't turn up. Not that I expected him. But he
had put on a show for me and I wanted to repay the compliment.
Seeing his name on a letter brought him back in a swoop. He
was no cave artist: there was great sophistication in the burnt
umber, slate-grey and bottle-green surfaces of this self-taught
painter who had raised the scratches on soiled brick walls to an
art which was all his own. The scumbling was masterly. I saw
again the cruelly incised snouts, collapsed toothless mouths,
ratty hair. The collective face of a lost tribe rise in my memory.
Like Lowry, he understood how much white there was in satanic
landscapes.

His letter made me laugh aloud with the pleasure of
recognition, and yet it could have been aimed at anyone.
There was a complete absence of personal chit-chat. Not a
single drop of ink was wasted on his 'news', though I would
have dearly loved some. He had been to an exhibition and had
got gloriously drunk on it, falling headlong through the joyous
gauzes and liquors and flowery light of a domain that no one
would have thought to associate with him and his world. It was
this that he now itched to convey. But why to me?

Without preamble his letter kicked off:

> While in London went to the Royal Academy where they
> had an expo of Pierre Bonnard, and never enjoyed a show
> of paintings so much in my life. Acres and acres of bosom
> and belly and bottom, of thigh and tit, in bed, on sofas,
> in baths: perfuming, sitting – all but performing, all but
> shitting – wonderful. Went thru room after room hunting
> for those naked ladies in crayon colours, Van Gogh
> colours, bird-bright colours – salad-green and mauve and
> iris-blue and corn-on-the-cob yellow. Kept looking again
> and again at those ladies – not coy – not the kind to laugh

at – nor to nod to – they were supremely ordinary yet ladylike and unashamed – not at all flashy, neither were they shy. Kept thinking where have I seen them before? I think they were the same one over and over, but couldn't tell so well. Too dizzy, too old. There was a lady with a wee wash basin. With an iron water-holder. In a zinc bath half-filled. With coloured towels to tread on. Mauve faces flaxen hair; rosy faces russet hair – all provincial – French provinces. Plump not fat. Couldn't imagine them ever being owt but ladies; never children nor virgins nor tarts nor old – eternally ladies like the toilet sign – pregnant I'm sure, for she was well gone in one and in others with a dog, a cat, a child, snow, the garden, bowls of fruit, spring flowers, the cottage. Like a spilling-over basket. And in so many of them the naked lady was wearing nowt but her high-heeled shoes – coming out of the bathroom you can imagine her saying Well look at me, all fresh and sweet – and the fellow saying You've still got your shoes on, do you bath in your shoes then? – and her saying Don't be daft, no of course I don't, but I'm not getting my feet dirty now I've had my bath . . . All the best from me and Dagmar, Joseph Meckler.'

The phone rang below in the haunted empty shop quarters of the building. Sighing, I put down a watercolour brush.

I was experimenting now with watercolour, entranced as never before by this translucent, silky, sunny medium, which seemed so in harmony with the womanly sea, the wide skies full of rainy light, the crystals glittering in rocks, the lichen mottling the trunks and twigs of trees. Laying down magical washes of colour made me believe I was capturing the very world I breathed, ruled and ravished by the seasons, the night and day, by white moons and starry kingdoms, as well as dead afternoons dragging by like lead, mornings rotted by the tick of the clock into grey divisions. The clang of a hot sun, a light quivery with fish, with flowers, I could run it all together in wet happy sweeps and imagine it as calm and round and simple, a completion, like a great face telling everything. It delighted me too that I could touch on things so lightly and effortlessly with the drift of a feathering brush, as I pitched around on my inner sea.

The 'Luna' painting, now a motif, spawned so many watercolours and wash drawings that I was soon obsessed and tyrannised. It meant that I took it to bed with me, chewed at it during meals – when I remembered to eat – and was tugged along on walks by it as if by a panting, voraciously greedy dog.

To regain a measure of control I tried treating the new motif with humour and a certain contempt. I did drawings of a baroque Rembrandtesque self-portrait, with wild curls and scratches coalescing around a pair of disillusioned elephant eyes which were fixed hungrily on a moon woman covering her breasts with a shirt. In one drawing there were two naked females who appeared close together, one embracing the other with soft insistent glances. In these two friends I saw a resemblance to Vivien and Celia. The sinuous figure of one with its ardent bones swam for the plump ovals of the other, who was swimming alone in her own night, her rudimentary nipples flat as blanched eyes.

The phone went dead. Then it rang again. It was late evening, late September. The summer had come and gone, and now the holiday crowds were dwindling rapidly. Every morning I considered a breakout. Fairly late at night I was extending my walks. Once I went as far as Devil's Point, overlooking the river mouth, behind me the white cakey walls and turrets of a large convent.

Out of breath, I panted into the phone, 'Yes?'

'Hallo, it's me.'

'Vivien.'

'What's the heavy breathing for?'

'The stairs. It's a long way down to here from where I work.'

'Can't you have the phone moved?'

'Yes, I intend to,' I said, lying from habit. I had no need to lie to my sister.

'Have I stopped you working? I'm sorry, Francis,' she apologised.

'I'm not. It wasn't going right.'

'Can I ask what?'

'You can.' And I stood holding the phone, laughing to myself.

Vivien laughed herself. 'Oh all right, be like that. What a thing, secrets from your own sister. Can't you even give me a hint?'

'I will if you really want me to.'

'In that case, no. It's too much of a responsibility. Francis, I've rung to warn you of a more serious disruption of your life. Are you ready?'

211

Notwithstanding my love for Vivien, I stiffened automatically in resistance. 'Break it gently,' I managed to joke.

I heard her swift intake of breath. 'You mustn't be angry or worried. It's just that I'm coming to see you.'

'Yes.'

'Is that all you can say?'

'Yes, good. Wonderful. I mean it.'

'Don't you want to know when?'

'When?'

'You did ask me you know, ages ago.'

'I meant it. I do now.'

'Listen, there's a way to avoid disturbing your routine too much, and that's for me to stay in a small hotel. Please, let me. Book me in somewhere fairly near that's small and quiet. For once I've got a bit of money saved.'

'Come as soon as you like, Vivien, truly. But why now? Is it a crisis?'

'No, it's my raging discontent. I think of you there at the edge of the sea and I think how good it would be for me, how soothing, how nice. With you to talk to as a bonus. London's so big, such a turmoil, it stretches so far. When you're milling around inside yourself it can be quite nightmarish. Can you understand? Tell me you understand. Yes, you can, of course you can.'

'Get on a train and come.'

'Oh thank you, bless you, Francis.'

I thought I heard distressing sounds. 'You're not crying, are you?'

'Yes. I cry when I'm happy, it's all right.'

'Just ring and tell me when your train gets in, and what day.'

'I will. Goodnight.' She hung up.

22

I thought of myself as alone, but strictly speaking I was not. My two cats were with me; that is, when they deigned to put in an appearance. They had transferred well from Cornwall, after a fortnight of intense fearful distrust of every shadow, seeing ghosts in all corners, leaping neurotically for cover without reason.

Letting myself into the shop area from the street, I would forget to take care. I banged the door behind me. One cat or the other would rocket away for the rear window and scoot through to the rotting backs and leggy faded weeds of the nether regions, where there was a sunless, shut-in yard littered with rubbish. I had no access to the rear of the property. I left the narrow window open just for them. More than once I had the urge to squirm through and follow, to stand in that weird stagnant space in the lifeless silence and find out what it was like to be a cat.

Early in October, the endlessly soft mellow weather proved so seductive that I went out on impulse one Thursday morning, working my way along the foreshore without once taking my eyes from the glittering and stirring Sound. What I admired above all was its vast repose, its giant animal breathing. No one else was dawdling. The promenade stretched ahead, as empty as a country road. The flights of stone steps and terraces of shrubs laden with bright berries looked especially attractive, their varying levels enticing me as if I were a boy with a boy's craving to scramble up things. I left the road and climbed straight up over the great grassy hump of the Hoe. On the broad tarmac plateau along which sightseers promenaded I let my legs carry me past the war memorial and the statue of Drake to its right. My limbs seemed aware before it dawned in my mind that I was about to embark on an adventure.

In my jacket pocket was the picture postcard which had come by the morning post from Vivien. All she had written was, 'Arriving 8.12 pm Plymouth North Road. Love, Vivien.' On the reverse side was a replica of Cézanne's 'Blue Vase', no doubt chosen to please me. Certainly I was pleased, and more so than she could have guessed. After a lifetime of being virtually blind to Cézanne, suddenly an eye I never knew was there had opened in my being. It was like finding religion, yet there was no mystery, no revelation. His paintings pulsated so modestly, with such quiet colours, and yet were so dazzlingly alive and powerful that I wanted to jettison Van Gogh, Bonnard, Nolde, Matthew Smith, in fact all the sun worshippers I had loved for so long, and keep only him. A passion I had known in my youth burned again and I longed to experience, as he had surely done, the world's virginity. Alas, I thought, such miracles can no longer happen, How has this come about? Man is victor and vanquished, both together. Miracles have been exchanged for

213

pipe-dreams. Nature lies defiled, or else is captured on film for us to wonder at. Innocence is a lost realm, or an aphrodisiac.

I walked to Stonehouse down a big greyish white street, between docks and the black hulls of ships on one side and the towering slab of a flour mill on the other. Opposite the marine barracks with its deserted parade ground I turned into a side street. This petered out after a hundred yards at a gas lamp, slate steps and a concrete slipway awash with the scummy water of an incoming tide.

I sat for nearly an hour in the lean-to cafe. In the mild sunny weather, whatever I did was pleasant. Instead of chafing at the long wait before the next ferry I swapped words with the woman serving tea and stared round at the cafe's tiny interior. Since my last visit they had installed a juke box. Though I had caught the little passenger ferry across the river to Cornwall on a number of occasions, I had the feeling I was doing these things for the first time.

After three quarters of an hour, I heard an engine roaring in reverse and then the clank of iron and a shout. Soon the few ferry passengers trailed up the street past the cafe windows. I got up. 'See you again.' The dark haired woman bunched up her cheeks in a broad smile. 'Goodbye, love.'

I went out and there was the ferry, white and trim, riding at anchor. I climbed up the slatted boarding plank, clutching the handrail.

Halfway across, cut loose from the city and its fixed grid of streets, standing in the bows of the rolling boat, bits of spray hitting my cheek, I pulled out Vivien's postcard again. Holding it between my fingers like a talisman I gazed ahead seeing nothing, blinded by the emotional thought that I was adrift and tugged this way and that by unseen forces, and that once one became aware of this then all was well. I smiled into the stiff breeze, unable to apprehend the sense of my own thought. Were Vivien's words between my fingers, the gentle blue spirituality of the Cézanne and the complex slow dance of the ferry acting on me separately or in unison, I wondered, and what were they telling me?

I lost the vision, or whatever it was. Yet what my eyes saw was every bit as perfect and desirable. We were sidling nearer, on a fierce dragging current, to a vista which looked as softly alluring as the Promised Land. The green earth ahead with its trees and rising hill and country house set back in ancient parkland had the hazy beauty of a mirage. The shaggy youth at the prow slung his hook and missed. The second throw was better; we squashed home against old bus tyres hanging from chains, the ferry now curiously weighty and large again. In the choppy tide race of mid-river the boat had felt light and frail as a shell. I heard the dry grate of the hook over the ribbed cement and my knees stiffened in readiness for the jolt. A feeling of regret passed through me. I was sorry to give up the sense of watery voluptuousness I had known, standing straddle-legged with the deck yielding beneath my feet in a mysterious rhythm of its own.

I walked up the short jetty and pushed through the turnstile at the ferry house. An old bus waited against the railings to run up the long hill by the side of the estate, then around mudflats and creeks in the direction of an unseen open sea. I decided not to bother; there was no hurry. Later on I would tramp into the soft countryside at my own pace.

To my left was a shingle and grass crescent, with water lapping over the pebbles of a miniature beach. During bank holidays the spot was crowded with trippers. Now there was only one distraught-looking woman in her forties pacing up and down. Her unpinned brown hair was being lashed by the wind into her face as she advanced to the water on bare pasty legs.

I squatted down on the low bank in the sun, meaning to watch the water, the birds, a far-out ship anchored beyond the breakwater, or else moving so slowly that it appeared stationary. But instead of doing any of these things I watched the woman. It is difficult to ignore the actions of someone who is behaving compulsively. The knotted varicose veins of the woman's calves made a sad as well as an ugly impression.

I sat puzzling over her antics. I was even angry with myself for not enjoying the play of light on the water. Somehow the strange woman's vacillations had become a matter of some urgency. She marched down to the lapping water, backed away, marched forward again, walked deliberately away from the ferry house, twirled in her tracks and came trudging towards it. Then she began the ritual all over again. Her movements were sluggish, as if her uncoordinated thick body was wading through dreams.

Disturbed, I sank into myself, hoping to escape the too-vivid picture of a mind's confusion. After all, my presence there was of no more interest to her than was that of the circling gulls. Closing my eyes, I thought at random, I wish Vivien would get out of

London for good. This thought was so immediately attractive that I let myself imagine my sister arriving at the station with a huge suitcase, not the weekend bag I had been expecting. Her eyes shone, and on her face was a seraphic smile telling me that my wish had come true.

Losing track of time, I sat up with a jerk. Dazed by the flood of light in my eyes, I got up. I moved forward instead of sideways, nearly bumping into the woman, who was sunk in thoughts or memories of her own, her dress hitched up over her thighs by a hand she had evidently forgotten. 'Beg your pardon,' I mumbled.

'When is Vernon coming back?' the woman asked at once. She was staring into my face so intently that I felt bound to answer.

'Soon, I expect,' I found myself saying.

'I'm here every afternoon without fail.'

'Yes. Then you're bound to see him.'

'He might be drowned.'

I was now, without knowing why, under a compulsion to deny her suggestion. 'No,' I said.

'Who are you?' she asked, in a sudden rage; and then tittered.

'Nobody at all.'

'Where are you going?' she called after me as I retreated hastily.

'For a walk.'

This at any rate was true. I set off up the deserted road in the direction the bus had taken some time before. Reaching the low white railing of the estate boundary, I stopped to look back. The slowly gyrating woman stood dabbling her bare toes in the grass. Her head hung down. She had forgotten me.

I came tramping up laboriously in a muck sweat from the shadowed green depths of a steep twisting lane. Emerging was like clambering from a narrow hole straight into pure sky. I shaded my eyes, my gaze sharpening, stretching, exulting. It was as if I had brought into being what I now saw – one effortless surge of creation off the tip of my largest brush.

I was on a high macadamed road, abandoned by the army at the end of World War Two and now in general use, flanked by gorse and a wire fence. To my left the bosky cliff went dropping away steeply for three hundred feet, above a swooping coastline that was dazzling and pure in line. The sea was occupied with its task, laying out the long beaches of freshly washed pale sand, blotted here and there by rocks and pools.

A few bullocks, young and curious, sore-eyed, stared from behind a gate. Going by them I grinned, the light and freshness expanding my breast. Ahead was the finely drawn rapture of the horizon line, hard and yet elastic. The vast Channel ran between, a sea-sky creature, glinting like steel but feathery. As if I had reached the hub of a wheel the whole of reality came to rest, both around and within. The sensation lasted for the faction of a second, leaving me tramping with aching muscles as before, fructified without knowing why.

A hand-painted signpost pointed a finger 'To Tregonhawke'. There was nothing in that direction except the sea. Then I saw a path winding through the grass and bracken. I crossed the road and began to follow it, dropping down at once quite rapidly. The track took me down to an idyll, a little sunken meadow surrounded by a ring of gaily painted and felted chalets, each one with its simple picket fence.

Leaving this settlement I wound down still further until I came to a long low timber bungalow bearing the name 'Lohengrin' in gothic letters. Then I saw the 'For Sale' notice. It was empty. I decided to explore. The bungalow was built on a deep grassy shelf tucked into the cliff, edged with dry stone walling. Except for the galley kitchen tacked on at once end, all the windows were sealed by shutters. Disappointed, I walked about on the bumpy turf, becoming aware of a silence that cast me off from myself in a way I feared, and seemed intent on burying me where I stood. To avoid this imaginary fate I kept walking round in a circle compulsively like the woman at the ferry, gradually becoming more and more intimidated by the huge bright wall of ocean endlessly toppling at me from this angle. I left by the same gap in the stone pen, glancing fearfully once again down from the edge on to the immaculate sand below. Then I went scurrying back up the path stricken by a delight that was partly fear.

Below the lip of the cliff road, the toy shanty town on its meadow was waiting just as I had left it, queerly suspended in time. I went on, stepping gravely and precariously between the clustered huts over the cropped grass as if sidestepping spirits.

I sat with Vivien in my improvised sitting room. Since I was not usually there, it could hardly be called a living room. The

217

October evening was warmly golden. I was a few days from my fifty-second birthday. The folding pearly screen was stuck away in a corner gathering dust.

The flying visit I had been expecting had transformed itself into a week. Now we were near the end of it. We sat back replete after a chicken cooked by Vivien. I had forgotten what home cooking tasted like.

'That was very good.'

'There's some cheese,' she said. 'Would you like some?'

I shook my head, plaiting my fingers over my sweater. 'I couldn't find room for any. I've got a small stomach.'

'What rubbish.'

I smiled at her and at myself, disconcerted yet again by my own self-consciousness in the face of this unaccustomed domestic bliss, settling round me like the golden weather. Vivien's eyes were on mine. Sometimes her gaze, at once penetrating and curious, was hard to meet. So were her sharp critical judgements. Facing her for any length of time could be more than a little daunting, I was beginning to realise. Under her scrutiny I felt as slovenly as an old slipper. She was good to behold, with her clear skin and shining hair. I made a vow not to apologise or make excuses for myself. That path could lead to resentment. I was what I was. Yet because her presence filled me with self-indulgent emotion I wanted to prolong the condition, even if it meant pleasing her in ways which were fundamentally anathema to me. For instance, I was looking uncharacteristically spruce, shaved and combed, and our conversations were becoming interminable. This garrulousness I took to be a peculiarly female trait or passion, and indeed felt at times that we were like two women talking together about everything and nothing. I excused it on the grounds of expediency. She would soon be gone, I reminded myself.

'You know what our father used to say,' I said enigmatically.

I paused so long that she cried out, exasperated, 'Go on! Am I supposed to guess?'

'A clean plate is the best compliment a cook can have.'

'Is that so?' she said mockingly.

A little later, over coffee, she said, 'Have you lost weight?'

I smiled uneasily. 'I always say no to that. I'm damned if I know.'

'Anyway, you're well.'

I nodded. 'Next time you come I may be vegetarian.'

Vivien's sharp alert face broke into laughter. 'When did you think that – during the chicken? Was it the leg you were gnawing?'

'I'm serious.'

'You're funny.'

'All right, laugh.'

'I'm sorry, it was the way you came out with it.'

'I said, with a touch of spite, 'What's Celia?'

'What is she?'

'Is she one?'

'Oh yes, she is.'

'There you are. Is that laughable?'

'What an illogical mind you have!'

I looked at her speculatively. 'I think I've always been one. I just haven't got round to it I suppose.'

When she was animated, Vivien's face became impish. 'Francis, I accept you in all your metamorphoses, so there.'

'Tell me what Celia eats. A lot of raw stuff?'

'Some.'

'Carrot juice? I draw the line at carrot juice.'

'Oh, I don't know. I remember once she ran out and bought a hunk of topside beef. She said a carnivorous lust had toppled her into depravity. She came back from the butcher's with this parcel dripping blood, and then couldn't even unwrap it.'

'Are you actually poking fun at her?'

'Well, it is hilarious in retrospect isn't it? But no, I'm not really. I could never do that. Everything she does is extreme, and so desperate. I'm always too scared and too worried to laugh. I thought her eating habits were absurdly puritanical, but when she did that I was deeply shocked. More than shocked. I felt disgusted with her, not for wanting to eat meat of course, but for letting herself down, and me too. If you like, for betraying her principles.'

'Has she ever stated these principles?'

'No, no, she's not the type. How could I ever like someone who stated principles? Those she holds she embodies. She *is* them. To a crazy, sometimes destructive extent. But whatever she does I accept and I love her, I can't help it.'

'You make her sound awesome.'

'She scares me stiff. Oh God, I can't help wondering it she's long for this world.'

'Why do you say that?'

'I don't know. She's so – breakable. That terrifies me. I smell doom, disaster in her. I'd like her to fly off, anywhere, but then I'd lose her. Sometimes she's so beside herself and I can't bear it. God help me, I've even wished her dead, out of her misery. She's like a bird thrashing round in a bush, hurling herself on thorns.'

'On her own thorns?'

Vivien laughed a short laugh. She said, 'Yes, naturally. Don't we all torment ourselves? Oh you could blame her father, who may have passed his depressive nature on to her, tainted her, who knows? She feared and loved her father, and she despises her mother. What strength she has, and it's quite a lot, derives from this determination she has not to be like her mother.'

'What's she like, this mother?'

'I've not met her. Celia's convinced her mother wants to ruin her, for some reason I've never fathomed. Jealousy, hatred, but why? Her own fate, a sense of her own vileness, a hideous loneliness perhaps? She's a solitary drinker apparently.'

'Do you see any hope for Celia at all?'

I had been looking down at my hands. Raising my head I saw Vivien begin smiling weirdly, as if Celia's unhappy spirit had entered her. 'I wouldn't be surprised by anything she did, good or bad.' Then she said, in a changed, caressing voice, 'The other week she sent me a note. Would you like to hear what it says?'

'Only if you want me to.'

She got out her handbag and rummaged through it, then pulled out a crumpled sheet of notepaper and read: 'I intend to conquer the world of art. I have this craving in me to excel, to be the best. If I wake up one morning convinced of my mediocrity I shall have to kill myself.'

I thought for a moment, then said, 'Does she go on about purity a lot?'

'Yes! All the time. How clever of you!'

'Not really. It just means she sees herself as corrupt, perhaps vile like her poor mother. Does she often say she disgusts herself?'

'That too.'

'Hence the vegetarianism perhaps.'

'I don't know. She's on such a razor's edge. One day she'll slip, and that'll be that.'

'I'm afraid for you.'

'Why are you?'

'You make her sound like your Angel of Death.'

She was shaking her head. 'I don't mean to, no, it's not like that.'

'It could be that she derives her energy from drawing close to death,' I suggested. 'Like the Plath woman. Have you thought of that?'

'Maybe she does. Stop frightening me.'

'It doesn't mean she's going to follow in her idol's footsteps.'

'I wouldn't like to say. My God, her ears must be burning tonight! I wanted to say something else, what was it? You've mixed me up. It wasn't about death.'

'I'll shut up a minute.'

'Oh yes – she's a mythomane. That's my conclusion, my final word on her.'

'A what?'

'She creates a myth of herself, and then proceeds to live it.'

'That's dangerous. So's her too-powerful conscience. What a combination.'

'I know, I know, you're quite right.' She let out a moan. 'God knows, I've tried to help. I really have. I've tried so hard. If I oppose her, I alienate her. All I can do is understand. And I do.'

I struggled to sympathise, but failed. The more I heard, the more I was irritated by the sacrificial aspect of Vivien's mission to save her friend from herself. I said in a neutral tone, 'It seems to me you're in danger of living your life through Celia.' As I pronounced Celia's name my throat tightened.

'Oh no, you're wrong, it isn't like that at all.'

'She engulfs you. You're totally wrapped up in her.'

'Only from choice. I have free will, Francis.'

'Not if you're hypnotised.'

'Oh, really!'

I felt I was about to be rejected and should pull back. I said gloomily, 'Maybe you're a kind of soror mystica.'

'I am? What's that when it's out? It sounds rather nice.'

'Well, if she's a real poet, that is a sort of alchemist, then that makes you an alchemist's companion.'

'I suppose it does. So that's me, is it? A soror mystica. How lovely!'

I said, suddenly jealous, 'I wish I knew what you see in her.'

'Wisdom.'

'Are you serious?'

'Perfectly.'

'Is she sick, would you say?'

'Yes, she is. What do we mean when we say that?'

'I want to hear more about her wisdom.'

'I didn't say she had it. I see it in her as a goal, that's all. For all her craziness and perversity, she strives for wisdom. Why? Don't ask me why. It's that conscience of hers probably, that gives her no rest.'

'Conscience about what?'

'Oh, herself. Something's eating away at her all the time. She condemns herself. Waste, waste of herself, that's the sin. She can freeze her feelings, and does, and then it's awful. Wise, detached people are often horribly cruel, aren't they? Then there's the world and how to live in it. Celia sees the adult as a Jew in a concentration camp I think.'

'That's Plath again.'

'Yes, and it's her too. She's full of imaginary horrors. I doubt if she's got a sense of humour, but she does have a sense of fun, believe it or not. In her mind she plays with these awful ingredients, these bogies, and her poetry makes a kind of celebration out of them. That is, when it doesn't all get twisted up to near screaming point by those tortured nerves of hers.'

She fell silent, and I thought she had finished. Then something secretive and yet smiling appeared in her gaze. She went on, 'I expect you'd like to know whether we've ever been lovers, or if we are now. Any man would, after listening to all I've been saying. The answer is no, not really. There's an almost laughable decorum between us. It seems to be what we both want. Or it could be fear of breaking a taboo, in other words convention. Then once at my place we got more than a bit drunk on vodka and lime. She seemed weirdly reckless and happy, she's got an infectious giggle laugh now and then that makes her sound like a different person entirely. It was my fault, pouring those drinks. I would have done anything to see her taste the joys most of us taste as a matter of course. Anything she had asked for that night I would have given if I could. A delightful child had taken the place of the dark diabolically cunning creature she normally was. Or was this the norm, was she simply set free, released into happiness? Somehow when we were undressed and ready for bed she ended up in mine. I cuddled her, it was glorious, innocent, like a dream come true. She wore one of those absurd baby doll nighties. When she came in from the bathroom with it on we both howled with laughter. "Jake bought it, did you ever see anything so ridiculous?" she shrieked. Then her face changed. "Make love to me." She stretched out her arms so forlornly that my heart broke to see her. "You're drunk," I told her. "Come to bed and behave yourself."

'In bed she lay beside me demurely and I cuddled her. I remember rocking her to and fro as if I had a baby in my arms, rocking out its pain and woe. Suddenly everything changed. From being weak and pliable and helpless she became strong and cruel, authoritative, she tore at my pyjamas, slapped my face when I protested, stripped off her nightdress and swarmed all over me. She wriggled like a fish. Her hands were everywhere. It was obscene what she did. I fought her off as you'd fight off a rapist but she kept coming back, clawing at me with her nails and making animal noises. Then she passed out, lying on top of me. I crawled from under her, covered her with the duvet. She lay on her back unconscious. Francis, did you notice that she's virtually breastless?'

'Yes.'

'It's as if the top part of her hasn't developed, the feeling, nurturing part, as if she stopped herself at a certain age from following in her mother's footsteps and becoming a woman. With her will I think she could stop anything. In her body there's a ferocious war going on between her bad and her good side. I've often wondered, does her denial of sex give her a perverse enjoyment? Is it a form of sex appeal, like some women's cooking? I know what men call females who dangle sex in front of your nose and won't deliver the goods. That's too simple. She's got the anorexic's urge to do away with the body. For someone like her to be pregnant would be like choking to death on her own flesh. She orphans herself out of pride, slaughters her parents in her mind and then dreams of having them back. Spirituality, that's her besetting sin. Lying beside her I thought crazy things. In the small hours all kinds of nonsense comes into your mind. What if she has no womb, just a gaping void in there? What if she was never properly born and ever since has been trying to achieve birth through her will, out of her despair? Wouldn't that explain the anguish? Towards dawn she began to snore, on her back with her mouth open. I stuck it for half an hour and then levered her over. She was surprisingly heavy, a dead weight. So you see, my love for her has even triumphed over her snoring! In the morning she got up, hung over and suicidal,

223

looked at me once with the utmost loathing and then went off without a word. Either she had blotted everything out, was too appalled to speak of it or just couldn't remember a thing. I've not mentioned it since, and she hasn't once referred to it. We resumed our usual decorum.'

'Do you still think about her in that way?' I asked.

'Naked, you mean? Possessed by demons? Oh, I'm not fooling myself, I'm quite certain I brought it about. It was my fault, my doing.'

'You wanted to be lovers?'

'Francis, I keep telling you, I love her. I've given myself up to her without conditions. In or out of bed makes not the slightest difference.'

I paused a moment before asking, 'Can you see her being happy with anyone?'

'Celia? No, never.'

'Not even you?'

I heard Vivien draw breath. She said quietly, 'Isn't that a sadistic question?'

'Probably. It's my jealousy.'

I had spoken frankly because I was certain she wouldn't believe me. Then with her intelligent quizzical eyes on my face I floundered into silence, as uncertain of my own feelings as I was sure of hers.

She smiled tenderly. 'I've been babbling away like a perfect fool. Were you about to say something?'

I came stumbling back with, 'Nothing I could put into words.' In her eyes I saw a fascination that was part childish, contradicted by the high butting forehead with its uncompromising steady attack. I thought too that the wriggling demonic fish I had seen leaping from her story was indeed the very friend I had depicted in my watercolour, perhaps by an act of telepathy, with wide exuberant hips and a schoolgirl's flat bosom.

On Vivien's last day, I came out with something I had been turning over in my mind each time I took her back to her hotel. 'On your next visit you must stay with me. It's daft, look at all this space going to waste. You won't disturb me, not a bit. Think of the money you'd save.'

I had come to realise that my sister, whom I saw as essentially direct and caustic, could also be frivolous. 'Wouldn't you mind, really?' she asked playfully.

'I'd like it.'

'Now don't be rash. You might regret it later. What I regret is not being allowed to see your latest work. Can't I just have a peep?'

'Plenty of time when you come . . .' I fumbled, and then laughed at myself.

'Yes?'

'I nearly said "for good".'

Vivien shot me a warning look that was at the same time full of yearning. 'Oh, don't,' she moaned. 'What's come over you all of a sudden? Don't tempt me with my own dreams.'

'Why dream? Why not act? If you seriously want to get out of London, then do it. What's wrong with down here?'

'Look who's talking! You take ages to decide anything, then as long again to get moving. I'm a gypsy compared to you.'

'Well, it's a thought.'

'You mean here in Devon?'

I began to stutter and stammer in my excitement. 'Yes, that. But here, in Basket Street. Here, in this dump. Here with me!' I said raising my voice in my agitation. 'Listen, I know it's a mess, but think of all the room going to waste, on the ground floor for instance. Does it have to be such a shambles? All it needs is an organising brain – that's you! You could help me civilise my life.' What would it feel like, I was wondering, even as I spoke, to have a woman moving and breathing down below me again?

Vivien was shaking her head and laughing. 'You're insane all of a sudden. But I won't say it hasn't crossed my mind this past week, I've loved it so much.'

'There you are. It's as good as settled.'

'Look, hang on. I'd have to suss out the job prospects.'

'Yes, of course. I should imagine supply teaching is available here, the same as anywhere else. And after all it's a big city.'

Vivien said abstractedly, as if to herself, 'You're a wild man.' She gazed round at her unpromising surroundings. Clearly preoccupied with thoughts of her own, she said warily, 'Now let's get something straight.'

'Go on, dear.'

'Are you really sure of the consequences of what you're so recklessly suggesting?'

'Consequences – what consequences?'

'Well, for one thing, I'm not the easiest person to live with. So I've been told.'

'Did you imagine I was?'

'Where would I live exactly?'

I made a pretence of brooding over the problem, but in fact I had often pictured us together under one roof. 'Leaving aside the ground floor for a moment, wouldn't the space behind that partition there make a good-sized bedroom? I believe it was one once. There's a double bed round here somewhere, I can unearth that for you. You'll sleep in style. Then you'll want a chest of drawers, a wardrobe.'

Vivien cried out in a mixture of fright and pleasure, 'Steady on, my man! This needs plenty of calm serious thought.'

I nodded agreement. 'I know, you're wondering how you can put up with me. Let me reassure you, if you can put aside my track record for a moment. Most of the time I'll be up above out of sight. You'll forget sometimes what I look like.'

She brushed my egotism aside. 'No, I was wondering how badly I should miss my London friends.'

Crouching over where I sat, I felt a pang of contrition. I said, 'Michael, Celia?'

'I'm not involved with Michael any more,' Vivien said proudly. 'As for Celia, wherever I am, she is.' She burst out laughing at the alarm on my face. 'In here,' she added, tapping her temples. Then she sniffed at the air. 'What's that gluey smell?'

'Oh that – I've been sizing a couple of big canvases.' I had also done some painting during her stay, working once far into the night after escorting Vivien to her hotel. One was an oil sketch in the inexhaustible 'Luna' series, began out of ignorance of the motif's scope. This was a silent drama of jealousy I called 'Amanuensis', decked out with deceptive innocence in spring colours, and no sooner dry than abandoned, because too literary. Titles were nearly always a sign of failure. The painting showed a long looming nose and morose eyes glued to an invisible window and the bare back of a dancing houri. Her clapping hands above the round rapt head were vestigial – and no castanets. The only detail I still liked was a huge ragged poppy, bluish-black-hearted, bloodily drooping its skirts on a level with the dancer's navel. Overhead a pale green moon floated serenely, its soft oval indistinct. Through fantasy I discovered again what I already knew and heard playing in the flutes of my bones. In fantasies, as in our sleep, an ancient past resurrected itself. Desires roamed at will over boundaries, copulating with anything that moved. Skeletons embraced maidens, hetaeras turned into maenads with a lust for entrails. Abominations and raptures, like disease and love, danced hand in hand over a sweet earth that was one gigantic grave.

Getting up too suddenly, I winced at a stab of pain in my lower spine.

'What is it?' Vivien asked at once. 'Have you hurt yourself?'

I was thrilled by her concern. 'It's nothing. Just tension.'

'Why – what are you tense about?'

'Everything. All the time.'

'I'm serious,' she said sharply. 'You ought to take better care of yourself – '

'At my age,' I finished.

'At any age. What exercise do you take?'

'Walking about. Running up and down all these stairs.'

'Why don't you try Yoga?'

'Would that be any good for a fifty-odd year-old back?'

'Marvellous!'

I was touched by her enthusiasm. 'Will you teach me?'

'It's something you need to read about first, and ponder. I'll bring you a book, shall I?'

'Yes. Bring it when you move in.'

She was standing in a fall of light, her fine hair which she found such a nuisance looking freshly spun. Seeing that bright halo, I was filled with absurd hope.

'Oh you're a cunning devil,' she said, 'and no mistake.'

'Half a devil,' I said, not knowing what I meant.

Vivien parted her lips thoughtfully. How was she taking my extraordinary proposal? Could the powers of telepathy be at work again? Was it, if the truth were known, more her idea

227

than mine? My own motives remained obscure, hidden from my conscious mind. Why had I blurted it out now, instead of waiting? After all, my work was at stake. I hastened to console and mock myself, thinking, She'll rejuvenate as well as feed me. All I shall be expected to give in return is brotherly love and the rudiments of a home.

Later, on the platform beside her northbound train, I looked up into her face smiling down at me from a carriage window, 'I'll be in touch,' she said, already with that hint of detachment a traveller has when the journey beckons. As the train moved out, she called, 'What if you have second thoughts?'

'Or a second birth,' I laughed, and imagined my face grimacing like a gargoyle.

I waved goodbye until her arm, flapping up and down in the distance, failed to convince me that it was attached to her.

The few passers-by I encountered as I retraced my steps glanced curiously at my face, or was it at my clothes? Or my expression perhaps? Maggie had remarked – and so later on had Della – on the wild-eyed look I turned on her at times, if the difficulty I was tussling with in my head wouldn't come right. I went on up the rise and down the long bald slope of the pavement in a rush, carried along by the stampede of my thoughts, though what exactly I was thinking I couldn't have said. I wondered once or twice if I was talking aloud to myself without being aware of it. Plunging back into the friendlier atmosphere of my own small-scale district, with its medieval-sized alleys and patches of worn cobbles, I noticed more rude staring and glanced nervously down the front of my trousers. Had I left the zip of my flies open again?

Nothing so obvious. The light now was incredible, and I escaped to some extent from my self-consciousness. An enormous sun smouldered down behind some ochre chimney pots which were blackening as I watched. It was still fairly early, so I marched past my door and kept on. I thought I heard the phone ringing, but as it caught my attention it ceased.

I took the route of my habitual late morning walks, letting the tubular rails my hands lingered over guide me up out of the shut-down Barbican and around the first bend at the top of the hill. I gazed seaward, but by the movement of my legs could have been blind.

Nothing soothes like the sea at this hour, I thought gratefully; nothing to beat the water in this mood, shining and white, peaceful as milk. The sun fell down behind Cornwall, the sky running with a green so staggering that it must, I always thought, have been the despair of countless painters. For one thing it was too profound. It gave one the urge to kneel, to stop struggling, almost to cease to exist. My throat constricted. I wanted to tell Vivien that her coming would make all the difference in the world to me, but if she had been here, would I have found the words? I cursed my pride, my vanity, for making my love sound like the expression of a whim. My mind recoiled in idiotic dismay from itself.

Leaving the rail I climbed the steep curving road beneath the granite walls of the Citadel. There facing me was the darkening shrubbery, the evergreens I disliked, the soil littered with ice-cream wrappers. I spotted the Michaelmas daisies, those thick clotted blooms I always associated with the north. The massed purple, yellow-eyed stars blazed passionately through all my young autumns, bringing back Nottingham and its fogs, its false starts, its sick heart in love with love, mistaking mirrors for loved persons. In my older but no wiser heart I tore at this memorialised virgin self as if to pluck it from my past and be free of illusion at last. Shaking my head, I stared at those memorial clumps. An old woman selling bunches of them in a restaurant swam up in my mind. Hands in my pockets I sauntered back in the direction of Basket Street.

On the broad expanse of black tarmac, raised up to receive the tattery flames of a half engulfed sun, I decided on a quick looping detour around the white black-capped column of Smeaton Tower, now a historic monument. The fairy-tale door at the lighthouse base was showing a Closed sign. I wanted suddenly to go swarming up, round and round the stone spiral on those treads worn hollow and treacherously smooth. I pictured my missile-figure bursting out on the tiny circular railed balcony and arcing into the light. Its velocity would be a measure of my joy in Vivien's capitulation. Or was it mine?

I had gone up there only once, in broad daylight. The little platform when I emerged was thick with children squabbling and elbowing for the best view. A young woman teacher with a pinched face warned them not to lean out, her voice shrill. Her near hysteria was contagious. I felt sorry for her, then unnerved. No one noticed me. Dizzy and sickened by vertigo

I stood back against the stone, my fingers trying vainly to cling to it. The terrifying forms of clouds rolled around my head like great sails as I fell into the gulf of space behind my eyes.

As I got back in, the phone was ringing and ringing. It was now deep dusk. The phone rang with a peculiar urgency – how could this be? I snatched off the receiver and called, 'Hello, hello!' and as I called and no one answered I heard the urgency in my own voice, echoing the phone's. Maggie was there at the other end of the line. I knew it before she spoke. When she did answer she could hardly catch her breath.

All this year I had been in touch with her, though not literally because we hadn't exchanged a word. I could say unwillingly, for she dwelt in my thoughts, she was on my mind, she wouldn't leave me in peace. I am certain it was her concentrating on me and not the other way round. Of course I did want to resume contact with her, but not if she was now settled and happy. She belonged now to someone else. I could have pestered her, got her to concern herself in my affairs for old time's sake, played on her sentimentality. I didn't, I left well alone. Slowly her grip on my spirit had weakened.

'Hello!' I shouted. My conviction wavered. Perhaps no one was there. But the line wasn't dead. Yes, it was her, breathing. Did she just want to hear my voice?

At last she said, panting, 'I'm in a call box. Where have you been? I rang and rang. The phones in these streets are all vandalised. I had to run to get into this one before somebody beat me to it. I don't like him, he's a skinhead.'

'Who is?'

'The kid waiting outside. He just pulled a face. I don't think he wants the phone, he wants to mug me.' I heard whimpering. 'Oh, Wes.'

'Maggie, calm down and listen. Why aren't you ringing from home?'

'Why d'you think? Gregory's there.'

'Couldn't you wait till he went out?'

'I did, I did. You didn't answer, you weren't there. Or were you? Have you got someone living with you?'

'No, no. But I might have soon.'

'I thought so. I'm going.'

'Wait, let me explain!'

'This phone needs more monies. I'll put in all I've got. Go on, explain. You can't make me more miserable than I am already.'

'It's not what you think. Vivien's talking about coming here – moving in with me.'

'Vivien, your sister?'

'That's right, yes. She's considering it.'

'Wes, I like her. She came to see me, wasn't that nice?'

'Yes, she told me. She's been here for a short break, staying here. We were talking about you only yesterday.'

'Speak up, this line's bad.'

'I can hear you perfectly.'

'You can what?'

I began to bawl. 'Is that better?'

'Too loud. It's all right again. Wes, I'm sorry, I know you hate emotions. I just wanted to feel in touch with you.'

'Is that fellow still outside?'

'Who?'

'The one you were worried about. The punk.'

'No, he's gone. He stuck his fingers up and left. Charming. A black lady with a little girl's waiting. I'll have to go in a minute.'

'What's making you so miserable?'

'Not Gregory, if that's what you think. He's got a heart, not like you, and he loves me, he does really, even though he sees other women who don't mean anything to him. He says I'm the one and I believe him.'

'I don't understand.'

There was a blank silence. Then I heard a gasping sound, which became weeping. I stood listening, holding the phone away from my ear. In desperation I cried angrily, 'If you don't stop I'm going to hang up.'

'I've got to go anyway. We'll be cut off in a minute.'

'Ring me again from home, when you're private. I'm always in, Maggie. Ring afternoons or evenings.'

She wailed down the phone, 'I want to know you care about me! If you don't, say so. You won't hear from me again, ever.'

The pips sounded rapidly. 'Wait a minute, give me your number!' I shouted. The phone went dead. Then I heard the humming sound.

24

It was a new year. I went downstairs to feed my cats – the early evening ritual. It was either that or have them come up yowling and importuning from the doorway. When I did finally stop work and attend to them, their untrammelled ecstasy would shame me.

I used to feed them on the ground floor, under the back window I kept permanently open. Vivien had changed that. Since she moved in they had been fed in the kitchen part of the living room, something I found distasteful but kept tactfully quiet about.

Feeding them was the first thing she did when she came in from her teaching. She had gone to London for the weekend, so it was my task again. When she was home, I would first hear the engine of her old yellow car splutter and die, down in the street, and then her quick footsteps climbing up through the building.

Once, during her first week, I asked her, 'Do you like cats?'

'I don't dislike them,' she answered, and this told me what I wanted to know. She was no cat lover. Maybe I was only one myself in my imagination. I saw how faithless they were, how they fraternised with all and sundry. I suppose what I admire is their assumption of superiority. They lay about like slatterns, and then I utilised them as models. Indian ink sketches of them, with heads resembling fox cubs, or goats, were tacked up on walls flanking the stairs, over the bath, in the lavatory cubicle and in the kitchen. One of these days I was going to attempt a full-blown painting of a 'cat-soul'.

If they jumped on my lap in Vivien's presence I shoved them off when she wasn't looking. Because I was unable to approve of these anti-cat tendencies in myself I tried now and then to project them on my sister. In fact her attitude puzzled me. She would seem like me, aloof in her feelings, almost cold, then at other times she nearly drooled over the cats. It was the inconsistency which I found baffling.

Probing none too subtly, I said once, 'I've seen women shudder if a cat so much as brushed against their legs.'

'So have I.'

'If you'd been one of those I'd have had problems.'

'I don't mind them.'

'I knew of a cat which always sucked the buttons on women's cardigans. Not men's.'

'Are you trying to tell me something?'

'You wouldn't put up with that.'

'How do you know?'

'I'm guessing.'

'Guess again, know-all.'

'Would you?'

'It depends on my mood. The amorous rubbing around cats do is something they do to anybody, even to the leg of a chair. It's just them.'

'That doesn't sound like a cat-lover.'

Instead of being amused, she said stiffly, 'They get properly looked after, don't they?'

'Better than when I did it, yes. They get two meals a day now,'

'Good.'

I headed disconsolately for the stairs. What else could I say to ruffle her feathers? Forgive me, Vivien, I thought, I'm not nice. My work with its endless false starts was the trouble. Frequently these days it rounded on me with a speciousness I thought quietly terrible. To lie down and go to sleep inhaling its smell and treachery was no doubt an idiotic thing to do. It was a habit I found hard to break. Vivien swore the air was toxic and once made for the window to throw it open. I kicked up such a fuss that she retreated, muttering that I was certifiable. The other night in a dream I fell soundlessly through one canvas mirror after another. Leaves, ashes, gushing out from my surrogate's chest, emptied me in a matter of seconds. I was left with a body dividing like water, that went floating mutely after its darkness and seed, shrivelling to lie curled up in the light and dust. Waking to a grisly dawn light my fingers touched a stickiness on my inner thigh. I had had a nocturnal emission.

Hovering in the doorway like one of my cats, I said, 'Another thing they seem to like is licking the armpits of woollen jumpers.'

Vivien was knitting away at a garment in sage green. 'This isn't a jumper, it's a scarf.' To me, all knitters looked infuriatingly philosophical as well as half sedated.

'Oh, I see.'

Her fingers worked steadily. It struck me that she was under a spell. Was I envious?

233

'Where are you off to?'

'Upstairs.'

'See if you can think of anything else that might disgust me,' she said slyly, without raising her head.

'Or me.'

At this time, without being aware of it I was entering the uncharted waters of a new crisis. I ploughed blindly on, with frequent outbursts of irritability, as far as Easter. One day, coming in from Benny's café, my feet weighted like a diver's, my mouth sugary from the jam doughnuts I had been stuffing into myself, I stood irresolute with my hand gripping the door knob. The key inserted in the keyhole refused to twist. I glanced wildly up and down the street. The truth was that I could no longer face my top room, where everything spoke with one voice telling me that the desire had catastrophically died.

I became clumsy at mealtimes, knocking over glasses and cups like a baby. Shaving once every few days I often cut myself. Once I nicked the lobe of my ear and the bleeding wouldn't stop. Making the blood congeal became a major obsession. Vivien laughed. How could a tiny pinprick be the cause of so much neurosis? Evidently she saw me as an overgrown child brother whining for sympathy, which indeed I was.

I was finding her strange contentment increasingly hard to take. Vivien tended her house plants, the African violets and geraniums, a bowl of hyacinths, or she sat reading a book or knitting. She finally drove me upstairs more or less permanently when she came in one evening with a portable television, bought second-hand from a colleague. I was caught now in a cruel dilemma. The only way to avoid her company, desperately though I longed for it at times, was by shutting myself up with my failures.

I still came down for meals. Hearing Vivien call I would descend with my shame like a condemned man, sit opposite her at the table and bolt down the food without appetite, my head lowered. Made guilty by her role of servant, though she didn't complain, I got up the minute I was finished and lingered by the sink ready to do the washing-up. One evening I was so far ahead of her, fidgetting uselessly at the back of her chair, waiting to snatch up her plate, that she lost her temper. 'This is stupid, crazy!' Her knife and fork clashed on the stone plate. My shoulders shot up round my ears.

'What is?' I whispered. These days, as I became more and more reluctant to speak, my voice seemed to issue in a kind of sighing.

'You, standing there. How can I enjoy anything, how can I eat with you haunting me? I keep getting indigestion – it's you! Can't you just *sit down?*'

'My knees ache,' I whispered.

'Francis, sit down.' She pointed angrily at my chair. 'I want to know what's going on.'

I said, 'Nothing's going on. Worse luck.'

'What did you say?' She craned forward, glaring, as if longing to land a blow. 'Speak up, man.'

'Nothing.' I rose blindly. The chair grated, toppled.

'Now look what you've done! What the hell is it? What's the matter? What's wrong with you?'

'Leave me alone,' I shouted weakly, plunging for the stairs.

Hearing noises from below the next morning, I came down to explore what should have been empty premises at that hour. Vivien was sizzling bacon and eggs in the frying pan. I watched in bewilderment.

'Want some?'

'I thought you'd be at work – '

'It's Good Friday,' she said. 'I'm on holiday for two weeks.'

Aghast, I escaped. A desert of exile in my workroom stretched before me.

Driven by necessity, I somehow managed to come to terms with Vivien. Each day of the next fortnight brought a crisis, but at least these erupted outside myself. Almost I relished them as a reminder that other forces were at work. I ran the gamut of moods I could barely control and wasn't aware that I had, from a mad scratching irritability to the half imbecilic docility which I hoped would convey the tenderness I always felt for her in the depths of my being.

I was on the point of regressing to childhood and knew it. I went round tugging at my fingers and hair and gnawing my lower lip, craving reassurance from anywhere. In the privacy of my workroom I grabbed one of the cats and tried to nurse it, for some creature comfort. But it was the intransigent black witch's cat. It immediately twisted off, affronted. It stood in the middle of the floor staring at me with its baleful wide yellow stare. I threw a ruined brush at

235

it, nearly crying out, wanting to weep in sheer frustration.

Also I bathed a lot, trying to relax knotted muscles, creeping down when I thought the coast was clear. To be seen at all, let alone naked, was a growing horror. At Vivien's insistence I had had a washbasin installed alongside the bathtub. As yet there were still no enclosing walls. An avenue led through the junk from the stairwell. Once, after Vivien protested vigorously, I stood the folding screen round the tub as a compromise solution. It stayed there.

A long shelf on rusty brackets, on one side of which I left my toothbrush and shaving gear, now carried a row of richly blooming fuschias in terracotta pots, on tin lids and saucers. Looking sideways at the blaze of colour one morning – outside it was blowing a gale and sluicing down – I saw the luscious red and purple hung bells as Vivien's message to me. In my unhinged state it was as if she had delved into the secret softnesses of her own body and produced them. Was this a kind of incest? The flowers hung like women's secrets, available yet hidden, a delicate blushing array. Where had they come from? Was she attempting to revive me by seduction? Could she be my inspiratrice?

Later that day the sky cleared and flashed blue, before white timid clouds scudded over. I ventured out and was in time to see the rainwater vanishing down drains, trickling and gurgling like the tea in my quaky guts.

On the first corner as I plodded submissively uphill I was brought face to face on the uneven paving flags with an elderly Pole I knew only by sight. I understood he was a survivor of the camps. He always hailed me with continental enthusiasm, nodding his over-large head with its gush of thick white hair. Today was no exception. 'Good day, Mister! Nice wedder now!' He was chewing the ragged stump of an unlit cigarette he had perhaps forgotten.

I was enlivened simultaneously by the Pole's simple exuberance and the patch of torn blue I could see now appearing over a rooftop like a flag madly waving. This broke me out of my prison for as long as it took my legs to go past the foreigner. Then I fell back into thoughts as intricate and senseless as my dreams. I trudged with bent head, following the road because I had nowhere to go, because my will, if it existed, swung in me like a broken compass. I had one task, and that was to kill time.

Finally, up in my retreat, I was reduced to copying. It was how I had first begun, with the aim of mastering techniques, before I knew what if anything I was meant to create. I inked away at an owl. The snapshot, torn from a magazine, was lying close to my right hand. The owl's inky black eye represented my own blackness until I travelled beyond it, transfixed by the pinpoint of light in each furious pupil. I scratched away at the lint surface, and at something beyond reach within myself, where I was blindly trapped.

I heard sounds. Vivien was calling me. 'Yes?' I shouted. I could hear her climbing nearer. Then she entered my room, something she never did unless expressly invited. My pen dripping blots, I twisted round to see.

'Are you deaf? I've been yelling blue murder down there.'

'Why, what's wrong?'

'Who said anything was wrong? Look at you – like a wild man. Your hair's standing on end.'

She seemed peculiarly bright-cheeked. Her eyes glowed and she looked keen with purpose. Everything about her mocked my inertia. She stood in the doorway confidently, but didn't advance further. If she was waiting for permission, I thought grimly, she had picked the wrong moment.

'Did you want me for anything?'

She said brusquely, 'We've got a visitor. That's all. I'd like you to come down, if you can possibly spare the time.' She was bustling away in the act of speaking.

'Wait!' I shouted, filled with panic. 'Who is it, for God's sake? Not for me I hope?'

'Come and see,' she called, her voice floating up.

I dived downstairs in pursuit of her. Going into the kitchen I caught my toe in the frayed carpet and entered the room off balance, with an ugly jerk. The stranger, sitting with her back to me, jumped violently on her chair. It was a young woman.

'We're about to treat ourselves to a very English afternoon tea,' Vivien said. In her voice I heard the notes of a strange coquettishness. After my siege-like existence of the past two weeks this struck me as quite grotesque. Disorientated, I wondered whether it was for my benefit or the visitor's. Vivien added politely. 'Would you care to join us?'

Then I understood the reason for her joyfulness and teasing. Celia sat in our kitchen. I edged closer for a better view, since she sat so unmovingly. I scarcely recognised her for the Celia I had met in Holland Park and then again in her well-appointed loft at Chalk Farm. Her face had lost its chubbiness, and she was now a blonde, with straight, quite long hair, cut neatly in a bob with side parting. She wore a dark full skirt, and a raspberry padded jacket with mandarin collar and tapes dangling. There was a bulky hood to the jacket, giving her back a rounded look.

I fixed my gaze on the jacket's embossed metal buttons rather than her face. 'I didn't realise it was you, Celia. It's your hair I think.'

Celia laughed. With her terrible unconvincing calmness she said, 'Blondes have all the fun.'

I noticed that her smaller-than-expected mouth was unsteady, and switched my gaze hastily to a point above her head. Then, remembering Vivien's admonitions – I drove her mad, she said, with my straying glances when we were in conversation – I returned to the buttons. I feared Celia's emanations, flooding now as a stammering confusion across the room, dreading more than ever their power to trigger off my own instabilities. Why has she come, what's she doing here? my racing thoughts were demanding to know, and above all, how long will she stay?

Feeling the need to say something, anything, which would produce a response, I said, 'I'm sorry, I tripped, I didn't mean to frighten you.'

Vivien gave me a cup and saucer, which I was grateful to be able to hold, though I didn't want the tea. 'Sit down, Francis.' She gave me a stiff encouraging smile.

'When was that?' Celia asked. 'I didn't notice anything.' Smiling compulsively, she gave Vivien a pleading look, as if to say, 'Save me from this brother of yours.'

'It doesn't matter,' I mumbled in confusion. Looking from one face to the other, I added, 'You'll have things to talk about, so I'll get back to work.'

'Nonsense,' Vivien said. 'Celia's only just got here. Stay and be civilised for once, it's a nice change. Have a scone. I know how you like strawberry jam.' Astonishing me still further with the picture of serene domesticity she was presenting, she said to Celia, 'I hardly ever see him these days, he's so busy.'

I took a gulp of tea and nearly choked on it. When I did leave after a few more minutes of painful tension, Celia was being divested of her padded jacket by Vivien, who handled her with the careful caution one brings to invalids. As I left the kitchen Vivien sought my eyes and spoke to me dumbly with a look of gratitude. For what? I asked myself. But I went out gladly, feeling I was about to be drawn in a drama in which my role had not been explained or the plot made clear, but where my participation was mysteriously required. That meant I had value after all, and not just as a lone artist. My work might be dead and finished but I lived. In a tumult I walked up to my room, a room no longer hateful or dreaded. Paintings and drawings, even those tossed aside as worthless, seemed all at once to acquire value, to contain possibilities for development which I had inexplicably overlooked. I looked from one to another, picked up sketchbooks and flicked through dozens of pages. Each picture, each image, whether complete or perfunctory or abandoned, suddenly possessed the power to excite me. Everything had unaccountably altered.

'I'd like her to stay here for a little while, with us,' my sister said. Clearly she was determined, but she had made her expression warmly attractive and her voice compliant, since it was my place after all. She asked mildly, 'Would that be all right with you?'

We were sitting in an area she had made more pleasant by degrees over the past few months. She referred to it mockingly as the parlour. Yet the very mockery was an indulgence, suggesting the extent of her pride. I glanced about appraisingly, surprised and pleased by her home-making skills. I was in a nest. It had all happened under my nose. Had I really sunk so far and so low, not to have noticed before this?

Away from the tall rear window, which rattled madly during gales, was the doorless opening to her bedroom. The long curtains in there were always drawn because the room overlooked the narrow street. She refused to bandage the glass, as she put it, with net curtain.

I sat silent a moment. As I sat there marvelling at her, I expected something of significance to be revealed, at any moment to be rocked back on my heels. 'I don't see why not,' I said noncommittally.

It was late afternoon, the day after Celia's arrival. Celia's belongings were strewn untidily on the floor beside the military-looking hold-all she had brought with her.

'Good. Thank you. I'll ask her when she comes in.'

'Is she likely to say no?'

A hint of laughter showed in Vivien's eyes. 'You never can tell.'

'You might have told me she was coming.'

Vivien didn't hesitate. 'In the atmosphere we were living in? Francis, be fair. You weren't in any kind of communication with me. I was beginning to think you loathed me.'

'Was I that bad?'

'Don't you know?'

'I think so. I wasn't even in touch with myself.'

'Are you feeling better now?'

'I suppose I am. I'm too superstitious to say.'

'I wanted to help you – I just didn't know how.'

'If my work stops or goes rotten, so do I.'

'You're working again now?'

'Not exactly. But the thought of it enlivens me. I'm not disgusted any more. I live in hope.'

'Francis, I've missed you. Your mood's changed, I can tell it's better, and it's changed your face. You look years younger all of a sudden. Oh dear, what a precarious life you lead.'

'We all do. It's just more obvious with some than others.'

'Yes. Like Celia. Seeing her again must have given you a shock. I'm sorry.'

'Sometimes a shock to the system is what we want.'

'What do you make of her? Tell me.'

'Celia? She's jumping out of her skin as usual. I know now what that's like. Where is she by the way?'

'Oh, out somewhere, walking around, seeing where she is.'

'That's funny, I'd have sworn she was indifferent to her surroundings.'

'That's because you don't know her at all.'

We talked on. Pleased with each other, deeply relieved and thankful to be back in touch, we kept breaking into smiles.

I looked at her in a new observant way, noticing how the bones of her face were emphasised by the severe cut of her hair, which left her small ears naked. I sat pondering the fresh evidence of her ears for a possible drawing. They were set flat against her head; they looked impatient. I was as startled by them as by the new situation, developing as though of its own volition. How had I come to be reprieved? Who or what was playing a trick on me, I wondered, smiling wryly to myself, willing to be tricked.

'Is it likely to help her, do you think?'

'Is what?'

'Being here.'

Vivien shrugged. 'I don't know. Has it helped you? Forgive me, I didn't mean it to sound like that.'

'It's a good question. I'm not sure if I can answer it.'

'I suppose a place can help if we're open to help. If we've closed the hatches and crash-dived, all we can do is lie on the bottom and hope for a miracle.'

'Is that where she is?'

'I wish I knew. Perhaps being here will be a good thing, perhaps it won't. I just want to look after her.'

'She's still with Jake?'

'Theoretically, yes. Poor devil!'

'You don't see him as the enemy any more?'

'God, no – did I ever? How can you have got that idea in your head? Misguided, yes, wrong-headed certainly, but no man's a saint. Look what he's had to put up with from her. That sounds terrible too, but you know what I mean. The truth is they're disastrous as a couple and always have been. It's like an awful joke, putting two such people together and saying "Love one another". They bring out the worst in each other. Narcissists in love – what a recipe for disaster. Though I doubt if Celia has ever known what we call love. I can't believe she has the word in her vocabulary.'

'I don't remember you saying this before.'

'I don't either. I do my thinking by talking aloud. But it's the truth and I accept it, I'm not loved, I don't expect to be loved. I just want to be allowed to love.'

'And are you?'

'Well, aren't I? She's here. She's come all this way on the train to me, hasn't she?'

'To be looked after by you?'

'Yes. Basically.'

'What if she changes her mind and won't let you? I mean, how will you feel?'

'Well, that's happened before, and more than once. Anything's possible. We'll have to see.'

We fell silent then, like conspirators who could go so far towards a common goal and no farther. I was about to ask where Celia would sleep, then decided against it. Where had she slept last night? Had they shared the double bed? For some reason I found this thought satisfying, before it became alarming. I

241

went away to consider the implications in private. Where she slept was of no consequence, but my curiosity was stirred, and so was an emotion I identified as jealousy. Now that I had found Vivien again and been reconciled, feeling closer, warmer, more at one with her than ever, was I now to lose her, and on my home ground? But when I tried to imagine facing Vivien with these fears I couldn't, because of the necessity of appearing to be her ally. And surely, in some deep sense, I was?

Celia seemed to be avoiding me for most of her short stay, ducking out of sight into the bedroom when I appeared without warning once or twice in the refurbished 'parlour'. Since she never joined us for meals I began to wonder if she ever ate, or did she manage to exist on milky coffee and aspirations? Apparently one of her phobias was an inability to eat in front of others. I wasn't offended, I ceased to question things. The changed circumstances, together with a new hopefulness as spring stirred underground and a fresh cold light announced itself, the grass beginning to grow, trees taking on a hazy fragrance which would soon be leaves, all these things put a kind of trance of acceptance on me. I was prepared to go on with things simply because they had come into being.

Then one day I became aware that Celia was no longer with us.

'Has she gone?' I asked, careful not to sound relieved.

'Temporarily, yes.'

'Where to?'

'She's got friends in Bristol, a doctor and his wife. I think Jake and Tom have known each other since school. They're both Bristolians.'

'But she's coming back?'

'She said so, yes. Are you sure you don't mind?'

'No, I don't mind. I hardly see her. She can stay as long as she likes.'

'Thank you. She does love it here.'

Surprised, I said, 'Did she say so?'

Vivien smiled ambiguously. 'In as many words.'

We sat together a while longer, alone and yet not. Celia may have departed but her unquiet spirit lingered in every corner. I went upstairs, back to a painting I had begun in a state of wintry grace, of some abstracted leggy flowers, cut daffodils and freesias, stroking at them with my brush to draw my own sudden glad influx of spring out of them. Life died, and was renewed. Raising up these dead flowers was like trying to resurrect oneself. The models I had bought weeks ago for Vivien in a fit of remorse, then apologetically scrounged back. They stood withering among encrusted paint cans in the window, their heads fizzled out, in the blunt cylinder of a vase stuck with ceramic vines – a relic of my Chycoose days, when I would poke about in the entrails of junk shops for props, unable to say what I was looking for.

On my walks now I had taken to circling the old harbour in the opposite direction, marching for once away from the sea. The sharp early spring air quickened my stride. Bulbous cobbles underfoot jolted my spine. Soon I arrived in the thick of close-packed stone warehouses jutting out on the harbour frontage, skirting the mess of ropes, the cranes and storage tanks on the wharfs. I traipsed up and down the dull alleys and was sliced by the edges of cold shadows.

One day, suddenly feeling that my surrender to fate had released me into a new space, full of peace and freedom, I began to trot and then gallop. I broke into the open and then was calmed by the monumental dignity of old stones. I still went for another fifty yards as fast as my legs would carry me, coming to a halt gasping and glowing.

A young workman emerged from the mouth of an open blister-shaped shed stacked with buttery yellow timber directly ahead of me and sat on an upturned crate. By the time I drew level he was picking at his soggy parcel of fish and chips.

The sun worked free and splashed down. My eyes met the youth's, and he winked. Or he may have been squinting at the light. 'Just the job,' he said affably. He tucked in.

The painter in me admired the lad's features, noting the unashamedly ravenous teeth, the stuffed pouches of his fresh cheeks, his black hair shining with health. He spread his legs, sunning his thighs with the animal pleasure of one of my cats. I went past and on, to where there was a blind corner.

'You'll drop off the edge,' I heard behind me.

'Beg your pardon?'

'Dead end that way. Unless you fancy a swim.'

'I don't think so.' I had to retrace my steps, crossing in front of the overalled figure a second time.

'Fancy a chip? Here y'are. Dig in.'

Our eyes met again. Out of courtesy I helped myself.
'Thanks.'

'You're a teacher, right?'

'Not exactly,' I laughed. 'I've got a sister who is.'

'Not a bad try. I like to guess what people do. I could tell
you was educated.'

Before long the problem of how to extricate myself began
making me anxious. Thanking my new friend again I went off
sucking my fingers, back to an activity I had managed not to
disclose.

25

In no time it was May, the growing year full of swiftness
and grace, the green earth heaving up. Every stick hung out
leaves, waved and flowered. In the stale air and paint stink of
old struggles I stood taking stock, suddenly among plenty. The
season of despair for weak dreamers lay down its challenge: live
or die.

Ceila hadn't returned. It was becoming easy for me to forget
she had ever been here. Vivien explained that she had gone back
home in a hurry because Jake's father, ill with cancer, was close
to death, and I saw her suddenly in a new light. And I kept
seeing dandelions everywhere.

Vivien came up. She stood in my doorway, stopped by an
invisible wire. Unnerved by this visit I beckoned her in with
what I hoped was a welcoming expression. She appeared not
to notice. She faltered there as if listening, perhaps sniffing
cautiously like a cat instead of seeing. She said meekly,
like someone seeking a penance, 'I should have come up
before this.'

Why should you?'

'Because I wanted to. It was important to me.'

Looking at her, I was seized by the idea that she was about to
say something extraordinary. At the same time, to my surprise
I felt hurt. 'Then why didn't you? What was stopping you? Am
I such an ogre?'

She shook her head. 'It wouldn't have been right.'

'Right?'

'Things were in the way.'

'Stop talking in riddles.'

'Difficulties. Obstacles. I didn't like myself.'

'I don't follow.'

'All right, I'll come out with it. I'm a little jealous of your sense of purpose. I don't have anything to compare with this world of yours.' She waved her arm to encompass the contents of my workroom.

'You're idealising. This isn't like you. I thought only men were idealists. You've got a purpose, you're a person. Get back to reality, Vivien.'

'May I come in?'

'Of course, I'm sorry, come in please, Vivien. Come in, dear. You're the one person who doesn't need to ask.'

I smiled encouragingly at her, the surrogate father who seeks to make everything right but is unsure of his ground. 'Now, can I show you anything?' I asked, like a too-pressing shopkeeper. She came up so rarely, and I was more nervous than I would have believed possible.

She walked in. I stood with foolishly dangling hands. She seemed to wake up with a little jerk. 'I don't know anything about art, I'm completely out of my depth.'

'This isn't like you.'

'But it's true.'

'That gives you a big advantage. Just respond honestly. Better still, don't say anything. Silence can be a form of communication. If it's shared, that is.'

I retreated before her, and the ruse worked; she came further in to the chaotic, pungently smelling room. Her eyes flew wide open and rounded, swimming hugely, regarding everything. Her vulnerability in my presence was something entirely new. On all sides my signs and symbols lost their potency, meanings blew away. I stood with things fallen to dust and lying somewhere out of reach, my hands empty, my heart overturned, touched by my sister's curious awkwardness. It was the first time I had seen her at a loss. I pitied her, unhappily in love with Celia, pitied her stuck with me. She deserved better; we all did.

In a drowsy, half absent voice which seemed to lift me up, she said, 'What a lot of dandelions.' Her gaze travelled round the walls. I wanted to hug her, and I wanted to open my mouth and hear a stream of laughter pour from it, standing there as if dejected with nothing to say, certainly nothing striking, and beyond the walls the whole of May's beauty laid out like a banquet.

The dandelions out there had kept coming and coming. They were on the patches of vacant ground between gashed streets where bombs had once ripped into them, and on steep banks, and even squeezing from the fissures in wrinkled asphalt. These brassy ignored sunflowers with their flat-ended petals would send me spinning back and forth to my task on their yellow cogwheels. Before long I was obsessed. I threw them down straight from the tube in thick gobbets trailing ghostly bled stalks, arranged singly in long rows and phalanxes. They swam up in blues and greens, with pale tails; they were melting, like the hot hearts of bonfires, they spread themselves in half hemispheres, in fat golden cushions. I couldn't pile them up high enough. Now I saw them as my gift to Vivien.

'Do you like them?'

She frowned, perhaps made uneasy by my intense nervous anticipation. My question was no sooner out of my mouth than regretted. What did I care whether she liked them or not? I had heaped them up because spring makes you crazy, and now I wanted to pour them over her.

'I don't really know,' she said. 'I don't have the right words.'

What words? I cursed her for a fool, a dithering female who took everything too seriously, who thought I was expecting her to pronounce like a critic. 'Say anything. The first thing that comes into your head.'

'They aren't representational – if that's the word – but I can see of course what they are. They seem to stand for something else, and that's worrying.'

'You like them to be one or the other?'

'I think so. I don't know. I told you I know nothing.'

'One of the old New York intellectuals, a man called Rosenberg, used to say that the painter now, in this century, was at liberty to foul up the canvas. In other words, not everything one does has to make sense.'

She made no reply, but wandered around more interestedly, examining this and that, as if she had suddenly granted herself a freedom.

'Art's hard,' she whispered.

'Is that Celia speaking?'

246

'I haven't heard her say so. I'm sure she'd agree. But I wouldn't have to ask. Knowing her, I can tell.'

'What's the hardest thing I wonder?'

'I could never do it. It's all the stripping, the letting go. I wouldn't be ruthless enough. There's so much to love in the world.'

I thought how clean she looked, freshly nautical in her near white trousers and trim dark blazer. She watched me expectantly. I marvelled at her smartness. She gave off an aroma which I had only gradually registered. I became aware of her breathing, of her difference. She came into her own as a woman.

Directly behind her was my mattress bed. Vivien dropped down on it, as though obeying an impulse of frivolity to compensate for all this art. She folded her legs like a yogi, sitting up very straight. She dug a hand into her blazer pocket and it came out clutching a chocolate bar in a bright orange wrapper. This acted like a signal and we smiled idiotically at each other, ringed around by the dandelions of my second childhood. Like a person who had given up free choice I wondered happily what she would say next, in the strange mood she was in. She unwrapped her chocolate bar with careful fingers. 'Would you like to paint me one day?' she asked.

'I've wanted to for years,' I answered gladly and at once.

With a perfectly straight face and in the same serious tone of voice she said, 'Would you like a bite of my Crunchie?' Like a small girl she held it out.

At bad moments, neither awake nor asleep, I would think myself still gripped by the nightmare which had gone on for so long. But no, my good fortune was a fact. Slowly but steadily the quality of my life improved. Some knot, or dispute, though I couldn't have said what it signified, had it seems been dissolved in the centre of my body. Vague though this was, its effects were definite and good. For one thing, the sight of my bare feet when I rose to get dressed no longer saddened me. For another, I was overjoyed to find myself in motion again. The desolate empty feeling which had been such a feature of my days still existed, but was now transferred to my work and there transformed. I was able to shape it like space, it possessed both spiritual and aesthetic value.

247

Other dealers apart from the Montague were beginning to seek me out. One even knocked on my door. I opened the high window stealthily and peered down, not answering. Later the peevish letter of reprimand which came seemed to indicate that I'd been spotted.

Another source of stimulation was the prospect of my first New York show, towards which I was now working. Arrangements for this debut had been set in motion by Della. Even with an ocean between us she was still a fixer. She loved problems, loved to banish them. Meanwhile, Vivien was talking with scarcely disguised enthusiasm of finding a place in the locality for herself, or possibly herself and Celia.

'You're going to share the expenses between you?'

'Well, we haven't exactly discussed it. But if it happens, yes.'

'Will she get a job here?'

'Are you being sarcastic?'

'It's a serious question.'

'I haven't the faintest idea, is the answer. Why do you ask?'

'Because you know she won't, or can't, and you'll be landed with the bills for everything and I think you should consider this step very carefully.'

'Oh you do. What am I supposed to be considering?'

'How about your sanity for a start?'

'You're being vile. Just because you want me to stay here.'

'Who says so? Just because I've got used to seeing you every day doesn't mean I can't break myself of the habit.'

'In other words you'll miss me. Look, Francis, I won't go far. Just think, you'll have the best of both worlds. Don't worry, we'll be able to meet any time we like and I won't be under your feet when you can't stand the sight of me.'

'You're never under my feet.'

'Liar!'

'I don't want you to go. I've got used to you.'

'Now don't be mean. Celia's in London, she's alone and helpless.'

'So am I.'

'That's not true. You've got your work.'

'I still think you're a fool.'

'Call it what you like. And for your information, Jake's promised to give Celia an allowance.'

'That's nice. Is he so desperate to get rid of her?'

'Francis, stop this. I hate arguing, especially with you, it's ugly.'

I couldn't stop. I felt a nervous compulsion to hang on to the subject of Celia, even if it meant wounding Vivien. Was that the point, did I seek to punish my sister? No, I didn't think so. Celia represented a darkness in our lives which refused to go away. Though I wanted to get rid of it, an instinct in me kept returning me to it with the insistence of a recurring dream. The reductive water which turned dark as I swilled out my brushes, nights of terror and violence mounting in my sleep, Celia and her death poems – were they one and the same stuff? Was death the clue to life?

I asked, 'Will he ever divorce her, do you think?'

'Jake? I doubt it. He still wants her, on any terms, at any price.'

'Just like you.'

'Oh Francis, I ought to hate you but I can't. You're always voicing my thoughts. Even as I spoke about Jake I was thinking, "Vivien, it's yourself you're talking about." Life's full of jokes. We both love her and she doesn't want either of us.'

Just as I had sought to make myself hard and cold, facing reality without illusions, I now felt more strongly a contrary urge to console Vivien, to aid and abet her in whatever her heart desired. I said, 'You don't really believe that. You're probably indispensable to her.'

'You're like a cat, like one of your cats. One minute cruel, the next kind.'

'No, I'm an eye, I see things.'

'Oh really. Then swivel it around and find me somewhere to live, will you?'

'If that's what you really want.'

'It is.' She said, 'What are you grinning at?'

'Nothing much. I met a man only the other day as a matter of fact, in the Mermaid – he's got a boat moored against the harbour wall. It's for rent, he told me. I think I know the one, a small slim yacht painted black and white, with a low cabin and a tiny galley. Interested? How do you fancy living on a boat?'

Vivien's face expressed amazement and then excitement at the idea of this revolutionary approach to her problem. 'A boat. I never thought of a boat. Could I? Oh I don't know. What's its name?'

249

'The boat? I didn't ask – he didn't mention it. Does it matter?'

'Yes of course. It's of the utmost importance.'

Inspired by her enthusiasm, I thought of something else. 'Then there's a chalet up on the cliff at Tregonhawke, made of wood but quite sound by the look of it – only that's for sale. I wouldn't mind it myself. Beautiful spot. Nothing in front of you till you get to France.'

'Oh Francis. What would it fetch, have you any idea?'

'No more than a caravan. Now that would have plenty of room for two. And there's a fireplace.' I remembered the brick chimney piece, well built and freshly pointed.

'Who owns it?'

'I don't know. We'd have to go up there and find out. A notice was stuck to the kitchen window but I didn't bother to read it.'

'Let's go this weekend!'

'It might be sold,' I warned her.

'No it won't, it can't. Is it nameless, like the boat?'

'It's called *Lohengrin*.'

Vivien stared, pop-eyed. She clapped her hands and cried out, *Lohengrin*, Tregonhawke, Cornwall! Imagine that for an address. Fantastic!'

I came on Vivien one silent Sunday afternoon taking a bath. It was pure accident. She took care to announce her intentions loudly and clearly, shouting her head off if necessary until I answered. One time when she did this and it slipped my mind, she heard me approaching down the stairs and hollered furiously, 'I'm in the bath, keep out of here!'

The folding screen was in position but slewed round. I was intending to get in myself, in the act of unbuttoning my shirt. I stopped still, sensing another presence. Wisps of steam drifted up. I tiptoed nearer, expecting to find her dozing. No, she was smiling almost seductively at me, her eyelids heavy and her eyes drugged with self-indulgence.

'What did you want?' she asked, with the drowsy voice of someone waking up in bed.

'I was going to have a bath.'

'I'm in it.'

'So I see. You didn't say anything, did you?'

'I forgot. Anyway I thought you were out.'

250

Until this moment I hadn't seen her naked. I still wasn't looking, keeping my gaze fixed firmly on her face, on which was mixed tired experienced lines and the innocence of youth.

'You know you said I might draw or paint you?'

'What about it? Oh, no – '

'Stay where you are. Don't get out, don't move.' I sprang away and up the stairs, hurrying back in a matter of seconds with a sketchbook and a stick of litho chalk. She had rolled on to her front. By the look of her near flawless back and dimpled buttocks I knew she was displeased.

'Please turn over. I want to make a few quick sketches.'

'No. Go away, I'm getting out now.'

'Give me five minutes, just as you are.'

'The water's nearly cold.'

'I'll pour some hot in. Hang on.'

She moaned. 'You're a beast. I don't want this.'

'Let me put some hot in shall I?'

'I don't like my body!'

'What woman does? Why, what's wrong with it?' I was already feverishly at work.

'I want to be longer. I'm too short. It's my legs!'

'Anything else?'

'Lots of things. My breasts aren't right.'

'You'd like them bigger?'

'No, no. They went up like balloons once, when I was on the pill. Horrible – I was top-heavy. It hurt when I ran. How would you like it?'

'Aren't you ever pleased with your body?'

'Only when I forget what it looks like.'

'That's because you're not outside it, fretting over it, but inhabiting it,' I suggested glibly, simply as a means of keeping her occupied with thoughts. I considered switching the conversation to a different topic but I was too absorbed in what I was doing. The soft chalk went down insidiously between the cleft buttocks of my facsimile. I felt the urge to map the moles, the nodules of her spine and even the fine hairs with accuracy, with a hard pencil or a sharp pen: I had neither.

She lay supine, and I thought my will had triumphed. Then she rose up all dripping and venomous, her mouth twisted by a cry. One wet long-nailed flipper clutched at me for support. I was left staring at her clear footprints on the dusty boards.

251

26

In New York, the heat was diminishing but not the smog. It was the end of summer, the beginning of fall, that favourite season of New Yorkers. For the second time around I had landed in America, braced for the impact of another planet. I felt keen and glad and in control of things. Here for a month, supposedly for a vacation but in reality to help arrange and then attend my show, I had made up my mind beforehand to wholeheartedly enjoy the experience. In order to do that, I told myself, it was vital to turn my face westward and leave England behind. But stepping down on to the new mustard-coloured cement at Kennedy Airport I knew I hadn't. It was in my innards, England, it shaped my thoughts into ironies, it was on my tongue whenever I opened my mouth.

Sending off picture postcards, I went up to the counter clerk and asked about stamps. 'To merry ole England?' he said, a fat middle-aged cherub who rolled the yellows of his eyes, mulberry thick lips clamped on an extinct cigar butt. On the broken paving outside I approached the corrugated tin hutch on its steel pole and posted my cards home.

Leaving one's mother country was like leaving one's mother. I felt drunk, irresponsible, light-headed, given up to a freedom that in England was vestigial. A wild hilarity rose inside me at the sight and sound of the astonishing raw foreignness of everything. Then I felt a pang of regret and wished I had persuaded Guy Franklin to accompany me, since he had never been here but only dreamed of it and it would have been like seeing it all again for the first time. How all the signs of dereliction would have staggered him! He would have inhaled it, reeled about in it, delighted, horrified, all his prejudices confirmed, his movie myths exploded. Seeing how much of it was falling to pieces would have made wonderful mad sense to him. He would have loved the freaks too, even the ugly nightmarish ones.

I had another reason for wanting to bring Guy along, and that was to provide a buffer between myself and Della. But Guy had moved to Exeter and we were temporarily out of touch. I understood from one or two fractured phone calls that he was in the throes of a domestic crisis. In fact, the buffer wouldn't have been necessary. Della was, nearly always, elsewhere. She provided me with accommodation at her house in Larchmont and then she left me to my own devices.

The Larchmont house was of white-painted wood and stone. On the ground floor she kept an apartment for herself. Guests were installed upstairs and were expected to fend for themselves. There were generous open stairs and light-flooded landings. Della appeared briefly, sweeping in like a queen, displayed her handsome beaky profile and disappeared in the direction of Manhattan. 'So help me, Francis, you don't change,' she called over her shoulder. She drove off. On the enormous ice box was a cellotaped notice: 'Help yourself to contents. A good little restaurant on Main Street called Chanticleer. Have fun!'

Also staying in the house were Robin and Tinker, a young, mysteriously quiet couple. When Robin did speak it was with the curious impersonality I had become accustomed to in Americans. She wore a dark blue cotton dress which exposed her knees. The deep V would have revealed breasts, but she didn't have any. Her pecking witty smile came and went for no obvious reason. Rimless round glasses drew attention to the cleverness of her sharp tanned features.

Robin's husband, Tinker – she called him Tink – earned his living as a sessions pianist. He also composed. Once or twice I heard him splashing away vigorously at a piano in an upper room. It was difficult to think of them as married. They were like two self-contained resourceful children who had been given the run of the house by indulgent parents.

The house stood in a select little estate or court of detached residences arranged round a leafy cul-de-sac. Standing on the porch I was treated to an almost English vista of gently stirring trees and the cream blotches of late roses. At the front the lawns were fenceless, while at the back the grass looked different, alarmingly coarse and untamed, and I thought sinister. Out there was some weather-stained garden furniture and an air of neglect.

I went in to Manhattan on the commuter train and came out again, exhausted by so much avid staring. The chaotic city seethed on a rigid grid. I gaped at the arrays of Jewish bread and sour cream on the other side of the glass in a Ratner's. Crossing the torn and blasted street I admired a four-storey high mural of geometric design on the end wall of a scarred block in the Battery. One day I intended to take a trip to Brooklyn Heights, an area I love. I never did so. The tranquil scene at Larchmont and the warm peaceful weather, turning mellow almost by the hour, encouraged me to sit on the stone steps of the porch, stretch out my legs and tell myself I was loafing.

My jacket was too warm when I walked about in it. I found a store in Larchmont called Lipman's and bought a denim jacket with metal buttons. It fitted as well as anything ever did.

'Not bad,' the storeman said. 'You got narrow shoulders, but this time of year you need things loose.'

'The sleeves are on the long side,' I mused rather than protested. I was resigned about clothes.

'Nothing much. Make a cuff if you want.' He did it for me, while I stood obediently. 'Okay?'

'How much?'

'To you, twelve dollars.'

I walked out wearing it. Would I pass for an American? As on the last occasion when I had stayed, and that time for much longer, it seemed to me that my psyche was failing to engage. Could it be that my soul stayed behind when I travelled, as Red Indians believed?

Next day I was sitting at the front on the parched grass, my new jacket peeled off. Robin came out silently behind my back and handed me an airmail. 'Thanks,' I said.

My white toes stuck out of my sandals. I wriggled them as I looked at Robin's bare splayed brown toes. She had surprisingly broad feet for such a small person. A boy on a bike coasted past for the third time in as many minutes, staring hard at both of us.

'Are you sunning yourself, Francis?' the girl asked.

I looked up. She showed her perfect white teeth in a smile. I said, 'Yes, I've decided to be a lizard.'

'I can never be too warm. I think I have a poor circulatory system.'

I scrambled to my feet. 'Excuse me,' I said, and went up to my room to read my letter in private.

A wave of homesickness mounted in my chest as I took in Vivien's words. By the sound of her letter she was in good spirits, and eager to bring me up to date with developments. She had actually bought *Lohengrin*, but not moved there. She wanted to redecorate, but felt in any case she should stay put and take care of my place till I returned. It was also, she pointed out, too far to come from Tregonhawke to look after the cats. 'Your paintings are quite safe, don't worry. The sloppy black and white cat hangs around your door now and then and lets out a pitiful miaow. I've given her a name, Harriet, so I can bully her properly. I think it suits her beautifully. That's because she puts on a helpless look like you when she wants to ingratiate herself. Helpless Harriet.'

Her letter went on to disclose that Celia was now back there at her invitation. This didn't surprise me, and in fact I had suggested it before leaving. 'Her temper these days is foul. Probably she's come here just to vent it. No point in being evil-tempered if you're on your own. She is frowning viciously over some epistle of her own at this very moment – or maybe it's a poem. Or a spell she's about to cast on me. I'll go black, I'll shrivel up. This is disgusting and bitchy and gives a totally misleading impression. When it is good it's very very good, and I wish you could see her then.'

Della suddenly returned. I was in the kitchen talking to Tinker. We heard the door at the front of the house open, then crashing noises, as if a large animal had got in. 'What the hell,' the young man said softly. Startled myself, I heard Della's raised voice, and stood up.

'In here, Norman,' Della said, leading in a shambling, ruined man, one of whose eyes seemed to be closed. The man was introduced as 'Norman Gorki from Chicago – the poet.' The poet was plastered. He sat down at the kitchen table and let his over-large head droop. He had a scrubby goatee, his grey crinkled hair was scraped back and stuck down with an oily lotion, and he wore a cheap summer suit, stained down the length of his right side as if he had fallen down in the road.

'You're the painter, right?' Gorki said. 'English guy.'

'Yes.'

'I caught Norman's reading tonight at Cooper Union,' Della said, 'and afterwards asked him back.'

'Appreciate, lady,' Gorki mumbled.

'He gave this terrific reading.'

'What was I like?' the man asked, through gritted teeth. It was like an expression of grief. He stared up at us briefly in turn with some obscure grudge.

'I have to say terrific.'

'I don't remember.' Then to me he said, still with his head down, 'A painter. I envy that. Only poets go round shooting off their damn fool mouths in public. When the words make you puke, and the paper, the typer, the fucking room, you get invited to read the crap. For bread. Which you always need. And it boosts the sagging ego, you hope. Biggest mistake there is.' I watched him fixedly, taking in the pock-marked skin on the loose flesh of his cheeks and over the fat spreading nose – a dull uneven purple – and telling myself this was a portrait, already making notes.

After Gorki passed out, and we abandoned him temporarily like a car smash, I asked Della in the sitting room what she proposed to do with her pick-up. Could she handle such a problem?'

'Why problem?' she answered impatiently. 'In a couple of days I take him on to his next reading, which is Staten Island someplace.'

Vaguely I hinted that I may go along too for the ride. To help me decide, she fished out from her shelves a book of poems by Gorki. I thumbed through it, a thickish volume entitled *Eyes of the Heart*. Listed inside were his other books, with facetious, sentimental, exhibitionistic titles: 'Islands in a Woman Sea', 'Love by the Balls', 'Gorki's Disease'. Though I hardly ever read poetry, the flavour of the words intrigued me.

Back in the kitchen, Della fetched a beer from the ice-box and a tumbler and banged them down beside Gorki's head. He sat up with a start and broke the seal of the can. Ignoring the glass he swigged at the triangular slit. The beer slopped down over his chin, ran into his beard and dripped off. I made my excuses and left. Morty Appel, the young organiser of my exhibiton, was taking me to a late dinner. Names of Americans never failed to delight me.

We sat in a new restaurant, opened that very week in a grim district full of blackened warehouses, by Houston Street on the edge of Greenwich Village. Friends of Morty from his college days were running the place. Inside, walls, furniture and curtains were snow white. Vines and variegated ivy twirled and climbed, rubber plants fanned out, baskets of curly ferns dangled on fine chains to within a few feet of the tables. Water trickled down a wall of rocks into a grotto. The whole interior, cool and crisp, acted on the senses like an immense green salad.

At the base of an elegant wrought-iron spiral staircase on an oval table was a pot of cyclamens, one blood-red flower seeming to imitate a bird or a hat, hovering above a cluster of mottled lead funnels. Under these airy blooms grew down a bunch of fat rubbery stalks. The cyclamen sketch I made on a paper serviette was the only work I attempted during the period of my stay. It was no good, I would soon have to go home. The discomfort of living without taking refuge in work of any kind was little by little rendering my being meaningless. So what was art if not a barrier between myself and the universe? Could that be justified?' Wandering the streets of New York it was possible to think that the world had gone mad and people everywhere carried on because that was all they could do. Did this describe my predicament? Only the rapture, tasted once or twice in the solitude of my workroom, could put these questions to flight. Meanwhile I trudged up and down on the dirty sidewalks with everyone else. There were no answers, there was just carrying on.

Another day I went shooting down freeways, steered by an imperious Della, slowing only for the toll stations. I sat in the back behind a near extinct Gorki. Norman Gorki was sober. In that state he became even uglier, a reptilian torpor to his neck and shoulders. Della at the wheel gleamed with an impressive cold efficiency, hauling us in a new direction at intersections, eyes peeled for the exits.

Gorki, jammed next to Della on the bench seat, would only grunt. With his blind back, his sullen silence, he had power over me. We were aimed at some college or other. What was a community college? More to the point, did I want to be involved, even to this extent? This ugly dog-faced man, who looked sixty but whom I estimated to be around my own age, fifty, touched me oddly. I saw a man as strange and foreign and sprawling as America itself. Meanwhile, Della was undeniably in charge, more and more regal as she sped through the filth and graffiti, then penetrated the sinister iron girderwork of bridges to hang us high over water, as arrogant as any creator. And as untouchable. Only when we began bumping over potholes of a bad section of road at the entrance to the college campus did she become human again, showing me her bad temper in the rear mirror.

Gorki said, 'Is this it?'

'According to the sign.'

'Give us a sign, Lord,' he said, showing his yellow teeth.

As soon as Gorki and I were on the tarmac she slammed the car into reverse.

'Aren't you staying?' I called.

'Another engagement!' she yelled over the squeal of tyres. 'I'll leave you men to your fun!'

It had happened and it served me right. I followed the other man as he headed for the nearest low buildings. We saw a sign saying 'Reception' and changed tack.

'This your idea of fun, Breakwell?'

I was still inwardly fuming at Della for leaving me stranded in this godforsaken place with no idea of how to get back to Larchmont. 'Tell you later,' I said, and cracked a smile.

'Grisly's the word. Listen, you don't need to eat the shit I serve up. I can see you're no poetry lover. Unless you like to witness obscene exhibitions. You don't look the type to me.'

'What do you suggest?'

'Let's find somewhere in this academic shithole where they keep the liquor.'

In the bar, mixing whisky and beer, Gorki said, 'Here's what you do, if you'll take my advice.'

'I'll take it.'

'Get your ass out of here, for my sake as well as yours. I can do without you as a witness. Book yourself into my hotel. I'll see you there after this little disaster is over. I feel better when they hand me the cheque. Got a piece of paper? It can't be far from here – let me write it down. There's a woman I'm expecting, Vida, an ex-mistress. If she's waiting I want you to introduce yourself and keep her warm for me. She's travelling a long way for this fuck-up. Christ knows why. Soft spot for me. Soft in the head. Jesus, I can't remember the surname she uses. Try Joplin. Only that's not it. No, it's Jackson. We haven't seen each other for six years or more. She may be the most godawful wreck.'

'Vida Jackson,' I said. I finished my brandy and got to my feet.

'Sounds right,' the beaten-up man said. 'Hey, that woman of yours has real style.'

'She's not mine.'

'Oh yeah.'

'Good luck with the reading.'

'It's a foregone conclusion.' Gorki waved his glass at me, but he had stopped looking in my direction. His wary concentration as he sank away inside himself reminded me of a tusked and armoured warthog squatting obscenely with its end in the mud. Above the fangs and implacable dead features were the sad eyes – enlivened now by an animal fear – which had first entranced me.

I found the hotel without any trouble, half a mile down the featureless highway, tramping by fence posts and glancing now and then at the curious rank grass I wouldn't have dreamt of walking on: it looked as if no human foot had ever been near it. A truck blared harshly at me, either for not being at the very edge of the deserted road or for existing at all outside a vehicle. Now and then sleek swaying cars whipped past. In a way I liked the eerie sensation of being on another planet, on the moon.

Yes, they had a room. I thought I might as well stay. There was no town, just a collection of dwellings on either side of the road, small frame houses and then this substantial building made of cinder blocks, air-conditioned when I investigated the interior.

I lay on the bed and surveyed the room. Better call it a chicken coop. Utterly featureless. I was glad of that. Other people's taste created burdens for the spirit: I told myself this sterility was better. Sprawling there only partially convinced on the anonymous sheets I indulged my latest obsession, touching at my front teeth with a forefinger to make sure they were there. Every time I paid a visit to my dentist at home, the short snip of a man mentioned that my front teeth were wearing down at a rapid rate.

'Can't you crown them?'

'Oh, I'd wait if I were you. It's because you've lost your lower teeth on this side. Chew on the other side.'

'That's what I do.'

'Manage all right like that?'

'Seem to.'

'Then I wouldn't worry. They're not unsightly, those front ones. Wait till they are.'

'When will that be?'

'Whenever you decide they are. Meanwhile, keep on doing whatever you're doing. They're quite sound.'

They weren't only wearing down, they've worn thin. My recurring obsession was that they might be disappearing altogether. I could only dispel this by touching, unless of course I looked. They were always there, but maybe one day when I woke they wouldn't be.

Pushing into the noisy, smoky air of the hotel bar I found myself a chair and a vantage point. The atmosphere was so heavily male, even though the bullish men were dull and tame, chinking the ice in their glasses, that I couldn't imagine an unaccompanied woman coming in. In the entire room there was one woman and she was elderly, in horn-rims, listening submissively to her loud-hailer husband.

I didn't have long to wait. Gorki shoved in, his face dully aflame and blasted, yet his lipless mouth actually smiling in a cruel, dangerous cat smile. By his side was a woman. I lifted my arm and they came over.

'Here, this is the guy, remember I was telling you about him? Hey, baby, are you with me?'

'Hallo mister. Norman, do we have to drink here?'

'What's wrong with it?'

The woman was smoking a cigarette. She wore a dark dress, out of which she jutted, solid and reassuring. She was tough, imperturbable, I thought; the sort of woman who had seen it all and accepted whatever there was. She glanced at me, nodding indifferently. Her smile was weary. Her rather heavy cheeks sagged a little. Her eyes softened and smiled for Gorki – she came up to his shoulder. I saw the man's transformation, how he gleamed now, his looks public, expecting reactions. Although very drunk he acted as though he was meant to be looked at. At his throat was a loose-knotted reddish satin tie I hadn't noticed before.

'I don't like it here. Let's go up to our room. Wouldn't that be cosy, hon?'

'If you want, go ahead,' Gorki said.

'Aren't you hungry?' Vida asked. 'Norman, when did you last eat?'

'If you're hungry, go and eat.'

'Not without you. I came two hundred miles to be with you.'

'I didn't ask you.'

'I wanted to.'

He went over to the bar and came back with three beers. 'Vida, you drinking with us or not?'

She was perched on a stool. 'Hell, that's a stupid question,' she said, chuckling suddenly and leaning over to him.

Forced, and too soon, into the strait-jacket of my spectator role, I struggled to free myself. 'How did it go, the reading?'

'He read all the wrong poems,' Vida said.

'What's wrong?' Gorki said, smiling wolfishly. He was loud. 'What's right or wrong about a poem?'

'You never read your best poems.'

'How would you know?' he asked brutally. 'Since when did you become a literary critic?'

'I don't care if it makes you angry. I was there on the front row willing you to read your best poems, and you didn't. Nothing's changed. Are you ashamed of your best work, is that it?'

His cat smile was glittering. Labouring to speak, he said, 'Stupid cow. When did you ever know a good poem from a wet fart?'

'I love those poems you didn't read, Norman. I nearly called out to you. That other stuff, it's rancid, it's all about your hate for yourself. That's not the Norman I came to hear.'

'I don't have to hear this.'

'It's the truth, though – '

Still smiling, without taking his eyes off her, he straightened his arm suddenly. His bunched fist caught her on the side of the jaw and her head wrenched with the force of the blow. She toppled on her stool to the carpet, a heavy surprised woman, her dark eyes filling with pain. Before I could help her up she had scrambled to her feet and was back on the stool, rubbing her face and making an effort to smile. 'Why, you bastard, Gorki,' she said in a low voice. 'That hurt. You don't know your own strength do you, you big punk.'

'You asked for it,' he said. He lifted his glass and drank. 'An old fart who's driven two hundred miles to tell me how to write.'

'I should lay one on you for that,' she said, rubbing her face, grinning.

I was in a state. It could have been my own public humiliation I was witnessing. Transfixed, I was too stunned to do more than flick glances at the other tables, where the swarthy and lithe and red-faced men in their white shirts went on talking and drinking. They might have been sightless for all the notice they took. Even now she was back, ruefully grinning and rubbing at her bruised jaw, I still stared down at the carpet where she had landed.

'Do you want more beer?' Gorki asked her.

'I want something, that's for sure. Have you been drinking all day?'

'All week. All year. When did I see you last?'

'Six years it's been.'

'That's how long.'

'I was a fool to come,' she said. 'There are things you'll never admit about yourself. Beautiful things you won't dare own up to. You'd rather live in a cesspool and blame it on the others, you'd sooner run – '

'How do I shut you up?'

'Get your beer,' she said, not flinching as he threatened her again, drawing back his arm. He got up and went.

'So there you are,' she said to me, seeming to notice me for the first time. I was now painfully involved and torn, with unsteady hands. 'Have you ever heard him read?' she asked. 'Do you know what I'm saying?'

'No,' I said.

'It breaks me up. It shouldn't I know, not after all these years, but it does.' She grieved, shaking her head, then laughed. 'The guy can't even remember asking me. Would I have come all this way without an invitation? He can ask very sweetly, believe you me. I got this call. I'm a sucker for this man. I ask for all I get.'

'Are you all right?' I asked. 'Have my chair, it's more comfortable.'

'That's okay.' She said, so ponderously that I knew she was drunk, 'My nostalgia brought me here, and I expect to pay for it . . . Listen, whoever you are, nice guy, don't go away thinking he's just an old lush.'

'Does it matter what I think?'

'Sure, sure it does. He thinks something of you. What you saw just now is only the liquor, know what I mean? He can be the sweetest man. Break your heart. I'm right about those poems.'

Now that she had my whole sympathy – it had lurched over to her in a sudden capitulation – I didn't care how long the old lush took to come back. I saw how unbudgeable she was, wounded or not. It was easy to see how she aroused Gorki's ire: there was no getting rid of her now, ever. Were her knees as massive as her breasts must be? Clearly she was hung up on the mulish suicidal vainglorious man heading towards us at this moment. The drink sloshing around in me, I thought her fixed gummy eyelashes caked with mascara looked sorrowful enough for us both: in fact for all the room. 'Here he is,' I said, as Gorki threatened the table in his effort to sit down.

'Steady on, you elephant,' Vida complained. 'Watch out for the glasses.'

Maybe because her voraciousness had to be justified somehow, now that I was established at last in her vision, she asked me, 'Have you ever noticed Norman's beautiful sad eyes?'

'Christ,' Gorki said. 'I'd forgotten . . .'

'What, baby?'

'That you were this stupid.'

'Isn't he gorgeous! So, okay, suppose you remembered way back and got it clear in your overblown fat head that Vida was this stupid, so what? Would that have stopped you inviting me?'

'You're crazy.' He was endeavouring to gaze round the room.

'I'm asking a straight question, Norman.'

'Then ask it.'

'I already did.'

'Which way is our room?' The man was on his feet and about to blunder to the exit. 'Come and join us for a drink,' he said, suddenly pleading with me. 'Don't leave me with this bonehead.' He told Vida, 'Bring some booze before it's too late.'

Vida was asking him for the key as they left the bar, with me following as if I had become fastened to them umbilically. Although my imagination had already gone ahead to the double room and created bizarre scenes for the three of us, in a muddle of sheets and clothing and indiscriminate emotions with the nametags thankfully missing, strangely enough this wish-fulfilment didn't include any hint of depravity.

The elevator was between floors so they went up the stairs ahead of me, Gorki hanging on to the handrail and Vida shoving him in the back as she encouraged him upwards, laughing and satisfied at last.

'Is your name Wesley?' she called back at one point in the ascent.

'One of them,' I said, snuffling out a laugh myself. It was better when you were on the move.

This was too difficult for her brain in its present condition. 'One what?'

'Never mind,' I said, impatient for us to arrive and begin whatever drama was in store. The nature of my involvement was as perplexing to me as ever, but perhaps now, in *extremis*, extraordinary things would be revealed.

In the drab, emptily waiting room with its two beds, vacant as if for emergencies, the tarnished mirror screwed to the wall over the wash basin reflecting without comment anything it might witness, the TV with the metal trim around the pushbuttons coming loose, we didn't seem to know why we were there. It was stifling hot. Vida went over and dragged at the catch of a window, cursing. Gorki stripped down to his undervest and then began to act ugly, as if I had already left.

'You can go any time you want,' he mouthed at Vida. 'I can't stand the fucking sight of you.'

'Have a drink,' she coaxed, coming over with a tooth-glass and a bottle. 'Poor baby, you've had a rough ride tonight.' She sat on the bed beside him as if nothing was wrong, desperately grabbing his hand and beginning to knead it. He let this happen for a moment or two, then tore his hand free.

'What did I ever see in you?' he said, aiming each word at her broad undefended face like a blow.

'Don't say things to me in front of your friend,' she warned in a low voice. I was moving back towards the door, about to leave a torture I refused to watch.

'Why shouldn't I?'

'I might just get up and leave. Drive back all the way home. You want me to do that, Norman?'

'Do it,' he said. But his head was sunk so low on his chest, she was able to ignore him.

'I can't leave you like this. You've been boozing all day, you great fool. Are you trying to kill yourself?'

In the long silence I stood noticing things of no account, such as the too-bright greens and blues of a framed landscape opposite the beds, like something out of a travel brochure. I kept my hand on the doorknob, hoping for a climax that would help me to turn it.

Gorki raised his head. His eyes gleamed cruelly, and he was pulling up the corners of his mouth into the cat smile. When the mask was more or less fixed he said, 'Haven't you gone yet?'

'Is that what you want? All right.' She looked round for her handbag and picked it up. Opening it, she pulled out a wad of Kleenex and went over to the wash basin. 'Oh Jesus,' she muttered, dabbing at her eyes.

'Come over here,' Gorki said. 'I've got something to say to you. Just keep your big trap shut about things you know nothing about, like poems. Don't shit me, you hear?'

'What is it?' she said, coming back to him eagerly and shooting a glance at me. I left the room. It was none of my business if she got beaten up. Shivering and twitching along my nerves I descended to the floor below and went up and down the corridors searching for my single room.

It was a room for brooding on existence in its most desolate aspects: on deformity (which I managed to turn to my advantage when at work), disease, the parched and aching spirit, smells of fear, failure, old grievances. I sat on the edge of the bed and resisted the worst effects by folding myself into my ego, and by intently listening. What if Vida left anyway – or was kicked out? Did her flesh quake when it was unloosened or was she built like a wall? I imagined scaling her while she tolerated me; I created doors and secret cavities I would unlock, astounding her grateful flesh. Instead of having to scale her like an unyielding cliff she would melt and come down to me, pouring liquid love until my complicated motives were washed out to sea.

I opened the door and listened, craning my neck upwards. Hearing nothing I went back upstairs in the direction of their room, trying to quell my hammering heart. I saw what I must look like, a common hotel sneak. I didn't stoop to the keyhole, though: I stood listening for sounds. There weren't any.

Nearly back in my rat-hole, I heard a door bang over my head. My heart banged violently again. Someone was on the way down. I shot into my room and then took up a spying position, trying to see past the door frame without being seen. When Vida came into view, hugging a thin summer coat to herself and sniffing, I moved and stood in the hallway where I could be spotted.

She was so wrapped in misery that she hadn't noticed me. Would she have bothered to stop if she had? I called out hoarsely, 'What's happened – what's happening?'

She raised her head. I saw her wet smeared eyes. She was dabbing at a split lip with a piece of pink-stained Kleenex.

'He's crazy. Don't know anything. It's the booze,' she snuffled, and started to trudge towards the next flight of stairs.

I went over to her. 'Where are you going?'

'Home,' she said. Her lip was swelling even as I looked at it. She cried bitterly, brief hard sobs, sounding angry with herself.

'Let me look at that,' I said, moving her hand away. It was a gesture merely; I had no suggestion to make.

'You can't drive in the state you're in,' I told her.

'Why not?'

'Too dangerous.'

'I ain't staying with him. He's crazy. He scares me when he's like this. I'd forgotten what a mean bastard he can be when he's boozed.'

'You've had plenty yourself.'

'I just wanna get out of here, understand?'

'What with the drink and your crying, you can't see straight. It's mad to attempt a long drive in the middle of the night like this.'

'So what d'you suggest, huh? Sit on the stairs till daybreak?' She was about to say more, but her voice broke. 'So long, honey,' she managed, moving away. 'Been nice knowin' ya.'

'Wait a minute,' I said, and took hold of her arm, experiencing her bulk though my fingers for the first time. 'Stay till morning, I should.' I said to her face, which listened dully, 'If you don't I shan't get to sleep for worrying about you.'

'Why should you care what happens to me?'

'I'm a worrier. It's my nature. Do me a favour and go in the morning.' I got this out while she gazed at me almost sourly, her puffy broken lip forgotten. I grinned shakily at the frank disbelief on her face.

'I don't get this,' she said, fuddled. 'Say what you gotta say.'

'I just said it.'

'Stay where?'

'Here.'

'If I asked for a room at this hour they'll think I'm a whore. Anyhow, I'm flat broke.'

'I've got a room,' I said, and pointed to my open door. 'There, look.'

She frowned, shaking her head in puzzlement. 'You want me to stay with you?'

'It's only a single, but maybe we could manage.' I went on hastily, 'Better than driving all night the way you are. Get some sleep, you'll feel better about everything in the morning.'

She swayed on her feet. 'Lemme get this straight,' she mumbled.

I took her arm and tugged gently. 'Let's do our talking in here. I just think it's dangerous, that's all.'

'Us in that?' she said, staring at the narrow bed, and started to laugh raucously, but her lip hurt. 'Ouch,' she complained, cupping her hand over it.

'Let me have another look,' I said, grateful for some obvious wound I could pretend to examine. To establish contact of a sort I pressed gingerly on the surrounding skin. It was a wide, naturally swollen mouth, the kind they call generous in romantic novels. Only this one, in spite of the treatment its owner had been subjected to – not only on this night but, I guessed, plenty of other times – threatened to split open at any moment and appreciate the funny side. Except that her weariness and an understandable dejection kept it mournfully dragged down.

'You'll live, I reckon.'

Her thick fuddled thoughts were nearly visible as she began to really gulp openly before me and let the tears come shaking out, and at the same time recover the will to live. 'That lousy slob,' she said, holding me by my thin shoulders. 'I oughta have my head examined, coming all this way. Where does he get off, kicking me out like a broad he can't be bothered with any more?'

'He's a funny bloke.'

'A what? Bloke? You from over there?'

'That's right, England. I've travelled farther than you.'

'Not today you haven't.' Then she said wonderingly. 'Have you?'

I shook my head, about to launch into a brief explanation, then stopped myself. Her eyes had glazed over and she was sentimentally weeping over what had befallen her. It took only a moment or two for her natural curiosity to intervene. 'You mean to say you like me?' she asked, and I saw the gleam of interest.

'Of course I do.'

This time her laugh full in my face at such close range was harder to take. 'Believe me, pal, it don't necessarily follow. If you get my meaning.'

I had drunk a good deal myself. Only my nervousness and the abnormal circumstances made me sharper than her. 'There's nothing wrong with you,' I said stoutly, unable to compliment such a brutally direct and loud woman, though there were more positive things I could have said. For instance, her amazingly rotund and solid body made me want to hug her, in this bleak featureless room with its blank planes you could skid off, right into the void. And the vicious-looking corners of the bed-head. The cheap matchboard locker and the scratched chest by the window fairly bristled with corners. It wasn't only the drink, I thought, that made her so unconscious of what her body offered to a man like me: a combination of home and amnesia. Well, that was part of it.

As if reading my half-thoughts, she said abruptly, 'Okay,' and peeled off her coat. Until I noticed the beads of sweat on her forehead I wasn't even conscious of the heat of the night.

'You'll stay, then,' I said, keeping my voice quiet. But the lift of joy in it made her beerily suspicious.

'Listen,' she said. 'I'm out on my feet, and besides, I'm not the kind of woman you might think.'

'How d'you mean?' I stammered foolishly.

'Don't get me wrong . . . it's just that you're too new. Know what I mean? I can't give you anything, okay?'

'Give me?'

'Like a good time.'

'I don't want anything,' I lied; but would have been hard pressed to say what it was I did want. At that moment it was the cessation of her unnerving scrutiny.

'Okay. Then I'm staying.'

'Good.'

'The way I'm feeling right now, I'd never make it to the exit.'

She unfastened her dress and it fell in a circle around her feet. She kicked off her shoes and then stood there, the elastic of her black briefs digging into her vast soft-hard hips. My downcast eyes took in her stumpy legs. Then I leapfrogged up past the bulwark of a torso to ask her which side of the bed she wanted to sleep on. 'If it's too cramped I can always stretch out on the carpet,' I said, willing her to talk me out of it.

'Suit yourself,' was all she said. 'I shan't know what's hit me when I get my head down. Boy, am I pooped!'

Clearly this was the nearest to an invitation I was going to get. She steered over and clambered in with the exceptional dignity of a large woman, or a drunk, then spoiled the effect by walloping the pillow about, labouring and groaning. 'Come on, then,' she said. 'It's your bed after all.'

It looked impossible, yet once I was on my right side, pressed up against her wide slabby back, I found I could hang on by hooking an arm over her belly, which slopped up and down with every breath.

'Are you in?' she muttered, her voice already foggy as she sank away from me. She had her face to the wall. Then the snores rose up, as her mouth fell open.

'In a manner of speaking,' I said aloud, though I knew she was conked. I spoke to comfort myself. When I tested her by asking, 'Do we need more than this one sheet?' I was answered by a loud snore and a series of grunts and choking sounds, as if she was being strangled. I stripped off the other covers and then grabbed her again, before I rolled out. The bed light was still on. I let her go again, to snap it off. Groaning, she squelched over, her back greasy with sweat, and in her sleep was crooking her arm round my neck. I stuck this unconscious passionate embrace for as long as I could breathe, in the pathetic need to believe she was aware of me after all. I was never much good at fooling myself. My bony carcass might as well have been outside in the terrible moonlight, stretched out by the verge and a police car screeching up. This gory melodrama got me nowhere either. I finished up literally fighting for air, prising her arm off my windpipe and shoving at her mindless flesh for several minutes like a vet struggling with a sick cow. She rolled back at last to the wall.

I had given up any idea of sleep. Instead of sinking my grappling hook into the various deep folds of her belly I shifted cautiously upwards until my hand was around what must have been the outskirts of a mountainous breast. I didn't know for sure, confused in the dark by its dimensions. The nipple when I reached it shocked me. Lost as I was in the night among these wastes of flesh, it seemed as personal as her nose. I began to caress it. The limp putty soaked in sweat crushed between my thighs was as dead, as lonely as the volcano I had scaled without love: out of a morbid curiosity I supposed.

I was reduced to pitying us both. Because of my tendency to identify, my desire remained dormant if my partner showed no response. This one was about as responsive as a monster hibernating at the bottom of a lake.

I must have passed out in the end. I opened my eyes to find my nose dug into the streaming wall of her back, and the daylight exposing me. I clung to her for another half hour, hoping vainly for another ration of forgetfulness.

After splashing at my face in the sink, hawking up once or twice quite deliberately because my need for company was so acute, I walked across, as indifferently naked as her, and shook her awake. Outside in the corridor they were going down for breakfast.

'Wadjawant?' she moaned. 'What time is it?'

'Nearly eight-thirty.'

'Oh my Christ. I coulda slept all week.'

'Coming down for breakfast?'

'Yeah, why not. I gotta get going anyhow.'

I dressed quickly, because she was exploring me with such curiosity.

'I can't figure you out.'

'Why not?'

'Why did you do it?' she asked, raking away at her hair with her fingers.

'Do what?'

'Let me stay in here.'

I was bored now with the stuff about the danger she would have been in. 'I felt like some company,' I said.

'Did you get any?'

'About five minutes' worth,' I told her frankly. What was there to lose? For an instant, laughing together, we were a couple.

She remembered her damaged lip and how she had earned it, touching it ruefully. 'My God,' she sighed. 'Vida, you're crazy.'

'You said you were broke,' I said. 'Look, have some of this.' I was rummaging in my pockets.

'No, honey,' she said. 'No, honest. I still got a bit of pride left.'

'Sorry.'

'It's worth more than dough to me, what you did.'

'See you downstairs,' I said hastily, getting myself through the door with my hypocrisy: not because I hadn't confessed my intentions fully, but for simpering there like a do-gooder, enjoying her gratitude.

In the dining room there was a scattering of men, two with propped newspapers. No sooner had I sat down than I was asked – by a pugnacious woman with a tired face – how I wanted my eggs. I tried to remember the password, the woman hanging irritably at my elbow.

'Sunny side up or easy over?' she prompted gummily.

'Yes – easy over.'

'Four?'

270

'Two's plenty.'

I caught sight of Gorki entering the room and making for me.

'I didn't expect you this early.'

'What's that supposed to mean?'

'Just that you didn't strike me as an early riser.'

All I got was a grunt. He was better drunk: anything was better than this cold sculpture: the congealed features and the body like a heap of dead ashes.

'Anyway, how are you?'

'What kind of damn fool question is that?'

'It's rhetorical.'

'Be back in a minute.' He blundered to his feet and left the room. He came back with a paper.

The surly waitress came up. As soon as she opened her mouth to ask about eggs, he said, 'Coffee, black. That's it.'

'I'll shut up, then,' I said, 'and let you read the news.'

'What news?'

'In there.'

'We're going to hell,' Gorki said. 'I just need print. I guess I'm an addict.'

'Get on with your fix, then.'

'Don't pay any attention to me, Breakwell. Talk if you want. It won't bother me what you do. Until noon I'm not even passably human.' He raised his head then, and made a glugging sound in his throat. 'Even then it's a matter of opinion.'

Tucking into my eggs, I remarked, 'You're a sentimentalist – if you don't mind my saying so.'

'I don't mind,' Gorki said.

'Good.'

'I'm one of the few subjects that interests me.'

'You agree, then?'

'Who's arguing?'

'Right.'

'Got any more observations?'

'It's a bit early for me too. No, I don't think so. Not at the moment.'

'Pity.'

'What are you staring at?'

'Those fucking eggs. I can't stand the stink of them, and the sight of them makes me think of road smashes.'

'You're lucky,' I said. 'I could have had four.'

Gorki bent his head to his paper.

Vida came up behind us. She was carrying her coat over one arm, and holding her bag.

'I'm going, honey,' she said lightly, resting her hand in a tender gesture on Gorki's shoulder. When he didn't acknowledge her, she stooped and brushed her swollen mouth against his stubble. 'Be good to yourself,' she murmured, so softly that I felt I wasn't supposed to hear. I waited my turn to say goodbye to her but she turned away immediately, gave a flick with her hand – which could have been meant for either of us – and was gone. Again the lightness of her step and her quick graceful movements surprised me.

Too disturbed to sit there any longer, I left the poet humped over his newsprint and made for my room. I felt ready to leave. Maybe I would bump into her again in the lobby, or outside. I caught a glimpse through the dining room windows of a large expanse of nacreous sky, beckoning with its washed purity like something out of the sea.

I kept my eyes peeled but there was no sign of her. I had nothing to collect, not even a toothbrush, but found myself idiotically opening the door of my room anyway, because that was where you went in a hotel after breakfast. About to back out again, I spotted a scrap of paper with torn edges on top of the chest. The biro scrawl merely said, 'Thanks, Mister Painter Man – from Vida.'

I wasn't prepared for the commotion it caused me – a mixture of regret and urgency, an intense dissatisfaction with the image of me she had carried away to incorporate in her unknown life. The transitory nature of our encounter, with its slapstick and burlesque elements, would go on existing now forever more, never amended by any real knowledge we might have gleaned about each other. It was intolerable to me. Yet I pocketed the miserable paper scrap – it looked like part of a used envelope – and went hurrying out to the road with it.

On my last day in New York I found myself walking springily, glancing about at scenes which might have already been consigned to the past, since they affected me now with a sadly sweet nostalgia. Nothing could alter the fact that I was on my way home, my spirit no longer blighted by the consciousness of vast distances. In a few hours I would board the plane. What could I do to pass the time? I did what most tourists do on the eve of departure, I went looking for gifts; or rather one gift, for Vivien.

Tramping in and out of the Guggenheim and the Metropolitan I had noticed vistas of uptown streets with ritzy shops. I got a subway train to Central Park and emerged by the Zoo, sniffing first of all the menagerie smell, then the aroma of hot pretzels.

In a glittery shop crammed with glassware, lit by a huge chandelier, almost the first thing I took in was a Nile-green amulet on a gold chain. Three naked figures stood in hieratic postures, looking quaint and diminutive and touchingly vulnerable on their velvet pad. I read the inscription glued to the lid: 'Isis, the young Horus and Nephthys . . . commissioned by the Ashmolean Museum . . . an ancient Egyptian faience amulet in the shape of three deities . . . to invoke their protection for the wearer . . .' Half expecting the artificial substance of soapy-looking pale green to be soft. I picked up the replica. The figure in the middle, Horus, had genitals I would have needed tweezers to grasp. His hands were held by the females on either side.

Three dollars eighty. I carried it off for Vivien, who had signed her letter, 'Your soul-sister'. On the night flight, hurled into a gigantic sunrise which filled the cabin with ineffable nascent light, the quiet ecstasy of my homecoming somehow included the three tiny effigies, now nestling in velvet in their box. I took off the box lid and uncovered these silent witnesses to my lordly progress over the oceans of water and light, as I sat fingering a gin and tonic.

27

I passed through Customs without a hitch and reached the visitors' area. There was Vivien beyond the rails, waving, her face grave. I acknowledged her joyfully, then we embraced. She was unsmiling.

'Is anything wrong?'

She didn't answer immediately and seemed to hesitate. I thought of the cats, a fire, flooding, but then she said, 'It's nothing for you to bother your head about. Let's get to the car first.'

Driving out of the Heathrow road system and bearing south, she said, 'It's Celia.'

'What's happened?'

We halted in a traffic jam, then began to crawl forward. 'She's in hospital.'

'Ill?'

'Not in the way you mean. She's at Marytavy – you know – the psychiatric hospital out on the moors. She went in voluntarily, without saying a word.'

'When was this?'

'A week ago. She simply vanished. I sat tight and waited for her to get in touch – she always does in the end. She'd been to see a consultant at Freedom Fields in Plymouth, Henry Baines. He may have recommended it, I don't know. Look, give me my handbag will you – there on the back seat. You look really well, Francis.'

'I'm fine.'

'I'm so pleased to see you.'

'What did you want in here?'

'Open it up. There – that's it. A letter from Celia – I got it yesterday. You can read it.'

The letter said:

> 'Forgive me please for letting you down. I am so scared, but a nice man here with a club foot says I have nothing to fear. His sharp blue eyes – blue as forget-me-nots – prick at me through his mask without hurting. He says he is very hopeful about me. I am believed in, whether wisely or not. As you aren't here I am finding it hard to believe in your existence. I ran here to get away from the sea. The sea is an enormous cleanliness that runs in and out like a clock, a great unstoppable clock. It frightens me. Come and see me soon, and don't despair of your Celia.'

I replaced the letter in its envelope and then in Vivien's bag, zipping it up carefully. All the time I was being tossed about by my emotions, my thoughts obscured. Nothing to do with me, I thought, none of my business. But Vivien was. What was she feeling at this moment?

'Have you been to see her yet?'

'No.'

'When are you going?'

'Tomorrow afternoon. Visiting is from two onwards. Will you come with me? You don't have to.'

'Are you sure you want me to?'

She was dealing with an intersection, her face grim. 'Yes, please.'

'Is she so scared of the sea?'

'I thought she loved it. She does love it. Let's stop for coffee soon, shall we? Wouldn't you like some breakfast?'

'I couldn't eat anything I don't think. I'm down here but my stomach's still up in the air.'

'You feel sick?'

'No, it's all right, it's nothing, just a queasiness.'

'Tell me about your trip – was it a success?'

'The show's going well, they tell me. Success, what's that? I'm glad to be home.'

We pulled in at a Little Chef. In a sudden fit of wild euphoria I slipped off to make a phone call to Maggie. There was no reply. I listened to the phone at the other end ring and ring, picturing an empty room, and worse. In a more sombre mood I rejoined Vivien. Coffees waited on the tablecloth. She said anxiously, 'Don't you want anything to eat at all?'

'No, nothing.' Vivien, I saw, was being tempted by the sight and smell of hot toasted bacon sandwiches on the next table. 'Go ahead, I'll enjoy watching you.'

Laughing, she ordered for herself. I decided to stop worrying about her.

By the following day I was feeling better, calmer, more real. I had become adjusted to England again, to its mild manners and murmuring voices, its remarkable *kindness*, but underlying the safe feeling was a confused sense of danger lurking somewhere out of sight, at the outer edges of my life. That afternoon we set out to visit Celia.

The country bus was full of women shoppers returning home. It was noisy as a hen coop. I shouted to Vivien, beside me. 'What are they all talking about?'

'Their exciting day,' she said, nudging me to keep quiet. I was embarrassing her.

We had travelled eight miles, there was another four to go. My head buzzed, my bones ached, my eyes stung in the tobacco smoke. The bus too was roaring with noise. It staggered and rushed at the hills and seemed to fall half out of control down slopes, emptier after each stop. The brakes squealed.

At Marytavy village we got off. There were signs indicating the direction we should take for the hospital. The final sign said, 'Hospital Entrance Ahead'. We toiled up a steep lane. Vivien gasped in alarm as a herd of cows came towards us, bellowing and painful with the day's milk. We pressed back against the hedge to let them pass. Then more walking for about five minutes brought us out on the broad back of a tawny moor.

In the hospital grounds, taking a wrong turn we entered by a narrow tradesmen's door at the side of a low modern block. Brown lino went flowing off in the distance. A male nurse appeared. He was dark-haired, young, with a high forehead and bony cheeks. We were shown into the Day Room, a lounge carpeted and upholstered in heather colours like a dull family hotel. Early September sunlight flooded in from a line of windows over looking the valley and main road below.

The people sitting docilely around the walls were all female. A girl of twenty or so giggled incessantly and quietly to herself. One woman, her hair coming loose and with a certain puffy arrogance to her face, pointed in a hostile manner to a row of soft chairs with wooden arms. We went over and sat there as if we ourselves were patients. Vivien gave me sideways uneasy glances.

A young woman came in, her glance so keen that I thought at first she must be a member of staff. Her eyes lighting on Vivien brightened with recognition and instant pleasure.

'Here you are,' Celia said, sitting down next to Vivien and smiling across at me. 'Thank you for phoning up. I've been bored rigid for days. Did you have any trouble finding the place?' She looked quizzically at Vivien, who seemed too overwhelmed and happy and relieved to speak.

'Not really,' I said, and suddenly blushed, feeling the heat racing up through my cheeks to my brow. I must have been staring at her in amazement. How well, how alert she looked.

She laughed in my face. 'Good.'

'But you, how are you?' Vivien was asking.

'How do I seem?'

'Wonderful!'

I said, 'What's the treatment they're giving you? We might come for some ourselves.'

'Nothing, really,' she said lightly. 'Only talk and a few pills to make me sleep. I'm having a holiday.' And then she added, 'From myself.'

'You look wonderful,' Vivien repeated in a dazed voice.

Celia laughed again. 'Oh, Vivien, how worried you must have been.'

'When your letter came, I was, yes. Before that I assumed you'd gone to London. I didn't know what – how – '

'What to expect? No of course you didn't. Am I an awful let-down? Did you think you might find me in chains screaming the place down with my hair all matted?'

Vivien smiled. 'You're making fun of me. That's a good sign. That's very normal.'

We sat quietly together, oddly joined and prosaic. 'You've had your hair cut short,' I said suddenly, noticing.

'You artists are so observant,' she mocked.

'I like it,' Vivien said.

'It's for my fresh start.'

I said, 'My hair's falling out. When it's gone, will I be all set for my fresh start?'

Celia said seriously, 'Yes. You'll be a baby, bald and new again.'

'So how long will you be here?' Vivien asked.

'Oh, I shall probably discharge myself in a few days, from boredom.'

'Then you must come and live with me on a cliff, in a magic box full of light called *Lohengrin*.'

Eyes shining, Celia said, 'Sounds like a fairy tale.'

'Are you having interesting talks with Mr Blue-eyes?'

'Yes, very.'

'I'd like to know what he makes of you.'

'So would I.'

'Doesn't he let on at all?'

'One thing he says is that I'm a great verbaliser.'

'Is he impressed by your poems?'

'Not in the least. He's far too healthy.'

'So what do you do all day long?'

'Read a little. Walk about slowly. I listen to other people a lot. So many are desperate to talk, and have never found anyone prepared to listen to them. There are some terribly sad cases here, you know.'

She went on talking thoughtfully to Vivien, while I sat listening. For the first time I thought there could be another Celia, lying deep down and undiscovered, now that I was no longer fighting back my expected dislike of her. With her face

277

cleared of inner torment, its shape and pallor reminded me of the egg-like purity of young women in Flemish paintings. Sometimes they would be receiving news at an open window, or reading a letter, or they were pregnant.

'Shall we have tea?' she asked. 'I'll go and make some, we're expected to do that for our visitors.' We followed her to the door.

A chubby bald man out in the corridor who was coming past in a rush, his raw anxious face perspiring freely, stopped and said, 'Remember me?' He thrust his head forward as if desperate to be acknowledged.

'This is Charlie,' Celia said.

'He knows!' Charlie exclaimed, bobbing up and down.

'How are you?' I said.

'You remember, on the Hoe?' Charlie asked in a beseeching voice.

'Yes – yes of course.'

'This is better for me, here,' the burning man explained rapidly. 'I was getting too worried about my little nipper.'

'How is he?'

His face clouded over. 'Smashing, he is. Look, I've got to go, they're waiting for me.'

'Cheerio,' I said to his departing bowed back.

Vivien and Celia set up house together, in the wooden bungalow on the cliff which would have been out of the question if it had not been for Vivien's car. Idyllic it certainly was, but only if you looked straight ahead. Straggling over the cliff at varying levels were chalets and bungalows and shacks, a shanty town built largely during the war by dockyard workers who had moved out there with their families to escape the blitz. The whole area was now under threat from conservationists and planning authorities. Cynics said that nothing would happen, the compensation involved was too great. Over a hundred little properties waited, year after year, for their fate to be decided.

Out of the blue I had a visitor. Guy Franklin called to see me one evening. He pulled up outside the warehouse in a muddied Volkswagen of uncertain age, an old transit van with crudely painted white daisies in rows on both sides of the bodywork. One of the sliding doors had a bashed-in panel. There were chintz curtains on sagging wires at the windows.

I asked about Yvonne and he told me quickly that they were now separated. He lived, as I knew, in Devon, teaching art at a large Exeter comprehensive. He had lost a good deal of his élan, but was still looking rakish with his tanned skin and abundant brown hair. Startled by him, I wondered if he had changed and was now more knowing, less decent; or had I simply forgotten? He wore a crimson scarf or large handkerchief tied at his throat piratically.

'Frank, it's great to see you again. You look good. How's the work, still flowing?'

'At the moment, yes it is.' I reached out and touched the wood of the door for luck.

Pleased, fascinated as ever by himself, electric, he was like a handsome young cat. He smiled winningly at me. 'You're getting famous, you old bugger. They've even heard of you at Exeter. No culture there you know, except agriculture.'

I laughed. 'How are things with you?'

'Don't ask. God, it's been ghastly this past twelve months. Yvonne threw me out, that's more or less what it amounts to, and the crazy thing is she's the only one I ever wanted, the mother of my kid. She just won't believe me. All hell broke loose. Now I'm broke, I still have to provide for her, she's got the house.'

'I'm sorry to hear it. Still, you haven't cracked up.'

'I came near to it and I don't mind telling you. Now I'm just starting to poke my head up and trust people again. She moved her boyfriend into my house! It hurts to be hated, it bloody hurts, when all you want to do is love somebody.'

I stood awkwardly, caught in a false situation with these confidences I could do nothing about. 'Come and look at some paintings – or do you fancy a drink or what?'

Guy nodded. 'Both.' His lips were moist, his soulful brown eyes darting and restless. Under the self-pity he was calm, cold, unchanged, I thought, smiling at him uncritically and touched by him for all my scepticism. Was I simply lonely and glad to see a friendly face?

'Didn't you say on the phone you had your sister living with you?'

'That's right, I did. She's got a little place of her own now, it's perched right on the cliff at Tregonhawke with a huge bay at her front door.'

'Sounds terrific. Back to nature, that's the stuff. I'd like to see it some time. Is she on her own then?'

'No, with a friend, Celia.'

'You go up and see her I expect. The light must be incredible. Can you paint up there?'

'I've not tried.'

Guy suddenly said, his eyes working, 'My old banger's outside. Why don't we have a ride out there? It's a nice evening, what d'you say?'

'You mean now?'

'Why not?'

'They might not be in.'

'That's okay, we can still enjoy the ride.'

I shook my head at him, laughing. 'Have you got ants in your pants?' I grumbled as we made our way out into the street.

The van was high off the ground. As I hoisted myself aboard I noticed the mattress and sleeping bag stowed away in the rear. 'Is this where you sleep?'

A mixture of guile and ribald laughter showed in Guy's eyes. 'In a manner of speaking. This is my passion wagon.'

We set off into early evening, the sky stormy. I remember everything, every last detail, I shall never forget. By road it was a long winding journey. We left Plymouth and entered Devonport, went bumping through badly patched slummy streets near a vast dockyard and then crossed over the broad sprawl of river by means of a lugubrious iron ferry on chains, clanking and inevitable like fate. On the other side, a green land soon enveloped us in its fat folds and curves.

Guy had begun the drive by talking chirpily. Now he relapsed into a gloomy silence. I pointed out various landmarks to try to engage him in conversation. He seemed disinclined to speak.

We came within sight of the sea and were soon driving back around the huge crescent of the bay. We had come in a great circle and were heading again in the direction of Plymouth, although the city with all its streets and buildings was nowhere to be seen. Along the five-mile length of the coast road we saw no one. The open sea spread out to our right, shining under strange cold glancing light, full of weird menace and a sublime indifference. It moved and yet stayed still, eternal as death while it swung to and fro like a cradle.

I thought I glimpsed the roof ridge of *Lohengrin* below us for a brief instant before it sank from view. 'This is it! You can stop anywhere here, pull over on the grass I should. Look, that's Tregonhawke Beach below us.'

The light was failing. Guy stopped the van. Flopping over the wheel morosely he stared out to sea. I climbed down.

'Aren't you coming?'

'Where is it?'

'Down this path. It's going to rain I think.'

Guy jumped down. He made an effort and sprang into life, his feet skidding on the loose shale. 'Hang about, I'm right behind you. Lead on, Frank.'

A sudden wind whipped into me, stronger than I expected as I plunged on ahead. The sun sank out of sight as I watched, disappearing in the naked changeless sea westward. A shifting ragged sky was left empty. Desolate and unearthly feelings chilled my blood. I shivered, picturing myself a puny figure tugged by the wind, swamped by the loneliness any human being of no account in an immense seascape feels. The dull thunder of the incoming tide far below, battering at the base of the cliff, seemed echoed by the explosive thud of my heart. I turned, glad to see Guy scrambling towards me grinning idiotically. 'It's a terrific spot, oh boy!' he yelled into the wind, and then gargled something else, a joke, which the combined sea and wind noises drowned at once.

Soon the path began to drop abruptly, twisting between overhanging gorse thickets, and then the bungalow appeared directly below my feet. It looked quiet and abandoned, as if sunk in thoughts of its own. I stepped down closer, on crude steps hacked out of the earth and capped with rough boulder-like slabs of rock. The thought ran through my mind: perhaps they had gone to see a film, or to eat in a restaurant. I called out, 'Vivien?' An opening door or a curtain stirring would have revived my flagging spirits. All I achieved was a renewed sense of being lost. The bungalow had taken on an air of dereliction. It was lightless. Up on the road it hadn't occurred to me to look round for Vivien's car. Usually it was parked on a strip of flat turf close to where the cliff path began. Had I walked past a solitary bright yellow car without noticing? I was certainly capable.

Guy caught up with me as I stood hesitating. 'Hey, this is really something!'

There was a storm porch built on the side, looking like a sentry box. The door would stick and had to be shoved hard; I had told Vivien I would fix it. I twisted the doorknob and pushed, expecting to find the door locked. It was stuck, I pushed harder, I could see it wasn't locked. It gave suddenly and swung open.

Inside, Celia lay on the floor in the tiny living room, on her back with her mouth open as if dead. Naked from the waist down, her skin was grey, her hair sodden and darkened, plastered to her scalp like a cap. Her mauve shirt clung in wrinkles to her body. Rivulets of water had formed on the stained and varnished boards. As we entered in a dumbstruck silence, she opened her eyes wide. She began to gasp violently, then to scream. She sat bolt upright, struggled to her feet and made a mad rush for the door. Guy caught hold of her arm and hung on. She screamed piercingly, nonstop. He slapped her face hard, first on one cheek and then the other. Celia shrank back, arms pinned to her sides. Her eyes frenzied, glaring into his, she hissed, spat, 'Bastard, you filthy bastard, you – '

'Where's Vivien – what's happened – where is she?' I shouted.

Celia started to babble at terrific speed, words pouring from her in an involuntary stream. 'I wanted to die, why can't I die, I couldn't drown, Vivien held my hand, we were far out, then she let go – '

I felt a sick thrill of dread. On the move, I yelled to Guy, 'Call an ambulance, quick – a phone by the café – up the road – '

Later I couldn't recall how I had descended the tortuous cliff path at such a rate and in failing light. I slithered, tripped, close to the edge of a sheer drop, flung myself onwards and somehow managed to stay upright. The last steepest section I didn't even see. My eyes were straining ahead to the pale faint light above the tumult of breakers and searching for any sign of life on the beach, the few yards of it not yet covered by the tide.

Twenty yards out, among smooth rocks like the backs of seals that were nearly submerged and then revealed by the hissing and foaming waves surging towards the shore, a partly clothed body washed lifelessly about. An arm moved, fell back. The cafeteria on the beach, a wooden structure covered in a layer of huge round stones cemented together, was shuttered against the elements but showed chinks of light. I ran up, hammered on the door with a shower of frantic blows, screamed, 'Help!' Then I started to wade out. Soon I was up to my waist. The body of my jacket floated up and lay on the water around me. I struck out frantically with my slow breast stroke like a powerless frog.

Celia was found collapsed on the path halfway up to the coast road, babbling insanely to herself. The following day Jake Samuels rushed down from London. He took her back wrapped in a travelling blanket like an infant, curled up on his Volvo's rear seat so that it was difficult to know whether she was awake or sleeping.

Not for the first time, her swift recovery was extraordinary. At the coroner's inquest she stated categorically that she and Vivien had walked hand-in-hand into the sea in order to die by drowning. She made no attempt to come near me. For this I was grateful. I heard her say in the trembling voice of a woman holding back tears that it was her intention to seek further psychiatric help. I took this to mean returning to Marytavy. A week later I phoned the hospital. They had no knowledge of her whereabouts.

Except for calling Maggie to tell her what had happened I spoke to no one. I couldn't face other people or myself. Was it destiny speaking through me which had enticed Vivien south, or was it just greedy selfishness for which there could be no remission? My work ground to a halt, a sure sign of inner disgust. I drew what comfort I could from reading books, and from long walks on the moors. The sea was now anathema to me. I would take a bus to Tavistock and then get lost in the lanes leading out to Dartmoor. In a book by George Steiner I came across Nietzsche's observation that if one looks into the abyss, the abyss looks back into one's own spirit.

The suicide note – when I came across it by chance – was in a volume of Van Gogh's *Letters*, a second-hand copy found by Vivien in Charing Cross Road and given to me on my fiftieth birthday. Five months to the day after that evening of terror my dead sister spoke to me. I sat perfectly still, a little frightened bereft man, half pulverised by death yet still living, and read first:

Darling Francis,

When you find this we will both be dead. We have made a pact. I can't tell you how happy, how completed I feel by this decision, about to be merged in the same death with Celia, whose distress will at last come to an end as my love for her finds its fulfilment. Don't mourn for us will you, please. She wished it and I want it. There can be nothing more beautiful than now, this moment. Dying together we will be utterly one. To love life and to hate it is in the end the same wave, on which we shall be lifted up. Your loving sister,

Vivien

A postscript in Celia's shaky hand said:

I want to return to life by drowning in life. Drowning will return me to the sea from which we came. I don't want to go on like this, a cripple, I want to die, to die, to die. Instead of being detached in horror from life to be immersed and eternal in it.

She had failed – or refused – to sign her name.

EPILOGUE

I didn't know what to do with myself, and my imagination, fastened as it was on spectres, was no use any more, and I thought, If I see Maggie, if I can only be with her, all this will cease and I will be changed, made over, become all right as a man again. I began making trips to London, since I was now able to see Maggie on a regular basis if I wished. Once this development would have astounded me. Now nothing did. How pleased Vivien would have been, I thought.

It had come about as a direct consequence of Vivien's death. Maggie extended an invitation on behalf of herself and Gregory, and I accepted gladly.

Our reunion, after dreaming about it for so long, was at once joyful, fraught, and the most natural thing in the world. Unbelievably, the flat above the restaurant where I had last seen her looked exactly the same. Maggie stood up and came towards me. She was heavier, thicker, putting her feet down with the tread of a matron. Only her eyes were still youthful. But her hair wasn't grey, it was hennaed red as I remembered. It shocked me to see how the years had aged her. Did she have a similar disenchantment to cope with as she smiled in recognition at me?

Yet, reaching her, I said with absolute sincerity, not hesitating for a second, 'Maggie, I swear you haven't changed.'

'Nor have you, Wes.'

'Where are the children?'

'One's with her gran. Rina is out boyfriending, God help us. The last one she brought back was terrible.'

Her face was as dear to me as ever. How could I have forgotten its wonderful openness? I put my arms around her. She pushed her nose into my cheek. Not knowing what else to say, I rocked her back and forth, while a voice within me was asking, 'Now what?' As always, I had no answer.

A month later I called again, the second of many visits to come. It was getting dark. Gregory, who had put on weight and lost most of his fine black hair, got up, I thought to switch on the light. Instead he came back with a bottle of Greek wine. He poured a glass for me and one for himself. Delicious cooking smells were wafting in from the kitchen. Both the girls were upstairs.

'I didn't know there was an upstairs.'

'My brother George, he had a small flat up there. When he was made a father he moved out to somewhere bigger. That was lucky for us.'

Gregory began speaking in a way that was part communication, part musing. 'I would like you to stay the night if you can. Keep Maggie company, she would be very glad. I have to go out.' Lowering his voice, he said, 'She suspects another woman. She's right. In another way wrong. I lived with June before Maggie, now she's come back into my life. I don't want this complication and these lies. What else can I do? She threatens to come round here and make violent scenes, she has always been jealous and unpredictable. I have a child by her. Maggie doesn't know this. Why should she? I tell you this, Francis, I would like both women. Not one as a wife and one as a mistress, but both together in one house. You will think me insane I daresay. How many men would like two, three or even four women? In the west they already do this, but one after the other separately. My way is more honest. It can't happen, but neither can I give up one for the other. That's the truth, that's how I am.'

I said, 'What if both sexes want the same freedom in the end? Aren't women demanding it already?'

285

Gregory spoke half to me, half to himself, while his smile seemed to say, 'You're joking.' He said, 'Who knows what women want?'

'Not slavery.'

'They enslave us.'

I heard the phone ring in the other room. Then Maggie opened the door. 'Wes, it's for you I think. The line's bad, I can't be sure. What are you both up to in the dark?'

I got to my feet. 'Asking ourselves what we're up to.'

'I should think so.'

'Who's calling me here?'

'She didn't say.'

I reached the phone, lifted the receiver from the small table and said hello. A thin high voice, frail as a thread, strong as a spider's web, said, 'It's me. Celia. Can you hear me?'

She hadn't been in touch since Vivien's death. Once I picked up the phone and was about to ring Jake Samuels to enquire after his wife's health, but was so filled with rage that I had to stop.

She waited for me to speak, then said, 'I wanted to find out if losing Vivien had done awful things to you. She spoke about you endlessly. I never knew anyone so close to a brother as she was to you. Are you well, are you coping, Francis?'

Ice gripped my heart. I put down the phone. Maggie asked, 'Who was that, a ghost?'

'A ghost, yes.'

'A wrong number?'

'That as well.' Someone who should be dead but isn't, I added under my breath.

Maggie laughed. 'Stop mumbling. You always did talk in riddles. Now come and eat, come on. At your age you should be looking after yourself. You're too thin, you always were. Do you want your stomach to shrink? Gregory, tell him what you say.'

'What? Food explains itself.'

'Yes, that. That's what he says.'

Sitting round the family table, we ate, talked and laughed. Juices from each pleasure ran and mingled in the one repast. The wine fumed in my head. 'You're as young as the Mediterranean,' I told Maggie, and then added, 'both of you.'

Maggie blushed. Her young eyes full of motherly reproach, she said, 'Eat your food.'